friends for a season

BRAD GRABER

ISBN:
Paperback: 978-0-99760428-3
eBook: 978-0-99760429-0

DEDICATION

To my wonderful husband, Jeff

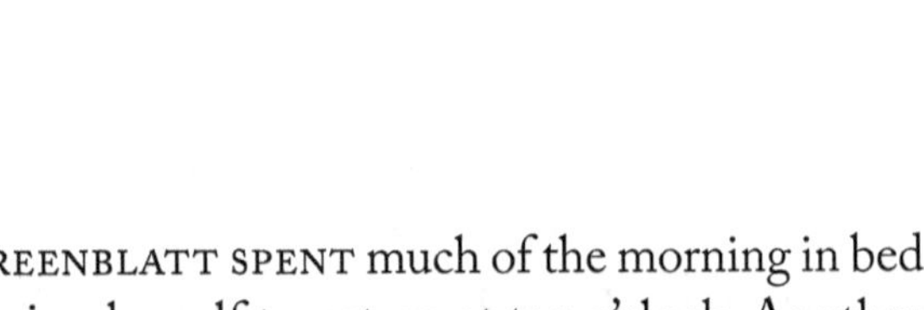

HELENA GREENBLATT SPENT much of the morning in bed before forcing herself to get up at ten o'clock. Another birthday, another year older. Birthdays had once been fun. Parties, cards, gifts. But at eighty-three, her life was quiet. Maybe, too quiet.

It had been a miserable night. So much on her mind. Memories from the past sneaking up and tapping her on the shoulder. She'd tried reading, but the book she picked up at Barnes & Noble failed to capture her imagination. The plot was as improbable as the reaction of the protagonist. She made a mental note. No more contemporary fiction. From here on out, she'd stick to biography.

She headed downstairs dressed in a pink robe and her favorite fluffy slippers, holding tightly onto the banister as she maneuvered the steep staircase. Once in the kitchen, she plugged in the percolator she'd prepared the night before. Three scoops of Maxwell House and four cups of water for the perfect pot of coffee. She made her way to the front door and peered through the glass trim. She spotted the rolled-up newspaper on the walkway. Stepping outside, she hoped no one would see her as she rushed along, quickly bending down to pick up the day's edition of the *Arizona Republic*. Back inside, she was dizzy as she steadied herself against the wall and took a breath.

Slow down, girl! she thought.

She could smell the freshly brewed coffee as she made her way back to the kitchen. She poured herself a cup, sat down at the kitchen table, and spread the newspaper out before her. She scoured the day's stories. So much heartache and tragedy. So much tension and disappointment. By the time she'd finished with the paper, it was eleven-fifteen. *Oh my, it's so late*, she thought as she headed upstairs to dress for the day. Her plan: stop by Safeway and do a little food shopping. Blueberries were on special and she was running low on milk.

She laid out her outfit on the bed: a white cotton blouse and a matching pair of shorts. *Cute*, she thought as she entered through the double doors into her ensuite. The ensuite had cinched the deal when she bought the house ten years earlier. A jacuzzi tub, double sinks, a walk-in shower, and custom cabinetry. She'd joked there was enough space to bathe, dress, and entertain a friend or two, if she wanted.

The last thing she remembered was looking in the mirror as she brushed her hair. When she next opened her eyes, she was lying on her stomach, a cheek pressed against the cold bathroom tile. She'd experienced another episode of light-headedness, but this time, there was no bed, chair, or sofa to catch her. She'd reached for the towel bar, but before she could grab it, the world had slipped away.

Oh shit! she thought, as the gravity of the situation settled in. How long had she been on the floor? Five minutes? Ten minutes? Half an hour? Her stomach gurgled. She hadn't eaten any breakfast. In truth, she was rarely hungry these days.

Gassy, yes. Tired, certainly. Achy, every morning. Hungry? Not so much. But she was hungry now.

She shifted about. A sharp pain shot down her leg. Had she broken a bone, a hip, or God forbid, hit her head on the tub? Her hands were by her face and her fingers throbbed when she made a fist. She had instinctually broken her fall, just missing the tub. Thank goodness. She took a deep breath. *Things could be worse*, she thought, trying to quell a growing panic. "You're safe," she whispered, keenly aware that the reality of the situation was very different. She recalled reading an article in the *AARP* magazine that described a fall for seniors as a life-threatening event. Brain bleeds topped the list of injuries for the frail elderly. *Frail elderly!* How she hated that term. Yes, she was in her eighties. Yes, she'd experienced weight loss over the last few months. Yes, she'd noticed muscle weakness during a recent gardening session. But wasn't that normal for a woman of her age? Did it necessarily translate to *frail elderly*? And why couldn't they name it something more dignified, like *advanced ager* or *life learner*? A name that conveyed respect for those who'd survived and thrived through the decades. But then she supposed with longevity, decline was inevitable. Or was that simply ageist? Surely not all seniors in their eighties are fragile. *Or are they?* she wondered as she eyed the bathroom floor. It needed a good mopping. But then, housekeeping had never been her thing, and frankly, it was the least of her problems at the moment.

She decided that she couldn't lie around all day. She had to get up. She had things to do. Places to go. Still, she didn't try to get up. Instead, she closed her eyes and rested, her thoughts turning to God. She'd never been much for organized religion and now she wondered if God was real. And if God was real, what might he look like? She loved HGTV and adored *The Property Brothers*. Perhaps God looked like handsome Drew Scott. Wouldn't that be a marvelous face to greet you at the heavenly gates? But then again, what if God was a woman? She imagined Eleanor Roosevelt, then Betty Ford, and finally settled on Maya Angelou. A strong, intelligent woman who was empathetic and wise.

Startled, she opened her eyes with a new realization. Perhaps her fall was God's way of saying it was time to let go. That her warranty had run out. Her coupon . . . expired. She would soon be going out of business like her favorite stores: Gertz, Gimbels, and Loehmann's. Her heart pounded. The blood rushed to her head. She steeled herself. *No. I'm not dying. Not today. Not here. And certainly not in this undignified manner.* But doubt lingered in the deepest recesses of her cerebral cortex. Was death near? Would her death matter? Was she ready to let go?

There was still so much she enjoyed. She loved her cactus garden and the hummingbirds that visited every night at five o'clock while she ate dinner. She loved to read, and the quiet adventures books provided. She loved her little house, decorated just as she liked with its yellow kitchen that looked onto a red flagstone backyard with a pool and tall bushes that partially shielded her view of a very green golf course. But she couldn't deny being lonely. Not that she didn't like her own company. She was fine by herself. But there had been too many long stretches without social interaction. Had the world forgotten her? Or more precisely, had her family?

She lifted her head. It ached. *Oh, yes,* she thought. *I'll be covered in bruises tomorrow.* Purplish black and yellow discolorations on the face and arms. She'd have to wear a hat and long sleeves to hide the hideous evidence. It would probably take weeks to heal. She might even need to go back to her doctor. "Oh, God," she whispered. She hated going to the doctor.

Over the years, she'd become her own diagnostician, guessing the cause of every random symptom. A backache could be the onset of kidney stones. A headache, the result of a brain tumor. A bellyache, pancreatic cancer. She'd undergone extensive testing, convinced that each symptom was a warning sign of impending doom. She'd even participated in a *Life Line* screening to rule out the likelihood of stroke or cardiac conditions. She'd recently had an endoscopy (Joan Rivers had died during such a procedure) and a colonoscopy (the prep far worse than the actual search) to ensure her indigestion wasn't due to a malignant growth. She excelled in her own misdiagnosis, and though she was grateful to be healthy, she scoffed when the gastroenterologist pronounced her "clean as a whistle." *Such a vulgar expression,* she'd thought. *A lady should never be described by a sound produced with puckered lips.* And now finally, her worst nightmare had come true. She'd fallen and was alone. *What had she done to deserve such an ignoble ending?* She was grateful she didn't own cats. She'd read that cats, when left alone too long with a corpse, will eat the face off of their dead owner. Or was that an urban myth?

She wiggled her toes. Perhaps she could stand.

Adrenaline shot through her body as she placed a hand below her shoulder, mentally mapping out her ascent as if preparing to climb Mount Everest. With a grunt and a twist, she pushed herself upward until she was lying on her left side facing the tub. Another breath and she willed herself to reach for the tub's edge. "Oh, no," she whimpered as a sharp pain shot through her shoulder blade and ran down her back. Cowed by fear, she eased back down and rested on her side, eyes closed, drifting neither here, nor there, nor anywhere; lost in a purgatory of regret. Regret that she was no longer young. Regret that she lived alone. Regret that her sons didn't live nearby. Regret that she was so darn regretful.

And then, she heard the voice.

If you could only see yourself.

She'd gone to a shaman to have the voice exorcised, but some things couldn't be eradicated. Especially if you were gifted the way Helena Greenblatt was gifted. Able to sense things other people were oblivious to.

The voice again: *It's a wonder you don't die of shame.*

Dead for thirty years, Ruthie sat perched on the edge of the tub looking down at her prostrated daughter. Her essence, unmistakable. The voice, unforgettable. Helena groaned. If timing was everything, the timing for this visit couldn't be worse. Not when she was, as they say, down for the count.

I've told you about the dangers of isolating.

During Ruthie's lifetime, she'd perfected the art of dire warnings. Motherly love baked into a spicy goulash best served to those with a cast iron stomach. A lethal combination of over-protectiveness and bitter recrimination. Tidbits of fear masquerading as wisdom; pithy sayings served as poisonous bon bons.

If you'd put yourself out there more, smiled now and then, you wouldn't be in this situation.

Helena doubted smiling would have prevented this mishap.

If only you listened to me . . .

Helena viewed her psychic gifts as a curse. Something she couldn't turn off. And while others might use such abilities for fame and financial gain, Helena had spent her days pretending she was like everyone else. Ignoring impressions. Discarding intuitive knowing. Turning a blind eye to the random incarnations that interrupted her naptime. A little ESP wasn't worth getting all high and mighty about. If anything, it marked you as odd. Broken. Possibly, mentally ill.

Ruthie was on a tear. *Face reality. Your health is faltering. My goodness. The dead have more get up and go than you.*

Helena was tempted to laugh, but she didn't want to encourage her mother.

Why couldn't you learn mah-jongg or canasta to keep yourself socially connected? And plenty of gentlemen would've loved taking you to dinner, but you preferred to microwave.

Helena was certain her current problem had nothing to do with card games or frozen meals. Besides, where was she supposed to meet all of these mystery men? Most men her age were at the cemetery. Below ground.

Marriage wasn't good enough for you. You had to do everything on your own.

Helena had tried marriage. The first time, with a high school sweetheart. That lasted five years. Robert died in a car accident, leaving her alone to raise two young boys. A devastating loss. And then, husband number two. Wasn't twice the charm?

Or was that, three?

David was brash; a stockbroker, daredevil-type. Eager to take risks. Fast cars, speedboats, motorcycles. Sixteen months into the marriage, he died in a scuba-diving accident. Very Darwinian. She'd never known a Jewish man who loved to scuba-dive; an activity Helena considered to be about as safe as skydiving. Still, that marriage turned out to be an excellent financial investment, if relationships could be measured in dollars and cents. He'd left her financially secure. Not bad for being together such a short time. She imagined David would have approved of the return on investment.

Ruthie held a Virginia Slim between her slender fingers. *You always had a lousy picker.*

Helena's left shoulder ached from supporting her body weight. She eyed her mother. "How can you still smoke? It's such a filthy habit."

Ruthie rolled her eyes and took a drag. Smoke billowed out of her nose as she assumed a pose—1942 Lauren Bacall. Very chic. Very sheik. Very seductive.

After the death of Helena's second husband, she joined a synagogue. With two dead husbands to her name, congregants whispered. People treated her like a black widow spider weaving a web to ensnare her next victim. She was gorgeous then. Shoulder-length blonde hair. A lovely figure. A dead ringer for

Elizabeth Montgomery from *Bewitched*. But her nose didn't twitch. Nor was she subservient to any Darrin Stephens. Married men stared and lusted. Some boldly placed hands where they didn't belong. Friendships faltered. Women were threatened by her presence. She dropped the temple membership.

Neither sons would have a bar mitzvah.

She pursued a career in journalism, landing a job as an on-air reporter. In her spare time, she wrote romance novels about a smart, independent, young widow. Within ten years, she was a *New York Times* bestselling author. Along the way, she gave up on men and their games. The sweaty, clammy creatures, grabbing, touching, reaching. Any sense of desire was sublimated into her alter-ego, Hannah Elliot. Each romantic adventure ended with Hannah learning a lesson on self-sufficiency. A heroine who defied romance's love-ever-after cliché. An iconoclast who captured the imagination of a generation of women intent on breaking the patriarchy.

Life was full then. She didn't need a man. She had her boys. She committed to her writing career and raising her sons. Given time, she warmed her hands at the fire of success. National speaking tours. television appearances on popular talk shows. Published opinions in *The New York Times*. Even a column in *Rolling Stone*. She was photographed at red carpet events and participated in civil rights marches. At one time, she *was* the news. Richard Nixon blasted her after she blamed him in print for the escalation of the war in Vietnam.

But that was a long time ago.

Did anyone still remember her?

Ruthie raged. *Stop feeling sorry for yourself and for Christ's sake, get up!*

Helena had no choice. She'd have to get back on her feet. Who would notice if she was missing? She'd no regular visitors. No weekly phone calls. No one was coming to the rescue. If she didn't stand, she'd die alone. "That damn doctor," she murmured, recalling the exasperated look on his face when she'd complained of dizziness. He dismissed her concerns as if advanced age had accorded her the right to be dizzy. She reached again for the edge of the tub, but before she could make contact, she spotted something moving by her legs. A cockroach was making its way toward her.

Ruthie's voice cut through Helena's shriek. *If Nick and Ben were here, things would be different.*

Helena shuddered. She hated bugs.

Your boys should be ashamed, leaving you alone. One mother can raise two boys, but two boys can't take care of one mother.

"It's not their job," Helena snarled, focused on the small brown intruder, its antennae vibrating as if transmitting messages back to the nest. *The old lady's down for the count. The coast is clear.*

Ruthie persisted. *What about responsibility?*

Helena refused to take the bait. Her boys lived out of state, and they weren't boys. They were grown men. Men with families, careers, and responsibilities. She'd known they wouldn't be there for her. She couldn't expect them to be.

The roach started to move, inching ever closer. "Stop," Helena hissed, convinced she could communicate with the brown interloper.

I'll do exactly as I like, Ruthie snapped, oblivious to Helena's visitor.

Helena groaned. Which was worse? An invading cockroach or a dead mother? Maybe the time had come to consider a retirement facility. Someplace where roaches would be banished, and dead mothers wouldn't pop in. But the idea of such a place terrified her. Disabled seniors with walkers shuffling along musty, urine-scented hallways. Images, far more frightening than a disgusting roach.

"I must get up," she cried out, once again extending an arm toward the edge of the tub, setting off a stabbing pain on the side pressed against the floor. Had she broken a rib? No. She was lying on something. Something that was digging into her. Her *Life Alert* medallion! Out of habit, she'd slipped it on when she first got out of bed as a precaution for maneuvering the staircase. She'd forgotten all about it.

She pulled on the necklace until the amulet was in her hand. With the push of the button, an alarm sounded somewhere. "Mrs. Greenblatt," a voice came through. "Are you okay?"

Such a silly question, she thought. "I'm lying on the bathroom floor, and I can't get up." She bit her lip. Wasn't that the line from the television commercial?

"Don't worry, ma'am. We're on our way."

In Phoenix, the fire department housed the EMTs. If needed, they'd call for an ambulance. She imagined a fire station of Keystone Kops. Men sliding down poles, rushing about, banging into each other, all for the purpose of lifting her one-hundred-and-thirty pounds of dead weight off the floor. She could no longer deny the truth. She'd taken a wrong turn down a dark alley. A turn anyone with good sense would've avoided. It was official. She was an old lady. A dues-paying member of the *frail elderly* club.

The roach stood its ground as Helena fretted about the appearance of the house. She spotted a used tissue on the floor that had missed the wastepaper basket. A dust bunny lurking in the corner. She would have tidied up if she'd known company was coming. She shut her eyes and visualized the handsome Drew Scott. Then, Maya Angelou. "Dear God," she whispered, "things just can't get any worse." And then with a jolt, she gasped.

She wasn't wearing a bra.

✧

The blare of a fire engine's siren ensured things were indeed about to get worse.

Helena's Phoenix home, located in a gated community on the grounds of the Arizona Biltmore Hotel, was at the end of a cul-de-sac. She imagined the neighbors gathering outside, worried about protecting their property from Arizona's deadliest threat . . . fire. The relief on their faces when the old woman, the neighbor they didn't know, the shut-in they suspected was a hoarder, the old gal who never smiled, the friendless grump who had no visitors, was hauled out on a stretcher like a supersized bag of Purina Puppy Chow. Perhaps they'd be reminded of garbage day when the Waste Management trucks rattled through the neighborhood picking up trash. Or maybe they'd be too busy in their homes to notice anything, glued to reruns of *Dr. Phil* or *Judge Judy*, sipping wine and nibbling on cheese snacks, indifferent to the tragedy occurring in the neighborhood.

The imagery of each possibility made her shudder with shame.

Fortunately, the EMTs had the good sense to stop at the guard gate and ask for the key to Helena's door. Even more fortunate, Helena had provided the guard gate with a spare key in case she locked herself out.

Lying on the bathroom floor, Helena could feel the vibration of approaching footsteps. Though she was grateful to be rescued, she couldn't help but worry about the carpets. They were new, and though she'd thought of going with a darker color, she'd foolishly opted for beige, hoping to brighten the place up. It wasn't her best decorating decision. Beige showed every bit of dirt. Had she met the EMTs at the door, she'd have politely asked them to remove their shoes.

If only . . .

There was a gentle rap on the half-open bathroom door. "Ma'am, are you alright?" The voice was deep. Masculine.

She'd have laughed if she wasn't so embarrassed. *I'm fine,* she thought. *I often lie on the bathroom floor hoping someone will stop by.* But there was no need for sarcasm. "Please come in," she meekly answered, clad only in an old pair of panties and the pink robe that had hiked up to her waist in the fall.

Slowly, the door opened. The cockroach, who'd held its ground until that moment, scampered up her leg, scaling the human hill, before darting off. Helena screamed and the medic stopped dead in his tracks on the threshold of the bathroom. "Ma'am?"

"No, no, it's alright. Please come in," she said, eyeing the EMT's blue boots with the thick white rubber soles. From her vantage point, the boots looked clean. She could stop worrying about the carpets.

The EMT crouched by her side. "Don't you worry. We're here to help."

She tried to shift about, but she couldn't move. Had her muscles atrophied since pressing the *Life Alert* button? Had she become a living statue? A *Venus de Milo* with two attached, but very bruised, alabaster arms? She imagined herself on display in the Louvre Museum. A horrifying vision. Oh, how she wished she could make the world disappear; be an ostrich with her head buried in the sand, or a turtle, head tucked in its shell. Anything to escape. Instead, she closed her eyes, unwilling to bear witness to the encounter.

Multiple voices surrounded her. One was that of a woman. "We're going to sit you up. Let us know if anything hurts." Strong hands gripped her shoulders. Another pair rested on her waist. Another on her calves. *Oh my*, Helena thought. *They have an entire squad here.*

"On the count of three," the lead voice directed.

Helena braced herself. She was lifted and turned until she sat flat on her butt. A hand supported her lower back. Another, her shoulder. She relaxed and slowly leaned backward until she rested against the tub. Someone covered her with a bath towel as she slumped forward and dry-heaved. A hand gently rubbed her back until she was able to lift her head.

"Take it easy. We've got you," the female voice said.

When Helena opened her eyes, three EMTs were crouched in a semi-circle before her. A solid shield of dark blue. Two men and a woman.

"I can't thank you enough," she said in a shaky voice as if it was all over. "I'm so sorry to be such a bother. I'm sure you have better things to do with your day."

"Are you taking any medications?" the medic to her right asked as the one to her left applied a blood pressure cuff. The third checked her pulse.

"No. I don't take any medications," she said, almost doubting her own credibility as she caught the surprised look on the female medic's face. "Honestly," she reiterated. "Not a thing."

Helena couldn't remember the last time she'd had so many people attending to her, let alone in her home. She only wished it wasn't happening in the bathroom. She resisted the urge to be a good hostess, which under the circumstances, was an absurd notion. But even if she could get up, she doubted there was anything in the pantry worth serving. No cookies. No cake. No soda. She made a mental note: *When next at the grocery store, purchase snacks for future emergencies.*

"Ma'am," said the lead EMT, "your blood pressure is very low. We're going to call for an ambulance to take you to the emergency room."

Helena nodded, too tired to be afraid as she yielded to events out of her control. "Whatever you think best," she said before passing out, her head dropping forward.

***

When Helena opened her eyes, she was in a white curtained-off area with an IV in her arm. She remembered the EMTs, and the horrible roach, but not the challenge of getting onto the stretcher, out of the house, and into the ambulance.

A young woman in a white coat pulled the curtain back and peeked in. "Hello, Mrs. Greenblatt. I'm Dr. Reynolds." Her black hair was braided and wrapped around her head like a crown. Her skin, a russet, reddish brown, was flawless and offset by a brilliant smile. Helena thought such a dazzling smile the gift of the truly blessed. Surely, any person with a smile like that could easily make friends.

"How are you feeling?" the doctor asked as she approached Helena's side.

Helena held up a wrist with the IV as if the doctor didn't know she was on a gurney in the emergency department. "As well as can be expected."

The doctor's eyes searched Helena's face as if anticipating something might have been missed on the intake form. "You've had a busy afternoon." She turned to inspect a laptop mounted on a stand—a rolling desktop. "I see Dr. Shin is your cardiologist."

"How do you know that?" Helena asked, concerned her personal data had been breached.

"I'm looking at your electronic medical record," Dr. Reynolds clarified. "Those of us employed by the hospital have access to the information."

Helena had liked Dr. Shin. At least up until her impromptu experience with the bathroom floor. "He's a lovely man, but I think he messed this one up."

Dr. Reynolds' tone shifted. There was an edge to her voice. Much like a teacher correcting a student. "You mustn't blame Dr. Shin. I don't think this has anything to do with your heart."

Helena wondered if all doctors stuck together, no matter what.

"You're dehydrated. That happens in the desert. But just to be sure, we're going to admit you for additional tests. We certainly don't want you to fall again. You were lucky this time."

Helena winced when she made a fist. "Lucky? What about my hand?"

"The x-ray was normal. A minor sprain."

Helena didn't remember having any x-rays. "And my ribs?"

"Just slightly bruised."

Helena didn't consider bruised ribs and a sprained hand to be lucky.

"An orderly will be in shortly to move you upstairs to a room. Do you have any questions for me?"

Helena did have a question. But, how to phrase it?

"Now don't worry. We'll figure out what's wrong," Dr. Reynold said.

But Helena wasn't concerned about her health. She knew she was in the right place with the right people. "By any chance," she asked, "is my mother in the waiting room? I know they don't allow smoking in the hospital, but I'm worried about her. She hasn't come back to see me. Can someone check on her?"

Dr. Reynolds tilted her head. The smile was gone. "Mrs. Greenblatt, do you know what day it is?"

Helena squinted, her confidence in the young physician suddenly shaken. "Last I checked, it was Tuesday. It's my birthday, today."

Dr. Reynolds nodded. "And can you tell me your age?"

"Well, of course I can," Helena said, growing indignant. "But that's already in my medical chart."

"Can you tell me your address?"

Helena didn't understand why she was being asked so many silly questions. "Now, why do you need to know that?"

Dr. Reynolds cleared her throat. "Not to worry," she said as she withdrew. "You're going to be fine. Someone should be in shortly to transfer you upstairs. It was lovely meeting you."

Helena relaxed. *Now, wasn't that strange?*

$$- \; 2 \; -$$

Zak Andrews struggled to stay awake in his morning biology class. The professor was covering genetics: X and Y chromosomes, dominant and recessive traits, gene variations. Had Zak not stopped at Starbucks, he doubted he'd still be awake. With his coffee cup nearly empty and eyes glazed over, he pinched a cheek, hoping a bit of pain might revive him.

It didn't.

Rows of students, tiered high, filled the Arizona State University lecture hall reminding Zak of six years earlier when his parents had taken him for his bar mitzvah to Las Vegas. He'd spent much of that weekend in the Bellagio suite watching cable television while his parents stayed out gambling. But one night, they all went to hear his mother's favorite singer, Celine Dion, at Caesar's Palace. The showroom seated four thousand people. They'd sat so far away from the stage, and so high up in stadium seating, that when Zak held up a hand and squinted, Celine Dion's entire body fit perfectly inside his thumbnail. Today, the professor's head fit inside Zak's thumbnail.

Zak suppressed a yawn. A late night of busing tables at The Windy Canyon Bar had nearly done him in. The blare of the new band, The Dirty Toenails, echoed in his memory as he tried to concentrate on the lecture. But all he could think about was the band's ridiculous name, as if the sillier a band's name, the better chance it had of making it big. There was Hootie & the Blowfish, the Butthole Surfers, and King Gizzard & the Lizard Wizard—three bands that had found success. Zak guessed The Dirty Toenails were onto something. But the heavy metal sound had been deafening. He couldn't imagine anyone enjoying the music.

Or maybe that was just him.

Being a college freshman was no picnic when you had to work your way through school. If he'd scored a scholastic scholarship, he could have spent his evenings studying in the library like his classmates. But he wasn't a great test-taker, and scholarships don't always go to the neediest. And so, by the age of eighteen, Zak had figured out that life wasn't going to be easy. But to be fair, his parents had already made that point abundantly clear.

He wished things with his parents were different.

He rubbed his gooey eyes and stretched a long leg into the aisle as he twirled a strand of black hair about his finger. He'd grown his hair shoulder length like Keanu Reeves in *John Wick,* one of his dad's favorite movies, and to his delight, when he was in his senior year of high school, a woman in the grocery store stopped him and insisted he looked like Keanu Reeves' son. He'd floated home on a cloud of pure joy that day, hopeful that even a geek nerd might be deemed good looking.

As the professor droned on, Zak mentally bounced from subject to subject. Did he really want to pursue pre-med? Wouldn't being a doctor require him to touch other people?

Strangers with various degrees of hygiene. Perhaps medicine wasn't his end game, but then what was he interested in doing? Whatever he did in the future, he'd have to earn enough money to live independently. He imagined himself single and alone the rest of his life. A definite possibility based on his mother's warning. Could creating names for bands be a career? It had to be more fun than sitting in a lecture hall with a pounding headache learning about the offspring of a fruit fly. If only he could've landed a different job. Something quieter. A job that didn't require working three nights a week and every weekend at a noisy college bar. He'd applied for various positions with the library, the campus bookstore, and the cafeteria, but Windy Canyon was the only offer that materialized. And if he wanted to stay at ASU, he had to work. There was no other option. He certainly couldn't go back to New York City. That door was definitely closed. *Why did I have to open my big mouth?* he berated himself as the professor diagramed the genetic combinations achieved by mating blue-eyed and brown-eyed humans.

Ahead of high school graduation, he'd come out to his parents. He'd thought it was the right thing to do. The honest way forward. But that night, standing in the hallway of his parents' New York City apartment, his father's shoulders seemed to stretch from wall to wall as Zak backed away. "Some secrets are best kept to yourself," his dad had shouted, eyes flashing with anger. "That's not how we raised you," his mother said moments before she slapped him across the face. And on this point, his parents were in perfect agreement: If that's how you choose to live your life, you're on your own.

Zak had been stunned. Why had his parents reacted so negatively? He really couldn't understand it. They weren't particularly religious. His mother never lit candles on Friday nights. They certainly weren't kosher. He couldn't remember the last time they'd gone to temple. Besides, he'd thought religion was mostly about one's belief in God. Not about sexual orientation. Or was their reaction based on voting Republican? But weren't there gay Republicans too? He was sure there must be. Besides, he had no idea how his parents voted. He'd never paid much attention to politics. It was all too controversial. Too ugly. Still, he wasn't the first gay kid to pop up in New York City, or for that matter, in America. He'd seen *Joe Bell* with Mark Wahlberg and *Love, Simon*. Weren't parents supposed to support their gay kid? Be grateful the secret was shared? He'd read that coming out was difficult for a gay teenager. But he hadn't expected his parents to behave so badly. He must have missed that chapter.

That June, Zak moved in with Allison, his best friend from high school. Allison's parents had consented to his staying in the guestroom as long as he understood it was a temporary arrangement. In the interim, he interviewed via Zoom for jobs in Tempe and landed the spot at The Windy Canyon Bar. In retrospect, he was grateful he'd waited until the end of high school to come out. God only knows what might have happened if he'd told his parents before they had paid for his first semester's tuition. Still, they'd made it clear that future expenses would be on him, including the one-way plane ticket to Phoenix.

Soon, it was mid-July. Standing together at LaGuardia Airport, Allison slipped $200 into his back pocket. "Oh no," he protested, pulling the money out and thrusting it back into her hand.

But Allison wasn't about to take no for an answer. With her brown hair pulled back into a ponytail, she looked even younger than Zak. Her eyes glistened as a warning of the tears to come. "Don't be silly. How are you going to manage?"

"I'm starting a job tomorrow night."

"You won't get paid for two weeks. There are meals and other necessities. You'll need cab fare from the airport to the dorm."

"I've figured it out," he said, feeling tremendous pride over his attention to detail. "Phoenix has a light rail system from the airport to the university and I've got enough cash for a few months. I should be fine."

Allison hugged him, slipping the money back into his pants pocket. "Just take it. I'll feel better and you'll have a bit of security. You can pay me back when you can."

Zak acquiesced. "But it's only a loan."

Allison squeezed him tighter. "I swear. You're the bravest person I know."

But he didn't feel particularly brave. Truth be told, he was terrified, which reminded him of a mantra he'd heard somewhere: fake it till you make it. At the time, he'd thought it was pure bullshit. But at the airport with Allison's arms about him, he realized that was exactly what he needed to do.

The professor rattled on about the process of mitosis as Zak leaned forward, elbow on the desk, cheek cradled in a palm. He squinted, imagining the bow-tied professor fronting for The Dirty Toenails. What instrument would he play? And then, as if the universe had heard the question, the professor approached the blackboard, picked up a piece of white chalk, and with a quick downward stroke, emitted a high-pitched squeak. The classroom let out a collective moan.

Hmm, Zak thought. *Perhaps The Dirty Toenails should add a blackboard to the band.*

After biology class, Zak headed to the campus library where he grabbed the first empty seat he could find. He opened his iPad and started to search ASU's online job board. He had to find another job. A job without the noise, rowdiness, and late-night hours of people who abuse alcohol. The openings were mostly for day shifts when Zak had classes. Other positions were off campus in Chandler and Mesa, places Zak had never heard of. Discouraged, he resigned himself to making the best of a bad situation. What other choice did he have? He needed the money.

Returning to his dorm, Zak crossed paths with Chuck, his roommate, a dark-haired, stocky guy from San Francisco. Chuck had a penchant for tie-dyed T-shirts and baggy jeans that barely clung to his hips. The daily maintenance of his close-cropped beard was the only clue that Chuck was at all interested in his appearance. A superior athlete, he was on a wrestling scholarship, reinforcing Zak's belief that they made an odd combination. While Zak had been a late bloomer with his tall, lanky frame, Chuck was thick and grounded like a fireplug with a sleeve of tattoos running down a well-muscled arm. He and Chuck had been randomly assigned through the ASU pool of students requiring housing. Zak hadn't anticipated rooming with a jock and though Chuck was friendly, Zak wished he wasn't so attractive. In tight living quarters, it was hard to ignore Chuck and his perfect male form.

The dorm room held two single beds pressed against opposite walls, anchored by matching closets and a chest of drawers. In the middle, there were two desks set back-to-back, so that each side of the room was a mirror-image of the other. Zak dropped his book bag on the floor and collapsed onto his bed. "I should have stayed here. I practically slept through the entire lecture."

Chuck pulled out a pair of Nike shorts from a drawer. He had nothing on but a white jock strap. "How late did you come in last night?"

Zak averted his eyes as Chuck slipped into the shorts. "Two a.m. I can't believe I didn't wake you."

"You couldn't wake me on your best day," Chuck said as he stroked the pelt of black hairs that covered his chest and stomach. "I could sleep through a rocket attack."

Zak couldn't believe he and Chuck were the same age. Chuck looked so much older. Maybe it was the beard or the well-muscled frame. Zak was certain Chuck had been part of the cool crowd in high school, while Zak mostly tagged along with Allison, never really part of any social group, always a satellite in constant orbit about Allison, the popular cheerleader.

Chuck slipped into a black T-shirt that stretched tightly across his chest. The T-shirt read: *Hands Off*. "So, how's the new job going?" Chuck asked.

"Terrible," Zak admitted. "I have to find something else. The hours are nuts and the noise is hurting my good ear."

Zak had shared with Chuck that he'd been deaf in his left ear since childhood. It seemed like important information for a roommate. Instead of merely accepting the fact, Chuck had wanted to know more. Zak explained that at age two the nerve had died during a bout of pneumonia. And though he wasn't sure, Zak thought Chuck's eyes glistened as he shared the details of his hearing loss. "My ear doctor in New York always warned me about the danger of loud noises. He'd say, 'No concerts and no headphones.' He'd probably have a stroke if he knew I was working at The Windy Canyon Bar. The noise level is unbelievable."

"So, what are you going to do?"

"I don't know," Zak said. "I've started to check out other options, but it doesn't look good. I may have to stay with the bar. I need the money."

"And your ear?"

"I guess I could wear an earplug," Zak said as the idea dawned on him. "Of course. That's it. Why didn't I think of that before?"

"What about the late nights?"

Zak had only one solution. "Coffee."

Chuck lifted a bottle of Red Bull out of his desk drawer. "Or you could try this." He tossed the small bottle over the two desks and into Zak's lap.

Zak checked the label. "Isn't this stuff dangerous?"

Chuck did a double take. "It isn't heroin. It's a stimulant. Perfectly legal. Carried in all the best stores." He pulled another bottle from the desk and held it against his cheek, pretending he was doing a commercial. "Need to cram for a test? Have an early morning class? Just one sip and your problems are solved."

Zak nodded. It was worth a try.

Gear in tow, Chuck zipped his gym bag. "I've got to get going," he said. "Wrestling practice."

Zak couldn't help but be envious. "You're so lucky to have a scholarship."

"Lucky! Do you know how much work it took to land that damn scholarship? The hours of practice and training. When I think about it . . ." There was a look of disgust on Chuck's face. "Well, I don't want to think about it."

Zak still thought Chuck was lucky.

"Wait for me before you go to dinner tonight," Chuck said as slipped the gym bag over his shoulder and headed out the door.

Zak wondered what Chuck's life must have been like growing up in the Bay Area. To Zak, Chuck was a complete mystery. It was as if Bigfoot had shown up on the first day of college and miraculously befriended him. While Zak had marveled at Chuck's hulking physicality, Chuck rambled on about being homesick and missing his mom. Zak instantly liked him. When Chuck made it clear that they were going to be pals by inviting Zak to join him for meals, Zak was awed. But how could he ever truly be friends with a guy like Chuck? Zak certainly wasn't a jock. Still, Chuck didn't seem to care. If anything, Chuck appeared to almost prefer that his roommate was a geek. Good news for Zak.

———— ∽∽ ————

Zak shoved a yellow earplug into his right ear. It was ten at night and The Windy Canyon Bar was packed. With the earplug tucked firmly in place, the noise level was muted as Zak circulated through the crowd, picking up empty glasses and plates, wiping down tables and chairs. Earlier in the evening, a drunken woman had left the contents of her stomach on the floor outside the ladies' restroom. Zak cleaned up the mess using a wet vac as he held his breath and suppressed a gag.

"Hey, you," a guy shouted, hand waving in the air. He was at a table with four other guys. "Get me another Tombstone IPA."

Zak held up a finger as he looked about for Melinda. Getting drinks was her job.

"Hey, buddy." The guy was now up on his feet, a nasty scowl on his face. "I'm talking to you."

Zak removed the earplug. It was instinctual. He certainly didn't need to. He understood the guy perfectly well with the earplug in. And for what he couldn't hear, he could lip-read, thanks to years of lip-reading classes sponsored by the New York City public school system. He'd attended those classes with kids who were profoundly deaf and who suffered noticeable speech impediments, leaving no doubt that their hearing was diminished. But Zak, because he had one good ear, had no speech impediment. So instead of being uncomfortable about his hearing loss, Zak mostly ignored it until he was forced to confront the problem, as in the case of The Windy Canyon's noise level.

"I'll get the waitress," Zak shouted above the din of the crowd. "She'll take care of you."

"No way," the guy said, his face contorted in a grimace.

"Okay," Zak conceded as he reached for the empty mug.

The guy pushed his hand away. "Get me a fresh mug, loser."

From the corner of his eye, Zak spotted Melinda making her way over. In the owner's absence, she handled the bar, waited tables, and mostly ran the place. She eyed the guy. "Not you, again. How many does that make? Three? Four? That's your limit. Time to say goodnight."

The guy stood and placed a threatening hand on Melinda's shoulder. In a flash, Melinda grabbed the hand, and with a quick twist and spin, the guy's arm was behind his back. Melinda sharply tugged the arm upward and the guy let out a yelp. "You want to play games?" she said, her voice menacing as she pulled the arm higher and marched the guy toward the rear exit. Zak followed along, holding the door open as Melinda, the tiny dynamo, readied the rude patron for a lesson in proper bar etiquette. With a hard shove, the guy went flying into the back alley as the door closed and locked behind him.

Melinda turned to Zak. It had all happened so fast, Zak was speechless. "And that," she said, "is how we take care of angry drunks and rude college brats. Any questions?"

Zak shook his head.

"Good," she said as she marched off, leaving Zak in her wake.

<hr>

When Zak had first met Melinda, she was on her knees, cursing a blue streak, one arm flailing underneath an overstuffed armchair.

"Lost something?" Zak innocently asked.

When Melinda looked up, strands of red hair swept across her face, reminding Zak of Cousin Itt from *The Addams Family*, a movie he'd seen with his dad when he was in grade school. "No, genius. I'm searching for spare change because my Apple Wallet is empty."

Zak was taken aback. There was no reason to be smug. "Just tell me what you're looking for and I can check around."

"Go away," she said as she stood up, a hand pushing the hair away from her face. She flipped the chair cushion and searched the corners. "Can't you see I'm busy? Go hit on someone else."

Zak realized the problem. A college bar. A cocktail waitress. It couldn't be easy. "Hey, you've got me all wrong. I'm an employee."

Melinda turned to look at him. Freckles covered her cheeks. Her blue eyes telegraphed suspicion. "Well, okay," she conceded as if Zak had passed some test. "Do you have a phone on you?"

Zak retrieved his iPhone from a back pocket.

"Unlock it."

Zak did as he was told. She grabbed it, and with a few quick jabs, Kelly Clarkson was singing "Invincible" from somewhere in the bar. Melinda headed in one direction, Zak the other, both in search of the lost Kelly.

"Here it is," Melinda shouted, prize held high.

"Great!" Zak said as he closed the gap between them. "Mystery solved."

She handed Zak's phone back. "Not really. Why were you all the way over there when my phone was over here? What were you looking for?"

Zak blushed. "Yeah . . . well," he muttered. "I'm deaf in my left ear. I only hear on my right side. I can never really tell where sound is coming from. Everything seems to always be happening on the right."

She looked at Zak from ear to ear as if his deafness might be distinguished by sight. "Why don't you wear a hearing aid?"

Zak hated the question. He'd been asked the same thing throughout his school years. "It's a dead nerve. There's nothing they can do."

"Oh," she said, in a sympathetic tone. "I'm sorry."

"Please," Zak said, hand in the air. "No need. I'm fine. Really."

She nodded, but her blue eyes lingered as if she wanted to know more. More than Zak was willing to reveal to a stranger.

She adjusted her T-shirt emblazoned with The Windy Canyon Bar logo—two coyotes howling at the moon. "I'm Melinda," she said, extending a hand.

Zak took Melinda's hand and immediately thought of Allison. Allison's popularity and good looks had provided him with a measure of protection as a closeted gay teen. As head cheerleader, Allison's zesty personality and curvy figure had buoyed her to the top of the class pyramid. The kids at school assumed Zak had a crush on her. He never corrected them, riding along on her coat tails.

Melinda's grip was surprisingly strong. "How come I haven't seen you here before?"

Zak tried to release Melinda's hand, but she held tight. "I've only been here a week. Mostly nights."

"Ah, that explains it." She twisted his hand back and forth as she studied him. "I've been in Chicago. My grandmother died."

"I'm sorry."

She smiled as she continued to engage his grip, pulling on his hand in a gentle tug-of-war. "You're very polite, aren't you?"

Zak's cheeks burned.

"Are you a freshman?"

Zak scowled. "Is it obvious?"

"Not so much," she teased as she pulled him slightly toward her, releasing his hand, causing him to be a bit off balance. "I've worked here for three years. I can usually tell the freshman from the rest of the crew. But you're different. I'm not sure what it is. You don't seem needy and helpless. Are you needy and helpless?"

Zak didn't know how to respond. Had his outward veneer of confidence fooled her? Was it his height of six two? Allison had told him that no one could spot that he was gay. That she'd never have known if he hadn't confided in her when he was fifteen. He imagined himself lucky. Nature had provided a sort of camouflage. He could hide in plain sight.

"Anyway, should you need anything, I'm your gal. Freddy, the owner, is usually out of town, so I'm the go-to person. You've met Freddy, right?"

They'd only met briefly. Just long enough for Zak to know his basic duties at the bar. "Well, sort of . . ."

Melinda leaned in conspiratorially. "He's a hard ass. You don't want to cross him. Which means you never want to be late. Otherwise, Freddy will tell me to *take care of you*."

Zak had no idea what that even meant. "You mean, dock my pay?"

"Oh, honey," Melinda cooed, her tone dripping with sarcasm. "Has anyone ever told you that you're adorable?"

Zak had no idea what to make of Melinda. "Are you also working your way through ASU?"

Melinda laughed. "Me! No, sweet pea. I'm thirty-one!"

Zak was stunned. There was nothing about Melinda—not the shapely figure, button nose, and bright smile, that hinted at such maturity. "I'm sorry," he stammered.

"Sorry? Don't be sorry. You just made my day. Don't get me wrong. I love looking young. I just don't like it when men assume I'm naive."

Zak couldn't imagine anyone mistaking Melinda for naive.

She tucked a lock of red hair behind her ear. "You know, not everyone in Tempe is part of ASU. Some of us work for a living. Some of us never even went to college. Some of us," she said as she lifted the name tag that hung around Zak's neck, "like it that way, Andrew."

Confused, Zak glanced at the tag inside the plastic cover. His first and last name were reversed. He'd never noticed it. "My name's Zak," he said, feeling like a fool.

Melinda seized on the moment. "Then who is Andrew?" she asked, breaking into a broad smile as if she'd come upon a secret.

"*Andrews*. That's my last name."

Melinda grabbed Zak's arm and pulled on it. "You're too much," she said with a laugh. "Has anyone ever told you that?"

Zak was unsure what to say.

"Well, you are," she assured him. "And from now on, you're going to be *my Andy*. That'll be my special name for you. So, you listen to me, *Andy boy*," Melinda said as she clung to his arm, squeezing his bicep. "We need to close ranks. This bar can be a tough place to work. And if you don't mind me saying, we need to get you to a gym. Management expects you to jump in if there's a bar fight. Don't make me protect you."

"Don't you worry about me," Zak answered, his voice deepening as he struggled to muster his confidence. Could he lose his job if he was unable to fight? He'd never been much good with his fists. "I can take care of myself," he bluffed.

Melinda grinned. She didn't seem convinced. "Well good for you." Her smile softened. "I better get back to work. See you around, *Andy*."

Zak watched as Melinda disappeared into the kitchen. Bar fights. Was she serious? No one had told him about that part of the job. Should a bar fight break out, he'd definitely slip out the nearest exit. He'd no intention of fighting. Violence was crossing the line, no matter how much he needed the money. *Dear God*, he fretted. *What have I gotten myself into?*

– 3 –

HELENA'S BRIEF STINT in the hospital generated a battery of tests but no answers to explain the dizziness and her subsequent fall in the bathroom. On the third day of the hospital stay, she was discharged. Her mood dipped as she returned to an empty house. The hospital had been so busy with staff coming and going at all hours. There'd been so many opportunities to interact with strangers. Interesting people she'd never meet during the course of a typical day. Everyone was young and energetic. So full of life. And so focused on her well-being. Back home, it was quiet. Deadly quiet. There was no one to talk to except the hummingbirds who populated her garden, and so far, they weren't talking back.

She was once again referred to her cardiologist, Dr. Shin, and on the morning of the appointment, sat in the waiting room turning through an old issue of *People*. She was shocked to read that Ben Affleck and Jennifer Lopez were once again a couple. She was in awe of Jennifer's courage to try another marriage, especially with a man she'd been so publicly aligned with years earlier. Two marriages were more than enough for Helena. She couldn't imagine herself having the courage to do a third, never mind exchanging vows with an old paramour. "Oh, how can that union ever last?" she mumbled to herself.

"Ms. Greenblatt." A nurse in blue scrubs stood with a clipboard by an open door. "You're next."

Helena followed the young man through the maze of Dr. Shin's back office, passing exam rooms, a nurse's station, a group of techs standing together in consultation, and a large open area with exercise bicycles, a treadmill, and floor mats. "You have a gym here?" she asked, not remembering the space from earlier visits.

The nurse swiveled about, an amused look on his face. "It's new as of last month. We just combined our existing equipment in one spot and took down a few walls. That area's for stress testing and cardiac rehabilitation."

Helena thought it marvelous. "You can tell someone is stressed by the way they ride a bike?"

"Oh, no," the nurse corrected her. "The treadmill is for stress tests. We measure your blood pressure as we increase the elevation of the track."

Helena nodded. "Of course," she said, laughing at herself for being so silly.

Once in the exam room, the nurse invited Helena to take a seat on the exam table as he logged into a laptop situated on the counter. "I'll need to confirm your birthdate," the nurse said.

"Oh, no you don't," Helena answered as she hopped onto the exam table, struggling to right herself as her feet dangled. "My age is already in the chart. Everyone has asked me for it, and up to now, I've been happy to comply. But I'm growing impatient with that question. Some women don't want to be asked their age over and over again."

"I'm sorry," he said. "But I need your age to confirm your identity."

"There's more to me than my age. Maybe there's another question you can ask."

"Sure," he said. "Can you give me the last four digits of your social security number?"

"Oh, no," Helena said, this time with even greater emphasis.

The nurse seemed surprised. "The last four digits?"

Helena wasn't exactly certain if the last four digits might be okay, or was it her Medicare ID number she wasn't supposed to share? Or her address? Whatever it was, it was something AARP had warned about. And AARP should know.

"Well then, let's just confirm your name."

Helena glared. "You just called my name in the waiting room, and I answered."

The nurse laughed. "Are you serious?" But once he realized Helena was indeed serious, he apologized. "I'm sorry. No one has ever pushed back on any of this. It's just standard. It's our way of making sure that the chart we're looking at belongs to the person we're treating. It cuts down on medical errors."

Helena became instantly alarmed. "Medical errors."

"Yes," the nurse explained. "There can be medical errors. Everything from drug interactions to entering medical data in the wrong chart. We try to avoid mistakes."

Helena sniffed. She didn't want to be disagreeable, but she didn't appreciate being treated like a cog in the wheel of a large healthcare system. She was an individual. A perfectly lovely human being who wanted to be treated as such. But she also didn't want to present as a pain in the ass. No one likes a pain in the ass. And above all, when at the mercy of others, she knew being liked was important. "Okay, then," she relented. "I was born in January of 1939. I'm a Capricorn. It was a cold and snowy day in the Bronx when I was delivered at Mount Eden Hospital. It isn't there anymore. The odd thing is, I have a burial plot at Mount Nebo Cemetery in Miami. Imagine that? I'll have spent a lifetime crossing from one mountain to the other. Proverbially, of course. I guess my life has been one tough trek," she said, laughing at this new perspective.

The nurse looked at her as if he was about to ask another question, but instead relented with a quick nod. "Well, it was nice meeting you," he said, preparing to leave.

"I'm sorry," Helena interrupted. "But we haven't really met. You see, I don't know your name."

The nurse paused. "My name is James."

Helena broke into a smile. "It's so nice to meet you, James. How long have you been working as a nurse?"

James rocked from side to side. "Ten years. I graduated from ASU."

"How wonderful. Your parents must be proud."

James beamed. "They are now. My dad thought I should've been a lawyer."

Helena titled her head slightly as she apprised James. "Oh no. You're the spitting image of a nurse. Handsome, energetic, and kind."

James blushed. "Well, thank you," he said. "That's nice of you to say." He paused, as if a fresh thought had occurred to him. "I want to apologize. Clearly my manners could be better. I should have introduced myself at the start."

Helena offered her warmest smile. "Well dear, don't be too hard on yourself. You know, we're all a work in progress. And being aware of our shortcomings is really the first step to correcting them."

"I suppose," James said, his face contorted in an expression that Helena could only assume meant *message received*.

～

Helena sat alone in the exam room for ten minutes until there was a knock at the door. Dr. Shin, a young man sporting a stethoscope around his neck, entered. At least in Helena's estimation, he was young. Dr. Shin was somewhere in his mid-forties. They'd met six months earlier when she'd first been referred by her primary care physician. Back then, Dr. Shin had mentioned he owned a greenhouse. They had a lovely chat about raising orchids. *Such a fine hobby*, she'd thought. And so wonderful that a man of medicine would be captivated by the art of growing one of nature's most beautiful treasures.

"Mrs. Greenblatt?" Dr. Shin asked. His eyes were dull. His tone, flat. His facial expression was that of a stranger.

Her heart sank as she nodded. The doctor didn't seem to remember her. She must not have made a favorable impression. Surely a woman in her eighties would be memorable. But then there were quite a few seniors gathered in Dr. Shin's waiting room. Perhaps it was unrealistic to expect the doctor to remember every patient.

"First, let's take a quick listen to your heart," he said as he pressed a stethoscope to her chest. "Deep breaths, please." He repeated the process on her back.

Helena did as she was told, suddenly eager to wrap up the visit and go home. She wanted to know what was wrong, and yet she didn't want to hear bad news.

Dr. Shin sat down before her on a stool positioned slightly lower than Helena. She wished she could change places with him. It didn't seem right to be looking down on his bald head.

"I've gone through your test results," he said as he crinkled his forehead.

Such beautiful skin, Helena thought. *I wonder if he's a vegetarian.*

"To be honest, I haven't found any heart-related issues that might explain your fainting episodes. The good news is that your tests are normal. Nothing unusual to report."

Helena absorbed the news. Nothing had changed since the last visit. The fainting was still a mystery. And if the doctor thought there was nothing wrong with her, who was she to argue?

"Have you experienced any further dizziness since returning home?"

Helena thought it an odd question. If she had, she would've gone back to the hospital. "No. I've been fine," she confessed.

"Well then, I think we should take a wait-and-see attitude," he said, standing up and turning his back to Helena as he typed away on the laptop, entering information into Helena's electronic medical record.

Helena felt a chill. She gripped the edge of the exam table as the room began to spin. Sure enough, just as the spinning stopped, Ruthie presented, standing next to the doctor, shaking her head. Helena tried to remain nonchalant, but Ruthie's appearance was as startling as it was intrusive.

Tell him you're going to sue his ass off if it happens again!

Helena shifted uncomfortably. "I won't say that."

The doctor stopped typing. He turned and gave Helena a quizzical look. "Excuse me. Did you say something?"

Ruthie stamped a foot. *She's not okay. Would she be here if she was okay? Maybe it's time for you to go back to medical school for a refresher.*

Helena swallowed hard. If only she could wish Ruthie away. "I'm fine," she answered the doctor.

You're not fine, Ruthie insisted.

"I am," she repeated.

The doctor seemed alarmed. "Maybe you should lie down. Can I get you a glass of water?"

Helena shook her head. "No, really. I just don't understand about these dizzy spells."

The doctor smiled. "Well, the human body is a mysterious thing. We think we know everything about how it works, but some things aren't cut and dry. I'd rather not play around with drugs and other treatments with a woman of your age if there'd be no benefit."

Ask him, Ruthie said in a huff. *Is that what he'd tell his own mother? Is that the diagnosis he'd give a man?*

Helena was slack-jawed. Ruthie needed to butt out. "I guess it's good news, then."

"For the moment," the doctor agreed as he reached for Helena's hand and gave it a gentle shake. "We'll schedule another follow-up in six months. Until then, you can find your way out when you're ready. Be sure to stop at the front desk and they'll set up the next appointment," he said as he exited the room.

Helena remained seated on the exam table, unsure what the doctor had meant by *for the moment*.

Ruthie crossed her arms. *It's called covering your ass.*

Helena snorted. Ruthie could be so suspicious of people.

❧

Back at home, sitting at the kitchen table and sipping a cup of coffee, Helena spotted a full-page advertisement in the newspaper for Ventana, an Arizona retirement community abutting the Arizona State University campus. *Live the Lifestyle You've Always Dreamed Of,* screamed the headline. *An exciting new experiment in aging that offers seniors the same amenities available to students of ASU. Access to the library and educational curricula with an intergenerational experience mingling with ASU students.*

Helena was intrigued. The timing of the advertisement, pure kismet.

Over the years, she'd come to dread the idea of living in a senior community, as if proximity to older people might have a deleterious effect on her body and mind. She recognized her fear as an innate prejudice, and like all prejudices, wondered if exposure was the only way to overcome it. But where did the fear come from? Was it rooted in the struggles with her mother, watching the aging process up close, seeing Ruthie becoming increasingly difficult to manage? Obstinate. Opinionated. Embittered. But then, Ruthie had always been difficult. So perhaps *we just become more* as we age. More set in our ways. More intractable. More determined. But why would only the negative traits become *more*? Maybe we might become kinder, more loving, more willing to embrace change. Could that also be possible?

Helena was excited by the fact that Ventana seemed to be offering something new. Something she could imagine herself exploring. An adult community for intelligent, active seniors, eager to be a part of an educational environment. The concept sparked memories of her youth at New York University, attending night classes, hearing national speakers debate the controversial topics of the times: the Cold War, Vietnam, the rise of Black Power and the civil rights movement. She imagined this could be the antidote to her isolation and loneliness.

No sooner had the thought presented than the familiar dizziness took hold. Helena placed her hands flat on the table and steadied herself. Thank God she was sitting. After a minute, which seemed like ten, she opened her eyes to find Ruthie standing by the coffee pot, a cigarette held high.

It's a great idea. You should definitely check that place out.

Helena took a breath. "You're back."

Ruthie scowled. *Well, that's not very welcoming.*

Helena chewed on her lower lip, a nervous habit she'd picked up after her second marriage. "Why are you here?"

That coffee smells great. Of all the things I miss, coffee is definitely at the top of the list. You'd think it might be a steak, or a chocolate chip cookie, or even mac and cheese. Oh, what I wouldn't give for a strong cup of coffee.

Helena stared at her mother's essence. "Then why the cigarette? Why not a cup of coffee?"

Ruthie glared at Helena as if she was an idiot. *Did you ever know a smoker who preferred coffee to a cigarette? My goodness, Helena, for an old woman you certainly know nothing about addictions or human nature. Besides, the cigarette's an illusion.*

Do you think a spirit can actually smoke? Honestly. Sometimes I wonder about your IQ.

Helena returned to her *Arizona Republic*. Maybe if she ignored Ruthie, she'd disappear. She scanned the newspaper, eyeing each story. One depressing headline after the next. Floods, famine, war. Why was the world in such a mess? Was there no end to the misery?

Oh, there's an end, Ruthie warned.

Helena had forgotten that when Ruthie was around, there were no private thoughts.

And trust me, dear. The way you live, you'll find out about that end soon enough.

Helena popped her head up. "Now why would you say something like that?"

Ruthie pressed a palm to her chest, wordlessly denying any ill intent.

Helena was ticked. "Well, I'm not scared. You have no power over me. I'm a grown woman, and grown women don't scare so easily."

Ruthie shook her head. *I'm just speaking the truth.*

"Your truth," Helena said as she turned her attention back to the newspaper. There, she spotted a small print advertisement for puppies. Gosh, she wished she was young enough to get a puppy. But there was no way she'd be around another thirteen years as a puppy aged into a senior dog. Ninety-six was definitely out of the question. Sure, it was possible for Betty White, Rose Kennedy, and Olivia de Havilland, but for the average human being, it was a stretch. And puppies require so much work. Adopting an older dog would be better. But then, how could she consider a dog when she was experiencing fainting spells? There was no way she'd put a dog in that circumstance. Still, owning a dog was such a lovely thought and perhaps a pet would provide purpose. Extend her life, as if remaining alive required one to have a long-term goal; a reason to rise and shine.

She'd never thought of herself as someone who was afraid to die, but she was keenly aware that she didn't want to go yet. There were still things for her to do. Read another book. Enjoy another dish of ice cream. Ignore another neighbor (or were they ignoring her?). She knew there were no guarantees in life. Nothing was permanent. She'd learned that lesson from burying two husbands, seeing her adult sons drift away, and watching a successful career slip through her fingers. *How odd life is,* she thought. Want, want, want, and more want. Can it ever be enough? Can we ever feel fulfilled? Or is fulfillment just an illusion?

The gentle scent of Jean Nate surrounded her. Ruthie's favorite perfume. *I may say it poorly, but I only want what's best for you.*

Helena surrendered to the moment. "What would you have me do?"

Move into an adult community where there are people nearby should you need them.

"I'm not ready," Helena said as she turned the page of the newspaper and spotted her horoscope. She stared at the words next to the sun sign of Capricorn: Today will be a good day filled with wisdom. Open your heart and mind to change.

Ruthie pressed on. *Don't wait for another emergency. Don't let the next fall be the one to put you in a nursing home. Helena, look around now and decide where you want to be for the rest of your life. While you're still alert and can make the choice.*

Helena had to admit Ruthie made sense. But was she ready to give up living on her own? Had she truly arrived at the point in life when such a decision was necessary? Dr. Shin had said her tests were normal. Couldn't she just go on managing on her own? Wouldn't it be simpler? Easier?

Ruthie was adamant. *You're a fool if you continue to hide in this house.*

Helena rubbed her eyes. Was she refusing to accept the future? Wasn't it inevitable that she'd need help as she continued to age? She could either hire strangers or move where she'd have access to help if needed. She flipped back through the newspaper to find the Ventana advertisement. Maybe Ruthie was right. Perhaps it was time to take a tour of the sparkling new building in downtown Tempe, Arizona. It certainly couldn't hurt to check it out.

– 4 –

THE THIRD WEEK into the semester, while working his Thursday night shift at The Windy Canyon Bar, Zak received a text from his friend, Allison Klein. She had wanted to come for a visit and once Allison made up her mind there was no stopping her. He'd barely stayed in touch, texting now and then when he could find the time. But Allison was not one to be put off. Her best friend was missing in action, and she decided that the only way to correct the situation was through an intervention. And everyone knows interventions are best done face-to-face.

Allison: *I'm at Phoenix airport.*
Zak: *What?*
Allison: *You don't sound happy.*
Zak: *Surprised. I'm working.*
Allison: *Working at 10 pm?*
Zak: *Yes.*
Allison: *LOL.*
Zak: *Take an Uber to Windy Canyon in Tempe.*

Allison: *Is that a place?*
Zak: *It's a bar. SYL.*
Allison: *SYL?*
Zak: *See you later.*

The Dirty Toenails were finishing their set when Zak spotted Allison at the door. The bar was crowded, and Allison, in a yellow Lilly Pulitzer dress covered in flowers, stuck out like a sore thumb amid the grunge of the jeans and T-shirt crowd. A very pretty, petite, sore thumb. Within moments, they were in each other's arms.

"You, handsome devil," she cried. "Why haven't I heard from you?"

"I texted," Zak said in his defense.

"That's not the same as calling. You definitely need to call or I'm just going to have to transfer to ASU. Do you hear me?" she said, shaking him from side to side as she tightened her grip about him.

Zak laughed. It was nearly impossible to hear anything in the noisy bar, but he could always make out Allison's high timbre. Anywhere. Anytime. Ever since they'd met in seventh grade, and Allison had learned about his hearing problem, she'd been asking him if he could hear her. Of course he could hear her. Everyone could hear her. As time passed, it'd became a throwaway line, more of a habit than a question related to Zak's deafness. *Do you hear me* was now synonymous with *I love you.*

Like a dog with a bone, Allison was not about to let Zak off the hook. "So why haven't you called?"

"I've been busy," Zak admitted as the band exited the stage.

Allison checked out the guys as they passed. *Cute*, she mouthed with a hand on her heart. "But all that noise. I can still feel the bass. It's so intense. How can you stand it?"

Zak pulled an earplug from his good ear. "This is how!"

Allison laughed. "How were you able to hear me with that thing in?"

"Lip-reading. You remember lip-reading," Zak said, though the earplug had only dulled the intensity of Allison's voice. Zak screwed the earplug back in as the house music came on. Allison covered her ears. "Grab a seat," he said as he started to pull away. "I'll see if I can get out of here early."

"What?" she said, her face contorted.

Zak pointed at an empty seat at the bar before rushing off to find Melinda. When he looked back, Allison was comfortably seated, facing away from the bar. A tall guy with a dark beard had already approached her. She cupped an ear and leaned in, struggling to hear, but from her expression, she looked to be having a good time. Zak guessed she couldn't understand a word the guy was saying, but then a good time was Allison's middle name. She always looked happy. That was her stock and trade.

⁓

Zak was glad Chuck was a sound sleeper. When he and Allison arrived back at the dorm after midnight, he was afraid Allison might wake Chuck with her incessant chatter. But Chuck, ensconced in the bed on the other side of the room, snored through it all, which only made Allison giggle.

"Quiet," Zak said, a fingertip pressed to his lips. He and Allison were lying side by side, looking up at the ceiling.

"I can't help it," Allison whimpered as she shifted, turning on her side to face Zak. "Could you move over a little?"

"I wish I could," Zak whispered, but the single bed was too small for two. He hadn't noticed it before, but the bed actually sagged in the middle. "If you'd told me you were coming, I could have found you a spot with someone whose roommate was leaving for the weekend."

"Don't be silly," Allison whispered. "I came to see you. We're here together. We might be crowded, but it's kind of fun."

"But how did you slip away? Don't you have classes?"

"You know me. I'm a free spirit. I can't be defined by a schedule. Besides, I'm a theater major. I'm not missing much. Have credit card . . . will travel."

Zak sensed there was more to the story, but didn't want to push. Besides, it wasn't his business if Allison wished to squander her money.

Chuck let out a loud snort and rolled over. Bed springs squeaked, followed by the sound of covers being kicked off.

"Tell me about him," Allison said. "Where's he from? What's he like?"

"He's from San Francisco. And he's a nice guy. Very friendly."

"Is he . . ."

Zak waited for the next word.

" . . . hot?"

"I don't know about his temperature. I've never touched him."

Allison gave Zak a bump with her knee. "You know what I mean."

"Yes, Allison. He is."

"Oh good," she said, snuggling closer. "I can't wait to see what he looks like in the morning."

"Like a hot mess. Just like you're going to look."

Allison jerked straight up. "Oh no. I can't let him see me like that."

Zak stifled a laugh. "How about we hide you under a blanket until he heads to the shower."

Allison laid her head back down. "The shower," she repeated as if she had a plan.

Zak rolled onto his side, turning away. Whatever Allison had in mind, he was too tired to hear about it. "I have to get some sleep. I have class at nine a.m."

Allison turned onto her other side, facing the wall. They were now back-to-back. She gently bumped his butt.

Within moments, Zak was asleep.

By the time Zak reached the lecture hall, class was wrapping up. Between Windy Canyon and Allison's surprise visit, he'd overslept and missed the session. *I'm such an idiot,* he thought as students rushed past. He pressed his back to the wall and slowly slid down until his butt touched the floor. There he sat, outside the lecture hall, as he assessed the situation. He was a college freshman who needed to work to stay in school. But what was the point of being in college if he couldn't stay awake during class, or worse, missed class? How could he become a doctor if he couldn't even get through Introduction to Biology? And how much of the class notes would be part of a future exam? The whole thing seemed absolutely hopeless. Yet, there was a small voice inside his head that refused to allow him to give up. If anything, he was more determined than ever to figure this whole college thing out. He'd just have to redouble his efforts. Gather himself up and take another stab at it. Figure out how to balance the job and his classes. Perhaps if he worked at night, he should study afterward, staying up until his morning class, and then sleep in the afternoon. If he shifted his schedule, he might be able to manage. Maybe, all he needed to do was think about his life differently.

Buoyed by a change in attitude, Zak headed to the student café to grab a cup of coffee before his Introduction to Philosophy class. Knapsack on his back, coffee on the brain, he was waiting in line to order when he felt a tap on the shoulder. He turned to find a guy with blond hair staring down at him. The guy had to be six-foot-four. Zak had seen him in biology class. You couldn't miss him. This week, his hair was blond. The week before it'd been streaked pink. The week before that, lime green.

"Aren't you in my bio class?" the guy said. His handsome face sported a dark stubble. "I saw you sitting on the floor in the hallway. That's one hell of a way to attend a lecture. Are you okay?"

"Not really," Zak admitted. "I'm a total moron."

The guy nodded as if he understood. "You need the class notes, don't you?"

"Yup," Zak answered as he stared at the guy's hairline. Was the color platinum blond or a shade of light gray? It was hard to tell.

"It's not natural," the guy chuckled without Zak asking. "So, do you live off campus?"

"I'm in the dorms."

The guy's eyes lit up. "And you still can't get to class on time? You need to learn how to set an alarm on your phone."

Zak laughed. "I already have a clock alarm by my bedside. What I need is an atomic bomb to go off."

"Your bed must be comfortable."

Zak thought of the sag in the middle. How sleeping on his side felt as if he was hanging onto a ledge. "I work late. It's eating into my sleep time."

The guy nodded. He had a nice smile. Big white teeth. Friendly. "Got it. Well, how about buying me a cup of coffee and we can stop at the library, and you can photocopy my notes. Unless you want to snap a photo of them on your phone. That's probably easier."

"That would be nice," Zak enthused, feeling suddenly lucky.

"Is there more?" the guy asked as if reading Zak's mind.

"I could really use the notes from the last two classes."

The guy nodded. "Not to worry. I've got you covered. By the way, I'm Marshall. And you are . . ."

Zak extended his hand. "A very grateful, Zak Andrews."

When Zak arrived back at the dorm, Allison was sitting at his desk, wet hair brushed back from her face, a cup of coffee in hand. She was skimming the latest edition of *Elle*. "Hey stranger," she said as Zak came through the door. She didn't bother to look up. "How did class go?"

Zak sighed. "I missed it."

"Oh, no." The words were right but the sentiment false as Allison continued to turn pages.

"But I have good news," Zak said, sitting on the edge of the desk. "I met a guy who offered to share his notes."

"A guy," Allison repeated, finally making eye contact with Zak. "That sounds promising."

Zak winced. "It's not what you think."

Allison swiveled about, offering Zak her full attention. "Why isn't it?"

Zak scrunched his face. "It just isn't," he said, hoping to change the subject. "Did you meet Chuck?"

"Oh yeah." Allison giggled. "He certainly wasn't expecting to see me."

"Whoever does? You just materialize out of thin air."

"Well, your big, strong roommate had come back from a shower, and when he dropped his towel, I poked my head out from under the covers and introduced myself. He jumped a mile before scrambling to get into his briefs. It was hilarious."

Zak didn't find it funny. "I should've told him before I left for class, but he was asleep. Big mistake."

Allison rolled her eyes. "I'm sure it's not the first time a girl has seen him naked."

"It's not that," Zak clarified. "You invaded his privacy. If the roles were reversed, you wouldn't find it funny. You'd call him a deviant. Shame on you!"

Allison eyed Zak with the special doe-eyed look that she'd invented to seek redemption for any mistake, great or small. Sad eyes. Downturned mouth. Pouty lips. An expression she'd mastered whenever she got into trouble. Like the time she was caught shoplifting at Walgreens. The manager let her go without contacting the authorities once she promised to never come back to the store. Or the time she slapped a friend across the face, pretending a mosquito had landed on the surprised girl's cheek. "As I remember," Allison said, "someone invited me to stay in his dorm room."

"I didn't invite you," Zak reminded her. "You just showed up."

"I distinctly remember you saying, when I handed you the money at the airport, 'Allison, anytime you want to come visit, you're welcome.' And last night, you definitely invited me to share your bed."

"Wait," Zak said, as he suddenly realized Allison's wet hair meant she showered and there was only one communal bathroom with four showers and four toilet stalls on the all-male floor. "Did you use the men's bathroom?"

"I'm glad you brought that up. Why aren't you on a co-ed floor?"

"Oh my God." Zak muttered. He should never have left her alone.

"Don't make such a big deal. The human body is a beautiful thing. You really need to get over yourself. You're so uptight. I'm sure no one cared that I was in the men's bathroom."

Zak sighed. There was no sense quibbling. He was bound to lose on a technicality.

"So, what are our plans for today?" she asked, as she closed the magazine.

"I've got a calculus class after lunch. You can sit in on it with me. And I'm working later tonight."

She hmphed. "Of course you are."

"After class, we can walk the campus and check out the sights."

Allison pretended to yawn, covering her mouth with her hand.

"Or we could hop on the light rail and head to downtown Phoenix and walk around."

"We're still walking?" Allison asked, her voice dripping with sarcasm.

"Well then, what would you like to do?"

Allison squinted as ideas seemed to tumble about in her head like the numbered balls in a Bingo game. After a moment, the winning ball revealed itself. "Shopping!"

Zak couldn't imagine anything more boring.

"Then lunch and a movie."

"Allison, I don't have that kind of cash. Remember: I work!"

Allison frowned. Even her frown was adorable. "Oh, don't be such a killjoy. You don't have to buy anything. I have a credit card. How do you think I planned my escape?"

Escape? Zak had no idea what Allison was talking about, but it was suddenly clear that she hadn't traveled from New York City to Arizona just to see him. There was another reason. Had something happened at the Manhattan School of Music? Allison had been so excited to be accepted in the theatre arts program. She'd often complained during high school about the rigor of private singing lessons, but her talent clearly shone through in the high school productions. She'd even contemplated trying out for *American Idol* until she realized the time commitment required to compete.

Zak approached the subject gingerly. As his dad often said when they went fishing, there was no point in scaring off the fish before you've even had a chance to bait the hook. "Is there anything you want to tell me. Something I should know?" Zak asked. "Why did you say, escape? What are you escaping from?"

Allison's eyes radiated innocence. "I have no idea what you mean."

Zak spotted the eye tic—a *tell* when Allison evaded the truth. He'd told her about it years ago, but she never believed him. She'd even looked into a hand mirror to see if she could spot the fateful tic, which failed to appear whenever she was looking at herself. "The tic," he shouted as he pointed at the fluttering eyelid. "You can't fool me. I'm so on to you."

Allison shook her head. "Stop it," she said as Zak's finger, the arbiter of truth, pierced her veil of denial.

Zak's voice dropped an octave. With a jabbing motion, he mimicked the actors on *Bridgerton*, with their dramatic gestures and British accents. "I implore you, Lass, to tell me everything!"

Allison buried her face in her hands. The tears flowed hard and fast. Zak crouched by her side and waited for her to calm down. "Look, whatever it is, you know you can tell me," he said, wishing he'd kept his mouth shut.

"My parents are getting divorced," she moaned, in such a high-pitched voice that Zak was sure all neighborhood strays were alerted. He took in this new information. He wasn't surprised about Allison's parents. He'd sensed the tension in the house when he stayed with them. He'd overheard her parents fighting. "It's just so unfair," she said. "How can they do this to me?"

Zak struggled to find the right thing to say as his thighs began to burn. He should've never crouched down. He was beginning to pay the price for that decision. *Perhaps your parents' divorce has nothing to do with you.* No, that sounded too harsh. Too all-knowing. He decided on a generic approach. "Well, sometimes marriages don't last."

As soon as the words came out of his mouth, he knew he'd made a mistake. If Allison were generating electricity, she could have lit up the city of Tempe. "Not in my family," she barked. "Marriage is sacred. Vows are sacred. I can't believe they're doing this."

"Well, they can't be sacred," he clarified, offering Allison a wan smile. Gosh his legs burned. Were his kneecaps about to pop off? "You know what sacred means."

Allison gently slapped his shoulder, causing him to wobble. He struggled to hold himself in place, keenly aware that the whole crouching idea was foolish. "Stop teasing me," she demanded. "This isn't funny."

"Of course not," Zak agreed, his curiosity piqued. "What did they say? When did they tell you?"

Allison, still seated at Zak's desk, leaned forward and wrapped her arms about Zak's neck, hugging him tightly as he struggled to maintain his balance. "We were FaceTiming. My dad blurted it out. My mom didn't seem upset at all. It was like they were part of a business arrangement that had failed and were announcing the dissolution of the company to their only employee."

Zak patted Allison's back as one might soothe a baby. Her grip on his neck tightened when there was a knock at the door. "Come in," Zak called out as the door opened behind him. He awkwardly shifted. Allison scooted to the edge of the chair and maintained a grip on Zak's neck as he wobbled. His legs were officially on fire.

The blond guy from Zak's biology class poked his head inside. "Hey, man," he said to Zak. Zak was glad he'd shared his dorm information with Marshall. The big guy was a welcome visitor. "I'm sorry, am I interrupting?"

"Not at all," Zak answered, eyes imploring Marshall to stay despite Allison's strangle hold. "Come on in. This is my friend Allison. We went to high school together." Marshall blinked. Zak could tell his explanation had failed to clear anything up.

Marshall stepped into the room. "I thought, if you had time, we might check out Tempe Town Lake. We can rent a rowboat and just fool around."

Allison let go of Zak. Zak immediately lost his balance and fell backward onto his rump. He moaned as he stretched his legs out, rubbing the thighs. "Gee, that sounds like fun," Allison said, her mood suddenly altered. "But we were thinking of going shopping." She made a pouty face for Marshall's benefit.

Marshall's face brightened. "Sure. We can do that instead. That sounds like a better idea."

Allison popped up from the chair, stepping over Zak who remained on the floor. "That streak of blond in your hair really suits you. I like your style," she said to Marshall in a tone that carried the authority of a beauty pageant judge gauging a new contestant. "Oh, you must be *Mr. Starbucks!*"

Zak's face burned.

Marshall gave Zak a wink. "I don't think anyone's ever called me that before. But that's fine. I'll own it."

Allison prodded Zak's thigh with the toe of her shoe. "Come on. Get up. We'll make a day of it. We'll take Marshall to Marshalls," she teased.

Zak looked from Allison to Marshall and then back to Allison. There was no way Allison, the queen of high-end retail therapy, was ever stepping foot in a Marshalls.

⌘

Allison arranged for an Uber to take them to Scottsdale Fashion Square. "Be sure to drop us off at the luxury end of the mall," she instructed the driver in a superior tone that implied any other entrance simply wouldn't do.

After lunch at Francine, the French restaurant voted best fine dining in Arizona by *Modern Luxury Magazine*, the threesome spent the rest of the afternoon wandering through Gucci's, Fendi, Cartier, Louis Vuitton, and Valentino. Zak gasped when Allison tried on a pair of blue Manolo Blahnik's with a jewel-encrusted toe, and then actually bought them. How a college student could ever use such a pair of shoes eluded him. Clearly, Allison was on a mission to punish her father by abusing his credit card. And though Zak cringed when he considered the amount of money she was spending, he decided it was her life and her relationship with her parents. He just hoped she wouldn't regret the decision the next day and ask him to cover his share of lunch, which in hindsight, was a mere pittance compared to the cost of those damn shoes.

"Now it's your turn," Allison said as she pulled Zak into Nordstrom.

Zak exchanged a worried look with Marshall.

"I think Zak already looks great," Marshall said, much to Zak's relief.

Allison didn't appear to be listening. "There's this amazing Balenciaga jacket that I want you to try on."

"Absolutely not," Zak protested. He'd never heard of Balenciaga, but any brand with that many syllables had to be out of his league.

"Don't be such a baby," Allison teased. "It'll be fun. Freshen up your look."

"I don't have a look," Zak insisted.

"Everybody has a look." Allison turned to Marshall and blurted, "Grunge."

"Thank you," Marshall said, seemingly complimented. "I wasn't really trying . . ."

"Oh, yes you are," Allison said a finger pointed at Marshall. "You have to work mighty hard to look that good."

Marshall broke into a smile just as Zak wondered if he'd lost his ally in the shopping wars.

"If we have time," Allison threatened as she gave Zak a fast once over, "we should give that mop of yours a trim."

Zak put a hand on his head. "Absolutely not."

Marshall draped an arm about Zak's shoulder and pulled him close. "Be brave. Own your truth."

Allison was undeterred. "There's a stylist in cosmetics. We'll ask her opinion. What harm can that do?"

After the Uber delivered Allison and Marshall back to the dorm, Zak rushed over to Windy Canyon to set up for Friday night. Sweeping the floor and wiping tables, he caught his reflection in a mirrored wall. Against his better judgment, he'd allowed Allison to press him into cleaning up his style. Or rather, putting one together. Maybe Allison was right.

Maybe he did need to step up his game. Ditch the baggy clothes. He examined the afternoon's collateral damage: new jeans, straight legged and fitted. New tee. David Briton. New haircut. Less Keanu Reeves, more Timothée Chalamet, off the face and combed back. He turned his head from side to side to get a better view. He didn't look half bad.

"Hey, good looking," Melinda teased when she caught him eying himself. "Looks like someone had a makeover." She spun him about to check out the new duds. "Are those AG Jeans? Honey, what have you done to yourself?" She touched his hair. "It's so much shorter."

"Everyone is wearing their hair short," Zak said as he pushed her hand away. "Don't make fun."

"Oh, I'm not. If you were two years older," she said, dropping her voice an octave and stepping closer.

Zak held his breath, hoping Melinda wasn't about to come on to him.

"I'd adopt you," she said, roaring with laughter at how easily she was able to unnerve him. "But where'd you get the money? I thought all your earnings were going into savings for next semester."

"Allison."

Melinda jerked her head back. "Your friend from back east paid for all this?"

Though Zak knew better, he couldn't help but defend Allison. "Why not? We're friends. That's what friends do."

Melinda's expression shifted. Zak knew the look. He'd seen Melinda use it on rowdy customers when it was time to cut them off. "We're best friends," Zak repeated, as if even a close friendship entitled someone to run roughshod over you.

"Okay," Melinda said, conceding whatever point she was trying to make. "It's not my business. But sweetie, don't let other people tell you how to be in the world. Be your own man. I like you just as you are."

"Allison likes me just as I am," Zak said as Melinda backed away, waving the white bar towel that she typically carried, as if surrendering. She disappeared into the kitchen.

Zak stared again in the mirror. He liked the way he looked. He thought the new haircut was flattering. Yes, it had been Allison's idea to make the change. That didn't mean he didn't agree. Or that he'd been forced into it. It wasn't like Allison had some superpower over him to make him change his mind. She was just being a friend. A good friend. And he was lucky to have her. After all, not many friends would go out of their way to hop on a plane and come visit. Or buy him gifts.

Yes, he was lucky.

Still, he couldn't help but wonder when Allison was going back to New York City. She hadn't mentioned a return flight. *That seems odd,* he thought as he shifted tables and chairs about, completing the bar set-up for the late-night crowd.

– 5 –

IKE ALL GOOD ideas, once the seed was planted about Ventana, Helena was unable to shake it. She'd promised herself to schedule an appointment to tour the property, but whenever she considered downsizing, she was overwhelmed by the thought of moving and selling her home. There'd be so much work involved. Too much work for someone her age. How could she ever manage it? Like a bad dream, the idea of relocating slowly became a distant memory as she slipped back into her old routine.

Thank goodness for routines!

Before dawn, she walked the neighborhood, enjoying the cool morning air. In the early morning hours, she felt invigorated. Joyful. Invincible. But as the morning progressed, her energy waned. By lunch, no matter where she was in the house, she struggled to stay awake. Though she resisted closing her eyes, eventually she'd succumb, falling asleep in odd places; sitting up, holding open a book in her lap in her favorite chair; at her desk, fingers on the keyboard, awaking after ten or fifteen minutes with a stiff neck, thanks to her refusal to lie down and take a proper nap.

Though she loved to read, she didn't read as much as she hoped. Instead, during the day, television became her constant companion. The voices of celebrities filled her space. Kelly and Ryan or Hoda and Savannah in the morning; Turner Classic Movies before lunch; afternoons with *Let's Make A Deal and The Price is Right*; dinners spent with *Wheel of Fortune, Jeopardy*, and then onto the evening sitcoms. Television was her company as she made the bed, cleaned the kitchen, vacuumed, and ironed. After a few days, she left all of the televisions on so that when she crossed the house to dust, heading from one room to another, she could hear voices that drowned out the ones in her head. Voices she'd contended with since childhood.

"You're special," her grandmother had told her. "It runs in our family. Skips a generation now and then, but we all have the gift."

Helena didn't want *the gift*. The gift frightened her. It drew strange beings into her life, sometimes waking her from a deep sleep. She was often startled as they hovered nearby, demanding her attention.

"All you need to do is tell them to go away. Say shoo. Shout it loudly and with determination. They'll take the hint. Shoo!" her grandmother had said, waving a hand as if swatting a fly.

Helena wished it was that easy. Ever since she'd been young, the voices had followed her. To school, and outside when she played. When she went through puberty, the visualizations started. Shadows morphed into transparent images, floating past, solidifying before disappearing. There were moments when Helena screamed, surprised by the energy that encircled her. "Shoo!" she'd call out. "Leave me alone!"

"You mustn't listen to your grandmother," Ruthie had scoffed. "She's just trying to scare you. When I was a young girl, there was a black cat on the roof. My mother swore it was an evil spirit sent to punish me unless I washed the dinner dishes. Honestly, Helena, you mustn't believe her."

But Helena knew what she was experiencing was real. Not "hokum" as Ruthie would laugh and say. She could physically feel their presence. The vibrations were strong, the messages demanding. Like the time the neighbor's dog ran into the street and was hit by a car. For weeks, Helena could see the poor animal following the family, trying to get their attention. It wasn't until she called to the dog that it peacefully crossed over the Rainbow Bridge. A simple wish and the dog was gone. That was when she'd realized the gift could be used for good.

But her mother couldn't be convinced. "You listen to me, young lady. It's all poppycock. No one has the ability to communicate with the dead. When you're gone, you're gone. There's no happily hereafter. It's just, lights out."

Helena often thought about the irony of that conversation when Ruthie appeared to her. If it was truly lights out, Ruthie hadn't gotten the message. And no matter how much Helena had loved Ruthie, her mother's perpetual presence had become unnerving and unwelcome. Eighty-three-year-old women don't need advice from their dead mothers.

Or do they?

∽

The next morning, Helena awoke with a start. She'd overslept and feared she'd have to chase the day to make up for the lost time. But by ten-thirty, she was back on schedule. The bed made. The kitchen tidied. The silence, deafening.

Sitting at the kitchen table, she sipped her coffee. What was there to do?

There was the Brad Meltzer thriller waiting on the side table by her favorite chair. Or should she grab her iPhone, listen to a podcast, and go for a walk? No, it was too warm in

September for a midmorning walk. The best time to walk was before the sun came up, when it was still cool. A walk was out of the question.

She thought about making a phone call, but there was no one to whom she wished to speak. Her sons were across the country, already at work, engrossed in their own lives. She could call one of her daughters-in-law, but neither of the ladies had ever seemed particularly interested in her. In their own mothers, yes. But not in Helena and her well-being.

Her four grandchildren were now adults with busy lives. Two were married with young families. One lived overseas. The other had struggled with drug addiction and was in and out of rehab. She'd relied on their fathers to keep her informed about their lives, but relying on adult men wasn't always the best way to stay connected to grandchildren. Her sons seemed to know even less about the children than she did.

Or so it seemed.

She stared out the window and wondered what had become of her life. What had she done to drive people away? Had she been a good mother? Well, perhaps, not the best. She wasn't always home. As a young reporter, she often worked late and missed dinner. Her boys learned to fend for themselves, reheating premade meals stored in the freezer. But did it take eating every meal with your children to qualify as a good mother? She'd done her best. Both boys had gone on to college and made successful lives with families of their own. Clearly, their success was worth a solid pat on her back.

She wondered if her loneliness was rooted in her focus on her career. *But I was a widow,* she argued with herself. She had to manage the family finances. True, but there'd been enough money from the brief marriage to her second husband to have carried them through. Could she have forfeited a career, stayed home, and *just been a housewife?* She scolded herself. *Just?* When she was growing up, expectations for women were limited to nurse, teacher, or housewife. Now she realized that being a housewife was the hardest profession of all. Nursemaid, bottle washer, chef, housekeeper, and maven of all things. But back in the 1970s, housewives weren't valued. Or at the very least, not respected. She remembered her eagerness to have a career as the women's movement came alive. All those marvelous, heroic, intelligent women, breaking down barriers and standing up for women's equality. Honoring a woman's reproductive freedom. She'd once had such dear friends. Women she'd admired. Women who were fiery and like her, bucked the patriarchy. So many meetings, planning, and organizing for passage of the Equal Rights Amendment to the Constitution. The deep frustration at the failure to ratify the amendment in 1979, and after the deadline was extended, the second failure in 1982.

There'd been a time in her life when she was on the phone constantly with friends, chatting about life, love, careers, and children. She missed those connections. The shared memories and the sense of being needed. There was laughter. So much laughter. But now, many of her friends had passed or moved away to be near their families. Still others had disappeared into the ether of retirement communities and nursing homes. *Live long enough*, she thought, *you're bound to be a party of one. There's no point in rehashing the past. I need to accept my life as it is today. I need to accept my circumstances.*

But it was hard to accept the quiet. She could still hear the boys racing around the living room in a game of tag, shouting, pushing, and wildly wrestling on the floor as she yelled at them to stop. On the weekends, she'd encourage them to go outside to play, or go over to a friend's house, anything to just leave her in peace to write. They'd watch television at night: guns, car chases, shouting, unending noise while she tried to read. She'd often been short-tempered, annoyed by the intensity of the male energy.

Helena took a deep breath. Was this how she wanted to spend the rest of her time? Sitting and rehashing the past.

Eating alone. Walking alone. Each day, the same as the next. Wondering how she'd manage if she once again had a fall, or God forbid, a major health emergency, like a stroke or heart attack. The very idea of being ill and alone was terrifying. *I must do something*, she thought.

Ventana popped into her head. She Googled the phone number. Today, she'd make a different choice. She'd choose not to be alone. She'd alter her present and change the future. She'd reach out and try to make a connection. Perhaps Ventana was the answer.

***

The staff at Ventana charmed Helena with their warmth.

When she arrived for the scheduled tour, the receptionist fussed over Helena's vintage sweater dress purchased at Saks Fifth Avenue in New York City in the 1980s. Helena had worn it to make an impression, but when the receptionist guessed it was authentic Chanel, Helena was surprised—until she learned the receptionist was a student working her way through ASU to obtain a BA in fashion design.

Helena was invited to take a seat in the lobby, which was sumptuously decorated in a mix of dark walnut and travertine marble. She was beginning to feel like a celebrity as strangers passed by and waved: active adults off to some important destination. Not a wheelchair or walker in sight. *Hmm*, Helena thought. *Maybe people just don't age here.*

She wondered why it had taken her so long to get up the gumption to visit Ventana. *This place is about as scary as Disneyland*, she thought, chuckling to herself about her own foolishness. There was nothing frightening at all. Just a lovely setting reminiscent of a Four Seasons Hotel. Upscale, yet luxuriously comfortable. And then, an older gentleman approached. Helena thought he was her tour guide. With wisps of gray hair atop his perfectly round head, she was reminded of a summer dandelion that had lost a portion of its crown after a stiff August breeze. The man's eyes, a deep shade of emerald, projected a luminescent merriment. "Hello," he said. "Now, why are you sitting here alone?" His voice, deep with gravitas.

"Hello," Helena answered, unaccustomed to such familiarity from a stranger. Was this her tour guide? If so, he should've introduced himself.

The man eyed her suspiciously. "Are you moving in?"

Helena was taken aback. Of all the conversations she'd practiced in her head, this was not part of the inventory. If he'd asked about her health, her financial status, even what kind of condo unit she was interested in, she'd have had the answers at her fingertips: not good, very good, two bedrooms and a den. But had she decided to move in? Wasn't that putting the cart before the horse. Certainly, in Helena's mind, it was. She stared at the man, her mouth open as she searched for the right answer.

The old gentleman ignored Helena's awkward pause. "You see, I'm also part of the social committee, and we like to greet our new owners and make them feel welcome. I had no idea someone so lovely would be joining us."

Helena thought the stranger unacceptably forward, his remarks ill-suited for a tour guide. Besides, she certainly didn't think of herself as lovely. At least not anymore. How could a woman in her eighties be flattered by such obvious affectation? Yet, she had to admit, she enjoyed the attention. Almost as much as she enjoyed the man's overall presence. #MeToo be damned. Had the sales manager sent him out as part of Ventana's strategy to persuade her to purchase a unit? Was she supposed to stare into those gorgeous eyes, be hypnotized, and fall in love? Did anyone still think that a mature, intelligent woman could be so easily wooed? Still, his dark green eyes were quite something. Helena couldn't help but stare.

"I've startled you," the gentleman said as Helena gathered her wits.

"Not at all," she lied. "I just wasn't expecting . . ." she had no idea how to finish the sentence. "The truth is, I haven't done this before."

His eyes twinkled. "Before?"

"I've always owned my own home."

"I see," the man said, a smile breaking across his lips as if two conversations were going on simultaneously: one about Ventana, the other about their personal chemistry. "There's nothing to be afraid of. It's a lovely place. Great people. But change is hard. We've all gone through *the change*."

Helena nearly laughed. Wasn't *the change* a biological event for women in their forties and fifties? She hadn't considered there might be more than one *change* in her lifetime. God knows the last one had been tough enough to survive. "*Afraid* might be too strong a word," she said, knowing full well that *afraid* was the correct word. "Let's just say, *I'm concerned*. This would be my last home. Once I make the decision to move in, I doubt I'll be going anywhere else."

"You wouldn't travel?" the man asked.

She hadn't considered such a thing. Did people travel once they moved into an adult community? If they felt the need to have proximity of care, how could they go anywhere?

"Ventana isn't a prison. It's not a nursing home. If you need care, it's all here, in one place. But many of us continue to travel. Some have second homes in Flagstaff or Sedona. Many of us travel extensively in July and August to escape the summer heat."

"Travel," Helena repeated as the concept sunk in. She'd always thought of these living arrangements as being so frightfully final.

"Whatever you're thinking, it's not how it is. It's much better. Much," the man said with a shake of his head.

Helena broke into a smile. "Well, that's reassuring to know."

"You come and go as you wish. The staff encourages you to stay active. Mix in with the ASU students. Mentor young people. Attend the lectures. Sign up for ASU classes. Use the gym."

"The gym?"

"It's all included," he said, standing straighter as if proving the value of fitness.

Helena laughed. "I can't see myself going to a gym."

"Oh, but you must. I swim every morning. They have a wonderful, heated pool. Very therapeutic. And there's yoga too."

Helena had to admit, the man looked the picture of health.

"You think about it," her new friend said as a young man in jeans and a pressed white shirt, sporting a name tag, approached.

Helena immediately picked up on the young man's energy. There was something sad about him.

"Hello, Mr. Goldfarb. How are you this morning?"

"Never better," the old gent said.

"I've scheduled us for dinner. I thought we might catch an Arizona Diamondbacks game tonight. I have two tickets set aside at the box office. They're playing the Dodgers. What do you think?"

Goldfarb's eyes lit up. "You're on. Same seats as last time?"

"Behind home plate."

Mr. Goldfarb pumped a fist. "Wow. It's going to be a great night. Oh, I nearly forgot. Any news yet?"

The young man shrugged. "Not yet," he answered, turning to Helena to include her in the conversation. "We're expecting any day now."

Helena beamed. "How marvelous."

"Yes," the young man said. "It's an exciting time."

Mr. Goldfarb patted the man's arm. "Just try not to worry too much. These things happen on their own schedule."

"I'll try," the young man said as he focused on Helena. "You must be my ten o'clock appointment."

Helena stood and extended her hand. "I'm Helena Greenblatt."

"Of course. I'm Alan Lane, the Executive Director at Ventana, and I see you've already met Mr. Goldfarb."

"Not formally," Helena said as she glanced at Mr. Goldfarb. "But he's been kind enough to entertain me. Thank you, Mr. Goldfarb."

"Oh no, please, call me Gilbert."

"Gilbert," Helena repeated, wondering if Gilbert frequently trolled the lobby in search of lonely females. Back in the 1970s, she'd have smirked at such a meeting, sarcastically referring to it as a staged Hollywood *meet cute*. Two souls destined to connect in an absurd way. But now, at this advanced age, such happenings were as unlikely as winning the lottery. Besides, there was nothing *meet cute* about a man introducing himself to a lady sitting in the lobby of a building waiting to tour the property. If anything, it was dull. Purely perfunctory. Sadly banal. Still, Gilbert Goldfarb was adorable for a late-August dandelion. The eyes. The cherubic shaped head. Even the slight bend in his nose added a certain delight to his face. Could it be possible he looked like a Disney character? Perhaps, one of Snow White's seven dwarfs. But taller. Much taller.

She turned to her young host for the tour. "Alan, congratulations to you and your wife on your good news."

"Wife?" Alan repeated with a confused look on his face. "I'm not married."

"Oh—then, your girlfriend."

Alan shook his head. "Did I mention a girlfriend?" He looked to Mr. Goldfarb, who held his hands up in a display of submission.

Helena struggled to explain herself. "You said you were expecting a baby."

Alan's confusion dissolved. "A baby," he said, eyebrows arched high. "My dog is having puppies. Petula, my apricot poodle, is expecting a litter any day now."

"Yes," Gilbert chimed in. "And Alan has agreed I might take one. Isn't that wonderful?"

Alan Lane escorted Helena through the three model units, peppering the visit with bits of conversation about the amenities of the building and introducing her to various staff members along the way. Helena encountered more smiles on young faces than she'd seen in a year. Everyone was exceptionally kind, as if they were the offspring of the Stepford Wives. When they reached the eleventh-floor dining room with its magnificent views of the city, Helena thought she'd arrived at a fancy supper club. The room was elegant with crystal chandeliers. The floor-to-ceiling windows showcased the views of the valley. She could almost imagine the tinkling piano of Duke Ellington as Alan pulled out a chair from one of the tables so she could rest.

"The menu changes every day, and we have our own chef on-site," Alan boasted. "Gluten free, low sodium, vegan, however you prefer your food prepared, it can be done."

Helena ran a hand over the white tablecloth. There was nothing like fine dining on a white tablecloth. "It's lovely," she agreed as she looked about in amazement. "And it's exclusively for seniors like me," she said in wonderment, as if she didn't deserve such marvelous accommodations. "It's certainly an upscale, expensive, retirement home."

Alan furrowed his brow. "We don't refer to Ventana as a *retirement home*. That has such a negative connotation. We're a retirement community, but only in the sense that no one here is dependent on earning a living."

Helena nodded, wondering if this was the moment when Alan would go in for the kill. A little lunch. A frightened senior. Another deal done.

Alan moved the empty crystal water glass at his place setting an inch to the right. "But being retired doesn't mean your life is over. Most of the people who live here are still quite active.

Some are trustees on company boards. Others, guest lecturers who travel. Many are involved in alumni associations, while still others are active in nonprofits, either volunteering or fundraising."

Oh my, Helena thought. *Will I fit in here?*

"Our owners like to stay busy and engaged. Many have hobbies. Some, second or third careers they've pursued past retirement. They may no longer be obligated to get up and commute to an office every day, but they're still mentally engaged."

Alan's speech seemed like something he lifted directly from a sales brochure. Still, Helena had to admit, the concept of Ventana was appealing.

"You're an author, so you must write every day."

Helena nodded. She owned a laptop, though she hadn't written a word in years. She mostly used it to watch YouTube videos and keep up with breaking news. Maybe the move might inspire her to start writing again.

"Well, how about some lunch?" Alan suggested as he nodded to the waitress who brought over a breadbasket and menus.

Helena skimmed the menu. She ordered the ahi tuna salad. "You're good at your job," she said, once Alan had ordered. "Have you always been a natural salesman?" The question was tinged with sarcasm.

Alan sat back in his chair. "You make it sound like you're about to be swindled. I hope that isn't how you feel."

Helena hadn't meant to offend. "Forgive me," she said, feeling as if she'd just swatted a puppy. "This is a lovely place and you've been very kind. I've truly enjoyed the tour."

Alan quickly recouped. "I hope it means you might consider joining us?"

Helena snapped a breadstick in half. She thought of Groucho Marx: dark bushy eyebrows, pacing about in a black tailcoat, waving an unlit cigar, muttering, "I refuse to join any club that would have me as a member." Clearly, living at Ventana would be an entirely different experience. Especially for a woman who'd always prided herself on being independent. Perhaps, she just needed more time. But how much more time did she have before being forced to make a move? Another year? Another month? Another week? Wasn't it best to just pick the spot while she was still sharp enough to make the decision? If so, why hesitate?

Why, indeed.

But she wasn't ready to commit, and the lack of clarity nagged at her. What more did she need to know? What might convince her? "I'm seriously thinking about it," she said as the tuna salad arrived.

Alan smiled so brightly she should've worn sunglasses. "Good. We can always use a new face."

"New face," Helena repeated as she pierced the tuna with her fork. "This face certainly isn't new."

"Perhaps not, but it is filled with history and intelligence. I could tell as soon as we met that there's something special about you. I Googled you last night. You were quite *the activist* at one time. I've made a note to read your novels."

Read her work? Well now he'd done it. He'd stroked her author's underbelly where the ego resided. Helena straightened her shoulders. "Why Mr. Lane, if I were younger, I'd swear you were coming on to me, and I'm old enough to be your mother." Though she knew she was old enough to be his mother's mother. But she couldn't bring herself to admit it.

Alan blushed. "Sometimes I get carried away. But to me, Ventana is one big family. I never had that growing up. My parents died when I was young. I was raised in foster care. That's not exactly an ideal setting for a kid." Alan looked about. "I sometimes feel like this is my home."

Perhaps that was the sadness Helena had sensed when she'd first met Alan. He was a big kid searching for a family and there was no doubt that Ventana provided ample opportunity to repair those missed connections. He seemed to be a fine young man, and if Helena had to live out the rest of her days at Ventana, there'd be nothing wrong with welcoming a friend like Alan into her life. Charming, handsome, energetic, and caring; he certainly brightened up the already wonderful scenery.

Helena gazed out the wall of windows onto the view of Camelback Mountain. She'd often hiked the rocky trail before she'd suffered a torn meniscus in her left knee at age sixty. She was well aware of the dangers that can present when human beings are surrounded by the beauty that they so desperately crave. "Tell me, Alan. If I were your mother, would you still recommend I move into Ventana?"

Alan looked away, avoiding her gaze. Had she said something wrong? Overstepped her bounds?

"I just love the place," he said when he turned back to her, his voice steady and sure. "I only wish they'd allow someone my age to move in. You have access to a great condo, terrific food, and wonderful people. Who could ask for more?"

Helena nodded. In life, things weren't always as they appeared. She'd spent the last few hours trying to uncover the myth of Ventana, and much to her surprise, all she'd found was exactly what the newspaper advertisement had described. "Well, Mr. Lane, I think you've earned a new owner."

Alan beamed. "I just know you'll love it here."

Helena glanced about the dining room. "Yes, I think I will. If I don't," she said turning to him, "I'll know who to blame."

Alan dropped his smile.

Helena was only joking, but could she have hit a nerve? "Forgive me," she quickly added. "I'd never blame you. Adults take responsibility for their actions."

Alan offered a troubled grin.

Helena made a mental note to treat Mr. Lane with kindness. Despite his gallant exterior, he was an extremely sensitive soul. But for the moment, Helena had no more time to focus on Alan Lane. She had plans to make. A house to sell. Packing to do. Movers to hire.

If she was going to change her life, she'd have to get cracking while the real estate market was hot.

– 6 –

THOUGH ZAK APPRECIATED Marshall sharing his biology notes, when they were alone together, grabbing a cup of coffee or walking to the library, there was an awkwardness. For one, Marshall was way too interested in Zak's friendship with Allison. How they'd met. Where they'd grown up. Who she'd dated. In short, Zak found Marshall's fascination with Allison a bit off-putting. To further complicate matters, Allison had said she was visiting for the weekend, and somehow, the weekend had extended into five days, leaving Zak wondering when she'd return to New York City. Exactly how long could he be expected to share a single bed? He was already struggling with late nights at the bar and early morning classes. Pressing up against Allison when he finally did lie down was doing nothing for his neck and back. Though Chuck hadn't said much about Allison's presence, Zak was beginning to worry that it was only a matter of time before Chuck complained about a third person in such a tight space. And who could blame him?

Even more confusing, Marshall and Allison had forged a mysterious bond. Allison's quick, playful wit and fiery personality had pulled Marshall right in. Zak understood Allison's allure. She was brassy. Bigger than life. It was all part of her charm. Men adored her. Heck, she was a theater major. Showy and full of vivacity. No wonder Marshall had fallen under her spell. Together, they disappeared during the day, doing whatever Allison liked, only to reunite with Zak later in the evening at The Windy Canyon.

"She's a bad influence," Zak shouted at Marshall after Allison headed off to The Windy Canyon restroom. He removed the yellow earplug from his ear. The music had amped up to a near-deafening pitch. "You missed class this morning."

"I like her," Marshall answered. "She's fun."

Zak nodded. *Yeah, she's fun,* he thought as he marveled at how quickly Allison had moved in on his territory. Not that he'd officially claimed Marshall. How could he? They'd only met the day before Allison showed up. Still, Zak wasn't certain whether Marshall was a friend or if there could be more. With Allison in the picture, he now wondered if he'd jumped to the wrong conclusion about Marshall based on a dye job. Straight men dye their hair. They certainly use moisturizers and grooming products. *It's so unfair,* Zak groused to himself. *It's nearly impossible to guess anyone's sexuality based on how they present.*

Marshall offered a mischievous smile. "Allison was telling me all about when you two hung out together after school. She said you loved going to the mall to check out guys."

Zak cringed. Why would Allison gossip with Marshall about their time together? The personal stuff. It felt like such a betrayal. "Actually," Zak corrected him, raising his voice to be sure that he was heard in the noisy bar, "she's a pushy camp counselor. Only fun, as long as she's having her way."

As soon as the words left Zak's mouth, he realized how true they were. He hadn't intended to bad-mouth Allison, and yet, there it was. Truth spilling out for Marshall to hear. Every word piqued with irritation. Alone, he'd never contemplated such thoughts. He'd always been grateful to be part of Allison's sphere of influence. He'd never much cared about his individuality. How could he? So much had been sublimated. Hidden from view. But now, as he and Marshall talked, he realized Allison wasn't all that easy to get along with. Perhaps she wasn't easy at all.

Marshall seemed oblivious to Zak's intent. As the drummer went into his solo, Zak glared at the stage. *Could it get any louder?*

"Am I taking up too much of her time? She came to see you," Marshall shouted.

Zak had no idea how to answer. Had Allison come to see him because of her parents' impending divorce? They hadn't talked much about the divorce. For someone who was upset, she wasn't acting that way. Was there more? Had something happened at school that would explain why she'd extended her stay. What was the big mystery? And why did everything need to be a mystery? Drama on drama. Zak wondered what classes were like for a theater major. Dancing, singing, memorizing lines? There had to be more. But he'd been unable to get Allison to open up. She didn't seem to want to talk about family or school. Zak knew all too well that when Allison didn't want to talk, there was nothing to be done. "I'm glad you two have hit it off. It's fine," Zak lied as he covered his right ear with the palm of his hand, hoping to diminish the noise level yet still hear Marshall.

Zak couldn't help but be jealous . . . about what, he wasn't sure. Was he jealous that Marshall was infatuated with Allison? Or was he jealous that Allison had found a new confidante? Either way, it didn't feel good, and it didn't seem fair, and it didn't feel honest. She'd invaded his private space and was taking over where he'd made inroads. He could feel himself slipping back into the role of second banana. A life existing on the outskirts of her orbit. The dutiful subject, destined to forever follow her lead. But he wasn't that boy any longer. Too much had happened since high school. Maybe the confrontation with his parents had been the major factor forcing him to take charge of his life. He wasn't certain, but there'd been a change, and he didn't like Allison's behavior. He didn't like it one bit.

The music hit a new crescendo as the drummer finished his solo and the band united in a booming uptick. Zak contemplated putting his earplug back in, but he didn't. There were tables to attend to and he couldn't stand around jabbering all night. Just as he was about to walk away, Marshall stood up and leaned in close. The scent of Axe body wash awakened Zak's desires. "I asked her how long she was staying, but she's been elusive."

Zak's heart skipped a beat. He imagined Marshall's lips pressed against his. He had to say something fast before Marshall pulled away. Anything to keep Marshall nearby. "I don't think my roommate is happy with Allison. She isn't quiet and she gives *invasion of privacy* a whole new meaning. She loves to show her body off. I've told her twice to cover up. I swear, sometimes it's like dealing with a child."

Marshall didn't waste the moment. "Would it be okay if she stayed with me?"

Zak was caught off guard. He hadn't meant for Marshall to take Allison off his hands. Was Marshall intrigued at the possibility of catching a glimpse of Allison nude? "I don't know," Zak answered, hesitant to appear too possessive, but unwilling to share Marshall.

The band finished its final set and left the stage. Zak's ear was ringing as the noise level dropped. But Marshall was not about to back off on the Allison invitation. "It wouldn't be a problem. We have an extra sleeper sofa in our house."

Zak had no idea where Marshall lived. Did he live with friends. Was he off-campus? Or at home with his parents? Why didn't Zak know any of this? Why hadn't he bothered to ask? Did Allison now know Marshall better than he did? They'd certainly spent enough time together. "It's nice of you, but really, it's not necessary. I wouldn't want to put you out. Besides, Allison is my problem."

Marshall didn't take the hint. "Nonsense. I'd like to do it."

Zak's hands were tied. It was late and he needed to clear The Windy Canyon tabletops and sweep up. He had no intention of staying after the 2 a.m. closing time.

Marshall leaned back and folded his arms. "Now, don't be mad. She's still *your best friend.*"

Zak thought that was an odd thing to say. Had Marshall misinterpreted his dour expression? He wasn't upset about losing Allison. He was upset about losing Marshall. "Do what you want," Zak said as he wiped a table with a damp cloth. "She's a big girl. She gets to make her own decisions."

Marshall nodded. "But where is she?" He checked his watch. "She's been gone awhile."

"I guess she's doing whatever women do in the ladies' room."

Marshall squinted. "Coke?"

"She's vegan. Her body's her temple. I doubt she's doing coke," Zak said with all the sarcasm he could muster.

By the last call, Allison still hadn't returned. Concerned, Zak asked Melinda to go to the ladies' restroom and check on her. "She's not in there," Melinda confirmed, her face twisted in disgust. "But *Andy* sweetheart, you better get in there and clean that bathroom before you leave. It's a freaking mess. I can only imagine what the men's room must smell like."

Zak hated that part of the job. Empty the trash cans, wipe out the sinks, refill the paper towels, clean the toilets, mop the floor. The whole thing was disgusting. Still, he could get it done in record time if he focused his mind elsewhere.

"She just called you, Andy," Marshall said to Zak, referring to Melinda who was standing right next to Zak. "Who the hell is Andy?"

Zak rolled his eyes. Who the heck was Andy? For that matter, who the heck was Zak? He only wished he knew. For the moment, he was nothing more than a work horse. Running from one filthy mess to another. Struggling to get an education. Trying to manage his way through college while hoping to find a boyfriend. It was one thing to identify as gay. Quite another to actually be gay. That required another person's participation. Preferably a man. Hopefully an attractive man.

"*Andy* is the new love of my life," Melinda teased Marshall, her eyes glowing as she linked her arm in Zak's and pulled him tightly to her side. Off balance, Zak stumbled. "I just sweep the boys right off their feet," she declared with a laugh.

Marshall exchanged a worried glance with Zak. He directed the next question to Melinda as if she was the bathroom whisperer. "If Allison's not in the bathroom, where could she have gone?"

"How should I know?" Melinda said, an edge in her voice. "Maybe she met someone. Went home with them. Maybe she went outside to get some fresh air and was locked out. She might be waiting for you in the alley. Or the parking lot. A lot of the kids hang out in their cars, doing whatever they do, with whomever they can."

Zak scowled as Marshall hopped up from his seat to rescue the damsel in distress. "I better go check the alley. See if she's out there."

Melinda turned to Zak as Marshall headed outside. "He's slow on the uptick, isn't he?"

"What do you mean?"

Melinda held a hand on her hip and gave Zak a *don't play dumb* expression. "He doesn't get that you have a crush on him."

"What? Where'd you come up with that?"

"I've got eyes. I see the way you're looking at him."

Zak sighed. "So what? It doesn't matter. He's under her spell."

Melinda looked toward the door. "Are you sure?"

"Well, he's been hanging on her every word."

"She is a very pretty girl," Melina pointed out. "Charismatic."

"Like a damn magnet."

"But so are you," Melinda said tugging on Zak's arm. "You're wonderful."

"But he's not into me. He's not into guys."

"Says who?"

"Isn't it obvious?"

Melinda cocked her head. "One thing I've learned. Nothing is obvious. Sometimes, you have to ask. Take old Fred and me. If I waited for Fred to warm up, I'd be alone."

Zak hadn't realized Melinda was in a relationship. "Fred. The owner of the bar. Are you two married?"

"Married?" Melinda groaned. "Hardly. I'm not that kind of girl. We live together. Five and a half years now."

Zak melted. "You're so lucky. Your life is settled."

Melinda rolled her eyes. "Hardly. Anyway, if you want to know about Marshall, ask him."

"I don't think so," Zak said as he marched off to the ladies' restroom to begin the cleanup. He had no intention of embarrassing himself with Marshall. Besides, if Marshall had been interested in him, he was sure he would've known by now. And if not, as the saying goes, there were plenty of fish in the sea. Men who'd help him find his way. Men who'd treat him with kindness. That was his last thought as he reached the end of the hall. When he opened the door to the ladies' room, he was overcome by the dank, fetid stench of vomit and feces. He stepped back into the hallway. Melinda was still watching him. He turned and they locked eyes. He scrunched up his face. She laughed as he hung the *Do Not Enter* sign on the door wishing he could heed the wisdom of such sage advice.

⁓

By the time Zak cleaned the bathrooms, swept the bar floor, and wiped down the tabletops and chairs, it was 3:00 a.m. The moon shone brightly as he crossed the parking lot, and though he tried not to worry, he was still concerned about Allison. Was Melinda right? Could Allison have met someone and gone home with them? Would Allison have done that without telling him? With each step, Zak became increasingly frightened. Maybe he should call campus police and report her missing. But she wasn't a student. Would that matter?

His mind raced through the possibilities. She could have been kidnapped. It wasn't unimaginable. He'd heard about college girls disappearing. There'd been something recently on BuzzFeed about a student who'd gone missing. Her body eventually turned up in the desert.

Zak checked his phone again. No messages. He texted Allison. Alone in an empty parking lot, he waited for her to respond. She didn't. *Where could she be*, he worried as a voice came from behind. Zak jumped.

"Sorry, sorry," Marshall apologized. "I didn't mean to sneak up on you."

Zak held a hand to his heart. "Where'd you come from?"

Marshall looked distraught. "I went back to your dorm. I thought she might be in the lobby waiting for us. She wasn't. And security wouldn't let me upstairs to check the room. How does she get past them?"

"She has a guest pass," Zak explained. Even so, Zak had no doubt she could talk her way in anywhere.

"Let's go back to the dorm," Marshall suggested. "Maybe she's in the room?"

Zak wouldn't put it past her. "I bet she's fine. Fast asleep. Doing what Allison does best. Making the whole night about her."

Together, they walked along the quiet campus streets of Tempe, each lost in thought, until Marshall broke the silence. "What are we going to do if she isn't there?"

Zak sighed. "I don't know. Leave it to Allison to make a mess of the night. She used to do this in high school. Up and disappear. It was so annoying. Her parents would be frantically searching for her."

Marshall seemed to marvel at this new bit of news. "No kidding. Where'd she go?"

Zak sidestepped the question. How could he explain Allison's wanton side? The teacher with whom she secretly met up with. The college jock she deflowered. The married neighbor who gave her money now and then. No. Any answer would seem disloyal. "I'm sorry about all this. She's my friend, but she can be really flaky sometimes. I'm sure she didn't mean to blow you off."

Marshall did a double take. "That's fine. We were just hanging out."

"Yeah, well, you were hitting on her pretty hard."

Marshall arched a brow. "Bro, you've got this all wrong. I'm not into Allison."

Zak was stunned. "You're not?"

"Absolutely not. She's fun. But hey, you introduced us. She's your friend."

Zak scratched his head. Had he made the whole thing up about Marshall and Allison? "Of course. Yes. Never mind," Zak said with a wave of the hand as they continued walking to the dorm. He was certain Marshall was merely saving face. After all, no one enjoyed getting publicly dumped. And though Zak loved Allison, he didn't like that she'd deliberately hurt Marshall, playing the field while playing with Marshall's feelings. She didn't get that most men, just like most women, were sensitive beings. He hoped one day she might have sons and understand how easily men could be hurt. Maybe then she'd have a better understanding of the opposite sex.

⁂

Zak checked his phone again as he and Marshall rode the dorm elevator to the fifth floor. "Still no word from her."

Marshall shook his head. "What could've happened?"

Zak had no idea.

"If she doesn't turn up, what should we do? Who should we call?"

"She'll show up," Zak said with a confidence that surprised him, since deep down, he was scared something might have happened to her. He couldn't remember a time when Allison hadn't answered a text. Maybe she'd lost her phone. Maybe the battery had run low. Maybe she'd turned the phone off like she did back in high school. Three maybes he was unwilling to expand upon as the elevator slowly climbed upward.

"Women disappear in this country every day," Marshall said, his eyes glued to the floor.

"Children do too."

Both men sighed in unison as the elevator doors opened to the fifth floor. They rushed down the hallway to Zak's room. Zak took a fast peek inside. The lights were off, but Zak could make out from the hall light that Chuck was in bed, asleep. Zak's bed was empty. "Well, there's nothing to do now. It's late," he said to Marshall as he checked his watch. Three-thirty in the morning. Not the best time to go searching for a lost girl. "You better go on home, and if she doesn't check in with me tomorrow, I'll go to the campus police."

"Let me know if she shows up," Marshall said with concern in his voice.

"I will," Zak promised. "She probably just went home with someone. A one-night fling." As soon as the words left his lips, he regretted them. Not only was Allison missing, but now he'd tarnished her reputation to a guy who seemed really interested in her, implying she was a slut. Great. Terrific. If she was truly in danger, he'd be the jerk of the year. Heartless, mean-spirited, a total dickhead. But then, it was possible she had wandered off with a stranger. And even though a one-night stand hardly made anyone a slut, it certainly made them a pain in the ass for disappearing without letting anyone know.

Once in bed, Zak tossed and turned. He tried not to worry. But he worried and worried until he grew increasingly annoyed with Allison. Not only had she moved in on Marshall, but now, she'd ruined his sleep with her erratic, self-centered behavior. He promised himself he'd have a long talk with her when she finally turned up. Some things simply could not be tolerated. Running out on Marshall at the bar, without a word to either of them, was reprehensible.

—⁓—

The next morning, Zak awoke to the sound of the door closing as Chuck left for class. Exhausted, he lay in bed staring at the alarm clock, struggling to fall back to sleep. He reached for his phone. Had Allison left a message?

There was still no word.

He decided to get up. Clearly, there'd be no sleeping with Allison missing. Naked, he searched for a robe.

"Good morning, sleepy head."

Zak turned and there she was. Lying in Chuck's bed.

"Allison!" he said, before realizing he was in his birthday suit. Grabbing a blanket, he covered his man parts.

Allison giggled. "Not too shabby," she joked as her eyes traveled up from his crotch. "I always thought you had a lot more to show than you let on."

Zak was aghast. Was nothing sacred? "What happened to you?" he asked as he searched for his pants, turning around and inadvertently mooning his friend.

Allison's voice was calm. "I was bored. So, I came back to the room. Chuck was here, and well, the rest is history." Her eye tic was back.

Zak slipped into his pants, dropping his blanket to the floor. "Well, I'm glad we're not slowing you down."

Allison smiled. "I couldn't help myself," she whispered.

Zak sat at Chuck's desk facing Allison who was stretched out in Chuck's bed. "And what are you going to tell Marshall?"

"Marshall?"

Zak nodded. "I thought you two were hitting it off."

"He's nice," Allison said, "but I'm not into him."

Zak was stumped. How could she lead Marshall on and then drop him? "Well, you better tell Marshall," Zak warned. "I'm not doing it for you."

Allison giggled. "You're so dramatic. He won't care."

Zak was glad he was gay. Immune to the games heterosexuals play. Free of the potential risk of being hurt by a woman playing the field.

Zak's phone dinged. It was a text from Marshall. He ignored it.

Allison was behaving exactly as she always had. No surprise there. Eternally the girl who chased boys to avoid facing her own issues. Whatever they were. Allison hadn't come to Tempe to hang out with him for the weekend. Not by a long shot. She'd chased after Marshall, and now, she'd extended her trip to sleep with Chuck. Three people in a very small dorm room. Zak hated the idea, even if that extra person in the room was his best friend from high school. The friend who'd rescued him when he most needed a friend. Zak didn't want to sit in judgment, but in judgement he sat. "You should be ashamed of yourself. You've managed to ensnare two men while you play your little *Allison games*. Both of whom you've met through me. I may love you, but I don't much like you."

Allison waved away his concerns with a flick of her hand. "You're just jealous. Chuck's gorgeous and he wants me."

Zak imagined any young woman who made herself so easily available could find a spot in Chuck's bed. It wasn't a relationship. It was sex. But instead of following up on her delusions of grandeur, Zak pitched the big question: "So when is this holiday of yours over? When are you going back to New York City?"

Allison at once appeared hurt. "You don't want me here?" she asked as if it were a total surprise.

Zak rolled his eyes. "That's right. I don't want you as part of my college experience. You need to get on with your own life." The truth had slipped out before he realized how it might sound.

"And leave Chuck to you?"

Zak turned beet red. "That isn't what I mean, and you know it." The room suddenly felt as if someone had adjusted the thermostat, turning off the air conditioner and switching on the heat. "Don't make this about Chuck. This is about you, Allison. You're running away. I don't know why you're here, but it isn't because your parents broke up. This is about you and your mess of a life."

Allison glared at him. He'd poked the tiger. Something he'd never dared in high school when Allison was Miss Popularity and he was Igor, the grateful lacky. Whatever was about to spill forth from Allison's mouth was going to hurt. Mama Goldfish loves to eat her guppies.

He braced himself.

"It must be awful to be gay and scrawny," she said as her head jerked to the right. "And that acne on your chin. Let's be honest. You're just a sad excuse for a gay man. All these years, I've been nice to you out of pity. No more. We'll let Chuck decide if I'm going to stay."

"Chuck's not deciding," Zak warned. "I'll let campus police know you don't belong here. Then, we'll see how that goes down."

Allison leapt to her feet. "You wouldn't dare."

❧

"When is she leaving?" Marshall asked Zak as students poured into the lecture hall.

"I don't know," Zak admitted. "But the conversation didn't go well."

"You two had a fight?"

"Oh, yeah," Zak confirmed. "A knockdown, drag-out fight. Our friendship is probably over. I doubt she'll ever talk to me again."

"Good riddance," Marshall said.

Zak was shocked. "Whoa. Why the change of heart? I thought you were into her."

"Hey, I admit she has a certain energy, but she doesn't wear well over time. Five days is definitely the limit. Trust me, you're better off."

Despite their differences, Zak hated to see the friendship with Allison come to an end. No matter what the cause, they'd been through so much together. "We've been friends a long time. It isn't easy making new friends."

Marshall nodded. "True. But you won't have any problems. People like you."

Zak was awed. He'd never thought of himself as someone people liked. He always considered himself more like pistachio ice cream; you see it in the freezer section and wonder what it might taste like, but you'd never buy it.

Zak opened his notebook. He was determined to take the best notes. "But she hasn't left yet. That's the problem of the moment. She's still connected to Chuck."

"Well, have you talked to Chuck? Told him how you feel?"

Zak hadn't. He thought his opinion about Chuck's bedmates stopped at the edge of Chuck's side of the room. "I don't think I'd be comfortable with that."

Marshall didn't hesitate. "You have to talk to him. Open communication between roommates is critical. You can't live with someone and not talk to them."

"Sure, you can," Zak blurted out. He'd done that for years with his parents. Lived with them, but never shared an important part of himself. It had all been too risky. And now, this conversation with Chuck was also *too risky*. Was that how life is? Veering from one challenge to the next, never feeling confident in one's place in the world? Refusing to let barriers drop? Protecting yourself? Accepting whatever comes your way from the people in your life and rolling with it, even if that means more rejection?

"You said Chuck is a good guy," Marshall reminded him.

"Right."

"So let him be a good guy."

The professor entered the lecture hall. Conversation stopped as the students directed their attention to the front. Zak was lost in thought. *What's the worst thing that could happen if I talk to Chuck?* He drew a blank. He couldn't imagine any scenario that would make it worthwhile to tolerate Allison's presence any longer. No. She'd have to leave. The sooner, the better.

"By the way," Marshall whispered as the professor stepped up to the lectern. "You really need to learn how to read the room. I was never interested in Allison. I'm gay."

Zak nodded, happy for that point of clarification.

HELENA SPENT A sleepless night tossing and turning. Had she done the right thing by buying into Ventana? Or was the decision a huge folly? She just couldn't shake the feeling she'd made a horrible mistake. That she'd been too hasty. Was it even possible for an eighty-three-year-old woman to be too hasty about moving into independent living?

She kicked a leg out from under the covers. Why was she second-guessing herself? What would it take for her to rest easy? Was she worried about the money? The initial paperwork had required an enormous cash outlay; the price of admission to Ventana. For the same amount, she could have easily purchased a single-family home. Still, the huge cash outlay guaranteed access to all Ventana had to offer; independent living, and should she need it in the future, assisted living and even skilled nursing care. The condo also had a monthly lease expense which was three times the monthly payment of any mortgage she'd ever held. She hadn't really purchased the Ventana condo. She'd purchased the privilege of living on the premises. Did it make sense to buy into Ventana and still have a lease payment?

She felt as if she was being snookered or was that just her native New Yorker talking? Still . . . why was it so expensive to be old? She'd never before spent so much money at one time in a financial transaction. Before bed, she'd checked her bank account, and the money had successfully transferred. Another important lesson. If you want to sleep at night, don't check your bank balance before bed. She chewed her lower lip as she shifted about. She had to remind herself that Ventana was not a real estate investment. Those days were over. It was more akin to a long-term health insurance policy. Should her health fail, she'd be looked after. And when she died, a large percentage of the initial cash outlay would be returned to her heirs. All in all, it was a win-win. Still, she didn't like thinking of her future in terms of illness and heirs. She didn't like it at all.

She checked the clock on her bedside table. It was three a.m. She flipped onto her back. Her thoughts shifted to the mechanics of moving. She dreaded the amount of work ahead. Wouldn't it have been easier to stay put? Not upset the apple cart. Hire in-home help and hope for the best. But who would she have hired? Where would she have found them? How could she have screened them? Would she have needed to go through an agency? And what agency would be trustworthy? She'd heard so many stories of seniors becoming dependent on caregivers who then went on to steal from them. How terrible to be vulnerable to someone you've invited into your home and who winds up taking advantage of your helplessness. The thought of strangers going through her drawers, checking the closets, searching through her things, was unsettling. Besides, she didn't need someone every day. She just needed someone in case she passed out. And there was no way to schedule help for that kind of spontaneous event.

How she wished she could stop second-guessing herself. Was it just fear talking? Fear of change. Fear of the future. Fear of 101 things she'd no control over. But then, had she ever had control over her life? Real control. She thought of Robert, her first husband. He'd died so long ago. They had met in high school and fell in love. Robert went on to college to earn an accounting degree while she dropped out to have their first child. He passed his CPA exam when their second child arrived. He was brilliant and she was proud to be his wife. Two children together and she couldn't imagine life without him. After five years of marriage, she'd become comfortable in the role of wife and mother. Familiar with the daily routine. He'd go to work; she'd manage the home and the children. Ruthie never thought the relationship would last. In a macabre way, Ruthie was right. During tax season, a truck ran a red light and T-boned Robert on his way home from the office. He was killed instantly, and Helena's world was turned upside down.

Then there was husband number two. She needed a father for the boys and the freedom to build a career. She was surprised the marriage only lasted sixteen months. Had she loved him? She never shed a tear when he died. Maybe she had been in shock. Or perhaps, she was emotionally shut down. Two dead husbands is enough to shut anyone down.

The faces of her sons flashed in her mind. Memories of their youth. Happy events. Birthday parties. Graduation ceremonies. Weddings. Times spent together in celebration. Other times when she'd just wanted to be alone. Childless. Quietly left to contemplate life. To write. Was it any wonder she'd ended up alone? Hadn't that been her grandest wish much of the time? To be left alone. Had she finally attracted her most ardent desire?

She searched through her memory for when her sons' lives had diverged from hers. There wasn't one specific moment that she could identify. It was more like a ship slowly pulling away from the dock and heading out to sea. A gentle slipping away. A silent glide through the waters of the future with nary a wave of goodbye.

Had she been a good mother? Wasn't that the universal mother's lament? Guilt for not being enough for her children. Guilt at wanting to have her own life. Her own career. Yearning to be free of entanglements. Yet, she must have done a good job. Weren't her sons independent? Wasn't that how it should be? Children launched into the world as capable adults. Fully equipped to lead their own lives. Perhaps she'd done a good job. Maybe even a great job. Produced two fine young men. Men with families of their own. Men who'd found love and successfully carved out a place in the world. Still, she couldn't quite decide; had she been a good or bad mother? Could both descriptions be true?

She stuffed the edge of the pillow under her chin. Why wasn't she sleepy?

So many things had once seemed so important. Activities that had drained her energy and patience. Working as an on-air reporter early in her career proved exhausting. The odd hours. The last-minute assignments. She knew then that she had to make a change. She was taking adult education classes in poetry at NYU when she attended her first women's rights rally. She was in the right place at the right time when volunteers were needed. The experience compelled her to write her first novel. Hannah Elliot was born. A character who faced the world with guts and savvy. She committed herself to giving speeches, marching, and once the novel was released, endless television interviews. She felt there was little choice. She had to raise her public image to attract readers. All those hours away from her boys hawking for the women's movement was a way of giving back. Or was it about ego? An escape from family responsibility?

She didn't want to think about it anymore. She stretched an arm out as if reaching for something she couldn't quite grasp.

She stared up at the ceiling and wondered what had become of the fans of her books. Had they disappeared into the firmament, never to be seen again? Or had they merely staggered into old age much as she had, wandering off somewhere waiting to die? Did they still think about her and the time they'd spent daydreaming about the life of Hannah Elliot? She already knew the answer. Of course not. So why had she done it? All that energy and effort. All that struggle to bring a novel to life.

Why, indeed.

Helena shifted. She still wasn't comfortable. If only she could turn her mind off. Quiet the busy thoughts. And though she had no wish to die, she understood why some poor souls might end their lives in the wee morning hours. The tossing and turning alone was maddening!

She fixated on her writing career. Why had she let it go? But then she wondered if she had let it go . . . or had it let her go? Oh, the horror of semantics. Ruthie used to say: "Say what you mean and mean what you say." But life wasn't that way. She wondered how much of what we understand about our lives is about trying to protect ourselves from some awful truth. There had been a time when her need to write had been as critical as her need to breathe. Her writing had been her therapy. She chewed on her bottom lip. Perhaps it was time to go back to therapy. She doubted she'd be up in the middle of the night if she had a good therapist.

She slipped out of bed and headed to the bathroom, waddling along on cramped feet, carefully navigating the tile floor, keenly aware that a fall could be disastrous. *Dear God,* she thought as she sat on the toilet, *when did I get this old?* It seemed as if her life had happened to someone else. Some quirky, other person who looked like her, but wasn't her. She was now purely an observer, no longer owning the past or her participation in it, as if she'd walked into Act III of the play of her life, untouched by the events in earlier scenes. Or maybe her story read more like a script. Scene, action, dialogue. A banal *Lifetime* movie she'd watched on television. Perhaps if she'd stayed in a long-term relationship, or maintained a career, or if friends were still nearby, she might feel a continuity with the past. Had aging narrowed her options? Or was her current circumstance about the choices she'd made?

She flushed the toilet, and with an *oomph*, was up on her feet. She washed her hands and then waddled back to bed and slipped under the covers, her mental motor still running at full throttle. She'd have to downsize before moving to Ventana. There was no way around it. Which created the dilemma of what to keep and what to discard. She had three sets of dishes: one from her mother, another she'd bought on a trip to France years ago, and a third for everyday from Crate & Barrel. She couldn't part with her mother's dishes. Nor the set from France. But the Crate & Barrel dishes were the ones she preferred. She'd have to let something go. But she couldn't decide. If she couldn't make up her mind about dishes, what hope was there for going through the rest of the house?

She gritted her teeth as the tension found its way to her jaw. Why did growing older require you to release the things you love? It didn't seem fair to spend a lifetime collecting possessions only to unload them. What was the point of all that? And who would ever love her things the way she had?

⌇⌇⌇

Helena had always believed if you focus on a problem with the right intention, the universe will send you an answer. For her, Rebecca Elert was that answer.

Helena was referred to Rebecca through a chance encounter with a woman she'd met at the nail salon. As she and the stranger chatted, Helena mentioned her upcoming move to Ventana. Upon hearing Helena's concerns, the stranger reached for her shoulder bag and dug out a business card. *Come Armageddon,* Helena thought, *the survival of the human race could be assured as long as women had proximity to their handbags.* "Her expertise is organization," the woman had said. "She works like an event planner. She'll handle the entire operation, arranging for charitable donations, packing, and scheduling movers. Whatever you need, she'll do. As little as necessary or manage the entire job."

Within a day, Rebecca, a short brunette with a face like a Boston Terrier, was sitting in Helena's kitchen, a mug of green tea before her. Helena guessed Rebecca to be in her early forties, though she was styled much younger, sporting sneakers, blue jeans, and a button-down work shirt: the sensible attire of someone who wasn't afraid to get their hands dirty. Rebecca jumped right into a discussion of her services, leaving the green tea untouched. She opened a large folder with a brochure tucked in one pocket and work charts in the other.

Helena, ever the perfect hostess, eyed the mug of green tea, wondering if Rebecca was waiting for it to cool before taking that first sip. Maybe the tea needed a sweetener. There was a jar of acacia honey on the table which Helena had ordered from Dean & Deluca. Try as she might, Helena could not open the jar. Rebecca, in the midst of explaining the importance of documenting charitable donations, held out a hand. Helena passed the jar. Rebecca lifted a teaspoon and banged on the lid. After a quick twist, she handed the open jar back to Helena without missing a beat in her presentation. Helena had no doubt Rebecca's problem-solving skills were first-rate.

"A lot of people don't realize how challenging it is to coordinate the details of a move. But let me assure you, Ms. Greenblatt, I have workplans that chart each step. There'll be no surprises if you hire me."

Rebecca's workplans certainly had steps. Pages and pages of steps. Helena doubted there was enough time to get through all those steps. A feeling of dread settled in as the reality of the upcoming move became increasingly real. She bit her lower lip, nervously chewing away, anticipating the work ahead. Uprooting wouldn't be easy. Perhaps she shouldn't have been so impulsive. Maybe she should have given the decision more time. Waited until she was absolutely ready. But waited for what? Another fall? Another health emergency? She took hold of herself. She had to be brave. There was no turning back. "I'm going to need a realtor," she blurted out, interrupting Rebecca who'd just started to review the activities under the section of the workplan labeled *Preparing for Your Moving Day*.

Rebecca didn't miss a beat. "I'd be happy to set up realtors for you to interview."

But Helena didn't want to interview realtors. She wanted the right realtor. The best one for the job. *Oh, my goodness*, she thought, as she realized that her Biltmore home would be the last home she'd own. Sure, there'd be the Ventana condo, but she really wouldn't own that. Besides, it wasn't a house. It was more of an apartment, and no matter how lovely a senior apartment building might be, it was, after all, a senior apartment building. Her current home was different. No shared walls. No concerns about neighbors. Privacy all around. Gosh, she'd miss the privacy. But wasn't privacy the whole point of moving? If she wanted to protect herself, she'd have to give something up.

She rubbed her temples. Was the weather changing? She had a splitting headache.

She suddenly realized she'd made a pivotal assumption. She was buying into Ventana with the expectation that the staff would look after her if she was unable to make her own decisions. Could she be mistaken? She hadn't asked when she toured if there was that kind of support. She'd been too busy inspecting the place: making sure the condo was the right size, the facilities first-class. Questions hadn't been asked about a potential healthcare ambassador to oversee her needs. How would that work? What guarantee did she have that someone would step in to help, should her health fail? Wasn't providing her with the appropriate level of care implied in Ventana's model of senior living? Why hadn't she even asked about it?

She bit hard on her lower lip, chewing on it till it was raw. She remembered the lunch with Alan. Asking about a healthcare ambassador had felt like a step too far. Like admitting she was alone in the world, forcing her to rely on the kindness of strangers much like Blanche Dubois in Tennessee Williams' *A Streetcar Named Desire.* A woman at the end of her options. But wait! She wasn't out of options. And she wasn't without means. She was just out of energy.

Proud . . . and out of energy.

Rebecca held up a flowsheet and spoke about the contents of Helena's Biltmore home. Helena imagined her treasures scattered to the wind. So many things she loved. Her mother's linen tablecloths. How many did she actually need? Her grandmother's lamps. Surely, she'd keep family heirlooms. What about her fine antiques and the rest? After she was gone, would her sons really want any of it? She doubted her daughters-in-law would.

Helena leaned forward with an elbow on the table. She rested her head in one hand and covered her eyes. She could no longer focus on Rebecca's maze of steps. It was all too overwhelming. Mercifully, Rebecca stopped talking. Helena exhaled, emitting a wheeze that sounded remarkably like an SOS call.

"I know this is a lot," Rebecca said, "but I find it's best to clarify details upfront. Then, after we sign the contract, there won't be any confusion."

Helena suppressed a moan. She'd no intention of hurting Rebecca's feelings but if anything was rife with confusion, it was Rebecca's array of diagrams.

"Once the house sells, things will move quickly," Rebecca promised as she rifled through her collection of papers.

Helena winced. What if buying into Ventana wasn't like buying into an insurance plan? What if, given time, she could no longer afford the monthly fees? Could they turn her out? Where would she go? And what if she developed dementia? Who would manage her money? That seemed like an awful lot of responsibility to hand over to a stranger. She'd heard of seniors financially ruined by lawyers, stockbrokers, and family members. Was she a baby gazelle in a field of hungry lions?

Rebecca scooted a little closer. She looked as if she might reach for Helena's hand which was at rest on the table. But she didn't. "May I ask you a question, Ms. Greenblatt. How old are you?"

Helena had often bragged about her age back when she'd felt indestructible. Certain anyone she told would marvel at her youthful presentation. But now, she feared that she appeared elderly, and though she'd tried to sit up straight, she was convinced her shoulders created a somewhat stooped silhouette. Based on what she already knew about Rebecca, the truth of Helena's age would not elicit a kind remark. "Eighty-three," she said as she held her breath in anticipation of Rebecca's response.

Rebecca's face went blank. Would a compliment be forthcoming. If so, would Helena require oxygen before Rebecca delivered it.

"My grandmother lived to be seventy-five. She was in horrible shape. The last two years of her life, she had two strokes. Then, she broke a hip."

The last thing Helena wanted to hear was a story of someone else's poor health. If God was kind, he'd let her die in independent living. On second thought, it might be okay to drop dead as soon as Rebecca left. Then, she'd avoid all this headache and maybe Rebecca would learn a valuable lesson about how to talk to seniors.

Rebecca's story picked up speed. "We couldn't afford to keep my grandmother at home . . ."

Helena wondered if it might be best to rent her home instead of selling it outright, just in case she didn't like living near the ASU campus. What if she felt trapped in a high-rise? Hated her neighbors? Couldn't make friends? What if she didn't like the staff? What if the shopping wasn't convenient and the traffic too intense in Tempe? What if, what if, what if. *Why*, she fretted, *are there so many what-ifs?*

Helena swallowed hard and reached for Rebecca's pen. "I'd better sign this now, while I still have the courage and all my marbles." Her hand shook as the pen hovered over Rebecca's contract.

Rebecca's tone turned warm and empathetic. "I know this is a hard decision, and if you want to give it some more thought, I'm perfectly fine waiting. But I promise, if you sign, I'll make the transition as easy as possible for you."

Helena wondered how erasing one's past could ever be easy.

"You have a lot to look forward to," Rebecca said with excitement as Helena handed over the signed contract. "A wonderful new beginning. Your next adventure!"

Helena winced. She wasn't going on a tour of Europe. She wouldn't be marching through the jungles of Africa on a wild game safari. Nor was she relocating to Israel to pray at the Wailing Wall. In her mind, the move to Ventana signaled no new adventures. If anything, future adventures seemed out of the question. "I think for the first time in my life, I feel old. Not older. Not growing old. But certifiably, one hundred percent, old," she admitted.

Rebecca's mouth hung open as if she were about to say something, but she didn't utter a word. She seemed to understand that the moment had arrived to listen. Helena thought it a wise choice.

Helena exhaled. The tension in her chest remained. "My past is slipping away. It isn't just about this house. My options are narrowing. I'm making this move because of my health, not because I'm eager to move forward into a new phase of life. I'm moving to Ventana because of physical limitations. Though it's a lovely place, I can't help but feel hesitation. Maybe it's fear. Fear about the next chapter of life."

Rebecca sighed. "I've worked with a lot of people who've gone through a similar transition. You need to be kind to yourself. Change is never easy. My grandmother used to say, 'The only one who likes change is a wet baby.'"

Helena thought Rebecca's grandmother very wise.

Rebecca continued. "When you think about it, no one knows what life has in store for them."

"True," Helena agreed. "But I once had the time to make a course correction, if needed. That window is now closing. My time is running out."

"As long as you're alive," Rebecca insisted, "you can do anything you want."

Helena thought Rebecca's perspective the luxury of the young who still have years to work out the challenges of life. She offered a wan smile. "I bet you thought an old lady like me would have made peace with all this by now."

"You're too tough on yourself," Rebecca answered. "Too alert about who you are and the changes happening."

Helena laughed. "Well, that's good news. At least I'm alert!"

⁓

The next morning, Rebecca showed up bright and early to start the downsizing process. Helena wasn't quite sure what to expect, though Rebecca had left a copy of the paperwork on the kitchen counter for her to review. "Today, we're going to start with the kitchen drawers," Rebecca cheerfully announced as if she were planning on taking Helena out to breakfast. "It'll be a challenge, but I know you're up to it."

Kitchen drawers, of course, Helena thought as if she were perfectly aware that it was the first step of the plan. Though Helena was a tidy housekeeper, she knew her kitchen drawers did not reflect that fact. If anything, she'd succumbed to the habit of using her kitchen drawers to hide an array of appliance booklets, warranties, recipes, loose paper clips, coupons, pads and pens, and all other odds and ends that threatened to clutter the countertop. Worse, her cutlery drawers weren't much better. She'd long ago ceased to separate the little forks from the big forks, or the teaspoons from the soup spoons, allowing them to nest together in a cluster of confusion. After all, she was only one person. It didn't really matter which utensil she used. Any size would do. Now she wondered if she should have organized the drawers before Rebecca showed up. Did she really want to reveal herself as being so disorganized on Rebecca's first day? Would Rebecca think her mind was as scattered as her messy kitchen drawers?

"Have you ever been to a therapist?" Rebecca asked as she opened the first kitchen drawer where Helena stored her large utensils.

"I have," she said, wondering where this line of questioning might be leading.

Rebecca held up a spatula. "Good. Then you know the benefit of talking to someone about your feelings."

Helena cringed. "Are you suggesting a therapist because you think I'm losing it?"

"Not at all," Rebecca quickly answered, pulling two more spatulas out. "I see a therapist. Do I look like I'm losing it?"

Helena gave Rebecca the once-over.

Rebecca broke into a smile. "Oh, you're funny. Very funny."

Helena chuckled. She was glad Rebecca got the joke.

"But seriously," Rebecca continued on as six spatulas now lined the counter. "I recommend therapy to all my clients going through this kind of transition. It's valuable to have a third party help sort it all out."

Helena frowned. "Isn't that your job?"

Rebecca stopped what she was doing to face Helena. "I may have great organizational skills, but for what's going on in your head, you need another kind of professional."

Helena wondered if talking about her fears would help. She'd met with a therapist when each of her husbands died. And when Ruthie passed away. But those circumstances were different. She'd been severely depressed. Wasn't this just a momentary problem? Wouldn't she feel better once the move was over? Besides, why dwell on the negative?

But Rebecca was not about to let it go. "You're an author."

"I *was* an author," Helena corrected.

"You know the value of putting your thoughts down on paper. Creative writing allows you to explore your unconscious. All sorts of things pop up that you might not otherwise be aware of. The same is true when you talk to a trained therapist. You might learn something about yourself," Rebecca said as she rummaged through her knapsack, retrieving a business card. She placed the card next to a red spatula, the last of the nine that lined the counter. She pointed to the card. "If you need a referral, I know someone who is excellent."

Helena sighed.

Rebecca opened another drawer. She retrieved a tenth spatula. "Do you really need all these spatulas?"

Some men loved going to Home Depot to buy tools. Helena loved Sur La Table. She especially loved the display with all the kitchen utensils. "Well, no," she admitted as she marveled at her spatula collection. "But if you cook, a spatula comes in handy." She reached for her favorite, a large metal one she used to flip pancakes.

"Good," Rebecca answered. "Select two more and we'll donate the rest."

Helena gasped. "I couldn't."

Rebecca pointed at the spatulas. "Unless you're opening a restaurant, you don't need all of these."

Helena balked. "You'd need a whole lot more for a restaurant."

Rebecca's face contorted into what Helena politely thought of as *the look*. Brows furrowed, a scowl on the lips, eyes sharp as a hawk zeroing in on its prey. Helena laughed. Maybe talking to a therapist wasn't such a bad idea. She picked up the therapist's card. Rebecca smiled from ear to ear. "Now, don't get too excited. I didn't say I'd go," Helena said as the opening lyric of her favorite Joni Mitchell song *Twisted* came to mind: *My analyst told me that I was right out of my head . . .*

———

Helena did not meet with a therapist. Wasn't it enough that she'd agreed to move to Ventana? Speaking with a stranger about her fears seemed like an added burden. Another expectation on the long list of expectations. One that Helena decided was beyond her limited capacity at the moment, regardless of Rebecca's Gantt chart. But Rebecca was not one to give up. Instead, she signed Helena up for a meditation class. Helena, not wanting to appear rude, accepted the gift. The daily meditation ritual proved to be a life saver.

On the day of the move, Helena was remarkably calm. When the movers arrived to pack her up, she assumed the philosophy of the Three Wise Monkeys; hear no evil, see no evil, speak no evil. When a mug dropped to the floor, she pretended not to hear the shattering glass. When the sofa was wrapped in plastic, she pretended not to see the dirty hands of the movers touching the fabric. When she caught the workers clowning around, she said nothing, although the crew was being paid by the hour.

The first night in her new Ventana condo, Ruthie's voice caught her by surprise. Helena looked about. There was no sign of Ruthie anywhere. The voice was manifesting from within.

I can't believe you've gotten rid of my good silver.

Helena covered her ears. Was there any way to blot Ruthie out?

I'm talking to you.

Helena rolled her eyes. "What does it matter? I wasn't using the silver. It should go to a home where it will be appreciated."

What about Ben or Nick? Maybe they'd enjoy it.

Helena laughed. "They don't want it. They barely have time for me. You expect them to polish silver?"

You were never strict enough with those boys. You let them run circles around you. The way they treat you!

Helena didn't want to hear any more. She reached for the television remote. Thank goodness Alan had arranged to have her cable set up on her move-in day. With the press of a button, the widescreen came to life. Helena breathed a sigh of relief. Distraction achieved. The last thing she needed was negative energy. She'd worked hard to make the Ventana move happen. She'd no intention of arguing with Ruthie about anything. Not the boys . . . or about the move, a subject which she was certain Ruthie would eventually get to. *It's like high diving,* she thought. *I've put on my bathing suit and jumped off the board. I'm in mid-air now, head over heels in a full twist. This is no time to lose focus. To let my mind wander.*

But the seed had been planted. Why was she on her own? Was she a victim of parental abandonment by her sons? Or had she done such a great job as a mother that her boys felt free to live their own lives without even a look back? She couldn't decide which was which and what was what as she chewed on her lower lip.

Had she been a good or a bad mother? And why, at this late date in her life, did it even matter?

– 8 –

THE TOENAILS WERE on a tear. Zak could hardly hear himself think, the music was so loud. Still, the crowd mingled about, seemingly oblivious to the noise, happily engaged in their cliques. Nobody appeared interested in the band. "Honestly," Zak yelled to Melinda as he gathered up empty beer mugs and wiped down a tabletop, stopping to rub his throbbing right ear. "Why are they so damn loud?"

Melinda put a palm to the side of her mouth like a megaphone. "Because they stink. Can't sing a lick. Can't play a decent note. Maybe they think no one will notice if they blast away." She pointed to the other side of the room, inviting Zak to follow her. Together, tucked in the corner, she asked him the million-dollar question. "What ever happened with your friend? The one from New York City."

Zak hoped Melinda might've forgotten the Allison debacle. It was the last thing he wanted to talk about. When he'd returned from afternoon classes, Allison was gone. She'd left a note on his desk apologizing for being a huge pain in the ass and hoping he could forgive her for being so mean. She wrote that she hadn't meant half of what she'd said. *Hmm*, Zak had wondered. *Which half did she mean?* She didn't say where she'd gone, but Zak assumed it was back to New York City. He was going to ask Chuck if anything happened between him and Allison, but on second thought, wasn't sure he wanted to know. He'd brought Allison into the dorm, which made him responsible for launching all the confusion, allowing Allison to bed hop from one side of the room to the other. Yes . . . some things were best left unspoken.

Zak twisted the bar towel in his hands that he used to wipe down the tables. "I don't know where she is or what happened to her. But she's definitely pissed at me. I kind of threw her out."

Melinda appeared surprised. "Well good for you, *Andy*. Someone's growing balls."

Zak grimaced. "Please don't call me, Andy. Really."

Melinda smiled the kind of smile one offers an adorable pup being housebroken.

Zak doubted his request registered. "I really feel bad about Allison," he admitted. "I think I just lost my best friend."

"Good riddance," Melinda said with a shake of her head. "Friends aren't supposed to intrude in your life. Move in with you without asking. Overstay their welcome. That's not a friend."

Zak agreed. But still, it didn't feel right. "She helped me when I needed someone. I should've tried to work it out. She was here just short of a week. What's a week in the course of a lifetime?"

"A long time when you're a college freshman. Not so much when you're my age." Melinda put a hand on Zak's arm. "Hon, don't blame yourself. There are plenty of people in the world eager to kick you when you're down. You don't need to be first person on that line. Be good to yourself. You did the best you could."

Zak guessed Melinda was right as he watched her stroll back to the bar to pick up another order of drinks. Unfortunately, the imagery of a line of strangers ready to kick him in the butt was now stuck in his brain. He imagined the Radio City Rockettes lined up to perform their high kicks. How many Rockettes were there? He bet those pointy-toed high-heels would be hard on his bottom. Or would the line be more like the queue at the airport during the Christmas rush; an angry mob wrapped around the lobby and out the door, bags pushed aside as they steadied themselves to kick him in the butt. How many people over the course of his lifetime would try to take advantage of his good nature? Were his parents at the head of the line? They'd certainly kicked him when he came out, making a difficult situation worse, just when he needed love and understanding.

And now, there was Allison.

Could his parents and Allison, the three most important people in his life, be right? Maybe he wasn't a good person, worthy of love. Maybe they knew him better than he knew himself.

Zak's mind wandered as he collected the kitchen garbage to dump in the outside trash cans. Should he reconsider talking with Chuck about Allison? Find out exactly what happened? Or should he just let it be? Was Melinda right? Was Allison really a bad friend who'd taken advantage of his kindness?

When Zak arrived back at the dorm, he was surprised to find Chuck awake. Zak checked his watch. "Isn't this kind of late for you?"

"Hey guy," Chuck said, stretched out in bed, his reading lamp on, a book open in his lap. "It is. But I wanted to talk with you. To be honest, I couldn't sleep."

Zak's heart pounded. *Oh no*, he thought. *This is bad. Straight guys don't ever want to talk. That's not very bro.* "Hey man, whatever happened between you and Allison, it's my fault," Zak quickly admitted. If he owned up to his share of the problem, maybe he could forestall Chuck wanting to change rooms.

Chuck squinted as if the light from the reading lamp was too bright. "About Allison . . ." he said with a sigh. "I hope you're not mad at me. I probably should have talked to you first, but with our conflicting class schedules, and you working at night, there wasn't time, and it just couldn't wait."

Zak was confused.

Chuck closed his book. "She had to go."

Zak nodded. "Of course. Sorry about that. She must have been really pissed off at me."

"You." Chuck sat up. His eyes were as big as saucers. "What did you do?"

Zak didn't want to rehash the whole thing. "I yelled at her. I told her to leave."

Chuck laughed. "Wow. Here I was afraid you'd be mad because I told her she had to leave."

Zak blinked. "Really?"

"Absolutely. She came back here all upset, hating on you, and to be honest, who wants all that drama? I told her she'd better hit the road. Life's hard enough without a woman coming between roommates."

Zak was amazed. Had he misjudged Chuck? He was more than just a good-looking dude. He had morals.

Chuck sat up in bed, one elbow supporting him as he twisted about to face Zak. "First, she's in your bed. Then she's in mine. There's something really wrong with that girl," Chuck warned.

Zak hesitated for a moment. What should he say? "Well, to be honest, she was *only sleeping* in my bed. That's all. Just sleeping." Why was it so hard to just tell the truth? He had no trouble explaining he was deaf in one ear. Or that he was Jewish. Or any other fact that simply described who he was. But the acknowledgement of being gay was different. He worried Chuck might have preconceived notions about gay men, negative stereotypes that might color Zak's admission.

But then, wasn't that also true about being Jewish, or being a New Yorker, or any of the other unique characteristics that made him different from everyone else? Still, Zak's parents had reacted so badly to the news, he was afraid to face the same consequences from a roommate. Would Chuck think he was interested in him? What if word got out in the dorm? Would he be able to defend himself in the wake of a homophobic reaction? There had been a kid in high school who'd really caught a lot of crap for being gay. Zak weighed his options. He clinched a fist and jumped into the fray. "I hope this isn't a problem, but there's something else I should tell you. I'm gay."

Chuck's face lit up. "Wow, you just let that fly right out."

"Sorry. If you'd like me to move or switch rooms, I get it."

"Are you kidding?" Chuck said.

"No, no. I'm just warning you. I am gay. I'm totally gay. One hundred and ten percent!"

Chuck smiled. "Wow. That sounds like you're really very gay. The king of gays. The Carl Nassib of gays. The Megan Rapinoe of gays. And you'd be willing to change rooms to make me feel more comfortable."

Zak nodded. "If that's what you'd prefer. But I hope you aren't going to ask me to move."

"Well, not to worry, my man. You don't need to move. I'm fine with it."

"You are?"

"Sure." Chuck stuck out his chin. "I grew up in San Francisco. Being gay is not exactly news to me. Besides, you're not the only one here with a secret."

Zak was thunderstruck. "You're kidding me. You're not gay."

"I'm not?" Chuck answered sarcastically.

"Then why'd you sleep with Allison?"

"She came back here drunk, and I couldn't get rid of her."

Zak knew she could be a handful. "She can be very persuasive."

"With some people," Chuck assured Zak. "But not with me. I wasn't going there."

Zak laughed. "Going there! Like a vacation you can't wait to take."

"More like a vacation you can't wait to come back from. Ever been to Aruba?"

"I haven't."

"I used to go with my folks. There's absolutely nothing on the island except a casino, lighthouse, and a beach. The most boring week of my life. Couldn't wait to get home. I felt the same way about your friend, *Aruba*. I couldn't wait to get her out of here in the morning. She was all over me."

"Aruba. You mean, Allison."

Chuck guffawed, his dark brown eyes glistening with tears of laughter. "No, bud. I mean *Aruba*."

⚬⚬⚬

The waiting room at Student Health Services was empty as Zak took a seat. He'd come between classes hoping the nurse would take a peek at his right ear. Whether it was the noise from Windy Canyon or his imagination, he was having a hard time hearing in the large lecture halls. There seemed to be an echo, as if he was listening to the lecture underwater. Worse, when he talked, he couldn't quite hear himself. He had no idea what was going on, but something was definitely off. More and more, he found himself relying on Marshall to share class notes, and even though Marshall kindly accommodated the request, Zak didn't want to be dependent. He'd been dependent on Allison and saw no reason to repeat the same mistake with Marshall.

After twenty minutes in the waiting room, a nurse finally appeared. "Next," she called.

He looked about. He'd been lost in thought and hadn't realized he was the only one in the waiting room. She pointed at him. He jumped up and followed her through a long winding hallway to an exam room where he was directed to wait. He paced in the small room trying to burn off nervous energy, stopping now and then to examine the anatomical diagrams hanging on the wall. It was all too familiar. How many hours had he spent as a child in similar exam rooms with his mother waiting for doctors who never seemed to be on time?

"Maybe we can play a game," his mother would suggest as the minutes ticked by. "Geography. I'll give you the name of a place and you use the last letter to name another place. What do you think?" He saw no value in playing geography when the office had a plastic model of an ear with removable parts sitting on the counter. How many deaf children had touched the model? How many were able to take it apart and put it back together? A sort of LEGO educational tool, the outer ear came off to reveal the middle ear, and the middle ear was easily removed to reveal the inner ear. He was fascinated with the inner ear's tiny structures. He held the vestibule, cochlea, and then the tiny plastic hammer in his palm. If he couldn't hear perfectly, at least he could slip each piece back into its rightful place to create the perfect ear. "Stop that," his mother would whisper as if they were being secretly watched by the office staff. "You shouldn't play with the doctor's toys."

The doctor's toys! Even at eight-years old, he knew the plastic ear wasn't a toy. Still, he did as he was told. He always did as he was told. The consequences of crossing his mother could be dire. She wasn't beyond giving him a sharp pinch on the arm when he didn't behave. Or a hard slap across the face. He needed her on his side in case things in the exam room got dicey. If the doctor probed too deeply into his ear, wiggling the instrument as he told Zak to hold still. Now, how could anyone hold still when something sharp was poking deep inside their ear?

There'd be a knock on the door and Zak would hop up onto the exam room table as if he were a fugitive, trying to avoid discovery. His mother, seated in a chair, straightened her short skirt as the doctor entered. It was showtime. "Good morning, doctor," his mother would say, all smiles, her face lighting up in a way Zak had only seen her do with his father. Why was she acting so strange? Being so friendly? So vivacious? "It's lovely to see you again."

Zak didn't think there was anything lovely about it. Being at the ear doctor was just the opposite of lovely. It was dreadful.

The doctor would stand before Zak, gripping Zak's head in his clammy hands, thumbs pressing against Zak's throat in search of something, exactly what, Zak had no idea. The man had the deft touch of a cannon being fired at close range as Zak smelt the doctor's fetid breath and counted the long gray hairs peeking out of his nose. *Rapunzel, Rapunzel, throw down your hair.* A quick turn of Zak's head and the doctor examined Zak's left ear, pulling hard on the ear lobe, as if by doing so, he could force the canal to reveal its secrets. Finally, the doctor would turn to Zak's mother. "We've looked through all the tests, and I'm sorry, Mrs. Andrews, there's nothing more to be done. The nerve is dead. There's no point in considering a hearing aid for the left ear. It won't help."

Zak's mother's expression would harden. He knew that determined look. Her child was imperfect, and she wasn't ready to concede. She'd cross her legs, exposing her shapely limbs as if a plea for special consideration. A favor that only a beautiful woman could seek. Her voice soft, seductive: "There must be something else we could do. Maybe another specialist might have a different opinion." Her statement was casual and friendly. Almost lighthearted. Smooth and easy with no hesitation. As if asking the doctor for the time of day. But she'd broken a cardinal rule. Patient's sublimate. But then, she wasn't the patient. She was the mother. And mothers don't sublimate when their only child's hearing is at stake. Not when their child is broken. Handicapped. Damaged. In need of repair. Not when there is a scintilla of a chance of fixing him.

The doctor would lick his lips as if his mouth was parched from uttering the same words to so many other mothers throughout his day. He'd then glance at Zak's mother's legs, just long enough for Zak to cringe. "Once the nerve is dead, there's really nothing more to be done. You won't find another doctor with a different opinion."

Zak couldn't bear the thought of going to another doctor. "It's okay," he'd say to his mother. "I'm fine. I can hear perfectly well with one ear."

The doctor would nod. "He's lucky. A high fever as an infant can leave a child totally deaf."

But Zak's mother wasn't about to concede. "What about a cochlear implant? Wouldn't that solve the problem?"

The doctor would then scratch his chin as he looked at Zak. The doctor was fine with Zak's hearing loss. He'd made no recommendation. So why did his eyes convey sadness as he placed a hand on Zak's shoulder? Zak was suddenly scared. "Mrs. Andrews, we recommend cochlear implants when there's profound deafness. Why not get Zak into lip-reading classes and see how he does? Being deaf in one ear is very manageable."

"But he's handicapped," his mother would insist, a dog with a bone. "Surely, he would qualify for an implant."

Zak's face burned. *Handicapped!* Was he handicapped? He'd never before heard his mother use the term in relation to his hearing. How could he suddenly be handicapped?

"I'm sorry," the doctor would say as he prepared to depart. "Be grateful your child is in good health and remarkably well-adjusted."

Zak squeezed his eyes shut. He didn't want to think any more about when he was a child. He was an adult now sitting in an exam room at Student Health Services taking care of what he needed to take care of, regardless of the outcome.

And there was no mother in sight.

⌁

Fifteen minutes later, there was a knock on the exam room door. "Yes," Zak called out as he straightened up and prepared to face the doctor. But when the door opened, it wasn't the doctor. It was the student health nurse. An older woman with frizzy gray hair and deep lines on her face, sporting an unusually bright red lipstick. He'd first met her when he'd arrived on campus. Because of his deaf left ear, Student Health Services had requested that he check in. It had all been perfunctory. *How long had he been deaf? Were there any surgeries? Did he have any need for accommodation?* Zak had winced. The last thing he wanted was another student with two good ears to follow him around and take notes. He was perfectly capable. Always had been and planned always to be. It was just a bad ear. One ear. Not the end of the world.

The nurse listened as Zak explained that he was having trouble hearing in the lecture hall. Everything sounded muffled. The nurse looked into his ears and then excused herself. When she returned, she had a syringe and a small plastic bowl filled with warm water. "You have wax buildup," she explained as she filled the syringe with water. She pulled down hard on his right earlobe and placed the tip of the syringe inside the canal, slowly pushing the warm water into the canal. There was a horrible whooshing sound followed by an uncomfortable fullness. She placed a yellow plastic receptacle below his ear to catch the watery runoff. A brown waxy plug popped out. "See?" she said, showing Zak the disgusting plug bobbing in the bowl. "You should be fine now."

Zak hoped she was right as he raced back to class, his right ear aching. At least the nurse had found the cause of the problem. That was worth the minor discomfort. Though he wished she'd explained what she was about to do before she actually did it. But then, he was used to medical people not talking to him. He guessed it must be annoying to have to deal with patients who are constantly presenting with problems.

The lecture hall was packed as Zak slipped into a fifteenth-row seat next to Marshall. The class had yet to start. Chemistry 101. Today's lecture was on polymers. *A good name,* Zak thought, *for a dog. Here, Polymer! Here girl. Fetch, Polymer. Good girl.*

"Are you okay?" Marshall asked as Zak took a notebook out of his backpack.

"All good," he said, not wanting to complain.

"What did the doctor say?"

"Nothing much," Zak answered. His ear had taken so much of his focus as a child, he didn't want to give it anymore attention.

Marshall nudged him as the professor entered the hall. All the talking stopped. In the quiet, Zak heard an odd ringing. Not loud, like a phone, but soft, like a tiny fan. Nearly imperceptible but very present. He put a finger in his good ear. He could still hear the fan. He pinched his nostrils and gently blew out. He'd been taught that popping the ears was an excellent way to clear the sinuses and any pressure imbalances. Still, he could hear the humming. The sound definitely was coming from inside his head as if the nurse had flipped some switch creating the low buzz of a self-cleaning oven. A buzz Zak had no control over.

As the professor led the class through various examples of polymers, Zak placed an elbow on the flip desk and turned his head to the left, right ear leaning in. He was barely able to catch a word. It didn't help that the professor was pacing back and forth while speaking, turning his back to the class as he wrote out chemical formulas on the blackboard. Though the professor was wearing a mic, Zak guessed it wasn't working properly. Perhaps it had shorted. Frustrated, Zak decided to move closer, descending the stairs from the fifteenth row only to realize there were no open seats upfront. There was only one solution. He sat on the third step in the aisle, notebook on his lap. If he couldn't hear at the back of the room, perhaps he might hear at the front.

The professor stopped the class. "I'm sorry, young man. But you can't sit there. It's a fire hazard."

Zak was horrified. The last thing he wanted was to attract attention. "I'm sorry," he said, "but I'm unable to hear you in the back."

The professor suddenly seemed concerned. He tapped the mic attached to his shirt. "Is this thing on. Can everyone hear me?"

A series of shouts from the students confirmed that the mic was indeed working.

The professor gave Zak a puzzled look as Zak stood and retraced his steps to the fifteenth row. "I can't make anything out from back here," Zak whispered to Marshall, his heart pounding, sweat breaking on his brow. Had he suddenly lost his hearing? Why was he unable to understand the professor? None of it made sense. He had to get back to Student Health Services. "I've got to get out of here," he told Marshall as he stood up, dropping a notebook to the floor with a bang.

Heads turned. "What's going on up there?" the professor called.

Zak felt the eyes of the classroom upon him. Why was he making such a commotion? Why couldn't he hear what was going on? He was sure everyone was laughing at him as he fumbled about, tucking the offending notebook into his backpack before rushing down the steps. He quickly crossed the lecture hall, passing in front of the professor. The two exchanged glances. Zak's was apologetic; the professor's, irritated.

When he was a child, doctors had warned that he could lose his hearing if he didn't protect his good ear. He'd always thought they meant sometime in the distant future when he was an old man. Not during his first semester of college. How could this have come on so quickly? Why was it happening at all? He'd always pretended to be like everyone else. Except for the visits to the ear doctor with his mother, and the lip-reading classes, he'd ignored his deafness. Blocked it out.

Some friends never knew he was hearing impaired. Some he never told. Or they'd forget. It was easy to forget when a person who is hearing impaired presents as normal. Speaks clearly. Appears to follow a conversation, even if he couldn't. He prided himself on being the master at faking his way through. He was *artfully* hearing impaired. Gifted at fooling others. Not handicapped, mind you. Never handicapped. But talented, nonetheless.

Get a grip, he thought as he cut through campus on his way back to Student Health Services. *You'll be okay. It's probably a passing thing.*

But he didn't feel okay. Not by a long shot. In fact, he feared he might never feel okay again.

– 9 –

HELENA STARED AT the view from her tenth-floor condo as she nursed her second cup of coffee of the morning. It was a beautiful day in Tempe, Arizona. The sky was clear. The mountains visible in the distance. A bustling city lay before her. She had everything to look forward to. After a few days of diligent work, the condo was shipshape. Her mother's good dishes were safely tucked away in the cabinet. Her bedroom closet was set up just as she liked it. Shoes snug in easy-to-reach hanging bags. Dresses to the right. Slacks and blouses to the left. With all the challenging work of the move behind her, she could finally rest easily knowing she'd taken care of herself. She imagined her sons grateful they didn't need to travel to Phoenix to help. After all, she was modeling self-reliance. Besides, how could her sons have assisted? They were too busy with their own families and careers. Still, secretly, she was hurt. At the very least, they could have asked to help. She'd never have accepted it, but it would have been nice had they asked. The thought haunted her, though she did her best to put it out of her mind. Negative sentiments, she reasoned, should have no play on such a lovely day.

She took another sip of coffee.

Now what?

She'd been handed a list of monthly activities by Julie Gold, the Ventana activity director, a spunky gal with short blond spiky hair. Julie's style reminded Helena of the edgy women of the late 1970s. Brassy rock n' roller chicks like Stevie Nicks, Pat Benatar, and Joan Jett. Women who cut their teeth in a man's world. Singing hard, playing hard, carving out their spot in the music pantheon. But this wasn't the 1970s and Helena doubted Julie played an instrument or even sang. Her energy was nonetheless fiery. Julie's mission, when they met, was clear: she wanted to get Helena connected to the Ventana community and active in the ASU campus. Though Julie clearly prided herself on being excellent at her job, the new tenant in 10A was not about to succumb to her charms. Helena wasn't quite ready to jump in and embrace her new resident status along with the socialization it required. Alone in the condo, she could pretend nothing had changed. She could come and go as she pleased, still the very independent lady. And though her health had faltered at the respectable age of eighty-three, she was as sharp as ever. So what if she'd moved into a senior community to protect her future? Didn't she deserve the security? The peace of mind such an arrangement brings when one is single. At least she wasn't a hostage in a nursing home, shuffling along in her pajamas. Sitting in a wheelchair parked in a smelly hallway waiting for her next meal. She was in a luxury building watching planes take off and land at Phoenix Sky Harbor Airport. She had her own kitchen, fully equipped with the latest Wolf appliances (oh, those red knobs!). Whole Foods had recently delivered her grocery order. She was still free, able to come and go as she wished, and she would come and go if only she wasn't so darn frightened. *I just need time to adjust*, she reasoned. And there certainly seemed to be plenty of time. Time to read a book. Time to sit on the terrace and enjoy the breeze. Time to watch Netflix. Maybe something sweet. Romantic. Or better yet, a documentary. Something devoid of violence. Uplifting. She had all the time in the world. Nothing had really changed. In fact, it was as if she were still in her former home, all alone, until the doorbell rang. *Now, who can that be?* she groused as she headed to the door, uncertain she was ready to welcome visitors.

"There you are!" Julie said as Helena opened the door. Julie was dressed in a tie-dye T-shirt of red, yellow, and blue, a pair of straight-legged jeans, black high-heeled boots, and a necklace of white pukka beads, the sort Helena had last seen being sold on a beach in Mexico in the 1990s. Julie's eyes twinkled behind a pair of pink-tinted eyeglasses. "I've been thinking about you." She peeked past Helena. "May I come in?"

Helena stepped aside, welcoming Julie inside with the wave of a hand. Julie settled on the sofa in the space which doubled as a family and living room. Helena made herself comfortable in an armchair, facing her visitor.

"I love what you've done with the place," Julie said as she looked at the grays and pale blues. Except for a piece of artwork here and there, the unit was a cool sanctuary, like what one might see in an Ian Schrager hotel. "You have a real talent for muted tones."

Helena couldn't help but smile. A love of bright colors was one thing she and Julie did not share.

Julie cleared her throat. "Now today, I was wondering if we might schedule a one-on-one so we can find out what classes you'd be interested in at ASU. You can audit any class. We also have a mentorship program that might be right up your ally. So many of our Ventana residents really enjoy mentoring students."

Helena hadn't yet looked at the flyer of available ASU classes. She wasn't sure how she'd even navigate the campus. It all seemed so vast, stretching over blocks of the city. Though she hadn't had another dizzy spell, the fear of fainting was still very much front and center. The last thing she wanted was to pass out in front of a classroom of students. She certainly didn't want to scare anyone. Nor did she want to be embarrassed. "I don't know yet what I want to do," Helena admitted. "Perhaps I'll start slow."

Julie offered a knowing glance as if Helena wasn't the first resident to rebuff her advances. "I understand. You want to relax and get adjusted. That's wonderful. But if you're available today, join me in the dining room for lunch. I can introduce you to our other guests. The chef is terrific. The food is wonderful. Salads, burgers, and a few specials. You do get two meals a day with your meal plan, so let's be sure to make use of that benefit."

Helena braced herself. Julie had an indomitable spirit. There was no point being rude and resisting her advances. She had to face it: she'd moved into a senior development with a lot of old people. Eventually, she'd have to meet them. Socialize with them. Be courteous, friendly, and welcoming. "I'd love to," she lied as her stomach did a cartwheel that would've impressed Simone Biles. "That would be lovely," she added, hoping her awkwardness would disappear as she slipped into the Ventana way of life.

Julie shifted expressions. The happy-go-lucky, devil-may-care smile was gone. In its place, a more serious note. "May I offer a suggestion?"

Helena raised a brow. What was this perky pixie about to say next?

"I know it can be hard moving into a new environment, and even though Ventana is a lovely space, this probably is a bit of an adjustment. Am I right?"

Helena froze. Had Julie read her mind? Was she about to be lectured by a young woman who clearly had no idea what she was going through? Wasn't it hard enough to face an uncertain future without listening to a twenty-something wax prosaic on life? Still, Helena thought it rude to be disagreeable. Clearly, Miss Rose-Colored Glasses had the best of intentions.

"We want you to be happy. You can do as much as you want, or as little, but I just want to be sure that you take advantage of what we have to offer before you decide you don't want to participate. Once you meet the other guests, I know you'll come to love it here."

Helena nodded even as she reacted to Julie's choice of words. *Guests? Why does she keep calling everyone a guest? Why not owner?*

"We're very proud of this place," Julie added. "Give it a chance. You'll come to love it."

Helena hoped so. But then, she really had no choice. She'd already sold her home. The hot Phoenix housing market had concluded the sale in record time. Her former life was now gone. Over. There was no going back. She'd have to give Ventana a chance. The entire Ventana experience. At least, as much as she could reasonably tolerate. Today, lunch with Julie was the one activity she could do with a smile.

She suddenly heard Ruthie's voice. *Life is short. Smile while you still have teeth.*

✦

The dining hall was abuzz when Helena entered through the glass doors. In the distance, Julie was chatting with a group of women. Helena took a deep breath. She'd dressed for introductions, wearing an Eileen Fisher outfit she'd ordered online: a basic white blouse over an unstructured pair of gray slacks. Simple. Elegant. Upscale. With her shoulder-length dark gray hair neatly parted in the middle and tied back with a ribbon, she imagined herself as chic as Diane Keaton. All she needed was a wide-brimmed hat and Diane's halting speech pattern and they could pass as sisters.

Julie hurried to Helena's side. "I love what you're wearing," she said with genuine admiration. "You look fabulous."

Helena's cheeks burned. Julie sounded surprised, as if she'd expected Helena to show up in a ratty bathrobe and fuzzy pink slippers. Now she feared she might have overdressed in an effort to put her best foot forward.

Together, they settled at a table for two in the center of the busy dining room. Helena looked over the menu, imagining that she and Julie made an odd pair. The very colorful Julie and the muted palette of Helena. Youth and enthusiasm, balanced by wisdom and caution.

"I'm so glad you accepted my invitation," Julie said. "There's so much we have in common."

Helena tried not to laugh. From her perspective, they'd absolutely nothing in common beyond sharing a table. Here was a girl at the very start of life, occupying space with seniors on the other end of the spectrum. That slippery slope that eventually beckons us all. *What a shame*, Helena thought. *Surely, a young woman as vivacious as Julie should be out in the world, enjoying life. Having adventures. Making friends her own age. Meeting men. Falling in love.*

Julie held her palms together in a reverential pose. "Years ago, I stumbled on a novel in the library in my hometown of Peoria, Illinois. I'd just entered high school." Julie rambled on about her favorite books when she was a teen. All the expected picks. *Jane Eyre. Little Women. To Kill a Mockingbird.*

Helena sipped her iced tea as she listened. She'd never been to Peoria. But she had been to Chicago. She'd attended the Democratic National Convention in 1968. The violence had inspired her to become politically active. Rocks and bottles in the air. Police charging on horseback, pushing the crowd back, wooden batons flying indiscriminately. She'd sought cover in Grant Park near a fountain as rioters stormed the police barricades. A clash of generations, a clash of wills, a clash of diametric opposites trying to find a way forward in an America that seemed to have lost its direction through the buildup of the Vietnam War. "I'm glad you like to read," Helena said, interrupting Julie's litany of classic novels, hoping she wasn't about to dip into the works of Shakespeare. "It's the sign of an intelligent mind."

"That's when I met Hannah Elliot," Julie said, leaning forward as if sharing a secret.

Helena was still mentally back in Chicago, thinking about that terrible year. The cold-blooded murder in Memphis of Martin Luther King, Jr. in April. The brutal assassination in Los Angeles of Robert F. Kennedy in June. America was a powder keg primed to go off.

"Hannah was my hero," Julie said with reverence.

Helena blinked. *Hannah Elliot? How could this youngster know anything about Hannah Elliot?* For all Helena knew, the novel was out of print, buried in the back of dusty bookcases. "I never imagined someone your age would even know about my work."

"Oh, yes," Julie gushed as the waitress approached to take their order. "I'd love to hear all about your creative process."

Helena wasn't prepared to discuss her former career. Instead, she ordered lunch when the waitress looked her way. "Egg salad on rye, please."

Julie didn't pick up on Helena's discomfort, so Helena redirected the conversation to the weather. The triple digit temperatures of summer. Helena's passion for gardening. The unique challenge of growing vegetables in a hot climate. Her love of hummingbirds. And dogs. Especially poodles since they're hypoallergenic. The amazing development of Tempe over the last ten years. After leading the conversation for some ten minutes, Helena finally relaxed. She took a breath, relieved she'd distracted Julie.

"Are you still writing?" Julie asked as Helena's sandwich arrived.

Helena blinked. There it was again. The big question. "I haven't written anything in quite a while."

"But why? You're so gifted. Your books are such page-turners. Stories of women who wanted more out of life than motherhood and marriage."

Helena smiled. It was her go-to expression when she wasn't sure how to answer a question. She'd hoped to avoid telling anyone at Ventana about her past. She saw no reason to bring it up. Being a one-time activist and author was a lifetime ago. A life someone else had led. What had happened to her writing career? Why had she given it up? She'd no interest in sharing those details with Julie. She wasn't even sure how to explain it to herself. Besides, some things were too personal to discuss. Some things were nobody's business. Still, she felt compelled to answer. "Times change," she finally said, as if one day the world had woken up and was no longer interested in what she had to say. "And so did my readers. More and more women were being published. Jacqueline Susann. Jackie Collins. All runaway best sellers. And then the blockbuster novels. *The Godfather* and *Love Story* were so popular. I couldn't compete. Or maybe I just didn't want to, anymore."

Julie seemed genuinely sad. "So, you stopped writing."

"Just stopped," Helena echoed, satisfied she'd effectively put an end to the discussion.

Julie shook her head. "That's a shame."

Helena pursed her lips as the impact of Julie's remark washed over her. "That depends on your perspective," she said, keenly aware that she'd somehow failed to live up to Julie's fantasy of what a writer's life should be like. And then it occurred to her: wasn't this lunch supposed to be an introduction to her next chapter of life? Not about judgment. Not about who she used to be. What was the point of looking back? What could ever be learned at this stage of life by rehashing one's mistakes? Wasn't regret just another way of feeling bad about yourself?

When she moved to Ventana, she'd been determined to leave the past where it belonged. In the past. At least, she'd hoped to give it a try. Or, as Ruthie used to say, "Let sleeping dogs lie."

"It's just too bad," Julie continued, her face full of disappointment.

"I thought the purpose of our lunch today was to introduce me around," Helena said in an effort to again change the subject.

Julie looked about as if suddenly aware that there were other people in the dining room. "Oh, yes. But before I do, I wanted to ask if you'd be a guest lecturer at ASU's Virginia G. Piper Center of Creative Writing. It's a wonderful program. Full of talented students. I just know they'd welcome hearing about your career."

"My past career," Helena corrected.

Julie's smile slipped. "You're upset. Have I offended you? I just thought being a guest lecturer would be a great fit. A win-win for you and the students."

Helena supposed Julie was only being kind, but discussion about her writing career had caught her by surprise. It seemed like bait and switch. Come to lunch, meet new people, and oh, before I introduce you to anyone, commit to discussing your former life as an author and why you decided to stop writing. "I'm sure you meant well," Helena said. "But I'd really prefer meeting some of the other residents."

"Guests," Julie corrected.

Helena nodded. "Yes. Right."

Julie clicked her tongue. "Okay. How about if I ask them to stop by our table on the way out? We can also set up a tea."

"Sounds lovely."

"Perfect," Julie said, her brilliant smile once again in place. "I'll just step away to talk with them before they leave."

"I'd like that," Helena said, keenly aware she'd agreed to Julie stepping away mostly to get rid of her. *Oh,* she thought as she nibbled on her sandwich, *simple lunches are never simple.*

～

Helena tugged on the front of her one-piece bathing suit. She couldn't remember the last time she'd been in a bathing suit. Had it gotten tighter or was she just not used to the clingy fabric? She crouched in front of Ventana's indoor pool and dipped a finger in the water. There was stiffness in her thighs and knees. She'd long ago given up yoga, but now she wondered if it would be worth starting again to improve her flexibility. She'd always considered herself somewhat limber, even enjoying dance classes well into her fifties. Great exercise for the body and mind. At some point, she'd decided she was too old for all that. Then, she developed sciatica. After that, she pulled a muscle in her back. Or was it that tennis injury that had sidelined her? She couldn't quite remember, but now, it felt as if she'd ceded her physicality to the enemy of time with barely a struggle, allowing mother nature to call the shots on how she experienced her body. Maybe she'd been wrong. Maybe those injuries were her body's way of telling her to slow down. Be kinder. Gentler. Learn to stretch, but don't stop all together.

A male voice called out to her. "You'll never get wet if you hover by the edge." It was Gilbert Goldfarb, the spry gentleman from the lobby. Her August dandelion. The president of the welcoming committee, or so he'd said the morning of the tour with Alan when Gilbert had introduced himself, flirting shamelessly with her. He was standing on the threshold of an open door that provided access to the pool.

"I'm still thinking about it," she admitted as she stood, a palm rubbing the ache in her left knee.

"You're very flexible," Gilbert said admiringly. "It's not everyone who can crouch down at our age to test the water with a finger. A toe, yes. But a finger? You know, you should be careful. Had you bent over, well, I don't need to tell you. Bending over can cause dizziness and result in a fall."

No. He didn't need to tell her. She knew all about dizziness. "I suppose you're also going swimming this morning. Is your bathing suit waiting for you in the men's locker room or are you stalking me?"

Gilbert laughed. "No, I'm not swimming. The pool is yours. I just happened to see you through this wonderful wall of glass that surrounds the pool, which is why this area is nicknamed the fishbowl. You seemed so tentative. I thought I'd better come in and offer encouragement."

"Oh, I see," she said as she took three quick steps along the edge of the pool and jumped in. The water was delightfully warm. When she popped back up, she gave her head a fast shake. She was instantly reminded of that awful day, decades earlier, when her white toy poodle, Muffy, had fallen into the backyard pool. Helena, fully dressed for an evening out, jumped in and fished her out, placing Muffy safely back on the flagstone. The poor thing looked like a wet rag. Helena didn't think she looked much better.

"Well, if you'll excuse me," the old gentleman said, "I'd better be on my way. There's a board meeting and my attendance is required."

Lovely, Helena thought, as Gilbert withdrew. She was grateful to see the back of his head.

She contemplated swimming laps. Or maybe one lap. Perhaps half a lap. Well, she'd see how she felt before firmly making up her mind. It had been years since she'd last gone swimming. Her home pool had become more of a water feature. An oversized fountain she loved to look at from her kitchen window. Oh sure, one could swim in it, but when the temperature outside allowed for swimming, the sun seemed far too strong. She'd long ago given up on all the preparation required to get wet. The sunscreen. The towels. The ice water to hydrate and wet washcloths she'd used to cover her eyes as she laid out and dried off in Arizona's summer heat. In truth, she'd always loved the ocean. The sound of the waves, seagulls swooping overhead at Jones Beach on Long Island. But that was a lifetime ago when she lived in New York City. Her last year on the East Coast, she'd still thought of herself as young, though technically, at fifty, she really wasn't. But what does age matter when you have your health? When you feel vigorous. She'd once thought she was indestructible, a force that couldn't be shushed into silence. Would her choices back then have been different if she'd known she'd have another thirty-three years on earth? She sighed. Odd how thirty-three years after fifty made you an old woman of eighty-three, but thirty-three years before, she'd have only been seventeen. So young, so supple. A mere baby. In hindsight, even fifty now seemed remarkably young.

She took a deep breath. Perhaps it was best to warm up. Holding on to the side of the pool, she kept her head above the water line, body fully immersed. Slowly she relaxed, allowing herself to luxuriate in the velvety feel of the water. She twisted her neck about, stretching each leg out as she offered a gentle kick. The next moment, she dunked her head under and pushed off the wall with her feet. She was gliding effortlessly, her muscles expanding and contracting as she pulled herself forward with the cupping of a hand, feeling her torso and hips twist along with the motion. One lap turned into two. Two laps into four. Her body had not forgotten. She discovered the once-familiar rhythm as she eased back into form. The delicious sensation of buoyancy as she was freed from gravity. Alone in a world of pure imagination. No longer an old woman. Not a woman at all. A sea creature from the deep. An eagle soaring across the sky. A gazelle racing across the savannah. Free to be whatever she wished. Free of the shackles of her aged form. Free once again to enjoy her physicality.

Breathing hard, she caught her breath as she clung to the edge of the pool, blinking to clear the water from her eyes. What was this new sensation? A gentle calm. A sense of accomplishment. A mastery of physical limitations. Whatever it was, she felt warm, confident, and protected. She was once again in charge of her life. Present to her sensations and desires. She'd made the right decision by moving to Ventana. She was certain of that now. The next step was up to her. She'd sign up for yoga classes. That would be the start of the new beginning. After that, she'd review the weekly activity listings. Consider auditing a few ASU classes. Suddenly, there was much to do. Because starting over required attention to details.

For the first time in a long time, excitement replaced fear. She'd started. Now, she wondered what else she could do as she awoke to the experience of life at Ventana. "It isn't over yet," she murmured to herself, a thrill in her voice. *There's still more left to experience. More left to still be,* she thought as the possibilities flowered before her.

～

Helena looked for a seat as the scent of freshly brewed coffee beckoned her to the back of the line. The Starbucks around the corner from Ventana was packed with students: laptops open, headsets on, doing whatever students in their twenties do as they sip coffee and eye computer screens, seemingly lost in their own world, blissfully unaware of those around them. Helena thought it simply marvelous. Such powers of concentration. She couldn't imagine herself working in such an environment, if the students were in fact working. Perhaps some were playing video games or streaming the latest Hulu release. Yes, she'd stepped into another world. The milieu of the young, and though the Starbucks staff had been welcoming, the place was not a social hall. At least not in the traditional sense. If anything, it was a caffeinated library where each member kept very much to themselves. There was barely any cross talk. Only the soft background music (was that Sinatra?) and the ever-present aroma of freshly roasted beans.

Coffee in hand, Helena settled at a table near the back. It felt good to be out and about, welcomed into this youthful oasis. Sitting with so many young people, she could easily forget her age. The blending was seamless, as if she'd returned to college, but without the headache of assignments, exams, and papers due. She closed her eyes. She was eighteen again, struggling to find her way. She was back at New York University. The future unchartered. Every possibility available, no clear path forward. She remembered being afraid. Unsure how she'd manage on her own. Scared about earning a living, fitting in . . . it wasn't an exciting time. The truth bubbled to the surface: unsure of herself, she'd married Robert and then dropped out of college. She did it long before she became pregnant. Looking back, it seemed as if she'd given up on herself. Had taken the easiest route out.

"Excuse me; is this seat taken?"

The woman's short brown hair was curled tightly as if she'd stuck her finger in an electric socket. She was pointing at the extra chair at Helena's table.

"All yours," Helena answered.

"Thank you," the woman said as she sat down. "It feels like I should be checking my iPhone." She eyed the other occupants of the room. "Just to fit in."

"Everyone does seem technologically connected," Helena agreed.

"It's a shame really," the woman said. "They text, Instagram, TikTok . . . do whatever they do . . . but can they actually talk to each other?"

Helena nodded. The same thought had occurred to her. "Maybe, this is how they connect. I suppose there's a proper etiquette to it all. We just don't know about it."

The stranger smiled. The lines about her mouth and eyes were pronounced. "You're probably right."

Helena clocked her new pal to be in her late forties. Tired. Probably in need of a vacation.

"My name is Aggie," the woman said, hand extended. "I've seen you around. You're new to Ventana."

"I am," Helena acknowledged. *Good guess*, she thought. But then she realized that anyone over sixty years old in this particular Starbucks had a 200 percent chance of being from Ventana.

"I work in the dining room."

Helena remembered. "Why, yes. Yesterday. You brought my egg salad sandwich."

"Right," Aggie said. "Most people don't actually notice me. I'm just part of the scenery in the dining room. Tablecloth. Napkin. Aggie Delano."

"I'm sorry. That doesn't seem right."

"Oh, don't get me wrong," Aggie explained. "I completely understand. Everyone is very nice. But my job is in the kitchen. I don't take the orders. I prepare the salads, put together the drinks, and make up the bread baskets. Then, I get the food out and onto the tables. I sort of come and go. It's hard to have a lot of interaction when your only conversation is repeating someone's order before you place the food in front of them." She mimicked herself in a high voice: "Meatloaf. Tuna casserole. Steak, well done."

Helena laughed. "I imagine that would be socially limiting."

"I've applied to be a waitress so I might soon be at the front of the house instead of the back."

"Well, I hope that comes through for you."

Aggie chuckled. "It's not exactly my dream job."

"No?" Helena said, her curiosity aroused. "What is your dream job?"

Aggie pointed her chin toward the Starbucks counter.

Helena couldn't imagine that a woman of Aggie's age wanted such a job. Wasn't that for young people? At least, Starbucks seemed to employ only young people. Was that by availability or design?

"They offer wonderful benefits and it's a solid company," Aggie explained. "I know, there'd be a lot to learn, and I'd need to get special shoes." She rolled her eyes. "You're on your feet all day long."

Helena thought of a bunion she had removed years ago. "Standing doesn't sound very appealing."

"Maybe not at the start," Aggie agreed. "But the day would fly by. I'd be with my peeps," she said, waving a hand.

Helena was confused. Except for herself, Aggie was clearly older than everyone in Starbucks.

Aggie leaned closer. "Peeps in spirit," she clarified. "I want to be . . ." Aggie lowered her voice, ". . . where the action is."

Helena looked at the young faces buried in iPhones and laptops. "Well then," she said, tongue in cheek, "this must be the place."

Aggie grinned. "You know, you're only as young as you feel."

Helena liked Aggie's attitude. "Maybe it's time to give that old adage a tweak. Maybe, *you're as young as you think.*"

Aggie raised her mug in a mock toast. "Oh, I like that. You're clever. You should be a writer."

Helena smiled. Why was her past always following her around? "I hate to admit it, but I used to be a writer."

"What do you mean *used to be?*"

"Well, I haven't written anything in years."

"Does that mean you've given it up?"

Helena thought about it for a moment. "Actually, it gave me up. Like miniskirts and go-go boots. Our time together came and went."

"What's your name?" Aggie asked.

"I'm Helena Greenblatt."

"It's nice to meet you, Helena. Now, we've got to start working on your thinking. You can be whatever you want. Look at me. I have a high school diploma and work at Ventana. Surely, for someone like you, the sky's the limit."

Helena supposed. "But I'm not sure I have any interest in writing again."

"Well then, fine," Aggie declared as she held her coffee cup up high. "You're doing exactly as you like. I say, bravo. But if there's a part of you that still wants to write, you should tap into that. Time is ticking. You only have so long to get those words down on paper."

Helena gasped. Who was this odd stranger who could speak the truth and still be light and airy?

"So, have you met the others?" Aggie asked.

"The others? You mean, the other residents?"

"Guests," Aggie corrected. "We're discouraged from calling them residents."

"Yes. I've been reminded of that," Helena confirmed. "Everyone I've met so far seems very nice."

"They are," Aggie assured her. "But busy. I've overhead some of the table conversations. Classes and mentoring students. A few are lecturing. Imagine that?" Aggie said with a hint of sarcasm. "The students must really enjoy having people from our generation share their lives."

Helena was surprised Aggie had suddenly aged herself into Helena's generation. "Our generation? You're not part of *our generation.*"

"The younger people imagine anyone over thirty is part of a monolithic group of elders. To be honest, I thought that way too when I was their age."

Helena wondered if Aggie was right. She looked at the students sitting at the next table swiping away on iPhones. "We may not be truly part of all this," she said, "but we're still here. I do think we have something to add."

"That's the spirit," Aggie cheered. "You're now part of Ventana. It's like drinking from the fountain of youth. Each day, you'll wake up just a little bit younger. More engaged. More active. Take advantage of what Ventana has to offer. It'll make the adjustment easier."

Following Julie's suggestion, Helena made up her mind to lunch every day in the dining room, inviting herself to join different tables as a means of getting acquainted with the other guests. After a few days of making the rounds, and with so many new faces, she employed little tricks to spark name recall: facial features, mannerisms, hairstyles, a Hollywood resemblance, all morphed into those hints. Walter was big on *winking*. Terri had a *terrible facial tic*. Marilyn spoke in a *breathy whisper*. Toni was a *sharp dresser*. Roberta wore her hair in a *bob*. The alliterations didn't need to be exact, and some of the choices were far-fetched, but they provided enough of a hint for Helena to associate a stranger with their name. On one occasion, Helena caught herself mid-sentence conjuring the wrong name despite recalling the correct hint. It happened as she said hello to a woman she'd met the day before. The woman had conveyed such a sunny disposition that Helena was reminded of *spring*. Unfortunately, upon meeting again at an evening lecture, Helena couldn't remember if the woman's name was April, May, or June. She split the difference, opting for May. Luckily, June was hard of hearing or perhaps too polite to correct the error. So, it wasn't exactly a surprise when Helena screwed up Babs' name. The short blond with curly hair rushed crossed the dining room to grab Helena by the elbow, pulling her over to join her table of three for lunch. Babs had talked incessantly when they'd first met in the Ventana library. This earned Babs the nickname *Blab*. Sure enough, Helena accidentally blurted *Blab* upon greeting her, but Babs was too busy talking to notice. Helena decided, in the land of eighty-three-year-olds, mistakes were bound to happen.

"So how are you adjusting to Ventana?" Babs asked as Helena took the empty seat at the table of four. "

Helena swallowed hard. How should she answer? Be pleasant and upbeat? Or truthful, sharing that moving to Ventana was like throwing ice cold water on your face after oversleeping. "It's an adjustment," she admitted, opting for door number two. "I'm afraid I've become accustomed to living alone. The good and the bad. This is a lot of socialization for me."

Babs appeared to understand, but then, she was also eager to talk. Was she even listening, or just waiting for her turn to share a story? "My first week, I was so depressed. I never knew what depression was until then. I could hardly get out of bed. But then Julie showed up. She's amazing. A truly old soul."

The others nodded, though Helena didn't particularly believe in old souls. The dead, yes. Disenfranchised spirits that showed up at the most inconvenient moment. Absolutely. But old souls? That was a bridge too far. Skeptical about anything she couldn't see or hear, Helena had no patience for fanciful psychic babble. After all, she remained a reluctant medium, certain that those who proselytized about auras and the like were full of hooey.

"It is an adjustment," said the woman to Helena's right. She had a long face and an even longer nose. "By the way, I'm Cynthia."

Helena made a mental note: it was a *sin* to have a face like *Cynthia*.

The woman to her left disagreed. Her white hair was beautifully coiffed in a short bob. Her make-up stunning. Helena wondered what she must look like in the morning before the paint job. Her perfume was just a little strong. "Didn't you girls ever go away in the summer? It was the happiest time of my life. I don't know why we can't just pretend we're on holiday at some beautiful resort in the Catskills. Or Atlantic City. Wait! What was that wonderful island? *Don't tell me.* Oh, yes. Puerto Rico! I've met some wonderful men in Puerto Rico. And those beaches!"

Helena had been to all those places and more, and in her opinion, Ventana was nothing like any of those gorgeous vacation spots. There was no lake. No ocean. No greenery. No sandy beach. No trees.

"*Don't tell me,* you've never been to Puerto Rico," Miss Makeup practically cooed. "Just *don't tell me.*"

Babs introduced Donna. Ahh, Helena smiled. *Donna, Don't Tell Me.* Of course.

"And who are you?" Cynthia said as she looked over the luncheon menu.

"I'm Helena."

"That's pretty," interrupted Donna. "Like Mount St. Helens in Washington State."

Helena gasped. Was Donna employing Helena's mnemonic trick? Could it be possible that Donna might one day accidently call Helena, Mount St. Helens? Helena chuckled. She'd have to gain a bit of weight to live up to the moniker.

"Go on," Cynthia said, tossing Donna a nasty look for the interruption.

"I'm just new here. Other than that, there isn't really much more to tell."

"Nonsense," Cynthia snapped as she looked at the others for confirmation. "There's always something to tell. You can't live this long and have nothing to say about yourself."

Helena took a breath. Cynthia's sharp tone was unexpected among a table of retired ladies. But then again, growing older didn't mean being gentle as a lamb. Wasn't that a stereotype? The grandmotherly type Helena had never considered herself to be. She searched for what else to add. She punted. "I'm a widow with two sons."

Cynthia wasn't having it. "You're not one of those women who defines herself by marriage and childbearing. Did you have a career? Did you ever work? I swear to God," she said, a fist in the air as she gave Helena her full attention, "if you dare say you were only a mother, I'll strike you. Or ask you to move to another table."

Helena's mouth hung open.

"You have to forgive Cynthia," Babs explained. "She lacks patience. She's an agitator at heart. Aren't you, dear?"

"I was a lawyer. A state prosecutor. A damn good one," Cynthia said with a scowl that emphasized her strong features.

"I wasn't a housewife, if that's what you're implying," Helena confirmed, angry in the face of such rudeness. "But there's nothing wrong with being a housewife if that's what a woman wishes to be. Wasn't that the whole point of the woman's movement? To be equal with men and make our own choices about how to live our lives? If a woman chooses to stay home and raise children, more power to her. That's not my cup of tea, but I wouldn't say anything negative about raising the next generation. It's a noble pursuit."

Cynthia made a gagging sound. "If it were so enviable," she said in a sarcastic tone, "men would stay home and raise children. Have you ever known a man to stay home and raise a child while his wife worked? Of course not. Being a housewife and mother can't possibly be a real choice if men aren't lining up to do it."

Helena thought of her two sons. They didn't seem capable of being a primary parent. For that matter, they didn't seem capable of communicating with their mother. As for her daughters-in-law, Helena didn't really know them well enough to judge. They'd always kept her at arm's length, as if the day they became engaged, the first brick was laid in an invisible wall erected to separate her from her sons. Perhaps, that was all good and right. After all, her sons' first responsibility should be to their nuclear families. Still, she'd hoped her sons might have shown more interest in her as she aged. Helena suddenly remembered something she'd read about Pete Buttigieg's husband raising their twins. "Chasten Buttigieg. He's the primary parent."

Cynthia clicked her tongue. "How do you know he hasn't hired a nanny?"

Helena had certainly relied on help when she was raising her sons. A woman to clean the house every week. Another to take the children to the park. Those women were lifesavers. How could she have ever had a career without them? "Hiring help doesn't diminish the role of primary parent. Plenty of families have nannies. Or drop their kids off at daycare."

"Gay men are different," Cynthia said, unwilling to yield.

"They're different alright," Babs happily agreed. "So creative, and very capable around the house."

Cynthia glared at her tablemate. "Honestly, Babs, some stereotypes needn't be perpetuated. I'm sure there are plenty of gay men who are boorish and can't cook."

"I'm an author," Helena interjected in an attempt to correct any misimpressions that she was a ne'er-do-well. "I was also active in the women's movement."

Cynthia eyed Helena with renewed interest. "You were? Well then you must be mad as hell with the Supreme Court striking down Roe."

"What makes me so mad," Donna added, "is no woman wants an abortion. But they do want the freedom to choose. I'm in favor of choice, but I could never have an abortion. But that's my personal view. *I don't have the right* to inflict my view on someone else. It's about my right to control my body; to make my medical decision without the government or my neighbors weighing in. Don't you all agree?"

"Well," sniffed Cynthia, "I'd like to go through the dresser drawers of all of those men up on Capitol Hill and find out what secrets they're hiding. How dare they try to tell someone else how to live? It's no one's business what a woman chooses to do."

Helena wondered how she'd ever eat lunch with such lively banter. First, women's rights. Then, abortion. What's next? Russia? Ukraine? The Middle East? The very thought upset her stomach. She didn't want to debate. All she wanted was a pleasant lunch with some light conversation.

Upon returning to her condo, she retrieved a bottle of Pepto-Bismol from the medicine cabinet. While the others seemed stimulated by the lunchtime discussion, she felt depleted, grateful to sit quietly and stare at the television with the sound off.

– 10 –

Zak raced across campus, nearly knocking over two trash cans and a few slow-moving students as he made his way back to Student Health Services. The nurse who had attended to his ear wax removal, now used an otoscope to check both of his ears even though he again explained there was no point in examining the left ear since he couldn't hear out of it, and as far as he remembered, he never could.

"Everything looks fine," the nurse announced, as if saying so made it true.

"You don't understand," Zak insisted. "I'm struggling to hear in the lecture hall."

"Are you seated up front?'

"No," Zak admitted, his face burning. "But I didn't have a problem at the start of the semester."

"You should probably move your seat."

Zak rolled his eyes. An obvious answer from someone who refused to listen and understand. "None of this is helping," he said. "Something's wrong."

"It might be clogged sinuses," the nurse said in a flat monotone. "Sometimes, when the sinuses are full, our hearing is diminished. In Phoenix, seasonal allergies can be year-round. Let's get you a prescription for a steroid to shrink the inflammation."

Zak breathed a sigh of relief. Yes, he had allergies. As a child, he'd taken allergy shots every week for three years. And yes, his sinuses were aching. Maybe the nurse was right. All he needed was a steroid. Relieved, he headed over to the pharmacy, chiding himself all the way. Why did he always default to the worst-case scenario? He was perfectly fine. He definitely needed to chill out. Still, he couldn't help but think, despite the nurse's diagnosis, that he had to remain vigilant. After all, he was all alone. Who else was there to worry about his good ear?

⚬⚬⚬

Over the course of the next few days, Zak's hearing grew steadily worse.

It wasn't long before he had difficulty deciphering the consonants of *s*, *f*, and *h*. Simple words, such as *so*, *for*, or *has*, were lost to him. Anxious, he created excuses for what was happening. He moved upfront in the lecture halls, certain he was compensating for a faulty mic or because a professor was prone to mumbling. He continued to rely on Marshall's notes to fill in the gaps of anything he might have missed, and increasingly, he was missing a lot. When he worked at Windy Canyon, he wore earplugs, even placing one in his deaf ear.

Back in his dorm room, he worked on a chemistry paper. Each student had been assigned a topic that required original research. Zak's topic was nucleic acids. His goal: explore how DNA evidence can be used in murder investigations to solve cold cases. Engrossed in the subject matter, he was unaware of Chuck's presence until Chuck sat down at the desk directly in front of him. "Jesus," Zak said, a hand over his heart. "You scared the crap out of me."

"You didn't hear me come in?" Chuck asked.

"I must have been concentrating."

"Or watching porn."

Zak blushed. "Of course not," he said emphatically as if he'd never watched porn. "What time is your wrestling match tonight?"

Chuck beat his chest like King Kong. He'd recently seen the 1933 Fay Wray version at a revival hosted by the ASU film school. Enamored with the mighty ape, Chuck had begun to incorporate Kong into his everyday communications. Today, Chuck pounded his chest like the great ape. Tomorrow, he might grunt and roll his eyes, pretending to be searching for the delicate Fay Wray. "I'm on at six-thirty. Come watch me wrestle before you head off to the bar."

Zak cracked a smile. "Sounds great. I can check out your teammates. Do you think any of them belong to our club?"

Chuck shook his head "Highly doubtful."

"But I can wish, can't I?"

"You can always wish. Just no touching. At least, not while I'm on the team."

"Oh sure," Zak laughed. "You have your hands all over them and I just get to look."

"And that," Chuck said as he slipped out of the chair and knelt to reach under the bed to retrieve a gym bag, "is one of the many benefits of rooming with a star athlete."

"What did you say?" Zak asked.

Chuck popped back up. There was a smile on his face. "*Star athlete*. Don't pretend you didn't hear me?"

"I didn't," Zak said. "Maybe you need to speak up?"

"Me? If I talk louder, they'll hear me down the hall. Either you can't hear or you're not listening. I'm not sure which it is."

"Hmph," was all Zak could manage. He hadn't been aware that he was missing parts of conversations or that Chuck was speaking louder than usual. "What about dinner tonight?" Zak asked. "Are you eating before the match?"

Chuck did a double take. "Not unless I want to throw up all over my opponent. I told you yesterday I wouldn't be eating dinner. You're on your own."

Zak shrugged. "No big deal. Marshall should be stopping by soon."

Chuck grabbed a pair of sweats from a dresser drawer, rolled them up, and shoved them into the workout bag. "He's catching a foreign film at Tempe Marketplace. Something French. By Truffaut. *Jules and Jim*. He told us that yesterday."

Zak didn't remember. Now he wondered if he hadn't heard it. "When did he say that?"

Chuck stopped what he was doing. "When we were at lunch. You must've been daydreaming."

Zak wondered how he could have missed so much. Yes, he was having trouble hearing in the lecture halls and now it seemed he was struggling with one-on-one conversations. But Student Health Services had said everything was fine. That there was nothing to worry about. Still, he was worried. But mostly about midterms. They were coming up and the late nights at Windy Canyon were eating into his study time. He'd always felt like he was behind his classmates, running a race that was impossible to win. He'd have to cram to get through exams. Maybe even pull an all-nighter. Probably everyone would. But with his work schedule, it was going to be twice as tough to find time to study.

Chuck snapped his fingers to get Zak's attention. "Hello. Earth to Zak. Hello Zak."

Zak exhaled. "I've got to figure out how to get time off from the bar."

Chuck zipped up the gym bag. "How hard can that be? Your boss knows students need to study."

Zak had no idea what Freddy knew. Mostly because he'd only briefly met Freddy. In all the weeks working at Windy Canyon, Freddy hadn't been on-site. Which hadn't seemed odd to Zak before, but now that he needed to talk to Freddy, he wondered why someone would own a bar and rarely set foot in it. Or at least not on the nights Zak was there.

With the gym bag hanging at his side, Chuck readied to leave. "Marshall said he'd swing by Windy Canyon after the movie."

Zak nodded, though he couldn't help but wonder when Marshall and Chuck had become so friendly. Sure, they'd met via the Allison fiasco, but now they seemed to have developed a genuine friendship apart from Zak. He tried not to feel jealous; after all, he couldn't control the friendships of his friends. But this felt different. It felt as if Marshall and Chuck were keeping secrets. Even if the secret was as unexciting as Marshall going to see a foreign film. "You two have become pretty friendly," Zak said. And though it was presented as a statement of fact, to Zak, it was more of a question. "Sharing secrets. Knowing each other's schedules."

Chuck grabbed his keys off the desk. "It's hardly a secret that Marshall is going to see a movie," Chuck said as he opened the door to leave. "But aren't we lucky? What were the chances that we three could have found each other on this great big campus?"

Zak had no doubt. *The Three Musketeers*: one for all, and all for one. Three friends who'd made their college experience special by bonding early in the process. That Chuck and Marshall were gay was icing on the cake. There was no need for Zak to hide his identity. He could relax and enjoy their time together. Revel in their mutual appreciation of the beautiful men on campus who caught their eyes. And even though the three were out to each other, Zak supposed they still remained fairly closeted to the rest of the world. Not that they'd deny being gay, but if they weren't asked, and it didn't come up, he doubted any one of them would feel compelled to announce their sexuality. After all, it was personal. No one's business. His parents certainly hadn't taken the news well. Why risk sharing the information with strangers? Besides, it wasn't like he was sexually active. At least, not yet. Much like his deafness, he could pick and choose who might need to know, and for the moment, the fewer, the better.

⁓

The Windy Canyon Bar was hopping when Zak came through the door at ten o'clock. The Dirty Toenails were onstage, but Zak assumed they were on break since the place was quiet except for the humming of a pair of faulty amps. Zak slipped in his earplugs.

Melinda barely said a word to him as he bused tables and wiped down tabletops. She'd texted him the day before that the ever-absent boss, Freddy, had agreed Zak could take drink orders. But it wasn't a promotion. He'd have to continue his regular gig, including the disgusting job of maintaining the bathrooms. Still, Zak was glad for the opportunity to grab tips. The more money, the better.

When Melinda came up to Zak on his left side, he jumped. She held a tray of drinks high in the air and mouthed something he couldn't make out. Was she asking him to mop the floor? He shook his head and pointed to his ear plug. "I can't hear you," he said, hoping she'd repeat herself. But she didn't. "Don't worry," he said, pretending he'd understood. "I'll take care of it."

He pulled out the mop and bucket from the storage closet and went about mopping a section of the floor where someone had spilled a mug of beer, creating a sticky hazard. He finished wringing the mop out and was about to roll the bucket back to the storage closet when a young man in a sport coat stepped in front of him. The man pointed to a table of new arrivals. Zak pushed the bucket aside and with an order pad in hand, prepared to take their drink orders. He removed his ear plug. Mouths opened and closed, lips moved, but he couldn't hear anything. The bar was unusually subdued, though people were everywhere. At a nearby table, a group of young women were especially rowdy. They banged on the table and appeared to be shouting to the band. But Zak couldn't make any of it out. Not the noise in the crowded bar. Not the music of The Dirty Toenails. Not the patrons who were screaming orders at him.

This can't be happening, Zak thought, sweat gathering on his brow. Images of the bar flashed before him as he felt the room begin to spin. He dropped the order pad and forced his way through the crowd to the rear exit. His balance was off; he could feel himself being pulled to the right as if he were a dreidel about to go into a spin. Alone in the alley, he struggled to breathe. He dropped into a squat, back pressed against the wall, eyes closed. But that only made the dizziness worse. He stood and scrambled to the nearby dumpster. He struggled to steady himself as his stomach flipped. He fell to his knees, leaning hard against the dumpster, waiting for the motion to stop. But it didn't stop as he retched up the McDonald's burger that he'd gobbled down on the way to work. Exhausted, he remained in a kneeling position, panting and praying. *Please God, help me. I'm a good person. I'd never hurt anyone.* But that wasn't true. He'd hurt his parents. Being gay had been a flashpoint in their relationship. His stomach twisted into a knot. Was this his punishment? Did he deserve to lose his hearing? He then realized he'd done something the doctors had warned against. He'd exposed his good ear to the noise of The Windy Canyon Bar. He remained in a situation that had put his good ear at risk. A circumstance he knew darn well was dangerous. *I've made a mistake. Please God, give me my hearing back and I'll never step foot in a bar again.*

But his hearing didn't return. Not in the alley. Not when the dizziness stopped. Not on his way back to the dorm. Not when he entered his room and failed to hear Chuck snoring. He stripped off his clothes and fell into bed, unable to sleep. *It'll be better tomorrow,* he thought, trying to comfort himself. But he didn't believe it. How could he continue to attend classes if he was deaf? What would Melinda say when she realized he'd ducked out on her? Would Freddy fire him? If he lost his job, how could he survive at ASU?

❧

When Zak awoke, he was shocked that it was noon. How could he have slept so late?

He fiddled with the clock radio, adjusting the volume. No news. No weather. No music. The darn thing must've died. He ran his hand over the top. It was emitting a vibration.

Then he remembered: the clock radio wasn't broken. He was.

Panic shot through him as he bolted straight up. Every nerve was activated. He was being chased by a stealth predator he couldn't outrun. Alone, terrified, and shaking from head to toe, he leapt from the bed, pulling the covers onto the floor as he frantically paced the dorm room, banging into the desk, bouncing off the closet, ricocheting into the dresser, trying desperately to work off nervous energy.

He had to think. But he was too rattled. Too filled with anxiety. He placed a hand on his chest, certain he was about to have a heart attack. Why hadn't he listened to his childhood doctors? They'd told him to protect his good ear. They'd warned against exposure to loud noises. That's why he'd stayed away from concerts. Covered his ear when emergency vehicles passed. Refused to wear earbuds. He'd always been careful about any noise that might affect his ear, and still, he'd taken the job at Windy Canyon. Why had he done such a foolish thing? There was no doubt. The deafness was definitely his fault.

Zak flopped down on the bed, burying his face in the pillow. He railed at God. Why had he allowed this to happen? What had he done to deserve such a punishment? Wasn't he a good person? A caring person? If he had to be deaf, why not later in life? After college, when he'd learned about himself and how to be in the world. It was so unfair. So cruel. This was not the way he thought his life would unfold. He made a pledge: if God would let him have his hearing back, he'd volunteer to mentor deaf students. He'd actively seek opportunities to spread good will. He'd do anything to prove his worth. Anything. As long as he could hear again. If only he could hear again.

He checked the clock radio one more time. Perhaps his deafness was a passing phenomenon that might miraculously correct itself. It was possible. Wasn't there a kid in high school who'd had an auto-immune disease that produced strange rashes? Maybe his hearing loss was like a rash that could be cured with the right diet. Couldn't that be possible?

Suddenly Chuck was in the room. He yanked out the plug of Zak's clock radio from the wall.

Zak focused. What was Chuck saying? *Why is the radio so freaking loud?*

Zak hadn't bothered to turn the volume down. The music must have been booming. Had others tried to get his attention? Banged on the door? He cringed at the thought of disturbing anyone; worse, about making a spectacle of himself.

Chuck's face was red, veins popping on his forehead. His mouth was moving, but Zak couldn't make out a word. He could tell Chuck was mad, but if he couldn't understand Chuck, what hope did he have with strangers? His terror heightened, Zak blurted out, "I can't hear anything." Had he said it loud enough to get Chuck's attention? He'd no way of knowing the volume of his own voice. He not only couldn't hear Chuck, but he couldn't hear himself.

Chuck's mouth softened. His eyes widened as he sat down on Zak's desk chair, next to the edge of Zak's bed. Zak leaned over until his forehead bumped up against Chuck's knee. Together, they sat. Chuck with a hand on Zak's back waiting for Zak to stop crying, and Zak certain he'd never run out of tears. After a few minutes, Chuck reached into a pocket and pulled out his iPhone.

Zak sat up and watched as Chuck punched in a number. Then, Chuck was speaking. Who did he call? Zak concentrated, as if by doing so he might hear what Chuck was saying. When the call ended, Chuck stood and handed Zak the pants he'd dropped on the floor the night before.

Chuck slowly mouthed, "Get dressed."

Zak did as he was told. Following orders seemed the best course of action for someone whose life had been turned upside down. Following orders made sense. Just as he finished dressing, Marshall mysteriously showed up. It took but a moment for Zak to realize Chuck had called Marshall. But where were they all going?

Chuck wrote it on a slip of paper: *ASU Student Health Services.*

～～

ASU's Student Health Services immediately referred Zak for a CT scan and then to an end of the day emergency appointment with Dr. Rod Peterson, a board-certified otorhinolaryngologist with a subspeciality in neurotology. Dr. Peterson, accustomed to patients who were unable to hear, placed a hand on Zak's shoulder and gave it a gentle squeeze. He held up an index finger, the universal signal for *hold on*, before slipping out of the exam room. Zak assumed the doctor was getting a nurse. Someone to help in case Zak had another emotional meltdown. He'd been crying most of the afternoon, and now, somewhat calmer, had to rely on his eyes to do double duty for his ear. If he didn't stop crying, he'd have no idea what was going on.

Peterson returned with a handout. A drawing that showed a growth in the middle ear. Zak had a cholesteatoma: a tumor that had perforated his eardrum. Though the hearing loss had come on suddenly, the tumor had been growing for some time. The doctor pointed at the heading of another handout labeled "Surgery." He then mouthed, *tomorrow.*

Zak nodded as if along with his hearing, he'd lost the power of speech.

The doctor pointed to a section on the surgical handout marked "Risks."

Zak didn't care about the risks. How could that matter? But then, he spotted something about *nerve damage.* There was a chance that the surgeon might sever a nerve, leaving Zak with a permanent facial droop. Zak knew he had to gamble that the surgery would come off without a hitch. Because if he remained deaf, how could he manage? It wasn't as if he'd been born deaf and learned American Sign Language. Besides, he knew his lip-reading skills left a lot to be desired. If surgery had the possibility of restoring his hearing, the sooner the better.

Peterson spoke slowly so that Zak could read his lips. "If we wait to do surgery, the hearing loss could be permanent."

Zak swallowed hard. One problem remained. How could he pay for the surgery?

The doctor pointed to a surgical form. Zak didn't know he was part of the student health insurance plan. His parents had paid the fee along with his first semester's tuition. The plan would cover the cost of surgery. Good news! And since he was over eighteen, the surgery didn't require parental consent. But Peterson pointed out, he needed a responsible adult to bring him to the hospital and to pick him up after the surgery. He also needed a place to recuperate. The only adult Zak knew was Melinda, but she worked full-time, and the bar was already short-staffed. With Zak out, things were only going to get worse. Besides, he was sure Melinda had already spoken to Freddy, and he'd lost his job. He wouldn't blame her for being angry. He'd run out on her the previous night without a word. She probably thought he was an irresponsible brat, not even bothering to resign. No, he couldn't ask Melinda.

Zak remembered Chuck and Marshall sitting in the waiting room. Could they fulfill the role?

A nurse retrieved Chuck and Marshall who joined Zak in the exam room. Zak couldn't quite make out the tenor of the discussion, but based on the doctor's expression and the energy between Chuck and Marshall, he could tell it wasn't going well. "What's going on?" he asked.

Peterson typed the answer on a small laptop with a screen that faced the hearing-impaired patient. *Sorry*, Peterson typed, *you need someone over 21. A parent.*

Zak locked eyes with Chuck. He then turned to Marshall.

Peterson continued to type. *It's not their fault. They're eager to help. We need to call your parents.*

How could he call home? There was no way he could manage an iPhone. And texting didn't seem the way to go. But if Chuck or Marshall called his folks, they could explain the situation. Let his parents know the surgery was critical. Ask them to fly out to Arizona. But would they? They'd been so angry when Zak last saw them. Surely, they must be over all that anger by now. But he wasn't certain. Neither parent had reached out since he had arrived in Arizona. But he hadn't tried to connect with them either. "I can't," Zak suddenly said, interjecting without knowing exactly what was being said between the doctor and his friends. "I can't ask my parents."

Peterson scratched his head. He typed on the keyboard: *without an adult to accompany you, I won't do this surgery.*

Zak eyed Peterson's expression. The doctor was not about to change his mind. Surely, there had to be a way to get the tumor removed.

I'll call your parents, Peterson typed.

Zak nodded . . . but doubted Peterson would make any headway.

"I've an idea," Peterson said so slowly that Zak could read his lips. "Leave it to me."

On the way back to the dorm, Zak struggled to come to terms with the new limits on his life. Everything was on hold until he could get the surgery. No classes, no work, no life. A cloud of despair settled in. Every step felt as if there were weights around his ankles and he was walking fully dressed through a deep pool. He knew Chuck and Marshall were concerned, but he couldn't follow their conversation. It was as if they'd given up trying to communicate with him, mostly talking together. Even with them by his side, he was completely alone.

Back in his dorm room, Zak collapsed onto the bed. He turned his face to the wall and fell into a deep sleep. When he awoke, Marshall and Chuck were gone. Zak checked his iPhone. They'd left a message. They didn't want to wake him. They'd gone to eat and would bring dinner back. *Hmm,* Zak thought. *It can't be any fun babysitting someone like me.* He laid his head back down. He couldn't get over how tired he felt. *God,* he thought, *being deaf is exhausting.* And then, he remembered Melinda. He sat back up and grabbed his iPhone. He texted Melinda. She'd need to know he wouldn't be coming in. More precisely, he wouldn't be coming back at all.

What's happened? she replied.

I need surgery.

OMG. When?

ASAP.

He watched the squiggly lines, anticipating she'd respond. But she didn't. How could she? The bar was probably busy and with him bailing, her workload had doubled. He felt awful letting her down.

All in all, it had been a terrible day. He'd been diagnosed with a tumor that had rendered him deaf. He'd disappointed Melinda, bailing on his job. He'd put Chuck and Marshall in an awkward position as nursemaids. He'd refused to contact his parents as requested by Dr. Peterson. And now, his depression was so severe, he could barely move. In a matter of twenty-four hours, his life had crashed and burned. His good ear had failed him. The ear he'd put at risk by working at The Windy Canyon Bar. The ear he'd always relied on. The ear that helped him make sense of the world.

When Zak awoke, it was ten at night. Chuck was at his desk, lamp on, studying. Zak sat up and watched as Chuck scanned the pages of an open book. He envied Chuck's ability to focus on something other than himself. Chuck didn't have to worry about his hearing or paying for tuition or undergoing surgery. His future at ASU was set. He was so darn lucky. Trouble free. Truly blessed. There'd be no hearing tests for Chuck. Or doctors poking in his ears searching for God knows what. If some people counted sheep to fall asleep, Zak could count ear specialists.

There were the surgeons who'd operated on the left ear when he was a child. Three operations that hadn't changed a thing. Then, there were the ENTs who'd treated his frequent ear infections in the right ear, which required tubes inserted into the eardrum to drain fluid and ease congestion. He'd spent hours of his life in auditory booths outfitted with headphones where he'd listen for imperceptible beeps, pressing a button each time he deciphered any sound, uncertain if the sound was real or imagined. The audiologists always insisted on also testing the deaf ear, even though the nerve was dead and there was nothing he could possibly hear on that side.

Zak needed to stand. To stretch. To move. Chuck was looking at him. He could see Chuck's lips moving. Zak smiled and waved. He felt the fool. Like a dog without the power of speech. Someone who wasn't expected to make himself understood. After all, if he couldn't hear, maybe he shouldn't speak. Why invite conversation when conversation was out of the question?

Chuck got up and came over to where Zak was now doing deep knee bends. He held Zak's iPhone in his hand and tapped it so Zak could see that Dr. Peterson had left a message. Zak leaned forward and the room shifted. His equilibrium was off. He closed his eyes, but that didn't help. If he was still, the spinning eased. He slipped into his desk chair, two feet flat on the ground, hoping to keep the dizziness at bay. He read the message: *Come to the office Friday morning at ten. We have a solution. We can schedule your surgery.*

Zak was shocked. Friday was a week away. How could he manage an entire week being deaf? And more importantly, what had changed? Did Dr. Peterson contact his parents? Had they committed to helping him? Would they be making their way to Arizona? Zak imagined his parents meeting Dr. Peterson. Their concerned expressions. *How did this happen to our son? How can he be both homosexual and deaf?* Or maybe they'd finally come to their senses. Sure, they'd treated him badly, but now they had the opportunity to make it up to him. Beg his forgiveness. Express shame at the way they'd acted. Zak had no doubt that when it came to his hearing, his parents would be conciliatory. After all, this was something his parents could understand. A tumor needed to be removed. Something to be fixed. Perhaps they were willing to let bygones be bygones.

The next morning, Zak awoke with a sense of excitement. Would he finally be able to get past the fallout with his folks? Would the ear surgery return both his hearing and his parents? He didn't care that the surgery might be dangerous or there'd be problems with him completing the semester. He imagined any difficulties could be resolved as long as he had his parents' support and could hear again.

H ELENA SHIFTED ABOUT, trying to get comfortable. The chairs in the ASU library were not made for older bodies. Talk about bone-on-bone discomfort. The metallic chair demanded firm glutes. Helena's tush no longer possessed the extra padding required for her to fall backward and bounce back up with hands extended in a graceful "ta-da." Any excess fat had long ago melted off her now wiry frame, dissolving her once shapely curves into a rather flat silhouette. Muscle tone aside, the hard library seat was killing her butt.

She'd gone to the library to see if she could begin writing again. A story. An article. Maybe even a poem. Anything to get the old juices flowing. Though she'd the best of intentions, all she could think about was the damn chair. In addition to her butt, it was also killing her lower back. Now why for God's sake would a library install uncomfortable seating unless they didn't want people to sample the contents of the shelves? It didn't take a genius to figure out that the chairs were counterproductive. Suddenly, it dawned on her: why not write a piece about the library chairs for the ASU student newspaper? There were no guarantees that it would be published, but at least, it'd be an achievable goal.

In no time, Helena pounded out 500 words on her laptop. After a considerable amount of editing, she reviewed the copy. *Ahh*, she thought, pleased with herself. *I still have the touch.* A quick print, and she held the column in her hand. It'd been a long time since she'd felt such a rush of accomplishment. As if what she had to say, truly did matter.

She stared at the headline: *Boney Bottoms Need Not Apply*.

Perhaps it wasn't her best, but it was an eye-catching play on words for her library chair dilemma. Worthy of a read and a chuckle. And maybe, just maybe, publication. Perhaps she could write on other topics. As long as she stayed alert to her surroundings, the possibilities were endless. She might even land a column. That, she suspected, would be quite the coup for Ventana.

She imagined her byline: *Granny Knows Best*.

She reconsidered. *Helena Speaks Her Truth*.

Or perhaps: *Ventana Maven Tells It Like It Is*.

The name of the column didn't really matter. The important thing was that she'd started writing again, immersed in the joy of creating. She was mentally engaged. Working on all cylinders. Full speed ahead. With the excitement of a cub reporter, she embraced the new day. Moving to Ventana had awakened something deep inside. She'd kicked off her orthopedic shoes and was now running barefoot through the grass, laughing like a girl, and excited about the next moment. She was underway, her mind clicking on future columns: ideas that would capture the interest of students and provide her with a creative outlet.

Life was beautiful!

Helena was delighted when her piece on the library chairs appeared in the ASU student newspaper. *Talent wins out*, she mused, committed now to a daily writing schedule. Her first stop, the local Starbucks where ASU students gathered. Laptop open, she was proud of herself as she indulged her creativity and enjoyed a blond vanilla latte. There'd been growing controversy in the national news over gender neutral bathrooms which made her think of Taro Gomi's children's book *Everyone Poops*. In no time, she knocked off five hundred words on campus restrooms. That was easy. Too easy. Maybe, if she focused, she had one more novel left in her. Was she up for the challenge? Perhaps she could write about an older woman who moves into independent living. It certainly was a topic she was familiar with. She jotted down a few notes, too engaged to answer her phone which she'd placed on vibrate. Adrenaline surged as she spent the next two hours sketching out an outline for a novel before deciding she was hungry. But she didn't want to stop for lunch. Not when the creative gods were favorably looking down upon her. Another latte and a slice of banana bread was the obvious solution as she toiled away, scenes popping in and out of her head, excitement building at every turn. Once she'd downloaded her thoughts on plot, she drafted the beginning of chapter one. When she finally checked her iPhone, she noticed a voice mail message from Julie: Helena, can we meet later today? Four o'clock at the rooftop bar. Text me if that works.

Helena checked her watch. It was nearly three. She'd been thoroughly engaged, lost in her own world. The writing had felt so natural. So easy. Once on a roll, she was unstoppable. Eager to get the next line down. Capable of generating paragraph after paragraph as she spun the very start of her tale. But now, she was at a good stopping point. She texted Julie that she'd meet her. How wonderful to have an appointment. To feel as if her social life and work life were coming together. She was proud of herself. Moving to Ventana had been a good decision. The very best decision!

As Helena packed up her laptop, she looked about. How she envied the young people around her. Not that she wanted to be young again. Oh, no. She was well aware that youth had its challenges. Insecurities, uncertainties, anxieties. But what they did have was time. She'd never considered that time held much importance. Maybe, that was because there had always been plenty of it. But now in her eighties, and with the excitement of a new novel starting, time had become a precious commodity. *I could have written at least five novels in the last fifteen years*, she thought, overwhelmed by opportunities lost. *Why did I let that time slip away? Why had I been so foolish?*

As if summoned from the depths of the great beyond to answer Helena's questions, she heard the familiar voice. Ruthie was standing next to a Starbucks display of coffee mugs. Helena braced herself. The dizziness had returned. She took two deep breaths as she struggled to maintain her equilibrium.

You still have time.

Helena tried to ignore the apparition. Maybe if she pretended not to hear, it would disappear. But Ruthie was not to be silenced.

Are you listening to me?

Helena looked over again.

Instead of regretting the time lost, embrace the time you have left. Be grateful for every moment. You're lucky. You may be old, but you still have a lot of get up and go. After all, you're my daughter.

Helena blushed. "Mother, please." A student sitting in front of Helena turned as if she was speaking to him. Helena nodded and he grimaced, returning to his open laptop with a grunt. Helena flinched. "Sorry," she whispered, apologizing for the interruption.

You're writing again. I don't know why you ever gave that up. You know, some people make themselves old before their time. They retire first from their careers and then from the world. Mark my words. Writing will extend your life.

Helena pondered how many more years she wished to live. Another ten might do. As long as she was healthy.

You should worry about your mental acuity.

Helena took a breath. *Here it comes*, she thought. First the loving caress, then the slap.

Those silly pieces about the university. The last article they published in the student newspaper about library chairs. Now the bathrooms. Really? With everything going on in the world, is that the best you can do? Surely there are more important subjects to write about.

There it was. The old Ruthie poke in the ribs. The jab that reminded Helena that only one voice and one opinion truly mattered. Her own. She couldn't expect to satisfy anyone else. It was a lesson she struggled to remember.

You should volunteer. Find people who need your help? Mentor a student. Someone who is struggling to adjust. You two would have so much in common.

Helena couldn't imagine having anything in common with the younger generation.

My darling daughter, Ruthie continued. *All around you are young people who've left home for the first time. It's all about change. And change is scary.*

Helena looked around the crowded Starbucks. There did seem to be a certain energy. Was that anxiety she was sensing? Anxiety about the future. About fitting in. About discovering who you are and want to be. Ruthie was right. Why hadn't she realized it before? Those were the same feelings she was going through. *Imagine*, she thought. *I'm a senior citizen going through the same stress as a college freshman.* Hmm. *Now there's a topic for my next blog: Why Are You and Your Grandmother Both So Anxious?*

～

Helena entered Ventana's rooftop bar to meet Julie for their four o'clock appointment. The richness of the dark mahogany walls and red leather booths created a moody, clubby setting, much like the fabulous New York City bars Helena had visited at the height of her writing career. The Bemelmans Bar at the Carlyle Hotel. The King Cole Bar at the St. Regis. Intimate places where New York City elites connected over cocktails and business deals. Piped into those bars was the music of The Great American Songbook: timeless standards by Cole Porter, Gershwin, and Berlin, accompanied by the stylish vocals of Ella Fitzgerald, Frank Sinatra, and Nat King Cole. True to form, stepping into the bar, Helena could hear the rhythmic crooning of Mel Tormé singing "Blue Moon."

"I'm so glad you could squeeze me into your schedule," Julie said as she stood to greet Helena. "I know this is very last minute."

Helena nearly laughed until she realized Julie was serious. It wasn't as if Helena had a busy schedule. She'd been writing, but other than that, her time was her own. She'd yet to create a Ventana calendar filled with classes and lectures as Julie had encouraged. If anything, she was slightly bored of her own company as she continued to limit her social interaction to one meal a day in the dining room.

Much to Helena's surprise, Aggie came through the door that led to the rear of the bar with an apron tied about her waist. Aggie hadn't mentioned to Helena that she had bartending skills. Perhaps, Aggie's dream of being a Starbucks barista wasn't such a big stretch. "How wonderful to see you," Helena said, assuming Aggie had received a promotion. "Is this your new gig?"

"I'm just helping out today," Aggie said, her voice steeped in annoyance. "It's on top of my other duties. So, ladies," she said to Helena and Julie before they even sat down, "what will it be?"

"A glass of water is fine. I really don't drink," Julie apologized.

Aggie fixed her eyes on Helena.

Helena enjoyed a glass of wine now and then, but not since the onset of her dizziness. But she was in a bar and a lovely bar at that. Would a martini go straight to her head?

She wouldn't be driving a car or operating heavy machinery. One drink couldn't possibly interfere with her ability to press an elevator button. "I'll have a vodka martini straight up with blue cheese olives. Stoli, please."

Aggie sighed. It was an unhappy sound from someone Helena imagined was used to delivering food rather than preparing drink orders.

"Is that okay?" Helena asked, concerned her order might be beyond Aggie's ken.

Aggie wrinkled her brow. "Perfectly fine," she said, though her expression definitely conveyed martinis were not her thing.

Helena and Julie sat down as Aggie disappeared behind the bar. "How lovely," Helena said as she ran her hand over the booth's cool, soft leather upholstery. She closed her eyes and could imagine herself thirty again; a black cocktail dress, black pumps, hair a light shade of honey blond. It felt like only a hop, skip, and jump from then to the present. All unwinding at lightning speed as she wondered why Julie had scheduled the meeting. Was she going to lecture Helena on the importance of being more social?

"I have two topics to cover," Julie began. "One good. One bad."

Helena couldn't imagine what Julie was getting at. "I'll take the bad first," she said, knowing she could never enjoy the good if the bad was hanging over her head.

Julie crinkled her nose. It was a gesture meant to be ingratiating, but Helena recognized the mannerism as the way some women soften the deliverance of bad news. A cutesy face that begged to be pardoned even as they clobbered you over the head. The other trick was to raise their voice high, to a girlish pitch. Or worse, they'd nervously smile when what they were sharing wasn't anything to smile about. In all her years on the planet, Helena had never seen a man crinkle his nose, fake a happy tone, or smile when delivering bad news. Nope. Never. Not once.

"You remember the piece you wrote about the library?" Julie asked.

Of course, Helena remembered. She was thrilled the student paper had printed it. Even more excited when the piece was so well received by the student body. Over a thousand likes and 235 online comments. Helena had hoped her humorous observations about the uncomfortable metal chairs might resonate. It was heartwarming that the piece was so well-received.

Julie continued. "We received a call from the dean's office."

Helena felt her chest bursting with pride. But then, there'd be no reason why something she'd written wouldn't have impressed the dean.

Julie flashed an impressive smile. All teeth and a lot of gums. "The dean was upset."

Helena's heart dropped. "For heaven's sake, why?" she asked. "The piece was well written. Barely edited."

"You were critical of ASU. We try not to do that. You see, they've sponsored this great Ventana experiment and hoped we'd . . . that you'd be mindful of the fact."

Helena pressed backward into the booth. She hadn't fully appreciated she was part of an experiment. She certainly knew it was a unique collaboration between investors and the university. But an experiment? Didn't experiments have start and end dates? Control groups? There was no way Ventana was an experiment. After all, she'd bought into Ventana. Since when did experiments require a buy-in?

Julie continued. "Some trustees read the piece and didn't appreciate the sarcasm."

Helena raised a brow. "It wasn't sarcasm. Have you ever sat in one of those metal seats. They're more appropriate for building a staircase than supporting a tender bottom."

Julie snickered. "I shouldn't tell you this, but I read the piece and thought it was very funny. But then, who am I?"

Helena took umbrage at Julie's comment. How could any modern woman apologize for having an independent opinion?

Though the jury was out on what Helena thought of Julie, she was unwilling to allow Julie to think of herself as *less than*. "Your opinion counts," Helena pressed, her tone forceful. "You're a smart, empathetic young lady, and I like you," she said as she stumbled over the last part of the sentence which perhaps was a touch premature.

Julie smiled. "I like you too. But going forward, we need to be more mindful of how your words reflect on Ventana."

"Well, perhaps I could have been more sensitive," Helena said, appearing conciliatory despite her shackles being raised. She nervously chewed on her lower lip. She'd no intention of upsetting anyone. She merely wanted to write something real. Something relevant. Something amusing.

Julie nodded as if Helena's statement was somehow an apology. "And now, for the good news."

Helena stretched her legs and straightened her shoulders. It had occurred to her that the university might want her to write a weekly column, and this was her reminder to keep it light.

"We need a volunteer to work with Student Health Services," Julie gushed.

Helena furrowed her brow. "Student Health Services? Do they want me to write a piece about the flu season?"

"Oh no, this has nothing to do with writing," Julie clarified.

Helena was stumped. What did she know about student health? Weren't the students already healthy? Afterall, they were young. How many things could possibly go wrong with a person in their teens and twenties? Bad knees? A broken hip? Sleep apnea? Hemorrhoids? All highly unlikely. She certainly was the spitting image of good health when she was that age. "I don't understand," she said, and for the first time in a long time, she actually didn't. "I know nothing about health, save for my own visits to the doctor, which frankly have been less and less productive. Why ask me? I'm not a doctor. I'm not a nurse. I'm not a medical assistant."

"It isn't that kind of volunteer position. We need an adult sponsor."

Helena pressed a palm to her chest. "Why would a youngster need an old lady like me to sponsor them? Are they trying out for the Senior Olympics?"

Julie let out a boisterous laugh as she bounced back and forth. Helena waited for her to catch her breath. "You'd partner with a student who's struggling with a health issue. You'd be the designated adult if there is no family nearby. Like an exchange program. Only, it would be temporary. You'd be like a temporary family member."

Helena balked. Temporary family. What the hell was that? If anyone needed a temporary family, it was her. She hadn't heard from her sons in months. It was as if she didn't exist. Besides, she'd just started writing again and needed time to get the new novel pulled together. Writing was a sensitive art. It couldn't be interrupted. That might break the flow. Besides, Helena didn't like going to the doctor. Wouldn't this require her to take on the care and worry for another individual? She already had enough on her plate with her own dizzy spells. Was this how she wanted to expend her waning energy?

"It's not what you think," Julie attempted to explain. "You'd be more like an ombudsman."

Student sponsor. Now, ombudsman. That made even less sense to Helena.

"You'd be the student's advocate. Someone who'd intercede on their behalf. Help them with doctor visits. Be a sounding board should they have issues."

Helena nodded. "But why me? There must be others far better suited for the role."

Julie blushed. "Everyone else is already committed. Either through classes, clubs, or other projects. You're new. Still untethered. We need someone who can step in right away."

Finally, the truth: she'd been selected based on availability. Not personality. Not energy level. Not skill set. The bar of expectation for the job was low. It seemed a bit insulting. If the position required no skill set, why had she, Helena Greenblatt, author, activist, and extremely old lady, drawn the short straw? Surely, she had some talent to share based on her years of professional experience that might be a better fit. Perhaps in the English department. "Is the student a writer?" she asked, still searching for a reasonable explanation for why the role was a match with her background.

Julie shrugged. "Truthfully, I have no idea. But I don't think so."

When Aggie reappeared, tray in hand, Helena was trying to figure out how to politely decline Julie's opportunity. She didn't want to be hasty, but the role was not a fit for her. Still, she'd been taught as a child if you turn down playdates, there is a great likelihood that no one will ever invite you again. It occurred to Helena that Ruthie might have invented that ploy as a means of getting her out of the house (gosh, mothers could be sneaky!)

"Well, there you are," Helena said as Aggie delivered a glass of water to Julie and placed a chilled martini glass with two skewered green olives in front of Helena. She poured the contents of a silver shaker into Helena's glass. Helena couldn't have been happier as she raised the drink to her lips. "Thank you, Aggie. This looks absolutely marvelous."

Aggie beamed as Helena took the first sip. She tried not to gag. How could anyone ruin a martini? Whatever Aggie had used, was not quality vodka, if it was vodka at all. Nor was there a hint of vermouth. With Julie looking on, Helena had no intention of embarrassing Aggie. Whatever she'd concocted, Helena was committed to imbibe, poisonous, as it may be.

Aggie lingered, waiting for Helena to take a second sip.

"Just wonderful," Helena said as she raised the glass in a toast to Aggie. "Here's mud in your eye."

The next sip went down like the first. So strong, Helena was afraid her teeth might dissolve.

"So, you'll do it," Julie announced with delight. "You'll be a sponsor."

"I'll think about it," Helena tentatively answered in a throaty voice as she plotted her escape from the bar without another sip of the demon drink.

– 12 –

AFTER A LIFETIME of ignoring his hearing impairment and pretending he was just like everyone else, deafness finally overtook Zak. With his Friday morning doctor's appointment days away, Zak could hardly wait to be whole again. Or as whole as he could be with the restoration of one working ear. Meanwhile, he struggled to understand Chuck and Marshall. His weak lip-reading skills had always required a bit of sound to decipher what was being said. He'd come to rely on the click of a tongue, the smack of lips, the rush of one's breath, to assist in the interpretation. Without any such hints, Zak was completely lost. His friends tried to speak louder, but it was only when they shouted that Zak could understand them. Hardly an optimal strategy for ongoing communication.

But Zak's inability to hear his friends wasn't the only problem.

He could no longer hear his own voice when he spoke, and if he couldn't hear himself, he was destined to struggle in pronouncing his words, especially complex words with multiple syllables, like cafeteria and auditorium. It wasn't long before he grew impatient with his inability to effectively communicate, and like the two-year-old who has a meltdown when words fail them, Zak's temper flared hot, and often. As a result, Chuck and Marshall stopped talking in generalities with Zak, limiting their interaction to mostly questions. Endless questions. And though *Yes* or *No* answers were easiest for Zak to manage, most questions in life are rarely satisfied by binary answers. But the more Chuck and Marshall's questions delved into sensitive matters, the greater Zak's resistance. His friends wanted to know why Zak didn't want to reach out to his parents. Was it wise to undergo surgery without their knowledge? And what about Allison? Was he still in touch with her? Should one of them reach out to her regarding Zak's condition? When presented with such personal matters, Zak turned away, pretending he didn't understand what his friends were asking. When the questions were written down on a sheet of paper, he ripped the paper up, unwilling to engage. Zak had decided that being deaf accorded him the right to *turn a deaf ear*. It was easier than trying to explain the situation with his folks or Allison. Besides, Zak wasn't sure why his parents had reacted so poorly to his coming out. Were they revolted by the idea of a same-sex-loving child, or just ashamed friends and family might judge them for raising a gay son. Whatever the reason, Zak's parents' shame had become his shame. His parents' reaction proved he was unlovable, and he had no intention of exploring these feelings with anyone. Not his friends. Not his doctor. And mostly, not himself. Certain wounds were best kept concealed under heavy bandages.

Sequestered in his dorm room, Zak was increasingly dependent on Chuck and Marshall to bring in meals and share what was happening on campus. And even though Chuck and Marshall were there to help Zak, both men were young, healthy, and socially active, which left Zak very much on his own. Alone with his thoughts, Zak's mind weaved scenarios his ears couldn't confirm. He decided his friends were growing frustrated and short-tempered with him. That he'd pushed his good luck by being so damn dependent. He was sure Chuck and Marshall regretted the friendship. Could that explain their dour expressions? Without any clear communication, he had no way of knowing what they were saying or thinking, but that didn't stop him from making it up. Every now and then, he caught them exchanging glances. What did those glances mean? Did they think he couldn't see them? That he wouldn't pick up on their growing bond, a friendship that seemed to solidify over his troubles? Lip-reading be damned, he seethed with frustration when he was unable to decipher what his two friends were saying to him or to each other.

Zak was racked with fear. Dr. Peterson had said there was no guarantee that surgery would restore his hearing, but without the surgery, the loss would be irreversible. Zak worried about the timing of when that loss might become permanent. Would it happen within a month? A week? A day? Had it already happened? He imagined the tumor akin to an octopus; tentacles wrapped about sensitive structures, tightly squeezing, destroying forever any chance of the surgeon being able to restore his hearing. How could he manage in a world where he couldn't hear? Was it too late to learn American Sign Language? And how long might it take to become ASL proficient?

Zak focused on the potential for surgical complications. *Dear God*, he fretted. *He could wind up deaf and disfigured.* He tried to quiet his mind, but the negative thoughts kept recycling, as if on autopilot. A vicious loop of circuitous thinking. Questions leading to more questions. Doubts, leading to more doubts. Fears, leading to more fears. Maybe it was time to reach out to his parents. Ask them to fly to Arizona. Beg for their forgiveness. Lie to them. Say, he wasn't gay. That the whole thing had been a mistake. An error of judgment.

Should he grovel? It had taken so much courage to be honest. Would they change their minds if they knew he needed them? Would that be enough to mend the relationship? He had no doubt that if the surgery were a gambit to turn him straight, his parents would stop at nothing to support him.

But wait!

Dr. Peterson had texted that he had a surprise. Had the doctor already contacted his folks? Had he done what Zak was afraid to do? Zak imagined the conversation. A learned physician educating his parents about ignorance and bigotry. How proud he'd be if a respected adult would speak on his behalf. Someone who might confront his folks with the gravitas that he lacked.

Zak worried about his class work. How could he continue the semester when he'd be missing midterms? If he needed to drop the semester, would ASU roll the paid tuition forward so the money wouldn't be lost?

Zak was convinced his entire future hung on Peterson's decision to schedule the surgery, and though the doctor's last text was positive, Zak still worried. After all, nothing in his life was guaranteed. He'd experienced one surprise after another. His parents' negative reaction to his sexual orientation. Allison's bad behavior when she visited. The sudden loss of his hearing. So many moments that had conspired to turn his life into a train wreck.

The day before his appointment, Zak stressed over his friendships. Chuck was getting up early for class and returning late. Marshall might stop by, but he didn't stick around for long. Was it because Chuck wasn't there? Were his friends now in a relationship together? He was certain they were avoiding him. And though both boys had made sure food was available for Zak, they seemed to have stopped trying to talk to him. Their relationship had been reduced to exchanging meals for money as if they worked for *DoorDash*.

"You don't have to leave," Zak said to Marshall when he dropped off a sandwich from the cafe.

Marshall hesitated at the door. He came back inside, pulling out Chuck's desk chair and sitting down.

Zak thought he looked tired. "How are you?" Zak asked, uncertain whether he was speaking too softly or too loudly.

Marshall shrugged. Zak couldn't blame him for being quiet. What could he possibly say that Zak could hear or understand?

Zak took a breath. What could he say to fix the friendship? To get back to the very beginning when they'd first met. When Marshall first tapped him on the shoulder and offered to share the class notes. "I haven't been a very good friend," Zak admitted. "I get that you and Chuck can't stand being around me."

Marshall's expression softened. He opened his mouth as if he were about to say something. But he didn't.

"I know," Zak said. "I can't understand anything. It's awful."

Marshall grabbed a yellow notepad on Chuck's desk and started to write. When he was done, he passed the pad to Zak. *We're not angry at you. When you have the surgery, everything will return to normal. Take it one day at a time. We've got your back!*

– 13 –

HELENA HURRIED INTO the dining room to join her friends for an early breakfast. As expected, they were sitting at their usual table, the same one they occupied at every meal. The three sipped coffee and chatted away as Helena slipped into the open seat across from *Babbling Babs*, with *Donna Don't Tell Me* to her left and *Sin of a Face Cynthia* to her right. "We still need a fourth for mah-jongg," Babs announced in a sing-song voice as Helena glanced at the breakfast menu.

Helena had resisted joining the ladies in their regular mah-jongg soiree. She didn't like losing, and after playing a game or two, was certain she'd never win. It was all too complicated for a novice. Is that tile a flower or a 1 bam? And why were the flowers numbered if the numbers didn't matter? But it was the mah-jongg card itself that was the real deal-killer. Row upon row of winning hands. How did anyone ever select the right hand to play and why were there so many complicated combinations? The mah-jongg card alone gave Helena eye strain. And as with all games, Helena knew strategy was key to winning, but who could concentrate on strategy when they were struggling to remember the name of the tiles and the hand they were playing? No. Helena would not be joining the ladies. Not if she valued her sanity. "I'll pass on mah-jongg," she said as she eyed the ingredients of a western omelet. She hadn't eaten one in years, but green peppers gave her indigestion. She'd have to make another choice.

Babs dug her heels in, refusing to take no for an answer. "Oh, Helena, really. If you want to have friends, you have to participate. It's the easiest way to connect with others socially."

Cynthia frowned, adding unneeded length to an otherwise horsey face. "Oh, leave her alone. If she doesn't want to, she doesn't have to. We're not all tied at the hip. Isn't it enough that we eat every meal together? Do we have to also spend every waking hour together?"

"Oh, you," Babs scolded Cynthia. "I just thought it would be fun. Us four girls together. This way, we won't have to play with Gilbert. He's so slow. How many times have we corrected him when he discards a tile? You'd think after three months of playing, he'd know you can't use a joker to make a pair. Men!"

Helena giggled at the thought of Gilbert Goldfarb, the "Ventana Romeo" with his head of August dandelions, sitting in as their fourth.

Aggie approached to take their breakfast orders. "It's about time," Cynthia complained. "I've been waiting fifteen minutes for a warm-up on my coffee." No sooner had those words left Cynthia's lips then Aggie turned and headed off to the kitchen. Cynthia's eyes bulged. Helena tried not to laugh. "What's wrong with that one? At the very least, she should have taken our orders."

"You scared her away," Donna said, a finger wagging in Cynthia's direction. "Honestly, Cynthia, you could be a little nicer."

"Nicer about what? I wanted more coffee."

"I think it's sweet that Gilbert tries so hard," Donna added, looping back to their initial conversation. "For a man in his late eighties, he's kind of cute. But those teeth. Let's face it. The man needs a dentist."

"Is something wrong with his teeth?" Babs innocently asked.

Donna made a face. "You never noticed?"

"No," Babs confirmed. "I'm playing my hand, not looking at the man's teeth. Dear God. Maybe you'd win more if you focused on your hand."

Helena had lost the flow of the conversation at the table as she decided oatmeal was a better choice than a western omelet. "What's wrong with your hand, Donna? Arthritis?" she absent-mindedly asked.

Babs, Donna, and Cynthia all turned to Helena. "We're discussing Donna's mah-jongg hand," Babs clarified. "My goodness. What world are you living in?"

Helena's heart dropped. She didn't like being teased. Part of the reason for not taking up mah-jongg was her fear that she might be in the midst of a mental decline. Misplaced keys. Lost reading glasses. Walking into the kitchen and forgetting what she'd gotten up for. She'd noticed the warning signs before she moved to Ventana. She assumed the cause was depression. But then, who wouldn't be depressed after being rescued from the bathroom floor by EMTs? Fortunately, after moving into Ventana, her depression had lifted. Still, she found herself misplacing the television remote. And so what if she missed a word or two of a conversation? It didn't mean she had dementia. Or did it? But now that she'd become more social, she was increasingly aware of how much she missed compared to her contemporaries. Especially when those contemporaries were eager to point it out. Was there a gentle confusion setting in? Something she couldn't fake her way through? Or was she merely distracted? It was hard to know which was which, and what was real.

"Ladies," Helena admitted, "I think I'm losing it."

Donna laughed. "I read your column yesterday on traffic in Tempe. Based on that little gem alone, I'd say you're still sharp as a tack."

Helena had been writing well. She'd secured a bimonthly column in the student paper: *Helena to the Rescue*. And her new novel was coming along nicely. She was nearly halfway through the first draft, excited to be back in the swing of things. Maybe Donna was right. Maybe there was nothing to worry about.

"You seem perfectly fine to me," Cynthia said with a huff. "You know, you're not the only one aging here. None of us is getting any younger."

"Thank God," Babs added. "Can you imagine if we were *actually getting younger*? Every day, you'd wake up and have this long life ahead of you. Holding a job. Raising children. Having a husband. Oh, I don't know about you three, but I wouldn't want to do any of that again."

"I would," Donna admitted. "I'd like to feel my body getting firmer each day."

"You can always go to yoga," Babs reminded her.

Donna laughed. "My knees wouldn't make it through the first downward dog."

Cynthia raised a brow. "Being young would come with so many complications. Wasn't once more than enough?"

"It was for me," Helena agreed.

"I don't know," Babs said mournfully. "None of us knows how things are going to turn out. We're still in the middle of our story."

Cynthia corrected her. "You mean, the end of our story."

Donna bristled. "It's scary. Comedians joke that Florida is God's waiting room. Which explains why I'm sitting here in Arizona."

"And that," Cynthia concluded with all the sarcasm she could muster, "is the update on our mortality for today. Personally, I'll take it one day at a time. The rest, I'll leave to God."

"The older I get," Donna admitted, "the less certain I am that there is a God. I've been a good Catholic all my life. I've never missed a Sunday. Gosh, I hope there's a God."

"Do you think you earn brownie points by following all the rules?" Cynthia asked.

"Who said I followed the rules?" Donna snapped back.

"Aren't you afraid of how this will all wrap up?" Babs said, a nervous quiver in her voice.

"You mean, am I afraid to *die*?" Cynthia said, the last word sounding like a curse.

Donna made a sour face. "Can't we talk about something else? Why does every conversation lead to illness or death? I, for one," she said, with a palm flat against her chest, "am too young to die. Much too young. And much too lovely."

All four women broke into laughter as Aggie approached the table with a hot carafe of coffee. "Aggie, what do you think about getting older?" Helena asked as Aggie made her way around the table filling coffee cups.

"I try to avoid thinking about it. What's the point? Aggie opined. "It's going to happen whether you like it or not. Thinking about it won't change anything. You've got no control over it. My mother always said, 'Only fools try to control the things they can't.'"

The group was dumbstruck as Aggie, head held high, withdrew back to the kitchen.

"She's right, you know," Donna finally said. "There's no point worrying about what we have no control over."

Cynthia nodded. "It's odd that a woman who's so terrible at her job can dispense such wisdom. Still, I wish you three would stop talking to her when she's working. She's so easily distracted. The poor thing needs to concentrate."

"Oh, she's fine," Babs said. "Be nice."

But Cynthia was not about to let it go. "Notice we still haven't ordered breakfast."

"I am getting hungry," Helena added as she glanced about. There was no sign of Aggie in the dining room.

"That darn fool keeps forgetting to take our orders," Cynthia grumbled.

Helena smiled to herself. Aggie was no fool. She was probably aware of Cynthia's jabs. Perhaps her inattention to the breakfast order was her way of getting even with diners who acted superior to the staff. She wouldn't put it past Aggie to torture little old ladies who should have learned by now how to treat others with kindness and dignity.

❧

Helena lingered at the table after the others left, sipping her third cup of coffee, knowing full well that too much caffeine was bad for her heart. At least, that's what the doctor said at her last visit. Ruthie whispered in her ear. *How can you stand those horrible women?*

Helena looked about. She was alone. No one anywhere.

I know you can hear me.

Helena took a breath. "I like them," she quietly said.

Babs is a bubble head. Donna, a dear heart. Cynthia . . . Hmm. Bitch comes to mind.

Helena smiled. Ruthie had no filter. On the brain, out the mouth.

You need to do something with your life.

Helena rolled her eyes. Her life had been full of achievement and now she was working on a new novel. She was writing again. Which was hard work. Shouldn't she get some credit for jumpstarting her life? Not to mention making the move to Ventana. It seemed she'd done a great deal of *something* so far.

Oh, that's all good and fine. But you're still hiding. All the writing has nothing to do with getting out there. Engaged with the world.

Helena bristled at Ruthie's expectations. Nothing was ever good enough. No amount of work or achievement, and here, at the advanced age of eighty-three, it seemed so foolish, so hopelessly ego-centric, to be more than she already was.

Hadn't her time for glory come and gone? Couldn't she just sit back and rest on her laurels?

Stop thinking your life is over. As long as you're drawing breaths, you've something to offer. You might have another ten years left. Maybe more. Do you want to spend the time you have left with those three airheads figuring out how to read a mah-jongg card?

Helena was shocked. Ruthie had always pushed her to learn mah-jongg and canasta. Anything to get her out of the house and into a social setting with other women. Besides, she'd already turned down the mah-jongg offer.

Mah-jongg was for when you lived alone. But now, you're at a university. You should be involved with the students. Tap into their life force. You should be putting yourself out there. Young people should know you.

Helena doubted young people would want to know her. Frankly, her own children and grandchildren didn't seem particularly interested in knowing her. Why would strangers?

You're a foolish woman, Helena. You think your life serves no purpose. I'm telling you that there are plenty of opportunities for you to make meaningful connections. To share your wisdom. Don't become a Ventana shut in.

Helena groaned. She'd no intention of becoming a Ventana shut in. Julie had pushed, and that very morning she had an appointment to volunteer as a patient advocate. And though Helena was initially reluctant about this new role, she found herself looking forward to doing something different. She'd already booked an Uber so she wouldn't have to walk across campus. It wasn't hard to do. It just required a bit of gumption, and of course, downloading the Uber app. That had been the new learn. When in doubt, search for an app.

Riding the elevator down to the lobby, Helena questioned why she still had such a strong psychic connection to Ruthie. These days, Ruthie was all about delivering messages. Egging Helena on. Making sure she stayed on track. In many ways,

Helena considered herself lucky. Ruthie's voice was forever bound with her own. She'd been the child of a strong woman and even though Helena lacked her mother's temperament, she appreciated her mother's tenacious drive. Ruthie may not have been a demonstrative mother, hugging, kissing, and touching, but she was certainly a capable prodder, directing Helena ever forward. Perhaps at this age, that was exactly what Helena needed. At least, Helena thought so as she crossed the Ventana lobby and spotted the Uber parked outside, waiting for her. She checked her watch. Eight forty-five. Right on time!

Dr. Peterson's waiting room was jammed with patients when Helena arrived at nine. She hadn't expected to wait alongside the others, believing the doctor's request for her services meant she'd bypass the reception area, but after twenty minutes, she was still waiting. Helena wondered if perhaps she should come back later just as a nurse appeared in the doorway. "Ms. Greenberg," she called out.

Helena looked about. No one answered. She stood up with a finger in the air. "Greenblatt?" she meekly questioned.

The nurse looked down at her clipboard. "Yes," she said, unaware she'd mispronounced Helena's last name.

Helena followed the woman through the maze of the back office, arriving at Peterson's private office where he handled consultations. "Dr. Peterson will be with you shortly. Please have a seat," the nurse said as she exited, leaving the door to the hallway open.

Helena looked at the certificates on the wall. A medical degree from Yeshiva University. An internship at New York University. A residency at Henry Ford Hospital. She took a deep breath. It was official. No backing out now. Julie had told her a bit about the role of patient advocate, but the specifics were sketchy at best. Helena found it unsettling to have signed up for something she didn't quite understand. And if there was anything Helena didn't like, it was not knowing what was expected of her. *Heck*, she thought, *I might as well be playing mah-jongg.*

Helena sat down in one of the two seats that fronted the doctor's desk. She shifted about, unable to get comfortable. There was something odd about the office that she couldn't quite put her finger on. She chewed her lower lip as she contemplated the new role. *How many hours would this commitment take?* Whatever the role entailed, she'd still need time to write.

"Hello," came a man's voice from behind. Helena turned and started to stand, two maneuvers that required more coordination than she could muster as a tall gentleman with gray frizzy hair waved at her to stay seated. She fell backward into the seat, knowing full well she was heading in that direction anyway. "And what can I do for you?" he asked as he came about the desk to face her.

"We have an appointment. I'm your new patient advocate," Helena said.

The man scowled. "That's impossible. We're already overstaffed. I've told my son that we need to cut expenses, but he just doesn't listen to me. He thinks my advice is worthless. I've tried talking to him, but it's like talking to a rock. Besides . . . aren't you a little long in the tooth to still be working?"

"I'm a volunteer," Helena clarified, her shackles raised by the mention of her age. "You're not paying me."

"A volunteer," the man sneered. "What's your training?"

Helena blinked. She suddenly realized the man before her was not *the doctor*. Perhaps he'd once been a doctor, but he was definitely not the doctor she was supposed to meet.

"I'm sorry for keeping you waiting," came the voice of a much younger man as he entered the office and shut the door.

Dr. Rod Peterson had jet-black hair, combed straight back to reveal a widow's peak. His broad shoulders signaled he may have been an athlete at one time. "Ms. Greenblatt, thank you for coming. My apologies for keeping you waiting. We're so busy this morning."

Helena stifled a laugh, hoping Ruthie wasn't about to make an appearance. "Yes. It certainly is busy," she said, enjoying the double entendre as the older gentleman moved over to stand by the window.

Dr. Peterson sat down at his desk. His demeanor cordial. "Thank you for agreeing to help us out. Has Julie told you anything about the position?"

"A little," Helena admitted.

The older gentleman leaned against the windowsill, not a foot away from the doctor's desk. He glared at Helena.

Dr. Peterson started at the very beginning. "Did she tell you why we need a patient advocate?"

Helena took a wild guess. "You need an extra set of hands."

Peterson chuckled. "Well, that's true. But no. This is a special position."

The older gentleman rolled his eyes and turned away, appearing to look out the window.

"Dr. Peterson," Helena interrupted. "Excuse me for asking, but has your father passed?"

Peterson seemed surprised. "Just recently. Were you one of his patients?"

The older gentleman shifted about, his gaze returning to his son.

"Were you close to him?"

Peterson grunted. "He couldn't stand me. I could never measure up. After he died, I realized he was in competition with me. You see, my father was also an otorhinolaryngologist. One of the best in the state. I was proud to be his son, professionally. But privately, well, it was an unpleasant experience."

A sadness emanated from the older man's eyes.

"I think your father regrets the way he treated you," Helena volunteered.

The older man offered Helena a wink.

"In fact, I wouldn't be surprised if he was nearby, watching over you."

"My father!" Peterson laughed. "Not my father."

The older man furrowed a brow.

"Forgive me for disagreeing, but I think he must have loved you very much and he's sorry for the way he treated you."

Peterson balked. "What are you talking about?"

Helena knew better than to tell Dr. Peterson about her gift. Why should he believe her? Most people wouldn't. "It's just a feeling. Forgive me for prying into your personal affairs."

Peterson squinted as he sized up Helena. "I don't believe in ESP or the hereafter or whatever you're trying to sell."

Helena sighed. ESP had nothing to do with seeing the dead. Nor could she read Tarot cards or perform aura readings. Her talent was focused. Her impressions, precise. Over the years, she'd tired of justifying herself or her gift, which was why she rarely shared her secret with strangers. Instead, she was content to deliver messages and let it go. If someone didn't believe her, that was their affair. She'd done what she needed to do, and sure enough, once she delivered the message to Peterson, the older gentleman faded into thin air. "My apologies," she said with a quick nod. She'd no interest in converting the doctor or anyone else. Let each person come to their spiritual truths in their own way. It wasn't her job to enlighten the world.

Peterson cleared his throat, as if resetting the conversation. "Now, for the matter at hand. We have a student at ASU who is going to need help. I'd like to introduce you two. He has no family in Arizona and has to undergo surgery. He's recently become deaf in his right ear due to a tumor. It's the only ear with which he was able to hear, but we can turn this around. The surgery is delicate, and as with all surgeries, the procedure is risky. We need someone to look after him before the surgery, and then, once he leaves the hospital. That's where you come in."

Helena nervously chewed on her bottom lip as she took in the severity of the problem. "What about his parents? Aren't they able to care for him?"

Peterson shrugged. "We've tried reaching out. They don't want anything to do with the boy."

Helena straightened up in her seat. She'd never heard of anything so cold and unloving. What parent wouldn't be there for their child?

Peterson reached across the desk for a notepad. He scribbled something down before tearing off the sheet and handing it to Helena. "Here's the boy's name and dorm information."

"Is he expecting me?"

Dr. Peterson glanced at his watch. "You'll be meeting him soon. He'll be here at the office at eleven."

Helena was stunned. "This is more than I anticipated," she admitted. "Much more."

Peterson smiled. "You'll do fine," he assured her. "Besides, we have no other choice. It's you or no surgery."

"Oh, that's unfair," Helena groaned.

Peterson cocked his head. "Perhaps you and I have something in common. You know, physicians can be intuitive too. Julie told me you were an unusual lady. A very kind woman. I can tell you are. But she never mentioned your talent with spirits. Of course, I think that's all nonsense."

Helena blushed. What else could she have expected from a medical professional grounded in science? Of course he'd never believe her. She certainly couldn't blame him. *This whole medium thing is so darn annoying*, she thought. It didn't matter if Peterson believed her. What mattered was that Peterson's father, with her help, was on the road to making peace with his son. *Wasn't that reward enough?*

With time on her hands before her scheduled meeting with the ASU student, Helena left Dr. Peterson's office and stepped outside to enjoy the cool morning air. November was such a beautiful time to be in the desert. Temperatures hovered around seventy. Cool breezes reminded everyone that Thanksgiving was just around the corner.

Helena strolled into the Starbucks next door where students were lined up for a jolt of midmorning java. She couldn't get over all the young people. They seemed to be a different species. Monolithic with their earbuds, iPhones, and backpacks; a futuristic representation of youth engaged in a common endeavor, but separated and disconnected, as if they'd walked into a shared space determined to remain in their own private worlds. Helena couldn't help but feel sad. One certainly didn't have to be old to be isolated and alone.

Situated in a corner chair, coffee in hand, she studied the room. She tried to remember being young. The time when every possibility lay before you, and you had no idea what was going on. Clueless, yet drowning in opportunity. Such freedom from a distance seemed exhilarating, but then, there's so much uncertainty. So many choices. She wondered why she'd chosen to marry when she was so young instead of continuing her college education. Was the curriculum too challenging or did she lack confidence in her abilities? Had she been scared to compete? And why for goodness sakes did she opt to have two children in what seemed like rapid succession? What had she been thinking? All she could recall back then was that she was lost *in the act of doing*. She'd been consumed by the needs of others. A husband. A home. Young children. Had all that activity been her way of escaping the uncertainty of life? Caught up in the flow of *being busy*. Lifted and carried along mindlessly until the death of her second husband. That second tragedy confirmed that no man was going to save her. She'd have to become her own hero. That's when she returned to NYU and earned a journalism degree. *There are so many choices in life*, she thought. *What we believe in. Whom we love. The career we'll pursue. The friends we'll make. All the while, you live moment to moment, unaware of the importance of those choices and how they will shape the future.*

When viewed objectively, Helena's life seemed like an experiment, and she, the reluctant guinea pig. Who would she have become if she'd never married? How would her present circumstances be different if she'd given birth to girls instead of boys or written her first novel after the death of her first husband? Are our destinies fixed or based on choices? So many questions and so few answers. And did any of it really matter as she approached the last chapter of life? And if none of it mattered, then did anything truly matter? And now, what was there left to do? What choices did she still have in front of her? Were those choices important in how she'd experience this next stage of life?

She sipped her coffee and considered all that might still lie before her, and though she didn't like to think about death, she knew time was running out. It may not be tomorrow, next week, next month, or even next year, but she wasn't long for the world. At least not in the way she'd once been. The clock was ticking. Memories had become more plentiful than new experiences. Her past was very much part of her present. Perhaps this new role as a patient advocate would ground her so she could stop floating between past regrets and fear of the future.

She finished her coffee. The caffeine provided the extra jolt she needed to get to her feet. *Life is good*, she thought, *rife with second chances*. Wasn't she lucky? Ventana was her second chance. Once again, she could be anything she wanted. Do anything, she wanted. She checked her watch. It was time to head back to Dr. Peterson's office. She was about to start a new chapter as a patient advocate to an ASU student. And who better for that role? She certainly understood how scary it could be to navigate the health care terrain.

Her confidence soared as she made her way with her empty coffee cup to the bin marked *Recycle*. On her fourth step, she became keenly aware that something was wrong. By the fifth step, she frantically looked about the crowded space for an empty chair. A student brushed past her on his way to the restroom, slightly knocking her off balance. Or was she already primed to go down as her knees buckled and the world slipped away?

– 14 –

Zak was a bundle of nerves when the morning arrived for his appointment with Dr. Peterson. There was a lot to worry about and worrying had become second nature. The silence of his world left him with few distractions. Would Peterson schedule the surgery? Would the surgery cure his deafness?

Sitting at his desk, he picked at a bowl of Cinnamon Cheerios. Had the doctor reached out to his folks and had they agreed to come to Arizona for his surgery? Zak wasn't sure how he felt about seeing them again. On the one hand, it would be a relief to know they'd forgiven him. But had he forgiven them? It'd been five months since he'd left home and there'd been no contact. No phone calls. No letters. No visits. What hope was there that they'd changed? Still, the doctor wouldn't have scheduled the morning's appointment unless he had good news and Dr. Peterson had said in his text that he indeed had good news.

Zak stepped into a morning shower. How strange it was not to hear the water splashing onto the tile. He washed his hair, but there was no squeaky-clean when he rinsed out the shampoo. Even his breathing was silent. All the sounds of his life were now but a memory.

With a towel wrapped about his waist, he returned to his dorm room to find Melinda sitting at Chuck's desk, her red hair tied back in a ponytail, eyes twinkling like the stars on a dark Arizona night. She smiled at him as if she knew a secret he'd failed to tell her. In a way, she did. After he'd run out on her at the bar, he'd texted that he wouldn't be coming back. But he didn't mention the tumor in his right ear or that he was deaf. He thought she wouldn't care. As if her only interest in her *Andy boy* was for him to clean up the Windy Canyon toilets. And since he couldn't do the job, there could be nothing more between them.

"Hi," he said, nervous to see her and embarrassed at his state of undress. It wasn't the warmest of greetings, but then, he wasn't in the warmest of moods. Melinda seemed unfazed. She said something or other that he tried to lip-read but didn't quite catch. "What are you doing here?" he asked as he grabbed his jeans from the bed and told her to close her eyes as he slipped them on. He hoped she wasn't too angry at him for running out on her.

Melinda got to her feet and pointed to the door. "Doctor," she shouted so loud Zak imagined he'd heard her.

Zak realized that Chuck or Marshall must have gone to Windy Canyon to talk to her. Of course, that's what happened. Was Melinda the big surprise they'd set up to take care of him? Had Chuck and Marshall given her name to Peterson? Had Peterson convinced her to sponsor him? Zak winced at the thought of imposing on her. But then, what other choice did he have?

He slipped into a pair of Adidas and pulled on a Calvin Klein sweatshirt. Together they walked to Peterson's office building on the other side of the ASU campus. Lost in thought,

Zak worried about Chuck and Marshall. Why hadn't they shown up to go with him to the doctor? He knew they had morning classes, but this appointment was important. Had he finally driven them away with his anger and sulking?

"Here we are," Zak muttered as they entered the lobby of the medical office building.

The waiting room was crowded as Zak checked in at the front desk. Melinda gently bumped him with an elbow as he signed the patient roster, offering a reassuring smile. But Zak didn't feel much like smiling. At best, he was about to schedule surgery, a serious procedure that could restore his hearing or leave him deaf and disfigured. The more he thought about the facial risks, the less inclined he was to move forward. Yet, he couldn't imagine his life living in a silent movie.

Seated next to Melinda, Zak kept an eye on the back-office door, waiting for the nurse to appear to call his name. An old man exited from the back and walked across the waiting room to sit in an empty chair across from Zak. Zak didn't make eye contact. What was the point? The man was in a totally different place in his life. He'd already lived with his hearing issues. How many more years did he have left to suffer? Zak imagined the old guy lucky, being so close to the end. How he wished he could look into the future and know how his life would turn out. Would he earn a college degree, find a profession, fall in love, have a family, and be able to hear again?

Melinda patted his knee. A nurse had called his name.

He was terrified as he followed the nurse through the back office to an exam room. He'd promised himself he wouldn't cry, but suddenly he was overwhelmed by emotion. There was so much riding on the surgery. *Why am I so frightened?* he berated himself, unwilling to accept the reality that even though he was in college, living on his own, he was still an adolescent. Someone's child. Someone's unwanted child. Someone's unwanted gay, deaf child.

– 15 –

HELENA AWOKE IN the back of an ambulance, the rocking so violent she was reminded of a carnival ride she'd endured as a child in Coney Island. At the end of that ride, she'd thrown up.

A female EMT stroked her arm. "Well, hello there. Feeling any better?"

Helena wasn't quite sure how she felt beyond nauseous from all the motion. "What happened?"

"You fainted," the EMT informed her. Her voice was kind. Reassuring.

Helena closed her eyes. She remembered. Starbucks. Coffee. Lots of coffee. Had the caffeine negatively affected her heart. Or was this the end of her life? Her last moments on earth. "Am I dying?" she mumbled.

"Hopefully not," the young woman said.

"Wait," Helena said, gripping the sides of the stretcher and attempting to sit up. "What time is it?"

The EMT checked her watch. "Eleven o'clock."

"Oh no," Helena sighed. "I have an appointment with a doctor at eleven."

The woman tried to calm her. "We're taking you to the emergency room. There are plenty of doctors there."

"No, you don't understand," Helena argued. "I was supposed to meet someone. Someone who needs my help."

"Not today," the EMT assured her. "Today, we're going to the emergency room."

Helena slid back onto the stretcher as the ambulance took another hard bump. "But I need to . . ." she mumbled, her voice trailing off as she resigned herself to the futility of her present circumstance.

At the hospital, Helena remained isolated in a white curtained cubicle in the emergency department as the staff scheduled a series of tests. She fretted about Dr. Peterson. *What must he think? I just slipped out of the office for a cup of coffee and never returned.* The very idea that someone she respected might think her a complete whack-a-doodle filled her with shame. *I should've stayed in the office. Sat and waited. Read a magazine. Enjoyed that home renovation show on HGTV. If I'd just stayed, I'd have been fine.*

Ruthie was back, lurking in the corner of the cubicle. *How you carry on!*

"Oh, no," Helena muttered. "Not again."

Where else would you expect a mother to be? My child's sick!

Helena had to concede that at least Ruthie had the best of intentions.

What did the doctor say?

Helena bit her lip. She wasn't going to admit to Ruthie that she'd been drinking too much coffee. "Nothing, yet."

After all this time, you still don't know what's causing those spells of yours. I think it's time to change doctors. Really. It's an outrage!

Helena tried to appease her mother. "Maybe they'll know more after they run the next series of tests."

Well, I should hope so, Ruthie said as she glanced about. *By the way, where are we? Why is it so damn white here?*

"Mother, please. Stop asking me all these questions. I'm tired. I need to rest."

You ungrateful child, Ruthie complained as she slowly evaporated.

"Hello." A nurse poked her head into the cubicle. "Are you alright?"

"Perfectly fine," Helena answered.

"I thought I heard you talking to someone."

"When you live alone, you talk to yourself. It calms your nerves."

The nurse nodded. "Good then. I just wanted to make sure you're all right. We have someone coming by who will transport you to x-ray."

"X-ray?"

"Just to make sure you haven't broken any bones in the fall."

"I didn't fall. I fainted."

"Either way, we can never be too careful."

Helena pursed her lips. "Any idea when I can go home? I'd like to leave as soon as possible."

"A social worker will be in shortly to talk with you."

Helena didn't want to talk with a social worker. She just wanted to leave. "You know," she said as she scooched forward and swung her legs over the side of the gurney, "I'm really feeling fine. This whole thing is silly."

The nurse was now inside the cubicle. "Not so fast," she said as Helena started her descent off the gurney. "We have to check you out."

"Oh no," Helena insisted. "I'm not going through a whole battery of tests today. I'll make a follow-up appointment with my doctor."

"But you can't just leave."

"Oh, but I can," Helena said as she slipped into her shoes. "I appreciate the concern, but I'm much too old to survive another day of being poked and prodded. And I'm far too young to be tended to as if I were a China doll about to break."

The nurse crossed her arms. "You can't leave without signing the discharge papers."

Helena was not about to take any gruff. "Fine. Bring them to me," she said as the nurse retreated. Once out of sight, Helena slipped out from behind the wall of curtains and made her way to the exit. Come hell or high water, she had an appointment to keep. And she was already late.

– 16 –

WHILE HELENA WAS planning her escape from the hospital's emergency department, Zak was passing a tense thirty minutes waiting in an exam room for Dr. Peterson to show up. With Melinda by his side, they sat in silence. After all, what else was there to do? Zak couldn't hear and he didn't feel like carrying on a conversation with Melinda via text. Instead, he cursed under his breath.

It didn't improve his mood.

He hated waiting for doctors. He hated exam rooms. He hated imposing on Melinda. But mostly, he hated himself for being deaf. And should he ever become a doctor, he swore he'd never make patients wait, especially when they were waiting for important news. Would Peterson perform the surgery, and if so, when? That's all he needed to know. Any other concerns, of which there were many, had suddenly become irrelevant.

When Peterson finally showed, he profusely apologized. Zak tried to suppress his irritation as he struggled to read the doctor's lips. Deafness had done little to improve his lip-reading skills. He didn't want an apology. Or the kindness that Peterson displayed, which Zak assumed was mostly for Melinda's benefit. Zak was too pissed for polite conversation. He just wanted to know that the surgery was scheduled. And the date.

Using a two-way laptop, Peterson typed away as Zak read the screen that faced him. Peterson had scheduled the surgery for Monday morning. Zak felt the muscles in his shoulders relax. What a relief. But wait! The patient advocate, the adult assigned to Zak's care and with whom he was supposed to meet, had failed to show for the appointment. Zak was grateful a solution had been found so that he could have the surgery, but was it a bad omen that the patient advocate had stood him up? Was that something Zak needed to worry about? Peterson didn't seem to think so, even though the man had a decidedly worried expression on his face. *This guy should never play poker,* Zak thought as Peterson assured him everything would be fine.

After the appointment, Zak was famished. Melinda took him to a small sandwich shop a few blocks from campus for lunch. She picked at a salad of mixed greens while Zak devoured a turkey club. Melinda started to speak, and then stopped when Zak offered a blank stare. He was tired. Too tired to read anyone else's lips. Melinda reached into her bag for her iPhone.

She texted: Are you coming back to work after the surgery?

Zak read the message. "I can't. It's too loud. It's not good for my ear."

Melinda texted: Are you dropping out of ASU? Going back to NYC?

Zak shrugged. How could he answer? At the moment, his future was a blur. All questions and no answers. "I don't know. I'm missing midterms next week. How can I continue at ASU?"

Melinda tapped away on her phone: Talk with your profs. Maybe you can take your exams later.

Zak thought, *easier said than done. I can't hear. How can I talk to them?*

Melinda reached for his hand across the table. Her lips were moving again, but Zak couldn't make a word out of what she was saying. He dropped his chin to his chest, ashamed of his emotional state. In all of his life, he'd never felt so sorry for himself. But then, feeling sorry for himself lately had become his favorite pastime. A new hobby of sorts.

– 17 –

HELENA PASSED THROUGH the emergency department's doors and into a long white hallway. She looked about trying to get her bearing. Which way to go? She turned right and followed the signs through what seemed like a maze that finally led to the lobby. There, she spotted a young man in a dark blue uniform dropping off a package at the Welcome Desk. "Excuse me, young man," she called out. "Is that your van parked out front with the Amazon logo?"

"Yes, ma'am," the driver said. His smile was warm and inviting.

"Can you help me out? I need a ride. It's not far from here."

"I'm sorry, ma'am. But that's against company policy."

Helena feigned surprise. "Really? Against company policy to be a good neighbor? That's a strange rule."

The young man blushed. "I wish I could."

"Well, then," Helena said as she linked her arm in his, "today is your lucky day. We're going to make that wish come true. You're going to pretend I'm your mother. Now, you certainly wouldn't say no to your mother."

"Mother?" The young man's eyes bulged.

"Okay, grandmother," Helena corrected herself, guessing the driver was probably in his early twenties. But just as he was about to say something, Helena held up a warning finger. "I'm not willing to go any older. I can't possibly be the age of your great-grandmother."

"Well . . ." the young man stuttered.

"How old is your mother?"

"Forty-five."

"And your grandmother?"

"She's seventy."

"There. What did I tell you? I'm eighty-three. Much too young to be your great-grandmother."

The young man nodded, though Helena knew she was only a few years short of qualifying.

"Now let's get a move-on," she said as arm-in-arm she led the young man out of the lobby and toward his van. "I have an appointment and I'm running late."

"But ma'am . . ."

"Now, if I were you, I'd stop worrying about company policy. Today, you have more important matters to concern yourself with. By the way, have any of the women in your family ever told you what a nice young man you are?"

The driver seemed taken by surprise. "Not really."

"Now that's a shame!"

"Ma'am, I think you're trying to manipulate me."

"Manipulate you!" Helena said in a mocking tone. "Me? Never."

"Do you always get your way?" the driver asked as he opened the passenger side door and offered Helena a helping hand into the van.

Helena reached for the inside door handle, and with a grunt and groan, hoisted herself into the passenger seat. "I guess that depends on your point of view," she yelled as the driver raced around the front of the van.

"You seem awfully pushy to me," the young man said as he buckled his seatbelt.

Helena pondered his remark as they pulled into traffic. "Young man, when you get to be my age, you realize the folly of taking *no* for an answer. There are some things in life you have to fight for. Beliefs. Ideals. Challenges that don't necessarily evaporate with age. And sometimes, even rides with kind, young men."

Yes, she proudly thought. *She was someone who knew how to take charge.* Women of her generation had to; otherwise, there'd have been no civil rights movement. No women's liberation. No struggle against the Vietnam War. No fight for the ERA. She'd been a warrior alongside the many women who'd struggled to gain political influence. Bella Abzug. Shirley Chisholm. Geraldine Ferraro. And even though she'd played a minor role as a novelist, she'd been there. It might seem ridiculous to consider commandeering a ride from an Amazon delivery driver as a radical move, but she'd been raised in a generation when women were expected to accommodate. Be homemakers. She was proud that today women were expected to have careers. Earn their own living. Lead their own lives.

"So now, where am I going?" the driver asked.

Helena chuckled. She'd forgotten to offer directions. Imagine commandeering a ride without bothering to inform the driver of the intended destination. "Dr. Peterson's office in Tempe," she said as the driver punched the doctor's name into Google Maps.

"The thing with your generation . . ." Helena started to say as the van left the curb.

"Wow. I'm helping you and you're lecturing me on my generation. The thing with your generation is you're entitled."

Helena did a double take. "You're fast on the draw. Good for you. You nailed me."

"My generation," he huffed as the van stopped at a red light. "I'm not a generation. I'm an individual."

"Exactly," Helena said with excitement. "You're very independent. When I was your age, we were a community. We worked together. We defined our issues and sought solutions. Today, you have those damn iPhones. Your generation assumes it is self-sufficient in an electronic universe. There's a lot to be said for connecting with others. Asking for help. I mean, here you are, the perfect example. You spend the day driving around delivering packages that someone, sitting alone somewhere, probably ordered on an iPhone. More and more, your generation is isolated. How can that be healthy?"

"There are times when I do feel lonely," the young man admitted as he tuned to make eye contact with Helena. "You might have something there."

"Of course I do," Helena said, reading his ID badge. "Bart."

Bart offered a quick smile as the light changed to green. "I spend my day rushing from place to place, delivering these packages, and no one ever says my name. Thank you. That was nice to hear."

Bart made a right turn and Peterson's office building came into view.

"Thank you, Bart. It was very kind of you to *break the rules*. I can't tell you how much I appreciate it," Helena said as Bart pulled up to the curb in front of Peterson's building.

The young man smiled. "You're welcome. I hope we meet again."

"Well dear, you might have to take me home with you if you don't come around to my side and help me out of the van. You know us older folks. Brittle bones. Balance might be slightly off."

In a flash, Bart was on the passenger side holding the door open, a hand extended. He even walked Helena through the front door of the medial office building. Like the rest of Bart's cargo that day, Helena was safely delivered to her precise destination.

~

When Helena walked through the door of Dr. Peterson's office, the receptionist at the front desk leapt out of her seat. "The doctor has been looking all over for you. Where have you been?"

Helena didn't like the woman's tone. "Living my life," she said rather defiantly.

The receptionist glared. "He needs to see you right away. He's a busy man and you've been gone for nearly two hours."

Two hours was a long time. Thirty minutes to grab a cup of coffee. Another hour or so to visit the hospital. *At least now,* Helena thought as the receptionist rushed her to Dr. Peterson's office, *I'm not going to be sitting in the waiting room.*

"You're back," the doctor said as he looked up from the paperwork on his desk. "I was worried we'd lost you. I wanted you to meet the young man you'd be helping, but he's gone now. We've scheduled his surgery for Monday morning. You have the weekend to get him settled. Earlier, I gave you his name and dorm information."

Helena nodded, patting her handbag where she'd placed the young man's information. But she still wasn't quite sure what the doctor meant by *getting him settled.*

"The plan is that he'll move in with you for a few days, and then, after the surgery, he'll stay with you for a few weeks."

"A few weeks?" Helena said as the scope of her role was becoming clear. "He's a young man. How can he possibly stay with me?"

Peterson furrowed his brow. "I thought you understood. You're going to take care of him while he recuperates."

Helena leaned forward. "I thought that meant I'd look in on him at his dorm room. Make sure he's taking his medication. Accompany him to follow-up appointments. I didn't think he'd be living with me. What do I have in common with a college student? Besides, I like my privacy. I'm a writer. I need my alone time. I can't be entertaining a stranger in my home."

Peterson frowned. "I don't think you appreciate the importance of this moment in this young man's life. He has few options. The surgery can't wait. We need a responsible adult to look after him. It'll just be for a few weeks. He'll remember your kindness for the rest of his life. Isn't that worth something?"

Helena wanted to kill Julie. What had that kooky activities director gotten her into?

"The next step," Peterson added, as if Helena was unable to think through the rest on her own, "is to meet the young man at his dorm, gather some of his things together, and get him settled in with you."

Helena chewed her lip. She'd have to get out of this. Perhaps she could use her dizzy spells as an excuse. Wasn't she just at the hospital? "I'm not a young woman," she said, stating the obvious.

Peterson leaned back in his chair and crossed his arms as if reconsidering the arrangement. "Maybe, you are too old," he seemed to almost gloat.

Helena winced. She couldn't yield to age. The very idea of presenting herself as frail and incompetent simply went against the grain. "Okay," she conceded. "You win. I'm in."

Peterson broke into a warm smile. An *I knew it* kind of smile.

She'd never felt more manipulated. Odd how the universe evens things out. She'd done a number on Bart, the Amazon driver and now Peterson had worked his magic on her. On the bright side, the wheels were in motion for this young man to have surgery. She couldn't back out. Maybe it wouldn't be so bad. What's two weeks in the course of a lifetime? The blink of an eye. She only hoped he was as nice as that kind Amazon driver. Heck, she'd have welcomed Bart into her home if he needed help. And she'd only spent ten minutes with him.

– 18 –

WHEN ZAK RETURNED to his dorm room after his lunch with Melinda, much to his surprise, Chuck and Marshall were entertaining a guest. An older woman was sitting at Zak's desk as Marshall took charge of the introductions. "This is Helena," he shouted so loudly Zak blushed. "She's here to help you prepare for surgery."

Zak scrunched his face. Was this the person he was supposed to meet at Peterson's office? She seemed so old. Really old. Unimaginably old. Peterson had explained that he'd arranged for someone to help him before and after the surgery, and that he'd be staying in their home. And when that person had failed to show for the appointment, Peterson suggested that she probably got sidetracked by errands and would catch up with Zak later at his dorm. But Peterson hadn't explained the woman would be an elderly lady. An old grandma. It seemed to Zak that he should be looking after her. Not vice versa.

Helena stood and held out a hand in greeting. "So nice to meet you."

Zak looked down at the stranger's wrinkled hand covered in brown spots. "No, no, no," he said, shaking his head and backing away. "This is all wrong. I can't do this."

Helena turned to Zak's friends as if they might have an explanation for Zak's reaction.

Marshall put an arm around Zak's shoulder and pulled him close. "What's wrong?" he shouted.

"How can I live with this stranger?" Zak moaned. "I can't hear. I don't know what's going on from moment to moment. And she's too old to help me. Much too old."

Helena put her hands on her waist, digging into the spot as if she were a fire hydrant about to be uncorked. "Old!" she barked so loudly that Chuck covered his ears, the sound reverberating off the walls of the tiny dorm room. "Don't you worry about me," she said, a thumb jabbing at her chest. "I can take care of myself, and I can take care of you. Just you try me."

Zak shook his head. He'd lip-read, *old*. And he caught *worry*. The rest was a garbled mess. But from Helena's brassy demeanor, he could tell he'd pissed her off. And though he himself was upset, that certainly wasn't his intention to upset her. Actually, he wasn't sure what his intention had been. All he knew was that he was frightened—of the surgery, of the hospital, and of the little old lady standing before him. The world was becoming a scary place. He couldn't help but lose his cool.

Chuck and Marshall exchanged glances and then words with Helena. "What are you saying?" Zak asked Chuck. "I see your lips moving."

Chuck grabbed his iPhone and texted Zak: *We told her you'll be okay. You need time to adjust. You're acting paranoid. It's your deafness speaking.*

Zak read Chuck's recap. Was it true? Did they think he was paranoid? Or had they really told the old woman they wanted him out of the room? Off the dorm floor. That he'd thrown a series of temper tantrums in the past. That he was losing it.

Becoming unstable. "I'm sorry," Zak said to Helena, as much an apology as an attempt to save his crumbling reputation as a decent person. "I appreciate what you're doing. But are you sure you're up for this?"

Helena shrugged and nodded affirmatively. "Absolutely."

Zak sighed. He had no choice. Who else was there to help him? The old woman was his only chance of getting the surgery. He just hoped she didn't drop dead while looking after him.

———❧———

"Can you believe this?" Zak said to Chuck as he packed a small roller bag. Helena and Marshall had excused themselves to wait for Zak in the lobby.

"It's pretty unusual," Chuck shouted back. "But she seems nice."

Zak winced. "She must be crazy to take me on. God only knows where she lives. Maybe a gingerbread house with an oven out back."

Together, they laughed. It felt good. There were just some moments when the absurdity of life needed to be embraced.

"My parents don't want anything to do with me, so I wind up with a woman who could be my mother's mother. Imagine that!" Zak zipped up his bag, turning his attention next to packing up his laptop. "Chuck," he said, stopping to sit on the edge of the bed. "I'm sorry about all this. I know it hasn't been easy and that we really don't know each other that well. I'm sorry I've been so tough to deal with. I'm really lucky to have you as a roommate. I just want you to know how much I appreciate your help. You've been a terrific friend."

Chuck nodded and pounded his chest with a fist in sympathetic King Kong connection.

"I just wish I wasn't so scared. I hope when the surgery is over, I'll be back to my normal self. If things don't work out . . ." Zak took a breath. "I'm not sure what I'll do."

Chuck made a face as if he'd sucked on a lemon.

Zak couldn't help but laugh.

"Try not to worry so much," Chuck shouted. "Peterson knows what he's doing. And that little old lady was nice."

Zak nodded. He'd caught exactly what Chuck was saying. Maybe his lip-reading skills were improving.

He lifted the computer bag and placed it on top of his roller bag. "Before I go, can I ask you a personal question? Are you and Marshall . . ." Zak hesitated, unsure how to finish.

Chuck crossed his arms and offered a crooked smile as if he didn't understand the question or had no intention of answering. Zak understood. It wasn't any of his business. Whatever was happening between Chuck and Marshall had nothing to do with him. Or his ear. And at the moment, his ear was the most important thing. "Never mind," Zak said. "It's okay. I get it."

Chuck pulled Zak into a bear hug. Zak, at first stiff, slowly relaxed. It was good to be physically comforted. An amazing feeling to be unconditionally accepted. When Chuck finally released Zak, he placed his hands on Zak's shoulders and gave him a gentle shake. It was a reassuring gesture, signaling that no matter what, their friendship would hold.

"I better get downstairs. Helena and Marshall are waiting for me." Zak scanned the room one last time, making sure he hadn't forgotten anything. "Imagine me living with a little old grandma. Maybe I'll come to like afternoon tea. Or learn how to needlepoint. I hope she doesn't ask me to sit in on a game of canasta with her friends. Hey, come to think of it, I'll finally be *the hot guy*," he teased. "The one all the women want to meet!"

"Grandmother types are perfect for you," Chuck shouted.

Zak smiled. "You'll come visit when you can, right?"

Chuck nodded. "I wouldn't miss it. I like older women."

Zak shook his head. He wasn't sure what Chuck had said.

Chuck grabbed a notepad and wrote it down.

"What's not to like?" Zak joked. "Golda Meir. Betty White."

"They're both dead," Chuck reminded him.

Zak sighed. He'd caught that. "Let's hope I don't kill this one. The odds are kind of running in my favor."

Chuck opened the door and jerked his head in the direction of the hallway, encouraging Zak to get a move on.

– 19 –

ELENA WONDERED WHAT the hell she'd gotten herself into, or more precisely, what the heck Julie had committed her to. A young man who couldn't hear was a most unlikely house guest, not to mention, a poor dinner companion. How would she communicate with him? The whole plan was sheer madness, and yet, she felt sorry for Zak. He seemed so helpless. So in need of attention. Maybe that was why Julie had brought them together. Perhaps Julie viewed her as someone who was also in need of attention. Someone who despite having two sons and grandchildren, had no real family around. After all, isn't that why she'd moved to Ventana? To ensure there would always be people nearby if she needed them? Still, she hadn't considered that someone as young as Zak could be so alone. That she, a senior citizen, and Zak, a college student, might actually share something in common.

"There you are," Helena said as Zak emerged from the guest bedroom and wandered into the kitchen. A batch of freshly baked chocolate chip cookies sat cooling on the counter. Her

Whole Foods magic trick. A frozen, premade, brown-butter batter pulled from the freezer and placed in a hot oven for fifteen minutes. Helena's secret weapon to communicating with a young man who couldn't hear. She'd coax him out of the bedroom with the aid of his nose.

"Those smell amazing."

She smiled, keenly aware that it was better to use facial expressions and hand gestures rather than her voice. If he couldn't hear, at the very least, he could see. "Help yourself," she said with the wave of a hand like Vanna White acknowledging the turn of a new letter on the *Wheel of Fortune* gameboard.

They were off to a good start as Zak gobbled down two cookies. Helena poured a tall glass of milk without asking Zak if he wanted it. Good—he took the glass and downed the milk. What else could they do together? It was only Friday afternoon and Zak wasn't due at the hospital for surgery until Monday morning at 6:00 a.m. How else could she entertain him?

Picking up a *People* magazine, she turned to a story on Michael Phelps. Zak looked at the cover photo and shrugged. She pointed to an inside photo of Phelps swimming in the pool. Then she pointed at Zak and put her palms together as if diving into a pool. "Do you want to go swimming?"

Zak shook his head. "I don't have a bathing suit."

Helena had an idea; she called Alan. "This is Helena," she said, fingers crossed. "By any chance, would you have access to a bathing suit for my houseguest?" Helena had spotted Alan using the indoor pool on a number of occasions and guessed he and Zak might be the same size. Sure enough, Alan had a clean bathing suit in his backpack and agreed to loan it to Zak. By four-thirty, Zak was in the Ventana pool swimming laps, and though Helena had no way of knowing if he was enjoying himself, she certainly knew nothing was better for relieving stress than exercise.

As she watched Zak through the glass wall that surrounded the pool, Julie sidled up next to her. "He's fast," Julie remarked as Zak took a turn off the pool's edge. "How are you managing? I meant to stop by, and then I thought maybe you two needed a little time alone. You've obviously got this under control."

Helena chuckled. "I feel like Gloria Swanson when she was a Mack Sennett starlet."

"I'm sorry," Julie said. "I don't understand."

"Gloria Swanson," Helena emphasized in a louder voice as if it might make anything clearer to Julie who'd never heard of Mack Sennett or the days of silent movies. "Never mind," Helena said, conceding that some references were lost on the younger generation. "How about Marlee Matlin?"

"You feel like you're deaf?"

Well, that wasn't exactly right. Helena could certainly hear. But, communicating with someone who couldn't hear did require a bit of pantomime and a lot of creativity. "It's a challenge," Helena admitted. "I don't want to stress him out using a voice he can't hear. His friends already warned me. Too much talking and he goes into a rage. I mean, who can blame him? He's been used to hearing his whole life and now, at eighteen, he's deaf. Unable to communicate. It's got to be a terrible thing for a youngster to face."

"But just look at him go," Julie said as Zak approached the end of a lap and with a quick flip, disappeared under the water line, gliding back toward the other end of the pool.

Helena smiled. "He's a strong swimmer."

"I just knew you'd be able to manage this."

Despite the compliment, Helena couldn't help but still feel annoyed with Julie. If anything, Zak's arrival was the ultimate imposition. "I appreciate your kind words, but honestly, putting this poor boy in such an uncomfortable situation where he has to move in with an old lady seems so wrong. My heart goes out to him, but I'm not sure I was the wisest choice."

Julie stepped back, a shocked expression on her face. "But I wasn't wrong. Here you are, handling this like a champ. And that boy," Julie said, pointing at Zak as he climbed out of the pool, dripping wet, "has for the moment transcended his personal troubles. He's lucky to have you in his corner. If you're angry at me, I can live with that, because I believe that you, like your peers in this building, are vital assets to the ASU community. Because unlike other places where seniors go to hide and die, this is not a retirement home. Not by a long shot. This is a place that requires you to be fully invested in life. Personally, I'd settle for nothing less."

Julie's impassioned speech rocked Helena to the core. She was instantly reminded of the women of her own generation. Their energy and commitment to bettering the world. Had she misjudged Julie? Had she misjudged the women of Julie's generation? Assumed that because they weren't marching in the streets, waving banners, that they were somehow less than? Perhaps, the Julies of the world experienced life in a more personal way. Person to person. Helena realized that Julie's perspective on aging was far more progressive than her own. Where Helena saw limitations, Julie saw opportunity. Yes, there was more to Julie than Helena had imagined. "I've upset you," Helena said sheepishly. "Worse, I've misjudged you, and for that, I apologize."

"Well, you wouldn't be the first," Julie acknowledged. "Some people think I'm a bubble-headed blond. Not that there's anything wrong with being blond. It's just another stereotype women have to deal with. Why is it so hard for people to believe a woman can be beautiful *and* intelligent? My goodness. Look at Beyoncé. Now who would doubt that woman has it going on? Or Lady Gaga. Or any Kardashian. Whether you love or hate them, they made money the honest way. Through brains and drive."

Helena thought Julie had a point. "You know, sweetie, the ditzy blond is a Hollywood creation men used to sell movie tickets. Jean Harlow, Marilyn Monroe, Jane Mansfield. There wasn't a dumb blond among them. It was all an act. No one could ever say Mae West was dumb. Do you know she wrote her own plays and film scripts. Her movies singlehandedly saved Paramount Studios from bankruptcy during the Great Depression. The woman was a genius. Well ahead of her time."

"I don't know any of those women," Julie admitted. "Well, I've heard of Marilyn."

"Everyone knows Marilyn," Helena said. "Whispery voice. Little-girl demeanor. Sexually alluring in a campy way. Non-threatening. I'm afraid that's how the world prefers to see us."

"Well, thank goodness those days are over."

Helena paused. Julie was right. She couldn't think of a present-day actress who had parlayed overt sexuality to build a film career. Not one. Perhaps there was something good to be said for the end of the good old days. Time had turned out to be the great equalizer. Women had made significant strides. If Julie was an example of the generation coming up, Helena was certain things were bound to get even better.

"I'm glad we had this talk," Helena admitted. "You've straightened me out on a few things."

Julie was unable to contain her shock. "Me!"

"Yes. Now, if you'd only tell me what to do with this young man for the next few weeks."

Julie didn't hesitate. "Teach him about life. How things don't always go your way. With each disappointment comes a lesson. Help him see that no matter how challenging life might be, there's always something to look forward to."

Helena nodded. "I wish I was as positive as you."

"Oh, but you must be," Julie insisted. "Just look at you. You've been a daughter, a journalist, an author, and now, you're a volunteer helping a young man through a dark period. You can do anything that you set your mind to."

Helena hadn't quite thought of it like that.

"Well, I better get back to work," Julie said as Zak came through the door, his regular clothes back on, a wet bathing suit rolled into a ball and dripping on the floor.

"Oh my," Helena said as she took the wet bathing suit.

"I've got this." Julie took the bathing suit and disappeared into the gym. A moment later, she returned with a towel wrapped about the wet suit.

Resourceful, Helena thought. *Very resourceful.*

By the time Helena showed up at the restaurant on the eleventh floor for dinner, the gang of three were deep in conversation. As Helena sat down, she caught the last few words. Something about age requirements. And though it had seemed like a lively discussion with Cynthia bobbing her head the way she always did when she started to lecture the others, once Helena joined the table, the conversation died. There was barely a peep as Helena looked about the table for an explanation. Something was off. But what, she couldn't quite determine. "What were you three old hens pecking at?" she teased as she glanced at the menu. She'd need to order something to bring back to Zak. He'd passed on joining her, preferring the company of a video game on his computer that involved lasers, robots, and God only knows what else. Helena had only caught a peek of it.

"Who are you calling an *old hen*?" Cynthia said in a huff.

Helena created a definition on the spot. "Anyone over eighty who is sitting at this table."

"That lets me out," Babs laughed.

"Me too," Donna agreed.

"Well, I'm certainly not eighty yet," Cynthia complained.

"Oh," Helena observed. "Then I'm the oldest one at the table."

"Yes, you are," Cynthia spat out. "You're the *oldest hen* here."

"That can't be possible," Helena insisted. "There must be others in the room who are in their eighties?"

"Well, there's Margaret Ann." Cynthia used her long chin to point toward a table across the way. "Poor thing."

Margaret Ann sat slumped slightly forward in her chair, one of the other guests cutting the baked chicken she'd ordered for dinner. Helena couldn't recall meeting Margaret Ann.

"She's visiting us tonight," Babs whispered.

Helena didn't quite understand. "She doesn't live in independent living?"

"She resides in assisted living," Donna corrected her. "Six months ago, she tripped playing pickleball. That game can be so dangerous. She broke a hip and then when she was in rehab, she had a stroke. She's never been the same. Believe it or not, she used to be the mah-jongg champion at Ventana. But look at her now."

Helena was doing just that. Looking. Margaret Ann's fork hovered near her mouth holding the tiniest bit of chicken. As the fork got closer to its destination, the shaking of her hand freed the tidbit, dropping it into her lap. "The poor dear can barely use her utensils," Helena observed.

"She has a long road ahead of her," Cynthia chimed in. "She needs speech and physical therapy and then she'll be back in the saddle again. Meanwhile, there's no point in her buying next year's mah-jongg card."

Helena gasped. "How old is she?"

"Your age," Babs announced as breezily as if discovering gifts under the tree at Christmas time.

Helena blanched what felt like a new shade of white.

"But not to worry, dear," Donna added. "Should anything happen to you, the three of us would help feed you if you were still interested in coming to the dining room. That's what friends are for."

Helena thought that little compensation for what looked like a miserable experience.

Margaret Ann suddenly shifted her gaze and made eye contact with Helena. She lifted a bony finger, and like an inchworm in Helena's Biltmore garden, made a weak yet determined wiggle in Helena's direction. Helena smiled, hoping she wasn't watching a preview of the future. "I'd prefer to just drop dead," she innocently said. "Let it be quick, and a surprise."

"Now that's rude," Cynthia snarled in her fiercest tone yet. "Are you saying lovely Margaret Ann is better off dead?"

Helena caught herself. Surely that had not been her intention, and yet, it certainly seemed that what she'd said could be interpreted that way. "I simply meant I'd rather not suffer."

Babs *hmphed.* "You think that's suffering? Look at her. She has a roof over head and clean clothes on her back. No doubt she's freshly bathed. And she's alive. Any other choice about her life would be the equivalent of aborting the elderly."

Cynthia inched forward. "You can't abort someone who is already born. That makes no sense."

"Perhaps not, but you can make comments that lead others to believe that seniors who face health challenges should no longer be here. We all deserve to live our lives with dignity. Even those of us who are infirmed," Babs said.

"What about those on life support?" Donna asked.

Babs didn't hesitate. "That's a family's decision. Not mine."

Donna clearly didn't care for Babs' answer. "What if the family doesn't want them around?"

Cynthia jumped in. "Well, that's why we have medical powers of attorney and living wills. To protect us from overzealous relatives."

Helena was curious. "Have any of you actually visited the assisted living floor?"

Cynthia pushed away from the table with a sudden jerk. "Of course not. Why would we?"

"I close my eyes whenever the elevator stops at three," Babs admitted. "I don't even want to see the hallway."

"I've been there," Donna said. "My husband was on that floor for two years before he passed last month."

Helena was surprised to learn Donna was a recent widow. "Last month. I'm sorry. How long were you married?"

Donna sighed. "We were married for forty-one years. Before you ask, I am not okay. I seem okay . . . but I'm not. But we have to go on living. What other choice do we have? I'm not going to crawl into the grave with him. Still, I miss him terribly. I've good days and bad days, but there's a secret to getting through this horrible grieving."

All three women leaned forward.

"Netflix!" Donna said with impish delight.

Cynthia's brow shot up. "Television?"

"Not just television," Donna explained. "Netflix has these wonderful Hallmark movies. There's love and romance and always a happy ending. Life might be disappointing, but Hallmark never is."

Babs sought clarification. "You watch romance to get through the loss of your husband?"

"I know," Donna admitted, "it's strange. But I find it so compelling. No one is ever sick. Everyone is young and beautiful. Love conquers all. What more could a grieving widow want to distract herself?"

"A life," Cynthia blurted.

"I think it's sweet," Helena added. "But I've never been much for romance. I actually don't believe in romance. Does that make me an awful person?"

Donna cringed. "That's a shame. Didn't you ever have romantic dinners with your husband or go on long walks? Or just sit together and talk about future plans."

Helena laughed. "My two husbands didn't live long enough for me to enjoy any of those activities. Raising my two sons obliterated any chance for romance. Being a journalist and then an author grounded me in realism. I can't really say romance had any part in my life. I'd always thought of it as a Hollywood creation to sell tickets. Real people lead real lives."

"That's sad," Cynthia said.

Surely, Helena thought, if anyone at the table was grounded in reality, it'd be Cynthia.

"Life is tough enough," Cynthia added. "A little romance can be a terrific way to spark things up."

Babs giggled. "Okay, Cynthia. Out with it. We want to know. Tell us all about your dirty little secret. We're all ears."

"Dirty secret, indeed. There's nothing dirty about a man and woman coming together in an intimate setting with a little soft music and a glass of wine to explore each other's needs."

Donna laughed. "I see a Hallmark movie in our future."

Cynthia continued. "He was tall, dark, and from Harlem. I was working late when we met. Grading papers. I taught a night-class at Queens College when I was starting out as a lawyer."

Babs gasped. "A student?"

Cynthia exhaled. "Yes. A college student. He was only seven years younger. It wasn't like I was robbing the cradle."

"Shameful," Babs joked.

"No, you were rocking the cradle," Donna added.

Babs giggled. "Rocking and rolling that cradle!"

"Does it qualify as romance?" Helena asked. "It sounds more like a roll in the hay."

Cynthia beamed. "I leave the rest to your imagination. Let me just say, having that kind of experience when you're young can warm your heart for years to come when you're older."

Donna looked over at Margaret Ann. "I hope she has some warm memories to keep her going."

"Me too," Babs said.

"But wait," Helena interrupted. "When I sat down, you three were talking about age requirements."

"Were we?" Cynthia said with an elusive look.

Helena was working on a plate of chicken Kiev when Aggie circled back to refill the water glasses. "Aggie, when we're done eating, would you please bring me an order of chicken soup, toasted rye bread, and rice pudding to go?"

"A little late-night snacking?" Babs asked, eyes wide in wonder.

"Oh no," Helena mused. "I meant to tell you when I sat down, but we got sidetracked. I have a guest staying with me. A young man attending ASU."

Aggie remained glued to the spot, notepad in hand, obviously mesmerized by Helena's news.

"Is he a relative?" Cynthia asked.

"He's a student having surgery Monday morning. I'm kind of his housemother for the next few weeks."

Donna leaned forward. "That sounds like fun."

"Nonsense," Cynthia demurred. "A college student doesn't belong here."

"You were talking about this when I sat down," Helena said, referring to how quiet they'd all become when she'd first joined the table.

Babs picked up the thread. "Gilbert saw you from a distance with a young man in the lobby. He asked me if that was your grandson. I told him, I had no idea."

Helena hadn't considered there might be a problem with Zak's visit. Wouldn't Julie have known if there was an issue? How else could she make such an arrangement? "It seems like this building is comprised of prying eyes."

Cynthia didn't miss a beat. "We have rules that limit the stay of family members. But a stranger? That's certainly not allowed."

"Don't be so darn mean," Babs chimed in. "I'm sure Helena isn't doing anything wrong. Are you, Helena?"

Helena wasn't sure. Still, there was no reason to appear anything but confident. "Absolutely not. Of course not. I'd never do anything wrong," she said with a clear conscience as she locked eyes with Aggie.

Aggie flipped her pen back and forth on the order pad. "An ASU student?"

Helena offered a weak smile. "Ventana is ASU-affiliated. It's not like I'm moving a stranger into my guest room. Besides, he needs my help."

Donna laughed. "Cynthia's young man from Harlem needed her help too."

Cynthia brayed. "How dare you! I told you that in confidence and now you're using it against me. Well, I just don't know if I can trust you." She crossed her arms defiantly. "This is a very disappointing turn of events."

Babs ignored Cynthia. "Tell us all about your student. What is he studying? Where is he from? How old is he? And where are his parents?"

"Is he cute?" Donna wanted to know with a twinkle in her eye.

Helena knew nothing beyond the basic facts: name, surgery date, and freshman. And yes, he was cute. The rest was a mystery. Though she'd been guaranteed by Dr. Peterson that he wasn't an escaped convict with a penchant for murdering little old ladies.

"Don't you think a student might prefer a cheeseburger and fries?" Aggie suggested.

"Absolutely," Donna agreed.

"Okay, then," Helena conceded. "A burger and fries it is."

"When do we meet him?" Donna wanted to know.

"I'm not sure. He's shy."

Donna raised her chin as if about to pronounce the winner of a presidential election. "If his surgery is Monday, that gives us a whole two days to get acquainted."

There was no way that Helena would expose Zak to the ladies at the table. If she knew him better, perhaps. But she didn't. "There's one problem . . ." she said as she worried whether it was a breach of confidentiality to reveal facts about Zak's health.

"He's afraid of older women," Aggie guessed as she looked at the occupants of the table before settling her eyes on Cynthia. "I completely understand. So am I."

Helena waved at Aggie to stop. "He has a significant hearing loss."

"Well, then he's perfect for this group," Aggie said. "There isn't anything said at this table worth hearing."

Cynthia pulled her head back as if she'd been slapped. "Now how would you know? You're never around to take our orders."

"You don't think your voices carry? I can hear you clear across the room complaining at every meal. *Where's Aggie? When will she take our order? What's the matter with her?*"

Helena blushed. Babs looked down. Donna covered her mouth with her hand. Cynthia straightened up like one of those inflatables announcing a sale at a used car lot.

"Shame on you, listening in on our conversation," Cynthia bristled.

"As if I had a choice." Aggie said as she turned and stomped off.

Cynthia's eyes bulged. "Oh my God. She did it again. She didn't take our dessert order."

***

After dinner, Helena returned to the condo. Zak was sitting in the living room, busy doing whatever young people do on their phones. When he looked up, Helena waved him over, setting him up for his evening meal at the kitchen counter. Zak hopped on a stool and without hesitation, dug in. Aggie had been right. The burger and fries were a hit.

While Zak ate, Helena stepped out onto the terrace. It was a gorgeous Arizona sunset, the sky a lovely shade of pink as the sun dipped below the horizon. *This is a good thing I'm doing,* she thought, proud of herself as she leaned forward on the terrace railing and admired the view. November's autumn air was dipping into the sixties at night, and for denizens of the desert used to the summer's triple-digit temperatures, it was nippy. Helena thought about going back inside and grabbing a sweater, but then she heard that voice. The one she'd known since the day she was born.

He's troubled. You know that.

Helena knew no such thing. As far as she was concerned, Zak was just a young man who needed a place to stay before and after surgery. Nothing more, nothing less.

Talk to him, Ruthie urged. *Get to know him.*

Helena rolled her eyes. Talk to him! That was easier said than done. She'd already struggled on the ride over from Zak's dorm room, thankful she had an expressive face. That alone bridged much of the gap. The rest was done through hand gestures and pantomime. Bad pantomime, if she had to judge.

He's done eating now and he's coming outside. Engage him.

Sure enough, the sliding glass door to the terrace opened and out stepped Zak. To Helena, he had a striking resemblance to a Hollywood heartthrob. The angular features. The dark hair. The square jaw. Maybe a teen idol from long ago. She'd searched her memory but couldn't quite put her finger on a name. But it was someone famous. Someone who she'd definitely know, if only she could come up with it.

"Hi," she said, palm up in a universal greeting.

"It's a nice night," he answered as he looked toward the horizon.

She nodded, the very least she could do. How could she connect with someone who couldn't hear? The only sign language she knew involved the middle finger. Hopefully, there wouldn't be any need for that.

Zak smiled. "Thank you for the burger."

Helena returned the smile. *Uh oh,* she thought. Would they spend the next few weeks smiling at each other? Was that how this awkwardness would morph and take over her life?

Zak continued to look straight ahead. "I'm sorry about all of this. Really. This whole thing snuck up on me. I've always been deaf in my left ear. That was no big deal. But this . . . being totally deaf is different."

Helena wondered about Zak's family. It was cruel for Zak to be on his own at such a young age.

Zak seemed to read Helena's mind, or maybe, it was the elephant in the room (or on the terrace). The topic that couldn't be avoided. "My parents have given up on me," he admitted. "And I've overwhelmed my friends. The truth is, my friends and I don't really know each other very long. I've been a complete pain in the . . ." Zak caught himself before uttering the last word. "Well, you know where."

Helena thought there was something awfully sweet in Zak's demeanor. Was it the shyness? Or that he was self-reflective? One didn't expect a handsome young man to be so vulnerable.

Zak turned to make eye contact with Helena. "I know I'm feeling sorry for myself, but honestly, it's so unfair. When I came out as gay, my folks wanted nothing to do with me." He closed his eyes.

Helena's heart sank. So that was it. The explanation for the absent parents.

Zak arched a brow. "I guess I can't blame them. It wasn't how I was raised. I should have known better."

Helena struggled to contain herself. But she couldn't. "You shouldn't ever apologize for who you are," she said. But Zak hadn't been looking her way. Her words had literally fallen on deaf ears. Realizing this, she placed a hand on his arm. He turned to her. She gave the arm a gentle squeeze to convey her compassion.

"You're very kind," he said as he returned to staring off into the distance.

Helena was disappointed in herself. She'd totally misread the situation. This young man needed more than her spare bedroom. He needed her guidance. There had to be a way to effectively communicate with him. She wouldn't rest until she figured out how to make that happen.

⌘

The next morning, while sitting at the kitchen counter sipping her coffee, Helena racked her brain to figure out what to do with Zak. Should she suggest a walk? Take him to the Phoenix Zoo? Perhaps he might enjoy a stroll through Phoenix's Botanical Gardens. Whatever she planned, she knew it had to be visual. Something they could do together that might distract him from worrying about his upcoming surgery.

You don't have to entertain him, Ruthie whispered. *Just let him be. He can figure things out on his own.*

"Absolutely not," Helena said. "He's a guest. I need to be a good hostess."

"Good morning," Zak said as he came down the hallway. "Are you talking to yourself?"

"You heard me!" Helena said, surprised.

Zak scrunched up his face and pointed at Helena's mouth. "I saw your lips moving." He offered a sexy, crooked smile. "My eyes work perfectly well."

Helena marveled at how strikingly good-looking Zak was when he smiled. Almost like Keanu Reeves. That was it! Zak looked like Keanu Reeves. Helena had been a big fan of *The Matrix*.

"Do you often talk to yourself?" Zak asked.

Helena blushed. The truth was, she did. Not necessarily because she was communicating with Ruthie. She didn't need to speak aloud to do that. Communicating with Ruthie could be purely a mental exercise. Still, she did from time-to-time talk to herself. A habit she'd developed living alone. Sometimes it was comforting to hear a voice, even if that voice was her own. Perhaps that was the ultimate definition of loneliness. The need to carry on a conversation with yourself, by yourself, for yourself. "I'm not quite sure how to do this," Helena said loudly as she tapped an ear. "How do I communicate with you?"

"It's frustrating, isn't it?" Zak answered as he read her lips. Helena concurred.

"We can write notes. If that's okay," Zak offered. "I can use my laptop, and you can type whatever you might want to know."

Helena thought the idea, genius. If there was one thing she was excellent at, it was typing. After all, as an author, typing was her gig.

"But first, is there any cereal or coffee?" Zak said as he rubbed his tummy.

Helena chuckled. All of her concern about being a good hostess and she'd forgotten to offer Zak something to eat. If the grandmothers of America ever found out, she was certain they'd tear up her membership card. She could see the headlines: *Senior Attempts to Starve Hungry College Student While Being a Horrible Hostess.*

After Zak consumed a bowl of Raisin Bran and had a cup of coffee firmly in hand, Helena sat next to him on the sofa and started to type. At first, the questions were basic: How old was he? Where was he born? Did he have any siblings? Slowly, the questions progressed. Zak shared the problems with his family. He described his job at The Windy Canyon Bar, his worries about pursuing pre-med as a major, the missed classes, and his upcoming midterms. On and on Helena typed away on the laptop. She asked questions and Zak quickly answered. Before long, Zak was asking Helena about her life. Where was she born? Did she have a family? Why had she agreed to help him? The laptop moved from one lap to the other as Helena typed her answers and Zak read them. With each exchange, Helena slipped in a bit of humor. She talked about experiencing a second childhood at Ventana. How she was learning to make friends all over again. How everyone was afraid of the third floor. About Babs closing her eyes when the elevator doors opened on three. Zak laughed when he read that part. And then the mood between them suddenly changed. "I'm really scared about the surgery," Zak admitted, his voice breaking. "I'm afraid I may never hear again."

Helena certainly didn't want to whitewash Zak's concerns. *Life is scary*, she typed, unwilling to deny his feelings and unsure if she should weigh in on the potential outcome of the surgery. What if it didn't work? What if Zac turned out to be permanently deaf? Should she offer false hope? But she also didn't want to discourage him. How could she recognize what he was going through, acknowledge his fear, and still provide emotional comfort? *Being scared is to be human. We're all scared at times*, she added.

Zak nodded. "I've been scared most of my life. Does it get better?"

Helena wondered how to respond. The simple answer was to say, *Of course it gets better*. And she did feel that to be mostly true. But *being scared* had also followed her throughout her life. Truth be told, she was a little scared as she sat on the sofa next to Zak. Well, maybe more than a little scared. After all, she was eighty-three, and even though she tried not to think about it, she did faint at the most unexpected moments. But then, did anyone ever faint when expected? Wasn't that only in those silly screwball comedies from the 1930s? And they don't make those movies anymore. But she was also scared of the next ten years. She'd tried to suppress the fear . . . to not look at it. It was the dark little secret she kept hidden in the deepest recesses of her mind. But it was a reality. Where would she be in ten years? She'd spent so much of her youth mapping out her future that the mere suggestion of a future at her current age was terrifying. Not simply because of death, though she didn't think that final moment would be much fun. But she was mostly concerned about remaining healthy while she finished learning whatever she'd come into life to learn.

You have your whole life ahead of you, Helena typed. *Of course, it's scary.*

"But does it get better?" he asked again, watching her lips. "They keep saying it gets better."

What could she say? She typed her answer. *Life isn't a straight line. It's more like peaks and valleys. Ups and downs. Sometimes it's scary, then other times, it's wonderful. Right now, you're facing a moment. The trick is to be brave and hope for the best.*

"But what if things don't work out?" he asked.

Helena sighed as she steadied the Dell on her lap. She hadn't expected such a tough back and forth. Why were Zak's questions triggering her own issues? *They always work out . . . just not the way you might expect. As long as you're alive, you have choices. If you don't like the result of a choice . . . you choose again. Through every hardship, there's a lesson learned. It might not seem fair. It might not be just. It might not be what you think makes sense. But there's always something . . . a kernel of truth to help you understand who you are.*

Over the next hour, the age gap between Helena and Zak melted away as two very different generations opened up to one another. Two minds connected through an understanding that life was an adventure, sometimes bumpy, sometimes smooth, but forever changing. After the hour, Zak leaned back on the sofa and stretched his arms overhead. "I think I'll lay down. I'm kind of tired."

Helena understood. She too felt worn out. On reflection, it seemed a miracle that she had survived the most difficult times in her life. Burying two husbands. Building a career. Writing her first novel. Watching her children leave to create their own lives. Losing Ruthie. So many moments when she'd picked herself up and started over again. Perhaps that was what life was about.

Starts and restarts. She'd spent so much of her life rushing about, too busy to give any of it much thought. But in the last decade, that had changed. She was frequently alone with her thoughts. And why was that? Had her sons simply abandoned her? Or was their distance a sign she'd done her job well? She couldn't decide if she was being too easy or too hard on them. And now, with the limited time she had left, did she have the guts and the will to revitalize a writing career? Would anyone be interested in what an eighty-three-year-old woman had to say?

Zak turned to her. "Can I hug you?"

Helena moved the laptop to the coffee table and shifted slightly on the sofa to face Zak. She opened her arms wide. Zak fell into them and there they both sat, Helena hugging a frightened young man, and Zak reminding an older woman that fear comes to the young as well as the old.

After a midmorning nap, Helena met the ladies for lunch in the Ventana dining room. She'd left Zak in the guest bedroom watching closed caption television. Closed caption was the trick she used to follow her favorite shows. It wasn't that she couldn't hear the dialogue, though sometimes that was true, but mostly because the actors tossed out their lines so quickly that it was nearly impossible to understand them. And then there were shows like *Ted Lasso*. Without closed-captioning, Helena wouldn't have a clue what the actors were even saying with those thick British accents.

"Where's your houseguest?" Cynthia asked with noticeable disappointment as Helena approached the table.

"He's resting."

"Oh no," Babs moaned. "We were all looking forward to meeting him."

Donna looked positively mad. "We were counting on it."

Helena was awed. Whatever made her think her mealtime companions might be annoyed at having a youngster in their midst? Instead, they evinced a level of empathy she'd rarely seen them offer each other. "Ladies, I'm touched," Helena said, a hand on her heart, "at your kindness."

"Nonsense," Cynthia snapped as Helena slid into her seat. "Kindness has nothing to do with it."

Helena nearly laughed. Clearly, the last thing Cynthia wanted to be accused of was being kind.

"You're just so lucky," Babs cooed. "To help someone in need. How blessed this young man is to have someone like you in his life."

"Frankly, I'm jealous," Donna admitted. "Don't get me wrong. I'm very active in the volunteer community. Last year, I pulled together quite a few items for the Phoenix Art Museum's silent auction. But Helena, what you're doing is so very special. You're actually hands-on, changing a life."

"I used to donate my time to the ASPCA," Babs admitted. "But now, I'm too old to even do that."

"For heaven's sake, why is that?" Cynthia asked with the huff and gruff of an old schoolmarm correcting a wayward student for forgetting to finish a class assignment.

"For one thing, my balance is off. How could I walk those large, high-energy dogs?"

"What about the cats? Cats need attention too."

"I've never been a cat person."

Cynthia snorted. "Seems like it might be a great time to start."

Donna interrupted with a hand on Cynthia's arm as if to hold back her latest diatribe. "Never mind about volunteering," she said. "I want to hear about the young man. Helena, what's he like?"

Helena wondered how she could sum up Zak. What might she reveal without revealing too much? "He's handsome. Tall, dark. A good-looking guy. He's eighteen. An ASU freshman pursuing a pre-med major."

"Eighteen?" Donna responded. "He's just a baby."

"Aren't they all," Babs reflected.

Donna wrapped her arms about herself. "Do you remember the first time you were with a guy?"

"Who can remember that far back?" Cynthia answered.

Donna scoffed. "Oh, don't lie. You remember. I remember."

Cynthia grumbled. "The first time is always awkward and scary."

Babs raised an eyebrow. "Not if you do it right."

Helena clicked her tongue. How could the mere mention of her houseguest lead the conversation into such unsavory waters. She looked for Aggie. Where was she? "Are we ready to order?" she asked the ladies, hoping Aggie might come by.

"Don't waste your breath," Cynthia said. "She's missing in action again."

"You haven't seen her yet?" Helena asked, concerned about Aggie's well-being. Despite Aggie's poor waitressing skills, she'd always been there. Even Cynthia had to admit Aggie's attendance record was exemplary.

"She must be out sick," Babs said.

And then through the swinging door, Aggie emerged from the kitchen.

"She's here," Helena said as she spotted Aggie coming their way.

"Yes, she is," Cynthia grumbled. "Here, but not *here*."

As if on cue, Aggie crossed the room, order pad in hand. "Good afternoon, ladies. Are you ready with your orders?"

"Yes," Babs said, "but can you tell me the soup of the day?"

Aggie scratched the back of her head with the pencil's eraser. "I'll have to check," she said, turning around and heading back toward the kitchen.

"Now look what you've done," Cynthia cried out. "I'm hungry. Who knows when she'll be back?"

Helena came to Aggie's defense. "You're much too hard on her. No wonder she toys with you."

"Well," Cynthia said. "You're sitting at this table too. She's also snubbing you."

Helena's stomach gurgled. Cynthia was right. And though Helena was also growing irritated with Aggie's shenanigans, the first thought that came to Helena's mind about her membership at the table was the old farmers' advice: when you wallow with pigs, expect to get dirty.

– 20 –

THE MORNING OF the surgery, Zak's confidence wavered. His last meal had been twelve hours earlier and he was hungry. No, not hungry. Starved. And though Helena had awakened him with a quick shake at five a.m., he hadn't slept well, tossing and turning all night, worrying. It wasn't until he was wheeled into the surgical suite on a gurney, IV hooked up and the anesthesiologist at his side, that he truly realized a surgeon was about to cut into his good ear. The ear he'd come to rely on all of his young life. The ear that allowed him to pass in the hearing world. And as he counted backward, waiting for the anesthesia to take effect, he had the horrible feeling that his life was about to take a terrible turn.

⌇

Opening his eyes in the recovery room, Zak was surprised to find Helena standing by his side, holding a cup of water. She placed a straw to his lips. He took a sip and closed his eyes, drifting off, content not to be here, there, or anywhere.

When Zak next awoke, he was alone in a hospital room. He shifted about, trying to sit up and relieve the pressure on his lower back. The IV in his hand was gone. In its place, there was a white bandage. Had he slept all day? Or was it morning? He wasn't sure until the nurse showed up. She said something he couldn't understand as she opened the blinds, allowing sunlight to flood the room. Zak's heart sank. She continued to talk but he couldn't hear a word. Nothing at all.

The nurse checked his temperature and pulse. *Your pulse is fast*, he lip-read as she checked the bandages on Zak's right ear that held the surgeon's packing. The ear ached when she pulled on the lobe and as she poked about, adjusting something or other, his breakfast tray arrived. Seconds seemed like minutes until the nurse was finally done with his slow torture and focused her attention on the portable bedside table that held Zak's breakfast tray. She shifted the table about until it was positioned directly in front of him. Orange juice and coffee in lidded disposable cups. She lifted a metal dome that covered a plate of scrambled eggs, bacon, and toast. He didn't feel much like eating. He didn't feel much like doing anything. As far as he was concerned, if he'd died at that very moment, it would have been a relief.

"I'll be back later," he lip-read as the nurse pointed to a button on the remote control that rested by his hip. The button had a cartoon drawing of a nurse's face. She said something else, but he had no idea what. He guessed the button was to be pushed in case of emergencies, but Zak wouldn't be pushing the button because the only emergency he had was being permanently deaf and that apparently wasn't fixable.

How easy life had once been. Simple. Uncomplicated. Now, everything had been turned upside down. He stared at his hands. Was it truly possible to communicate with one's fingers. Would this be the primary way he'd be interacting with the world?

When Helena entered the room, his eyes were closed. When he opened them, he jumped, startled by her sudden presence. Of course he hadn't heard her arrive, but then, how could he? She held a small vase filled with yellow daisies which she placed on the windowsill. She held up a hand in greeting and smiled. Zak was furious. How could anyone smile on such an awful day? The day when his world had imploded. Raging, he pushed the breakfast tray away, knocking the unopened coffee onto its side. He covered his eyes with his hands. If the world couldn't be as he wished, he could block it out.

Helena moved closer.

He sensed her presence. He dropped his hands from his face and watched her inspect the breakfast tray, righting the Styrofoam coffee cup. She caught his gaze. She spoke slowly so that he might read her lips. "Would you like a cinnamon bun from the café downstairs?"

Zak didn't respond.

"You can't hear me," she said softly as she stroked his arm.

He jerked his arm away as tears filled his eyes. It was all so unfair. What had he ever done to warrant such a punishment? His thoughts shifted to his parents. How angry they'd been at him for disappointing them. How they'd essentially ended the relationship. Was that his fault? Was he truly to blame for being gay? Could this be his punishment? None of it made any sense. Still, there had to be a reason why he was deaf.

Helena moved the portable table and made a spot for herself on the edge of Zak's bed. Zak let out a wail. His body heaved. Helena scooted closer to him. He read her lips. "Life is sometimes unfair," she said. "I'm so sorry."

He leaned into her open arms and wept as she gently rocked him.

"I need to speak with Zak's surgeon," Helena told the head nurse. "When do you expect him?"

The nurse checked the schedule. "I'm sorry. Dr. Peterson was here earlier. He won't be back until tomorrow. But the hospitalist will be making rounds later. About three p.m."

Helena winced. "But I want to speak to Dr. Peterson, directly. The surgeon. Not the hospitalist."

The young woman shifted her gaze as if the conversation was over. "I'm sorry. That's the best I can do for you, ma'am."

Helena gasped. There it was: that secret weapon. *Ma'am.* Helena suspected that the young woman thought by calling her *ma'am*, Helena might go away. Wasn't that how civilized conversations ended? Throw out a *ma'am*, and an older woman is supposed to shut up.

"Now, hear me loud and clear," Helena said, her heart beating rapidly as she raised her voice. "I want that hospitalist here pronto."

The nurse's expression shifted from disinterest to concern as she once again made eye contact with Helena. "Ma'am . . ." she started to say.

"Don't even go there," Helena warned, "otherwise, I'm going to throw the biggest stink this hospital has ever seen. And trust me, no one wants that. Do they?"

"Why no," the nurse agreed as she paged the hospitalist.

Helena waited patiently in Zak's room as the minutes ticked by. Fast asleep, Zak's breakfast tray remained untouched. She didn't have the heart to wake him and force him to eat. But he'd need to eat soon. After all, he hardly had any weight on his already lean frame. Just as she was plotting what to get him for lunch to spike his appetite, a young physician appeared in the doorway. "Were you looking for me?" he asked. "I'm Dr. Bigly."

Helena charged the door, pulling the doctor into the hallway. She gripped his arm tightly as if he might fly away at any moment. "Doctor, have you spoken to the surgeon. How did everything go?"

Dr. Bigly towered over Helena. "And you are . . ."

"I'm Zak's grandmother," she lied.

Bigly nodded. "The tumor was removed. Everything looked clean."

"Clean?" Helena asked. What the heck did that mean? You clean the floor. You clean the refrigerator. Well, some people do. But an ear. A tumor. How does clean work for that? "But he's still deaf," she said as if the hospitalist was unaware of Zak's condition.

"He's deaf for the moment. The ear is packed with antibiotic gel. Much like a thick Jell-O. But it will dissolve with time. Plus, the bandages are blocking out sound. He needs to heal before we know more. In the meantime, speak loudly. His hearing might be about fifty percent of what it was before the tumor broke through the eardrum."

"The eardrum?" Helena knew about the tumor but nothing about the eardrum.

"Dr. Peterson had to rebuild the torn eardrum using a graft from the inside of Zak's ear canal."

Helena nodded. The surgery had been more complicated than Dr. Peterson had shared with her. "But he will hear," she said, eager for confirmation.

"We certainly hope so," the hospitalist said. "But we'll know more when the packing is removed."

Helena sighed. It was hopeful news.

"Now, if you'll excuse me. I have to get back to my rounds."

She almost said *don't let me hold you* until she realized she was still tightly clasping onto the poor man's arm, delaying his departure.

When Helena returned to Zak's hospital room, he was gently snoring. She wasn't surprised that he'd be so tired. Nothing was more exhausting than being a patient in the hospital. The staff constantly interrupts your sleep, waking you up to tend to this or that, and though you might be lying in bed, the mattress wasn't a Serta Perfect Sleeper. If anything, the bed was more akin to a gurney sporting a hard, thin mattress with no give at all. An instrument of torture for those who had to endure it.

She slid a chair close to Zak's bedside as he opened his eyes. "Big news," he said with an alarmed expression. "I have to go to the bathroom."

Helena pressed the call button for the nurse. They waited for a response, but there was none. After a few moments, she headed down the hall to the nurses' station. The desk was unoccupied. Where could they have all gone?

When she returned to Zak's room, he was sitting straight up, the covers pulled back, feet touching the floor. "Whoa-ho!" she called out, one palm held up for him to stop what he was doing. She rushed to the bathroom, quickly returning with a yellow plastic jug that she waved in the air.

Zak shook his head from side to side.

Helena shook her head up and down.

"I'm not using that," he said emphatically.

Okay, she decided. If the plastic jug was a no-go, she'd have to do the next best thing. She positioned herself close to the bed as Zak scooched to the edge, the hospital gown hung limply in front of him. She focused her eyes on the floor waiting for his weight to shift off the bed. "Take it easy," she said as though he could hear her. "I've got you," she whispered as Zak stood to his full height. She grabbed ahold of his elbow as he leaned in her direction. The back of his gown parted like the Red Sea. "Slow," she warned as Zak glided along the floor, barely lifting his feet, his size and weight dwarfing her tiny frame.

"I got it," he said as he passed over the bathroom's threshold.

But she didn't let go until he was firmly planted on the toilet seat, her eyes focused on her reflection in the bathroom mirror. There she stood, nearby, and waited as Zak relieved himself, her back toward him until she heard the final tinkle.

"All done?" she asked as she turned to her young friend.

Zak's face was bright red. The kind of red she'd hoped for in the Pearson tomatoes she'd once grown in her Phoenix garden. "Thank you," came a small voice, barely recognizable as Zak's.

"No worries," she said as he struggled to stand up.

Once on his feet, she ran the water in the sink, handing him a soapy washcloth for his hands, and then a towel. With his hands dried, she readied herself for the return trip back.

"I'm sorry," he repeatedly muttered as they slowly made their way.

"There's no reason to be embarrassed," she shouted, hoping he might hear her. "We all go to the bathroom. It's normal. A healthy part of being alive."

⚬⚬⚬

On Zak's second day in the hospital, he awoke to find Melinda watching him from the chair in the corner. "Hello, sleepyhead," she said. "You're finally awake."

"You're here," Zak said. His voice sounded like he was in a tunnel, far off from Melinda.

"That's some bandage you've got on," she mused as she came closer to plant a kiss on his left cheek, avoiding the right ear. "How are you doing?"

"A little better," he answered. "My head doesn't ache as much. They removed some of the exterior bandages late last night. The final bandages will come off in another week."

"Good. Is there anything I can get you? Maybe something to eat?"

"What did you say?" Zak said with a sudden rush of excitement as he jerked straight up in bed.

"Do you want something to eat from downstairs?" Melinda repeated.

"Oh my God," he shouted. "I can hear you!"

Melinda smiled. "Of course you can hear me. Isn't that why you had surgery?"

"No, you don't understand," he sang out with exuberance. "I was certain I'd never hear again. When I came out of surgery, I couldn't hear, and now, I can definitely hear." He swung his legs over the side of the bed and started to get up.

"Relax, *Andrew*," she said. "Maybe you should take it easy."

"I don't want to," he said as he started to stand, faltered, and plopped back down onto the bed. "Oh . . . I'm dizzy."

"That's to be expected. How long have you been in bed?"

"Too long!" Marshall answered for Zak as he came through the door. His hair had a distinctive green tint. "Hey, guy. How are you doing?"

Melinda filled Marshall in on Zak's progress. "He's just discovered he can hear."

Marshall's face lit up. "That's great news!"

Zak was overwhelmed with joy. He lay back down in the bed as Melinda and Marshall chatted away. Sure enough, he could hear them talking about his good fortune at being able to hear again. It was all such wonderful news. He'd dodged a bullet. Now, he could go back to class. But then he remembered: he'd missed midterms.

"Where's that old woman who's been hanging around here?" Marshall asked Melinda.

"You mean, Helena," Melinda corrected him. Her tone, firm. "She has a name."

Marshall blushed. "I didn't mean anything," Marshall countered. "I was just asking."

Melinda glared at Marshall. "*That old woman*, as you so rudely referred to her, has been here night and day watching over Zak. She's been keeping me updated on his progress.

This morning when I stopped by at seven a.m., she was here. I suspect she spent the night in that very chair in the corner, but she wouldn't admit it."

"You're kidding," Marshall said.

"I wish I was. I sent her home to get some rest."

"Wow," was all Marshall could manage.

Melinda turned to Zak, a finger pointed his way, "You'd better be nice to her. She's special."

Zak nodded, though he was no longer tuned into the conversation. He'd moved on, focused on school, tuition, and room and board for next semester. How could he work that out? Why was it that once one problem was solved, two more popped up? So very whack-a-mole.

Another knock on the door and Chuck popped into the room. "Howdy, slick," he said as he walked up to Zak and gave him the once over. "You look good. Even with that bandage on your ear. You're really rocking that Frankenstein look."

Zak couldn't help but laugh. Chuck was about as subtle as a hurricane.

"How's our patient doing today?" Chuck asked the room.

"I can hear," Zak answered.

Chuck's face lit up. "You mean no more blaring radio? No more shouting to be heard?"

Zak nodded. It was a relief to have all that behind him.

"Where's Grandma?" Chuck asked as he looked around.

Melinda rolled her eyes. "You mean, Helena. A little respect. *She has a name.*"

Chuck nodded. "She's something else, Zak. She came to the dorm right after you went into surgery to get my cell phone number. Can you believe it? She's been texting me. That old lady . . ." he stopped as he caught the look on Melinda's face. Her eyes, poisonous darts. "I mean, Helena. She's been updating me. Can you believe she knows how to use an iPhone?"

"Yeah," Marshall chimed in. "She's been texting me too. Chuck shared my contact info."

"She came to the bar to find me," Melinda added, eyes wide. "The Dirty Toenails were in the middle of a set and she hopped up on a barstool and ordered a beer. A beer! I thought I'd keel over from shock."

"I guess old people are just like us," Marshall said. "I mean, we're all bound to get old one day."

"Older," Melinda corrected.

Marshall raised a hand to concede the point. "If you're cool when you're young, why would you be an old fuddy-duddy when you're old?"

"Because life kicks the shit out of you," Chuck reasoned. "I was watching that movie *Woodstock* about a concert held in upstate New York in 1969. All the top rock 'n roll artists played it. The people who attended were wild. Running through the mud naked. Getting high. Sex everywhere. Flower children. Hippies. It made me wonder. Where are those people today? They're Helena's age! Do you think she was at Woodstock dancing topless?"

"What are the chances?" Marshall asked.

"Zero," Melinda answered. "But I get your point, Marshall. Being older doesn't mean you're dead from the neck up."

"Just the neck down," Chuck joked. "Can you imagine having sex at that age?"

"Oh my God," Melinda grumbled. "I hope when I'm an *old woman . . .*"

"*You have a name,*" Marshall and Chuck both sarcastically yelled out.

Melinda ignored them. "I'd enjoy everything life has taught me. Including how to pleasure myself."

Marshall's and Chuck's mouths dropped open. "Eww," they said in unison.

"Anyway," Melinda said as Zak's eyes closed. "Our patient looks tired. Maybe we should give him a chance to rest."

"I just got here," Chuck objected.

"Me too," Marshall chimed in.

"Well, let's go downstairs and grab a bite and then we'll come back up. Rest up, sweetie," she said to Zak, kissing him on the forehead. "We'll be back."

Zak offered a weak smile. He wanted to think about how lucky he was to hear but couldn't focus on that blessing. He was already onto the next problem to be solved. Why couldn't he just be grateful for his friends and his hearing? "When will it get easier?" he mumbled, keenly aware of the challenges still ahead as he drifted off to sleep.

～

Melinda had insisted Helena go home and rest, but Helena was uncomfortable leaving the hospital. So instead of going home, she headed down to the cafeteria to grab a bite. After all, she was Zak's patient advocate and keenly aware most people visit a hospital at their leisure until the dullness becomes too much. That usually took less than an hour. Uncomfortable chairs, bland décor, and interminable boredom sets in and sends even the heartiest of visitors racing for the exit. And Helena believed it unwise to leave a patient in the hospital alone. She felt someone needed to be on hand at all times to commune with the doctors and nurses, ask questions, and help the patient remember what was being said about their care. Plus, she wanted to be close by for the simple things. Passing Zak a glass of water or a box of tissues. Helping him to the bathroom. But mostly, she was concerned about unintentional medical errors. Like administering the wrong medication. Or the delivery of the wrong meal tray. Or worse, when the meal tray was placed out of reach. Busy people make busy-people mistakes, and hospitals were full of busy people. Helena had no intention of allowing Zak to endure one bad moment as long as she was on watch. She certainly couldn't be in control of everything, but she could do her best to stay close.

"Oh dear," Helena muttered as she poked at the runny eggs on her plate. "This is disgusting."

Two women at the next table looked over. Helena blushed, offering a friendly nod just as she caught sight of Melinda's bright red hair heading toward her. She checked her watch. Melinda had lasted barely twenty-five minutes.

"Didn't we send you home?" Melinda said as she placed her tray across from Helena and sat down. The tray held a cup of coffee, a bran muffin wrapped in plastic wrap, and a small bowl of red Jell-O.

"Oh, I'm fine," Helena said. "You don't need to worry about me."

Melinda removed the plastic wrap from the bran muffin. "Looking after him will be a full-time job. At least you can get some rest while the nursing staff covers for you."

Helena nodded. There was no point in educating Melinda on the facts about hospitals. Melinda was far too young to have amassed significant hospital experience. She had yet to learn that nurses were hardly at anyone's beck and call, no matter how well intended.

"Is he resting?" Helena asked.

"Yes. Marshall and Chuck are walking over to McDonald's to bring him back an Egg McMuffin."

"Good," Helena said even though she doubted McDonald's was the most nutritious option for someone in a hospital bed. "Well, I'm glad we have this moment together," she confided. "He's worried about school. Midterms and how he'll pay for next semester."

Melinda sighed. "I know. I've been worrying about that too."

"I didn't want to ask him about scholarships. Is that still possible?"

Melinda shrugged. "I've no idea."

"What about his job? Is there any chance you can hold that for him?"

Melinda shook her head. "I wish I could, but he doesn't want to come back. I've already hired someone to replace him. I just couldn't go without help. We're so busy. Besides, what he earned at the bar barely covered his living expenses. It certainly wouldn't make a dent in his tuition. Do you know how much ASU charges per semester? It's outrageous. There's no way around it. He'll have to drop out."

Helena rubbed her temple. "It's just so unfair. He has no family, no job, and now he's missed midterms. He's probably lost the whole semester. He's out of surgery and his life is a mess."

"I wish he could've asked his professors for an extension on those midterms before his surgery. But then, how could he? He was deaf," Melinda said as she lifted the bran muffin to examine its underside. "Now how could they have ruined this? It's burnt on the bottom."

Helena had to laugh. "That's pretty black."

"But at least he can hear," Melinda added almost as a throwaway line.

Helena had no idea. "What? When? How?"

"Just now. I was talking to him, and he could hear me."

"Oh, my God," Helena blurted out as if her own hearing had been miraculously restored. "That's a relief!"

Melinda returned the muffin to the plate and pushed it away. "What if we work together to get Zak back on track?"

"You'd do that?" Helena asked, eager to team up.

"Sure."

"What about the boy with the green hair? Marshall."

Melinda offered a blank stare. "What about him?"

Helena chewed on her lower lip. "Is he at all interested in Zak?"

"He seemed gaga over Zak's girlfriend from New York City who waltzed through here at the start of the semester. I think her name was Alice. Or Allie."

Helena froze. Had she accidentally outed Zak by referring to Marshall? It certainly wasn't her place to discuss Zak's private life. "Oh—Allison," Helena said in an effort to cover her gaffe. "Of course."

Melinda held up a spoonful of Jell-O. It wobbled as if sending a secret message: don't eat the food here. "The last time that girl visited, they had a falling out, and then she suddenly disappeared. I can't imagine she's an important player at the moment."

"Right," Helena agreed, feeling somewhat off balance. Keeping her own secrets was hard enough. Keeping someone else's, pure misery.

⌘

When Zak opened his eyes, he was alone. His ear itched. It itched something awful. He was afraid to touch it. He moved his jaw in a circular motion as if doing so might stop the itch. It didn't. He yawned an exaggerated yawn. Then he coughed. Still, there was no relief. No matter how he tried to ignore it, the itching grew more persistent. Was a worm burrowing in his head? Three deep breaths, and the itch was still there. He panicked. Did the itch signal something was wrong? He buzzed for the nurse. And waited. And waited. And waited. Finally, Helena came through the door. "What's going on?" she asked, as if reading his mind.

"Something's wrong," he barely managed to eke out. "My ear . . ."

Like a flash, Helena was out the door. Zak had no idea where she'd gone as the itching intensified. Was the cochlear nerve dying? Was that something you could feel? He'd no idea. He just wanted the itching to stop.

"Alright, young man," the nurse said when she arrived, Helena trailing behind her. "You're having a problem?"

"Yes," was all he could manage to answer.

The nurse checked the bandage. "Everything looks fine."

"But the itch . . ."

"That's all part of the healing process."

"But what can I do to stop it?"

The nurse looked at Helena who stood on the opposite side of the bed. "The wound is drawing and pulling. But let's try a trick. We're going to distract the mind. You see, the brain can only process pain in one spot at a time." She demonstrated a technique which Zak followed. She pressed the fingernail of her right index finger into the knuckle of her left thumb. "Does that hurt?"

Zak shook his head no.

"Press harder."

Zak winced. Sure enough, the sensation that had nearly driven him crazy was replaced by the pain in his knuckle.

The nurse offered a thumbs up.

Zak sighed. "That's it?"

"That's it," the nurse confirmed.

Zak closed his eyes and let his head fall back onto the pillow. "Phew. That's a lifesaver."

⚬⚬⚬

Helena followed the nurse out into the hallway. "Thank you so much."

"You're very welcome," the nurse answered.

"But tell me. Is it true what you told him? That it's the healing process?"

"Let's hope so," the nurse answered. "Right now, he can hear through the packing and bandages when you speak loudly. That's great. But who knows how well he'll hear once everything is removed. I'm not saying you should worry. I'm just being realistic. It's anybody's guess, until it isn't."

Helena nodded. "So be cautious. Right?"

"Yes. Like everything in life. We'll know when we know. Things can't be rushed. Miracles in healthcare require expertise, great timing, and patience. Today, he has an itch. Tomorrow, he might have an earache. Or worse. Maybe a migraine. Let's hope not. But for certain, the tumor is gone."

"What do you recommend I tell him?"

"Follow the doctor's lead. Whatever he says, I'd repeat. That's the best advice I can offer."

The nurse excused herself and hurried off down the hall. It was good advice. Reasonable. But Helena wished for so much more for the young man under her charge. There seemed to be so many obstacles before him. Even with his hearing on the mend, he had personal issues to face. Thinking about Zak's life, she was grateful she was no longer young. How tiring life could seem! How very challenging.

"There you are," Julie called out as she meandered down the hall toward Helena, dressed as if she'd just stepped out of a 1980s Pat Benatar lookalike contest in a leopard print top, black leather pants, and black suede boots.

Helena wrapped Julie in a spontaneous hug. Being at the hospital with Zak had lowered her defenses. Brought out the maternal side. She suddenly felt protective of everyone under thirty, as if they were all her baby chicks. "What are you doing here?"

"I wanted to check on you." Julie said as she pulled away, a look on her face of disapproval, much like a teacher who'd caught her favorite student cheating. "I know you didn't come home last night."

"You do?"

"The front desk told me. I thought I'd better stop by and see how you're doing."

"I'm fine," Helena said, uncomfortable to learn she was being monitored. As an adult, she had every right to come and go as she pleased. Was Julie checking up on her because she was an older woman? Or because she doubted Helena was up to the role of patient advocate? Whichever way she thought about it, Helena considered it intrusive.

Julie looked about. "Can we talk privately? Is there somewhere we can go?"

Helena directed Julie to follow her to a lounge at the end of the hall.

"Well, this is nice," Julie said as she took a seat next to Helena on a dark gray sofa with the kind of hard cushions that offered no give at all.

Helena clasped her hands together as if she were a child about to be lectured, and like a child, she was prepared to rebel, already working through the words she'd choose to defend herself.

Julie let out a nervous giggle. Helena could tell she was uncomfortable. "First, let me say thank you for all you're doing."

Helena smiled. Maybe she'd misjudged the situation.

"That said," Julie continued, her shoulders seeming to reach up to her ears, "we can't have you sleeping here at night. It's too much for a woman your age."

Helena felt the hairs on the back of her neck stand up. Who was this young woman to tell her what she could and could not do? Julie had no agency over her. It was not only presumptive but highly insulting.

"I think it's best for all concerned if you let me relieve you here. We'll get someone else to help Zak."

"Relieve me?" Helena repeated, unable to hide her irritation.

"Yes. Just until you get some rest. We can talk about it again next week."

"You're firing me?"

"No. Not at all."

"Well, I refuse," Helena said, arching her back and assuming the pose of a British Royal. "I have built a relationship with this young man and neither you nor anybody else is going to interfere with that. He needs me. This is a critical moment in his life. Come to think of it, it's pretty important to me too. I'm not walking away from him."

Julie sighed. "I was afraid you might take that attitude. Can I do anything to dissuade you?"

"I think not," Helena said as she stood, signaling their conversation was over. "I'm sure you mean well, but that young man needs me. And I'm going to be there for him, come hell or high water. I hope you understand. But if you don't, well, too bad."

"I'm not the enemy," Julie said as she locked eyes with Helena, her voice pleading.

She's not wrong, Ruthie chimed in. *Your job is to look after him. Not solve all his problems.*

Helena hmphed.

Ruthie continued: *It's not like he's a blood relation. He's a stranger. An assignment. You'll never survive as a volunteer unless you emotionally distance yourself.*

Helena lacked the enthusiasm to argue with Julie and Ruthie. "I'll see you back at Ventana," she said to Julie as she walked out of the lounge, making her way back down the hall to check on Zak.

– 21 –

HELENA WAS EXHAUSTED by the time the Uber dropped her off at Ventana. It'd been a long day sitting with Zak as he dozed off and on. In the early evening, Marshall and Chuck returned for a visit, and though Zak seemed happy, Helena sensed he was uncomfortable in their presence. She couldn't quite make out why. Both friends seemed genuinely interested in Zak's welfare and Marshall even helped Zak make his way to the bathroom, an arm about Zak's waist to steady him. Helena had been impressed. *What young man knew to do that?* she thought as she caught sight of Zak's tush peeking out from behind the hospital gown. She turned to look out the window, reminded of Michelangelo's *David*.

As she crossed the Ventana lobby, making her way to the elevator, Gilbert Goldfarb intercepted her. "Well, there you are," he said as if they were old friends. "Where have you been hiding yourself?"

"Hello," she meekly answered as she continued walking, determined to press the elevator button. Gilbert followed closely along at her side. She didn't want to be rude. She just wanted to relax. Slip off her shoes. Take off her bra. Put on her favorite robe. Spread out on the sofa with a warm mug of green tea. Turn on Netflix. Disappear into something mindless. Just so she didn't have to think. Or talk. Or be.

Gilbert seemed alarmed. "Are you alright?"

"Yes, just fine," she said, hoping to bypass any discussion about the last few days.

"I was going up to the bar for a nightcap. Why not join me?"

"I'd love to," she lied. "But not tonight. I'm going straight to bed."

Gilbert checked his Apple watch. "At eight-thirty?"

Helena sighed. When had eight-thirty become early? Wasn't everyone at Ventana tucked away for the night? Why was Gilbert still roaming the lobby? "I've been thinking about getting one of those watches," she lied, hoping to throw Gilbert off track as she pressed the elevator button.

Gilbert puffed up. "They're wonderful. Do you know I can do my own EKG by just pressing this icon?" He did just that. Within the next moment, he tilted his wrist so that Helena could see the face of the watch.

Helena stretched her neck to get a good look. Yes, she could see the spikes of the EKG. "That's lovely," she said, having no idea what she was looking at.

Gilbert beamed. "I can track the calories I've burned walking today just by switching to this setting." He pressed something or other and offered Helena another peek.

Helena tried to appear interested, but she wasn't. All she wanted to do was go upstairs. Where was the damn elevator? "Fascinating," she said, hoping she didn't sound too smarmy. After all, if a man in his eighties felt it necessary to count the calories burned by walking from the dining room back to his condo, who was she to criticize him?

Finally, there was a loud ding as the elevator arrived. Gilbert reached for Helena's elbow. "Before you go, if you're not interested in a drink, why not grab dessert with me at the coffee shop?"

Helena considered the offer. The man had such kind eyes. She was going to nurse a mug of green tea anyway. What would be the harm in taking a few more moments with Gilbert? Besides, something sweet might be a nice reward for a long day. "Alright," she conceded. "Something quick," she warned. "I'm tired."

"Deal," he said as his watch flashed a message regarding his heart rate. It had suddenly spiked.

"Are you alright?" Helena asked as he examined the message.

"I can't understand this damn thing," he muttered.

"Maybe you should sit down." She grabbed his hand and led him over to a nearby chair.

Gilbert plopped down. His face pale as if he'd just seen a ghost.

"Take it easy," Helena said in a melodic voice. "Breathe."

Gilbert took three deep breaths. The color returned to his face.

"There you go," Helena said as she kneeled by his side and held his hand.

Gilbert's eyes lit up. "How can you still kneel? Doesn't that hurt your knees?"

Helena hadn't anticipated the change of subject. It took her a minute to understand what Gilbert was saying. "Not really. I've always been flexible."

"That's your secret, isn't it?"

Helena had no idea what he was talking about.

"To being fit," he clarified.

Helena didn't think falling in the bathroom and needing to be rescued by the Phoenix Fire Department was a sign of fitness. But she guessed for a woman of her age, flexibility was an advantage. And if Gilbert wanted to think of her as unique, she had no intention of bursting his bubble. "Are you feeling better?" she asked as she continued to rub his hand.

He blushed. "Yes. To think, all I wanted was to ask you to join me for a drink. Now here you are, holding my hand."

Helena was charmed. Not by what he'd said, but by the way he looked at her with that doe-eyed stare. Admiring, welcoming . . . ever hopeful. "Well, I'm glad I was here," she said as she released the hand. "I have to say, that watch is really something. How often do you get an alert?"

Gilbert smiled. "It happens quite a lot. Usually, it's my heart rate."

Helena was sad to hear that. "That's terrible. But what do you do with all the information?"

Gilbert seemed flustered. "Do?"

"Yes. Do you follow up with your doctor? Do you go to the emergency room? What exactly happens when you get an alert?"

Gilbert stared at her as if she were from another planet. "I turn the notification off."

Helena tried not to appear shocked. What could possibly be the point of owning an expensive piece of medical jewelry that provided healthcare alerts if the owner had no intention of using the information? "I don't understand," she admitted.

Gilbert seemed indignant. "I don't want to go to the ER. And I certainly don't need to visit my doctor again. No. This is just for my edification. I use the watch to keep me informed of my health status. That's all. At least now, when I get dizzy, I know why."

Helena nodded, though she thought the whole thing a terrible waste of money, not to mention bother and worry.

"I don't suppose you'd still like to go for dessert?" Gilbert asked, his dark emerald eyes shining with anticipation.

How could she possibly say no to a man she'd just rescued from a rapid heartbeat? "Of course," she said as she stood and offered Gilbert her hand to help pull himself up. *Men and their toys*, she thought as he latched onto her arm, directing her to the café. *Do they ever grow up?*

———◦◦◦———

"And that's what I've been doing for the last few days," Helena explained as she took another spoonful of her vanilla sundae smothered in cashews, hot fudge, and whipped cream. Too bad the café was out of cherries. She wondered why she didn't eat more ice cream. Why had she acquiesced to the tyranny of diets throughout her life? *For goodness sake*, she thought. *I'm eighty-three. Isn't it time to eat what I want?* Still, on the next bite she was already processing the calories of the sundae in her head. Perhaps if she passed on lunch tomorrow, the ice cream wouldn't do too much damage.

Gilbert licked a chocolate ice cream cone. Red, white, and blue sprinkles clung to the corner of his mouth. "Taking care of a teenager is a lot of responsibility. I'm not sure I'd take that on," he confided.

"It's only for a few weeks," Helena clarified. "It's not like Zak's moving in with me permanently."

"Still, I don't know if I could live with anyone again. Especially someone so young. You're going to have to feed him," Gilbert pointed out as if preparing a meal was a sin specified in the Bible. *Thou shalt not feed young adults.* "I suppose you could bring him to the dining room."

She wondered what Zak liked to eat. "I don't mind cooking. In fact, I rather like it. It's a nice feeling to prepare a meal for someone. To be useful. I never did too much of that when I was younger. I always had someone come in to help out. When you're a working widow with children, you either hire help or go crazy . . ."

Gilbert stopped her. "You have children?"

Helena was surprised. Wasn't that obvious? But then, how would it be? It wasn't like a woman who had children looked different from a woman who didn't. Well, perhaps a woman with children might look older, she mused. Raising kids was certainly hard on the figure and the mind, not to mention the wrinkles gathered from worrying whether you're a good mother, or worse, why you weren't acting more like a mother when you were busy with your career.

"Boys?" Gilbert asked, taking a guess.

"Men. Two fine men."

"Good for you."

"What about you?" Helena asked. "Any children?"

"I'm alone," Gilbert answered.

How odd, Helena thought. It was so unusual to meet a man who didn't have children. As if not having children was an indicator of some sort of social defect worth hiding. She wanted to ask more but thought better of it. Too personal. Besides, why bring up serious matters when enjoying a dish of ice cream? What could be the point of marching down that joyless path?

"I had a son," Gilbert admitted after a moment or two. "But he no longer talks to me."

Helena leaned forward. "Oh, no." Against her better judgement, she jumped in with both feet. "What happened?"

"I made the mistake of telling him that I didn't like his wife."

Helena thought about her dislike of her own daughters-in-law. "You didn't!"

Gilbert's eyes welled up. Helena panicked. Was Gilbert about to cry? *Please*, she thought. *Don't cry. I'm too tired to console you.*

"I could never get past that last horrible miscalculation," Gilbert explained.

Helena certainly understood how easy it was for an errant opinion to rip a relationship with your children to shreds.

"Tell me," Gilbert said as he took another lick of his cone, "what did you do to upset your boys?"

Helena wasn't sure she'd heard him correctly.

Gilbert clarified. "When was the last time you saw your sons?"

Helena squinted as if the answer was on the tip of her tongue. But it wasn't. Between Covid and life in general, it had been years. But she couldn't bring herself to admit it. If she did, she'd have to face the reality of her family dynamics. "Not too long ago," she said, hoping vagueness would be enough to let the subject drop.

Gilbert nodded.

She suddenly felt defensive. What exactly did Gilbert's nod mean?

"I speak to my sons every now and then," she said with a quiver in her voice. "After all, they're grown men with their own families."

"Aren't you part of their family?" he asked as he dabbed the corner of his mouth with a napkin.

Helena looked off in the distance. She was tired. She'd only agreed to have ice cream, because . . . well . . . she couldn't quite remember exactly why. But she had no energy for a serious conversation. And not with a man she barely knew. "I don't mean to be rude," she started, struggling to put forward her best face, "but I really am tired. If you'll excuse me, I'll say goodnight."

Before she could get up, Gilbert said, "You're wondering how I know about your sons."

Helena hadn't wondered anything of the sort. Besides, what he was saying about her sons wasn't true. Of course, she was part of their families. An important member, in fact.

"The longer you're here, the more you'll come to understand the dynamics at play with most of the owners. You don't spend this kind of money unless you're certain you're destined to be alone. We buy into Ventana to ensure someone is available to look out for us when that final decline begins. Usually, that's because family is nowhere to be found."

Helena felt a cold shiver run down her spine. What a way to phrase it. *Final decline.* "Well, Gilbert," she said as she rose, her heart rapidly beating. "It's getting late and I'm tired. I have to be at the hospital tomorrow bright and early."

Gilbert reached for her hand, but her hand slipped through his fingers. "I've upset you," he said, as if realizing his misstep.

"Not at all," Helena answered, determined to get away. "Now, if you'll excuse me, I must go up. It's been a long day. Goodnight."

"Will I see you again?" he asked as she stepped away from the table.

"We both live here," she called as she crossed to the café's exit, unwilling to commit any further energy to Mr. Gilbert Goldfarb.

The next morning, Helena showered and quickly dressed, eager to get back to the hospital and Zak. If all went well, this would be the day she'd bring him home to Ventana to recuperate. There was something exciting about having a teenager in her life again. When her sons were young, she'd been so busy working, she'd missed the chance to spend quality time with them. After the boys left for college, the gap in their relationship only intensified. In a way, they'd become intimate strangers. Helena couldn't quite put her finger on exactly what had gone wrong. Had they resented her for being *missing in action* during their childhoods? In those early years, she'd directed so much of her energy toward her career. Night school at NYU. Becoming a journalist. Then a novelist. Then a speaker. How else was she to manage as a single parent?

There could be no disappointment where there was no expectation and she'd shed expectations about her sons long ago, deciding instead to pat herself on the back that her boys had grown up to be strong, successful, independent men. She could take pride in having raised them well. Whether she'd been there a hundred percent of the time or not, they were still her boys. Her fine young men. Her knights in shining armor who'd gone off to the battle of life. And if she was being honest, she was grateful they'd matured into the kind of men who could take care of themselves. Now that she'd played her part as the mother, wasn't it time for her to have her own life? To stop being someone's mother?

Still, her life seemed somewhat smaller than she'd imagined it might be. No published essays in *The New York Times* or rave reviews for a new novel could fill the emptiness. Oddly, meeting Zak had offered her a second chance to experience her nurturing side. He'd turned her life in a direction she hadn't imagined. And for some odd reason, which she couldn't quite explain, she felt invigorated. Eager to experience each new day . . . happily, engaged in life.

"Good morning, young man," she said as she strolled into Zak's hospital room. Chuck and Marshall were already there, impressive considering it was seven o'clock in the morning. Marshall sat on one side of Zak's bed. Chuck occupied an adjacent chair, feet up, dirty shoes on Zak's blanket. One look at the sad faces and Helena knew something was up. "What's going on?" she asked as the three unhappy men greeted her.

"Allison's back," Marshall said.

Helena nodded. She'd heard about Allison. But why, for heaven's sake, was that a big deal? Wasn't she one of Zak's closest friends? How could her arrival have brought such a cloud of doom?

"I don't want to see her," Zak said.

Helena nodded. "Well, you don't have to. You can always make an excuse."

"It's too late," Chuck said. "She stayed at the dorm last night. She slept in Zak's bed."

"Oh," Helena said with a shrug, not wanting to appear provincial. In her day, plenty of young women would have pushed their way into the dorm room of a guy who looked like Zak or Chuck. A little coke. A little booze. An attractive man. It seemed like a plan. She was sure the three adorable monkeys before her would never suspect an eighty-three-year-old lady once had a sex life. "So, she's here. Big deal. What am I not understanding?"

Zak sighed. "It's too complicated to explain."

Helena scowled. *Oh, these young people. All drama, all the time.* "Well, try me."

Marshall took a stab. "She has a way of making everything about her. She dominates any space. Sucks up the oxygen."

Helena nodded. Young, attractive women could do that.

"Then she pushes her agenda," Chuck explained.

Helena got it. Allison excelled at manipulation. She must be quite a ball of energy. "Okay. But it's only a visit. How long will she be here?"

"We don't know," Zak answered.

Helena still didn't get the big deal. "Is she enrolled in college? If so, she can't be here for long."

"Right," Zak said, perking up.

Helena tried to put a positive spin on it. "For my two cents, I think it's lovely she came to visit. I'm looking forward to meeting her."

Three sour faces grumbled.

Helena changed the subject. "Now to the business of the day. How are you feeling, Zak?"

Zak lifted a brow. "Better. The itching is less and my hearing is improving."

"Wonderful. Has the doctor stopped by yet?"

"The nurse told me he's running late. He should be here in the next hour."

Helena hated to bring up a sore subject, but with Zak's hearing restored, it seemed like the right time for Zak to refocus on his classes. "Have you heard anything about those midterms?"

Marshall answered. "Melinda asked me to speak with the dean on Zak's behalf. He said it's up to the individual instructor about whether they'd allow Zak to take the exams off schedule."

Helena crossed her arms. Bureaucratic inefficiency had always driven her nuts. She made a mental note: Hunt down the dean. Wrangle a time for she and Zak to meet with him and get a firm commitment to allow Zak an extension on his midterm exams. Then, if necessary, with Zak in tow, speak to each of Zak's professors and nail down the date for those midterm exams. If there was one thing she knew, it was the art of overcoming objections. That was how she'd found an agent, editor, and book publisher. It was time to apply those skills. Speak up for what was right. If they wouldn't listen to reason, well, she'd cross that bridge when she got to it. Hopefully, with tact and diplomacy, she could influence the dean. *After all*, she thought, *if there's anything I excel at, it's tact and diplomacy.* She then heard Ruthie's voice. *Before you ride roughshod over the school, let Zak ask for your help. Don't be a buttinsky.*

Helena bit her lip. Ruthie was right. Why was it so hard to do the right thing when she knew the right thing to do?

✦

Helena had nodded off in a chair when Peterson finally showed up at eleven to check on Zak. She was awakened when the doctor's cell phone went off.

"Sorry," he said as he checked the caller ID. "Spam! You'd think the government could do something about all these damn robocalls."

Helena sympathized. In the last week alone, she'd heard from a grandchild who'd been in a car accident, an IRS agent who'd threatened to arrest her due to outstanding back taxes, and an insurance company trying to process a claim that required her social security number.

Zak was fast asleep as Peterson approached him. "Hmm," he said in a jovial tone to Helena. "He's really wiped out. Have you two been partying to all hours of the night again?" He gently shook Zak's shoulder.

"Yes, yes," Zak muttered, eyes fluttering and licking his lips.

Helena filled a cup with water and passed it to him.

"How are you feeling?" Peterson asked in a low voice. So low, Helena strained to hear him.

Zak didn't answer.

Peterson asked again, this time his voice louder.

Zak merely blinked.

"Can you hear me?" Peterson asked, this time much louder than any of the conversations Zak had participated in while Helena was in the room.

Zak's expression shifted from calm to sheer panic.

Helena gasped. "What's going on? He could hear earlier. His friends were here. There were no problems."

Peterson nodded as if Zak's poor hearing was totally expected. "There's nothing to worry about. We've used an antibiotic gel in the middle ear to prevent infection. As the body absorbs the gel, it shifts about so his hearing will vary. It's all normal healing."

Tears rolled down Zak's cheeks.

"Is there anything we can do in the meantime?" Helena asked.

"Nothing. The ear needs time to heal. The swelling has to come down. And his hearing will come and go, like a radio that needs to be finetuned. Until then, he might be dizzy. His balance might be off."

Helena flashed back to her bathroom floor. She could still feel the hard tile on her cheek. See the dust bunny in the corner. The dreadful cockroach with its brown cellophane wings and antennae.

"We're going to keep him one more night. Tomorrow, we'll send him home. But I want to see him in my office at the end of the week. Can you do that?"

Helena nodded.

"Until then, keep him quiet. Let him rest. He's been through a lot."

Helena reached for Zak's hand and gave it a squeeze. "You're going to be fine," she said so loud that she was certain the nurses down the hall at the nurses' station must have heard her.

– 22 –

ELENA STAYED WITH Zak until he fell asleep. He'd been so distraught about the change in his hearing that she considered staying overnight. Instead, the nurse provided Zak with a dose of anti-anxiety medication and thankfully, within thirty minutes, he could barely keep his eyes open. Helena dimmed the lights and promised to wait till he drifted off, only to wake up herself at midnight, muscles stiff from having fallen asleep in the corner chair. It wasn't until she was seated in the hospital lobby waiting for the Uber back to Ventana that she noticed the message on her iPhone: *Helena, it's Alan. I'd like to talk with you when you have a moment. Please stop by my office.*

Helena sighed. Julie must have filled Alan in. Now she'd get to hear the same lecture in stereo about her bad behavior. She supposed they had her best interests at heart. After all, she was beginning to feel the wear and tear from spending her days at the hospital. It wasn't just her limbs that ached. She was emotionally exhausted from worrying about Zak. She'd forgotten how tiring it could be when a loved one was in the hospital. How very draining. Caring for others required an enormous amount of energy. Energy she wasn't sure she still had.

Back at Ventana, asleep in her own bed, Helena dreamt she was lost in a forest. But she wasn't alone. There was a dark presence nearby. Then, it was chasing her. Which way to turn? Tall trees blocked the sun as she struggled to make her way forward. Would anyone notice she was missing? Would anyone try to find her? Could she escape this ominous threat which was closing in on her? She awoke with a start, lying in a pool of sweat. *Silly*, she thought as she gathered herself together and headed to the bathroom. *I'm safe. There's no boogeyman.* But the sense of uncertainty lingered. She struggled to fall back to sleep.

In the morning, as the sun broke over the horizon, Helena sat at her kitchen counter sipping a cup of coffee. She was determined to put the night's troubled sleep out of her mind. Instead, she fretted about the day ahead. Was it too much to wish for Zak's hearing to be miraculously restored? This would be Zak's last morning at the hospital. He was scheduled to be discharged at noon. She thanked her lucky stars that she wouldn't have to spend another full day in that gloomy place. It was getting to be too much. And she wasn't even the patient!

She quickly dressed, preparing to head out the door. *Just one more morning*, she thought as she stepped onto the Ventana elevator and pressed the button for the lobby. She sighed with relief as the elevator began its descent. Soon, she'd be back at Ventana with Zak at her side. When the elevator doors opened, she mindlessly stepped out, unaware of her surroundings. It took a moment before she realized she wasn't in the lobby. She'd gotten off the elevator on the wrong floor. The third floor. Just as she realized her mistake, the elevator doors closed behind her. Instead of turning and pressing the button for the next elevator, she wandered down the hallway, curious to see what the third floor was about. Aside from the central nurses' station, the third floor looked like any other floor until she reached the dining hall. There she saw the residents, some in wheelchairs, others with walkers, gathered around communal tables of eight. Some were slumped over. Some struggled to hold their dining utensils. Most were in their bedclothes. One man was yelling and pounding the table. A few had dazed expressions, as if lost in their own reality. Helena slowly backed away. Now she knew what all the fuss was about. It wasn't just about being housed on the third floor. That in itself wasn't so bad. The space was beautifully decorated, much like the rest of Ventana. But it was the vacant stares of the residents that haunted her, as if their souls had been whisked off by a higher power, leaving behind empty husks to be cared for.

Once in the lobby, she crossed to the corner café to grab a coffee to go. Inside, she spotted Alan and Julie, deep in conversation. When they looked her way, she reached deep down and offered a vibrant, "Good morning," though her instinct was to turn and flee.

"You're up bright and early," Alan said as he stood, waving Helena over to join them. When she approached, Alan pulled out a chair and offered her a seat.

Helena reluctantly sat down.

"Good morning," Julie said, a bright smile on her face.

"Are you on your way to the hospital?" Alan asked.

Helena nodded and braced herself. *Here we go*, she thought. *A lecture is coming.*

"Is there anything we can do to make this easier for you?" Julie asked.

Helena bristled. Their oversight was unneeded and unwarranted. She couldn't help but feel infantilized by their attention. Just because she was eighty-three, did that mean she was unable to manage her business and personal affairs? But then, wasn't that the reason she'd moved into Ventana in the first place? It was all so confusing. Still, she was convinced their attention was simply ageist. And ageist behavior was the last thing she'd expected from Ventana. "I'm perfectly fine," she insisted. "I'm bringing Zak home today. It's a good day!"

"I'm glad," Alan said. "But we've heard some disturbing news."

Helena's ears perked up. Not again. She hadn't written a blog since she'd been looking after Zak. Who had time? And she'd kept her promise to Julie. She'd slept in her own bed the previous night instead of at the hospital with Zak. Was this about Zak? Or was there something else? Suddenly, she was nervous.

Alan continued. "You've been overheard talking to yourself. Seemingly disoriented."

"I beg your pardon," Helena said as she looked over at Julie.

Julie raised her hands in the air, signaling she was innocent of such gossip.

"I don't understand," Helena said. "Who told you this?"

Alan Lane blushed. "I'm not at liberty to say."

In all her days, she'd never imagined anyone might question her mental stability, if that was in fact what Alan was doing. She couldn't deny her life had been challenging. She'd had her heartaches and disappointments, but she'd always thought of herself as a trooper. Someone who could face adversity and rise above it. Fiercely independent. So what if she talked to herself now and then? Big deal. She wasn't the first and wouldn't be the last person to ever do so. Though she did sometimes talk aloud to her mother. She'd done it for so long she wasn't even aware of it. Still, an accusation of being disoriented was untrue and highly offensive. The entire conversation was beneath her dignity.

Helena took a deep breath. "Well, I can't speak to a charge for which I have no way of defending myself. I was unaware there are spies in the building monitoring my every move."

Julie leaned forward. "It's not a charge," she said in a soft, sympathetic tone. "We're concerned. That's all. You really haven't engaged in the Ventana community in the way we'd hoped. You haven't signed up to audit classes. You haven't attended our lecture series. You're not involved in the social clubs of the other owners. And now you're super-involved with this young man, which is all fine and good, but you've gone overboard by sleeping in his hospital room at night, which is a problem. We've also heard about your supposed . . ." Julie raised her fingers in air quotes. "Visions."

Helena's heart skipped a beat. Should she defend herself or laugh it off as a misunderstanding? Or apologize? But apologize for what? She didn't understand exactly what was being asked of her. Or how to even address it.

"Why not let us take over Zak's care? The surgery was successful, and we can have someone else look after him."

Helena chewed on her bottom lip. She wasn't ready to let go of Zak. At least, not yet. Perhaps she should humor them. Yes, that might be the answer. Assure Alan and Julie she was absolutely fine and capable. Don't let them see she was upset. "You two are very dear to me," she started, employing flattery as her first defense. "I can't tell you how much I appreciate your concern. You're right about overextending myself. I promise, going forward, to be more mindful and to take better care of myself. Since Zak will be discharged today, I'll be resting later this afternoon in my condo. If Zak does need to stay another night at the hospital, I promise, Girl Scouts honor," she said as she held three fingers in the air, "not to stay later than an hour past dinner to make sure he eats. Now surely, that counts for something."

"And those visions?" Alan asked.

Helena laughed. "Really. I can't imagine such a thing. I don't even believe in a higher power. How could I see visions?"

Julie eased back in the chair. "What a relief. I feel so much better now," she admitted. "See Alan. What did I tell you? I knew Helena would understand."

"Good," Alan said. "After all, you're our responsibility."

Helena smiled, even though she didn't remember that being part of the contract she'd signed when she bought into Ventana. Where did it say she was their responsibility? "If you'll excuse me, I've got an Uber waiting," she said, manifesting her most courteous voice as she rose. "Perhaps we can reconvene when I have more time. But now, I have to hurry."

They both wished her a wonderful morning, seemingly convinced that Helena was more than capable to go on her merry way.

– 23 –

When Allison showed up at the hospital, Zak was on edge. How had she found out about his surgery? Their last time together hadn't ended well. He remembered the night at Windy Canyon when she'd disappeared into thin air, only to turn up in Chuck's bed. They'd argued. He accused her of overstaying her welcome. The whole fiasco made him sick just thinking about it. But now, as Allison stood before him with her adorable smile, eyes radiating genuine concern, Zak felt as if his old friend from high school was back. Not the selfish girl he'd kicked out of his dorm room. *Allison must truly care about me*, he thought. *Otherwise, there'd be no reason for her to be in Arizona.* "Hey, you," Zak whispered as she approached.

"I've missed you," she said, her voice velvety soft as she sat at the foot of Zak's hospital bed, sporting a new hair color.

"When did you go blond?"

She tossed her hair back and pointed her chin up with typical dramatic flair. "I had to do something to get noticed at that damn school."

Zak couldn't imagine anyone not noticing Allison. Being noticed was her specialty! When they were in high school, all eyes were upon her. If they weren't, she was the master at redirecting attention her way. A grand gesture, a bold speech, an outrageous joke. She had a delightful way of laughing that always made her the immediate center of attention in any social situation.

"You seem just fine," Allison said as her eyes went to his bandaged right ear. "You can hear me perfectly. Is this whole hospital thing just a wild bid for attention?"

Zak smiled. "My hearing comes and goes. I can hear fairly well today. But every now and then, there's a shift in the antibiotic gel the surgeon placed in my ear as its being absorbed by the body. I hear this popping and crackling and then suddenly my hearing changes. It's weird and scary. But it's better today. I'm reading lips too. Not bad, huh?"

Allison leaned forward, a hand on her heart. "I'm so sorry about your ear."

The last thing Zak wanted was pity. Sure, he felt sorry for himself, but that was his prerogative. After all, he was the one with the hearing problem. He didn't expect others to understand. That's why he rarely told anyone about his bad ear unless he had to. He didn't want to be pitied. And he certainly didn't want to be judged or have anyone think less of him. Sometimes when he told people about his deaf ear, they'd deliberately start to talk louder, some even shouting. He didn't want special treatment. He didn't want to be noticed. But now, unfortunately, there was no way to avoid it. "I'll be fine," he said in an effort to brush off Allison's sympathy. "It's not the end of the world. Once the packing is out," he said as he touched the bandage on his ear, "I'll hear perfectly again."

With that, Zak's ear popped and the volume in the room instantly changed, and not for the better.

"Let's hope so," Allison said. "But I have another surprise for you."

Zak wasn't sure he was up for much more. Truth be told, Allison was already draining his energy.

"Your parents are here," she said, wildly clapping. "I called them and told them what's going on."

Zak wondered if he'd misheard. How did Allison even know what was going on with him? Did she just say his parents were in town? "I don't understand. How did you find out about the surgery?"

Marshall appeared in the doorway. "That was me. I texted her."

Zak saw red. "Why?" he asked, without any thought to Allison overhearing him.

Marshall's smile faded. "I thought you'd want your best friend to know."

Zak turned to Allison. "You told my parents?"

"Your doctor called them, but they hadn't bought plane tickets yet. I asked my mother to call your mother," she said proudly, "and I guess my mother did a terrific job convincing her."

"Your mother?" Zak repeated just as his parents walked into the room.

Mrs. Andrews, a small woman of five-four was smartly dressed in beige, her brown hair cut fashionably short and close to the face. She gasped when she saw Zak with his ear wrapped in a bandage. "Oh, no," she moaned. "Are you okay?"

Marshall started to explain about the packing in the ear, but Mrs. Andrews had already moved on to hugging Allison while Mr. Andrews, a tall man with strikingly dark features like Zak, stood mutely by, staring at Zak, but not approaching the bed, as if his son had a contagious disease that Mr. Andrews was unwilling to catch.

"You're here," Zak said, stating the obvious as he looked from his mother to his father.

"We've come to bring you home," his mother said. She looked over at Zak's father, but he said nothing. She turned back to Zak. "You belong with us. And now that you're unwell, you should be at home."

Zak wasn't sure he understood everything his mother had said. She'd looked away when she was speaking so he couldn't read her lips. But he had certainly caught the word, *unwell*. "I'm not unwell."

His mother blinked as if the sun were in her eye. "Of course, you are," she said, an upturned palm in the air. Her tone, matter of fact. "We are in a hospital."

"I've had surgery and will be leaving this afternoon."

"Where to?" his mother asked. "You can't go back to your dorm room."

Marshall tried to explain about Helena, but Zak's mother talked over him. "Gerry," she said, glancing at the mute man in the corner holding up the wall, "tell your son he's coming home with us."

Mr. Andrews hesitated to answer, rolling his tongue around in his mouth as if searching for the place where he'd lost a filling. "We'll see," he finally uttered like one of those laconic cowboys that inhabited old Hollywood Westerns.

Zak glared at his father. "I'm not going home. You don't want me there. It was a mistake for you to come."

"Don't be that way, Zak," Allison said as she scooched up on the bed and placed a hand on Zak's leg. "Your parents love you. They want what's best for you."

"No," Zak grumbled, looking at his mother. "If they wanted what was best, they would have been here for the surgery. They've only showed up because your mother confronted them on their negligence."

Mrs. Andrews shook her head as she addressed Zak. "You've always been ungrateful. Even as a child, you wanted everything your way. So very selfish."

"Don't even try it," Zak warned his mother. "Your guilt doesn't work here anymore. I'm on to you."

"Don't you take that tone with your mother," Mr. Andrews said, an index finger pointed at Zak.

"Why don't we all take a break?" Marshall suggested, though no one seemed to hear him. "Give Zak a chance to rest."

Zak glared at Marshall. "See what you've done."

Marshall paled. "I didn't realize . . ."

"No. You didn't," Zak snapped.

"I guess I'd better be heading to class," Marshall said, looking at Zak as he excused himself. *I'm sorry,* he mouthed before leaving the room.

Zak clenched the covers in a tight grip. He shouldn't have been unkind to Marshall. Marshall was only doing what he'd assumed was best. But Marshall had no idea what he'd initiated. And what truly caught Zak off guard was his sudden, intense dislike of Allison. Her condescending way. Her showy manner. Her barging in where she didn't belong. He imagined his family rift was great source material for a future acting class. He couldn't bear to look at Allison with all her sugar-and-spice nonsense. And just when Zak thought things couldn't get worse, Helena showed up with her buoyant personality. He cringed at the thought of his parents and Allison meeting Helena. Surely the shit would hit the fan when they realized Helena was his surgical angel. The kind stranger who'd stepped in when there was no one else to help.

***

"I'm back," Helena announced as she strolled into Zak's room. Much to her surprise, Zak had company. Lots of company.

A young blond woman with a lovely face hopped off Zak's bed and offered her hand much like a princess might. "I'm Allison. This is Zak's mother, Betty, and his father, Gerry."

Helena's eyes shifted to the two adults. The man nodded and turned away to look out the window. He was tall and moody. He and Zak shared the same angular features and impressive jawline. If the man ever smiled, Helena imagined he'd be downright gorgeous. The woman in the chair by Zak's bedside was impeccably dressed. Her hair was cut short like Mia Farrow's in *Rosemary's Baby*. Her manner was regal as she offered Helena a faint smile. Helena sensed she'd interrupted at a key moment. The tension in the room was palpable.

"They've come all the way from New York City on the East Coast," Allison cheerily added as if Helena required a geography lesson.

Helena struggled to gain her bearings. After being at the center of Zak's care, she now found herself outside of the action, not knowing the players. She'd heard about Allison, but meeting the charming young woman was a totally different experience than hearing about her antics from Zak. Then, there were the parents. Helena hadn't heard much about them, but what she'd heard, she didn't like. Parents don't disown their children. Not real parents, no matter what the issue might be. For the second time that morning, after running into Alan and Julie at the Ventana Café, Helena put on a brave face. "How wonderful to meet you all," she lied. After all, what was the harm in a little white lie? As long as it helped someone. And based on the mood in the room, Zak needed all the help he could get. She introduced herself. "I'm Zak's patient advocate. I volunteer with his doctor's office. Zak will be staying with me for the next few weeks as he recuperates."

"Really?" Mrs. Andrews said as she turned about to check Helena out, giving her the once over, eyes finally coming to rest on Helena's black Nikes.

Helena wished she'd dressed better, but she'd assumed Zak's discharge would be an extremely casual affair. She'd no idea she'd be meeting people. Or be on display. A pair of jeans, a white blouse, and sneakers seemed to be more than appropriate. "Well, I see you've got a full house," Helena cheerfully added once the brief introductions were over. She did her best to ignore Zak's sad expression. She'd get to that in due time. "Has the doctor come by yet?" She directed the question to the room of visitors while Zak stared blankly off in the distance.

"We haven't seen him," Allison answered.

Helena struggled with what to do next. When Peterson showed up, it'd be awkward, to say the least. All she really needed to know was whether Zak was ready for discharge, but now, she'd be forced to deal with all these interlopers whose presence was doing nothing to enhance Zak's mood. Polite conversation seemed the only way forward. "Did you all come in last night?" she asked Zak's mother as Helena maneuvered her way to the other side of Zak's bed to get a better view of the room and have greater access to Zak.

Zak's father answered. "We got in at ten o'clock. Mrs. Andrews had a terrible headache."

Helena tried again to engage Mrs. Andrews, but Zak's mother's eyes remained glued on Zak as if she were deliberately ignoring Helena. "Is the hotel nice?" Helena probed.

"It's pricey," Mr. Andrews balked. "It comes with some sort of resort fee. What's that about? The place looks like an old Holiday Inn. No golf course. No tennis court. What's the resort fee for?"

Helena had no idea. Nor did she care. "Zak." She touched his shoulder and slowly mouthed the words so he could easily lip-read. "How did you sleep? Are you tired this morning?"

Zak's eyes told the whole story. Helena instinctively knew he was trapped in a room with three people he didn't want to see. Even if he was exhausted, he wouldn't sleep in front of these visitors.

"Aren't you going to answer?" his father bristled. "He's been difficult since we arrived," he complained to Helena. "Short-tempered."

Allison gave her mane a shake. "We don't know what to do with him."

Helena had an idea. "How about we convene in the lounge at the end of the hallway and have a little chat. Give grumpy head a chance to close his eyes and nap."

"But what about the doctor?" Zak's mother asked.

"I'll let the nurses know where we'll be. We won't miss the doctor. Don't you worry."

Like the pied piper leading rats away from an infested village, Helena led Zak's visitors down the hall to the empty lounge. The tension eased once they sat down. The three interlopers on the sofa and Helena in a chair angled next to Mr. Andrews.

"The doctor did call us," Zak's mother said, breaking the ice.

Helena nodded. "So, you were the one who filled Allison in on Zak's surgery." She directed the statement to Mrs. Andrews who had lost interest in their conversation and was searching through her bag for something or other.

Allison corrected Helena. "No. Marshall texted me. I then called Zak's parents. Actually, my mother did."

"We didn't know exactly when he was having the surgery," Zak's mother explained, her eyes avoiding Helena's but focused on Allison.

How could you? Helena thought. *You haven't talked to your son in months. You gave no indication to the doctor that you'd be willing to help out.*

Zak's father kicked his foot forward, just missing Helena's leg. "Now that we see he's fine, we're heading back tomorrow."

Helena was flabbergasted. "So soon."

Allison fidgeted, tugging on the collar of her blouse. "Zak's so angry. What else can we do?"

Helena sighed. Was this even worth her time? After all, her job was to be a *patient* advocate. To take care of Zak while he recuperated. Get him back and forth to his doctor's appointments. Make sure he was comfortable and supported. Was dealing with these three characters really part of her role? Wouldn't she be crossing a boundary if she got involved in Zak's personal relationships? She wasn't clear on the right way to proceed, but she had to do something to try and fix this mess.

"You two must be tired," she said to Zak's parents. "Why not go back to the hotel and relax? The doctor probably won't be here until the afternoon," she lied.

"No," Zak's mother said so weakly that Helena barely heard her.

"I could use a cup of coffee," Zak's father said. "Maybe we'll go see what we can dig up in the cafeteria."

Zak's mother looked at her husband with what Helena could only conclude was quiet desperation. Helena addressed Allison. "As for you, young lady, why not come back a bit later after Zak has a chance to nap? It's awfully difficult to sleep in a hospital. I'm sure he's exhausted."

Allison perked up, happy for any excuse to leave. "Fine," she said. "But first, give me your iPhone and I'll share my contact info."

As Helena waited, Allison confirmed Helena had received the text with Allison's contact information and accepted it. Helena was proud of herself as the three interlopers left the lounge. *Odd*, she thought, to consider Zak's parents interlopers. But if they weren't there to help, what else could she think? She headed back to Zak's room. At least for the moment, she'd be alone with Zak, able to determine what he'd like to do next.

"Tell me, Mr. Popular," she said as she sat in the chair next to Zak's bed. "What do you want to do about your visitors?"

Zak's face was ashen. He rolled his eyes as if exasperated.

"Can you hear me?" Helena asked, uncertain she'd made herself understood.

Zak sighed. "I can hear you. I just wish they'd all go. My mother wants me back in New York. I can't do that. They won't let me be who I am."

Helena didn't follow. "What does that mean?"

"They want me to be heterosexual."

Helena tried to maintain a neutral expression, though inwardly, she was shocked that Zak's parents might hold such outdated beliefs. It seemed so irrational. Silly. Cruel. Absolutely pointless. "Maybe, you just need to talk with them again."

"I don't think they'd listen."

Helena couldn't help but marvel at the irony of a young man who was struggling with his hearing explaining himself to parents who refused to listen. "But they're here now. Maybe it's time to give them another chance to understand."

"What more is there to say?"

"You can say you love them. That you had no intention of hurting them."

Zak squinted. "Hurt them? This isn't about them."

"Of course it is. They had expectations of what your life would be. Parents do that when they love their children. They create futures. And right now, that future isn't shaping up as they had hoped."

Zak scowled. "It's all about them."

Helena crinkled her nose. "At least for the moment."

"I can't change any of this. Not me. Not them."

Helena placed a hand on Zak's hand. "They must love you very much if they flew all this way to be with you. Don't you think it might be worth another try?"

———

Helena headed straight for the cafeteria to intercept the Andrews. If Zak was about to talk with them about his sexuality, she wanted to be sure they were ready to receive the information. Based on what she'd seen of the twosome, she already regretted the advice she'd so cavalierly dispensed to Zak. But what other choice was there? Zak was miserable. The parents, unforgiving. Clearly, it would be better for Zak's healing if he wasn't so upset. Maybe this was an opportunity to patch things up. And who better to take on the charge than an eighty-three-year-old woman who refused to mind her own business? Though she'd certainly met her fair share of dullards in her lifetime, people who refused to understand another's viewpoint, she knew this interaction with Zak's parents would be especially challenging. If anything, the current times seemed more laden with black-and-white thinkers than ever before. America had become a hotbed of *my way or the highway*. At the very least, Helena hoped to soften the family's position. If they couldn't accept Zak as gay, then at least they could let him remain in Tempe and help him financially.

Ruthie's voice echoed in her ears. *This is not your business. Stay out of it.* But Helena had to do something for that lovely young man. She was certain she was in the right as she strode over to the Andrews' table in the hospital cafeteria, morphing along the way into the most opinionated, know-it-all old woman ever birthed on planet earth.

"Has the doctor arrived?" Zak's mother asked as she caught sight of Helena. Mrs. Andrews half stood, gathering her purse.

"Not yet," Helena said as she pulled out a chair and sat down across from the couple. "His office texted me. He's running late. He won't be here for another hour or so."

"That's awfully inconsiderate," Mr. Andrews grumbled as he bit into a glazed donut.

"He's in surgery this morning," Helena explained. "It isn't personal."

"I want to thank you for looking after Zak," Mrs. Andrews said, ignoring her husband's grumpy mood. "It's nice of you to do this."

Helena checked her watch. She wondered how long this conversation might go on. She guessed Mr. Andrews had four more good bites left on that donut. Just enough time to get the ball rolling before the donut completely disappeared. "I'd like to talk to you about Zak," she confided. "I hope you don't mind if I get personal."

Mrs. Andrews tugged on Mr. Andrews's arm as he started to speak, interrupting him. "Let's hear her out."

"Your son has had a difficult time. Not just with his ear. He'd like to mend the riff in your relationship. He'll be talking to you about that today."

Mrs. Andrews' face lit up. "I'm so glad."

Mr. Andrews spoke. "Has he decided to give up all this nonsense and move back home?"

Helena locked eyes with Mr. Andrews. "What nonsense are you referring to?"

"You know what I'm referring to."

"The whole gay thing?" Helena asked.

Andrews nodded affirmatively.

"Hmm," Helena hummed. *Where to begin?* "Yes, I think he will, but only if you change your eye color from brown to blue. If you do that, I'm sure he can change from being gay to straight."

"It's not the same thing and you know it," Andrews charged.

"I know no such thing," Helena said.

Mrs. Andrews jumped in. "I've been reading about other families in the same situation with their children." She directed her comments to her husband. "If we continue down this path, we're going to lose him."

Mr. Andrews nodded. "I'm prepared to walk away."

Helena gasped. Surely the man must be joking. She refused to believe that anyone who loved their child could walk away. "You don't mean that."

"I do," Mr. Andrews said, his tone firm. "My parents would have never tolerated such insolence."

"And you?" Helena asked Mrs. Andrews. "What do you say?"

Mr. Andrews turned to his wife with a look that dared her to defy him. But the little woman from New York City was not about to be cowed. "I want to hear what my son has to say."

Like a flash, Mr. Andrews was out of his chair. "We're leaving," he said to his wife. "Now."

"I'm not going anywhere," Mrs. Andrews said, holding her ground. "My son is in the hospital and I'm going to meet the doctor. If you want to go back to the hotel, fine. But I'm staying."

Much to Helena's surprise, Mr. Andrews sat back down. His wife had called his bluff and the grizzly bear stopped dead in his tracks.

"Okay," he relented. "I'll listen. But I won't like it."

Helena raised a brow, keenly aware that her best intentions had indeed borne fruit. "Mr. Andrews, when you get to my age, you'll find there are a lot of things you don't particularly like that can't be changed. It's all part of this great experiment called life."

When Dr. Peterson stepped off the elevator, Helena pulled him aside for a private chat. She explained the circumstances with Zak, the arrival of his parents, and how the Andrews family seemed intent on his going back to New York City. Peterson listened, but Helena could tell he was distracted.

"Ms. Greenblatt, I have a lot to do today. If the parents want to take him home, let them. That's their affair, not yours."

Helena tried to interrupt, but Peterson was not about to let her. "You've become too involved. Your job was to make certain Zak had a place to stay after surgery. We wanted a responsible adult to look after him. We need someone who can keep a dispassionate distance. If I got involved in the personal lives of my patients, I'd never sleep at night."

Helena understood. Dispassionate caring. "I admit, I am overzealous," she agreed, hoping if she soothed Peterson, he might hear her out. "And I'm stubborn."

The doctor nodded.

"But Zak doesn't want to leave ASU and his parents are insisting he fly back with them. You must tell these parents that he's your patient and needs to stay in Arizona for follow-up care. They'll listen to you," she pleaded.

"I won't do that. There are plenty of ENTs in New York City who are perfectly qualified to follow up with him. I won't lie."

Helena caught sight of a familiar figure heading down the hallway. The older gentlemen nodded to Helena as he approached. Peterson's father was back.

Tell him about me. Remind him how he was raised.

Helena didn't understand. Why would that change anything?

Just tell him!

"Your dad is here," Helena meekly said, fully expecting Peterson to take off.

Peterson winced. "Don't pull that hocus-pocus mumbo-jumbo garbage on me."

"He wants you to remember how he raised you."

Peterson shook his head. "Don't do that."

Helena held her arms out. "I'm not doing anything."

"You are. You think by invoking my dad, I'll change my mind."

Helena wasn't sure how that could be possible, yet the younger Dr. Peterson was suddenly engaged. He wasn't leaving. Could that dispassionate outer shell be melting?

"My dad made life hard for me. He blocked me at every opportunity. He competed with me. Never once was he proud."

Helena held her tongue. Perhaps the less said, the better. Let Peterson ruminate in his memory of his father.

Peterson rambled on. "He left quite an imprint. Even today, whenever it feels like I'm behaving like him, I do the opposite. You see, I never want to be like my dad."

Ah, there it is, Helena thought. "Then he taught you an important lesson. What would your father say at this moment?"

"My father would have called security and had you physically removed. My father would have unloaded a verbal tirade on you that you wouldn't soon forget."

"Like father, like son?" Helena asked.

Peterson stared into Helena's eyes. His shoulders relaxed. His manner softened. "You don't play fair, do you? Okay," he conceded. "You win. I'll talk to the family."

"No," Helena corrected him. "*You* win."

But in truth, Helena knew the real winners were Zak and Dr. Peterson's dad. The apparition stood next to his son, flashing a bright smile. With her victory at hand, Helena winced when Peterson's iPhone beeped. "Crap! I'm running late for a meeting with the CEO," Peterson moaned upon checking his phone. "I'll be back in an hour," he said as he rushed down the hall and out of sight.

– 24 –

Zak was relieved when Helena cleared out his unexpected visitors. He had a lot to think about. Did it make sense to return to New York City with his parents considering his future at ASU was in limbo? At least with his folks, he was guaranteed a roof over his head. That is, if he were willing to deny his sexuality. But if he stayed in Arizona without a job, he'd soon be out of money. There was no way he could afford ASU tuition, never mind the price of housing if he was on his own.

"Anybody home?" Chuck said as he walked into Zak's hospital room. "Whoa, that's a long face. And I thought I had it bad, spending last night with your friend, *Aruba*. That girl is too much. How did you stand her in high school? She talks constantly about herself."

"She was different then," Zak said, knowing full well Allison hadn't changed. She'd always been self-focused.

Chuck pulled up a chair and sat across from Zak. "I get it. You were trying to pass as straight in high school. You probably put up with all of her bullshit and were grateful to be accepted."

"Right," Zak agreed before realizing Chuck's take didn't make the friendship seem honorable. "Wait a second," Zak protested. "I'm not sure that's exactly how it was."

"Think about it," Chuck said, as he stretched his arms overhead and yawned. "A lot of gay guys have female friends. That's okay, as long as it's a real friendship. But what kind of friendship is this with Allison? Did she encourage you to come out? Or was she happy to cover for you as long as you remained closeted?"

Zak was suddenly defensive. He wondered where Chuck was going with this line of questioning. "It wasn't her job to push me out."

"Don't you see. She used you as much as you used her. You were part of her show. A good-looking guy hanging on her every move. The other girls were probably jealous. And that works for a while as long as you're there for her. Helping her feel secure. I had a female friend in high school who was my buddy too. Until she came on to me. I told her I was gay. Trusted her. But that didn't stop her from trying to change me. It was a confusing time and when I wouldn't play along, she outed me. Nice, huh? I never saw it coming. My senior year was miserable."

Zak winced. "You were outed?"

Chuck shrugged. "I was a jock. I denied it. I didn't have your kind of courage. I still haven't told my parents. To be honest, I'm not sure I ever will."

Zak hadn't considered that he might be more courageous than Chuck. "But you're from San Francisco. Being gay isn't a big deal."

"Tell that to my dad. He's a cop. According to him, *we straight people* are the true minority. I couldn't tell him that I was gay. It would've broken his heart." Chuck let out a bitter laugh. "Or maybe, he would've broken me! I'm not sure that I wanted to hear what he had to say about me being gay. I guess that's why I haven't come out to my wrestling squad here. Who needs all the stress? I'm just living my life. I don't owe anyone any explanations. Maybe that's why I don't trust Allison. That, and all the other crap she's pulled."

Zak counted his blessings that Allison hadn't outed him in high school. He couldn't imagine having had that news delivered before he was ready. "She'd never have outed me."

"Maybe not. But that doesn't make her a great friend. Honestly, that's just the low bar for what you'd expect from a friend. How do you feel about Allison now?"

"Not good," Zak had to admit as he filled Chuck in on the arrival of his parents, but it wasn't until he started to talk about leaving ASU that he unexpectedly began to cry. Shame washed over him as the tears rushed forward.

"Right now, your plate's full. Don't future trip," Chuck advised. "Rest and heal. Tomorrow will come soon enough."

"It's not just ASU," Zak gushed between gasps of air. "I don't know how I'm going to manage without hearing perfectly."

Chuck grunted. "What are you talking about? You can hear me."

"It comes and goes," Zak admitted, wiping tears away with the back of his hand. "They say it's the antibiotic gel but I'm not so sure they really know. Sometimes, if you turn away, I'm not sure what you're saying. I have to read your lips to be sure. And I suck at reading lips."

"Maybe you'll need to wear a hearing aid. Look on the bright side. It's still a manageable handicap. One you can live with. Plenty of people have hearing problems. My dad wears a hearing aid."

"But he's old," Zak said, surprised how quickly he felt the need to point out the obvious.

"Who cares? I swear, you're the only one who cares," Chuck said as he whipped out his iPhone and tapped away before holding it up to Zak to see. "According to Google there are 11 million Americans who consider themselves deaf or with serious hearing issues."

It was hard for Zak to release his fantasy of being just like everyone else. "When I had one good ear, I was perfectly fine. I never considered myself disabled."

Chuck shook his head. "You were never perfectly fine. You just didn't let your hearing dictate your attitude. So why do that now? I'm sure there was plenty you didn't hear when you had one good ear. You just didn't know it. Has the doctor said your hearing won't come back?"

"Just the opposite. He said I'll be fine."

Chuck exhaled. "Then stop making such a big deal. God, you really know how to carry on."

Zak knew Chuck was right. If carrying on were a sport at the Olympics, he'd earn a gold medal. "I get it. You're right. But there must be something that totally consumes your focus."

Chuck didn't hesitate for a moment. "Staying in my weight class. I have to practically starve myself not to weigh out."

"But that's temporary. While you're in college."

Chuck seemed to take offense. "Hey dude, my scholarship depends on my athletic prowess. One major injury and I'm out of an education. How would you like to carry that around every day for the next four years?"

"I'm way ahead of you. I've missed midterms. I'm missing classes. I can't catch up. The entire semester is lost. The tuition money, gone."

Chuck shook his head. "There you go again. All helpless. I didn't know this was a competition."

"Sorry," Zak mumbled as he realized he wasn't the only one with challenges.

Chuck smiled. "Good then. Message received. Have you tried talking with your professors?"

Zak grunted. "Sure. Like I know them. Have you ever seen pre-med classes? The lecture halls are huge. It's like everyone on campus is in those classes."

"Wow. That's a gross exaggeration."

"You know what I mean."

Chuck crossed his arms, fists resting behind his biceps which only made them appear larger. "Whoa. These excuses are too much. So what? The classes are big. Get a note from your doctor that you needed surgery. Start with the dean. Tell him what happened."

"Marshall already talked with the dean. The dean said it's up to each professor to make the determination."

"Did Marshall give the dean a note from your surgeon?"

Zak shook his head. How could he? Zak hadn't yet asked Peterson to write the note.

"Then get on it. When you get out of here, go in and personally talk with the dean. Don't give up. Lobby your professors. See what they're willing to do."

"How can I manage that when I'm struggling with my hearing?"

Chuck rolled his eyes. "God, you're acting so pathetic. Find a way. How about if Marshall and I help out? He'll take two professors, I'll take two. We'll go with you. But you'll need to do the talking."

Zak considered Chuck's offer. "Who will go with me to talk to the dean?"

"Take Melinda with you."

"I can't impose on her."

"Then take the old lady . . . I mean, Helena. She'll do it."

"You think?"

"Are you kidding? She'll do anything to help you. Just ask her. She'd probably jump at the chance."

Zak leaned back in bed. Well, it was a plan. At the very least, he needed to give it a try.

———≈———

Difficult mornings may lead to difficult days, or so Zak imagined. And if there'd ever been a difficult morning, Zak had just experienced it by his parents' and Allison's surprise visit. But there was a bright spot too. Chuck had challenged his thinking about ASU. Made him see that he wasn't exactly powerless. Maybe there was a way to work through the ASU problem. Perhaps he could get an extension to complete the midterms if the dean and the professors were amenable. And where there was a chance, there was hope. And where there was hope, there was opportunity.

Zak began to think through what he'd need to do to get those midterm extensions. The planning proved a welcome distraction from worries about his ear. *One step at a time*, he thought in an attempt to ease his anxiety over ASU. Helena returned from the cafeteria just in time for Zak to ask for her help with the dean. But before he could get his request out, Helena appeared to have something on her mind too.

"So, those are your parents," she said, as she chewed away on her lower lip.

To Zak, her statement sounded like a judgment. "They're difficult," he sighed.

"Your mom's nice."

Zak *hmphed*. "That all depends."

Helena tilted her head as if by viewing Zak from a different angle she'd get a better understanding of the Andrews family dynamics. "Look kiddo," she said, "I've been around the block once or twice."

Zak made a face. "Around the block." He had no clue what the expression meant.

"And I know one thing. You can't force change. Your mom wants to mend this riff between you two, but she needs a chance to work on your dad. He's a little . . ."

"Gruff," Zak said. "Difficult. Mean. Hostile."

"It's sometimes harder for men to accept certain things."

Zak winced. "That sounds pretty sexist."

Helena spread her arms wide. "Okay. You got me. I'm sexist. What can I say?"

Zak raised a brow. Where was this all leading? What was the point?

"Maybe if you give your mom time to do her thing, she'll come through."

"And what would *her thing* exactly be?" Zak wondered.

"Work on your dad."

Zak doubted it. The idea that his mom might be more amenable than his dad was ridiculous. "She was there the night my dad went off. They both kicked me out of the house. It wasn't just my dad. She did nothing to stop it. And she smacked me across the face. Not a great way for her to exhibit her understanding nature."

"That's terrible," Helena said as she continued to chew on her lower lip. "Maybe, given a little bit of time, things will cool off."

Zak rolled his eyes. "They have cooled off. They've gone from cold to frigid."

Helena exhaled. "I'm sorry. There's no excuse for it. It's horrible behavior."

Zak took a breath.

"Sweetie, parents aren't perfect people. But the good thing is that people can change. We have to allow them time to change."

Zak wasn't buying it. "I'm sorry. I know what you're trying to do. Offer me hope. But I think it's too late."

"I know," Helena said, her voice dropping an octave. "I get it. You're young. Everything is black and white. Right and wrong. This or that. But I'll tell you something, even those we love, the adults in our lives, do and say the most foolish things. I've done it myself. Age doesn't make us immune to stupidity. Neither does being a parent. I know. I've made plenty of mistakes.

Adults are just grown-up kids. Some of us never mature. We act like scared children. Afraid of being different. Afraid of change. Afraid of being judged. Afraid of a hundred and one things we don't understand."

Zak's ear perked up. "Are you telling me that you would have treated your sons if they were gay, the same way my parents treated me?"

Helena gave Zak's question a moment to sink in. "Honestly, I'm not sure what I'd have done. My boys were raised in the 1960s. It was a different time. I hope that I might have been more compassionate, but I can't really say. Somehow, I doubt I'd have been kind about it. I'd probably have reacted like your parents."

Zak was shocked. "So, you agree with them!"

"Of course not. But that wasn't what you asked me."

Zak squirmed, unsettling the blanket. "When are they coming back?"

"They're downstairs in the cafeteria finishing up," Helena answered. She checked her watch. "They should be up here any moment."

"One thing more," Zak said. "I need to ask Dr. Peterson for a note explaining my situation so I can go to the dean and then my professors to secure an extension for the midterms."

Helena nodded. "That makes sense."

"But I need someone to go with me to the dean. Someone who can hear the entire conversation and help me make my case. Will you do that with me?"

Helena puffed out her chest as if she were about to salute the flag. "Why, of course I'll do that. Marshall filled me on his visit to the dean. So yes. I'd be happy to go. In fact, I'll set up the meeting and make sure Dr. Peterson gets that letter done."

Zak laid back, his body finally relaxing from all the tension of the morning. Maybe there was a way forward. Maybe all his worries could be addressed if he took one step at a time. He wasn't sure, but he was committed to finding out.

Dr. Peterson's timing couldn't have been better. He showed up to check on Zak a few moments after Zak's parents had meandered back from the café. Helena had ceded her usual position next to Zak's hospital bed to Zak's mother, opting instead to take the spot at the foot of the bed. Zak sensed something had changed. His mother was more upbeat; more connected as she tussled with his hair, running her fingers along his crown just as she had done when he was a boy. Mrs. Andrews, the dainty flower from New York City, had caught a glimpse of the bright Arizona sunshine and perked up, while his dad, ever the moody stranger, stood in the corner of the room with a miserable look on his face.

Zak did the introductions. "Dr. Peterson, these are my parents."

"Nice to meet you," Peterson said, nodding first to Zak's mother and then to his dad. "You and your dad look alike," Peterson observed as he turned his attention to Zak. "You can definitely tell you're related."

Mrs. Andrews was delighted. "He does favor my husband, doesn't he?" she said as she looked at Mr. Andrews. "The height and the dimples. You can't tell now," she assured the doctor, "but when Gerry smiles, it's the same smile as Zak's."

Zak stifled a laugh. Dr. Peterson had yet to see Zak's smile. How could he? There'd not been much for Zak to smile about. And by the dour expression on his father's face, those dimples were bound to be forever a family secret.

"Okay, Zak," Peterson said. "Time to check the ear."

A nurse stood by to assist with the unwrapping of what Zak imagined was the most special of ears. The Rafael of ears. The DaVinci of ears. The Salvador Dali of ears. With a gentle tug and a pull, the doctor removed the internal packing. Zak heard the squeaky wheels of a cart in the hallway as it passed. The ticktock of the clock on the wall. The hum of the HVAC fan. Then, the nurse's happy murmur upon viewing the sutures behind Zak's ear lobe where Peterson had cut through the skull to remove the tumor. Zak was back in the world. No Jell-O crackling. No popping. His hearing seemed sharp. Perfect. Exhilarated, ecstatic, enthused: he'd never felt so alive, so grateful, or so relieved, as if his reintroduction to sound was as miraculous as the Apollo moon landing, the creation of the internet, or the invention of the Apple iPhone.

"There," Peterson said as he applied a fresh packing to the ear and retaped it. "It looks great. Just a few more days and we'll take out the packing. But for now, everything looks fine."

The nurse nodded in agreement.

Peterson turned to Helena. "I think we can discharge Mr. Andrews to your care. We'll set up a series of follow-up appointments. Meanwhile, should you need anything, be sure to call the office."

Helena stood at attention as if commanded into battle. "Absolutely," she said with a huge smile.

"When will he be able to fly home?" Mr. Andrews asked.

"He won't be able to fly for at least three weeks," Peterson said, his face turning beet red. "Until then, I'll need him to remain here so I can continue to check on him."

Mr. Andrews exchanged glances with his wife. "We have an ENT at home who can follow up with him."

"I'm not leaving Tempe," Zak said firmly with a new confidence. "And I'm certainly not going home with you."

The nurse backed away as Peterson looked down, suddenly embroiled in a family squabble. "Your son really should stay until we're finished with his care," Peterson said in a low voice, barely audible.

Mr. Andrews moved closer. He nudged Helena to move over and make room for him at the foot of Zak's bed. It was the closest Mr. Andrews had been to Zak since arriving at the hospital. "If he must stay, okay," he said, directing his words to Dr. Peterson before looking over at Helena suspiciously. "But we certainly don't need a stranger looking after him."

Helena seized the moment. "Then why not let Mrs. Andrews stay with me? She can look after Zak. This way, he'll have the best of both worlds. Tempe, Dr. Peterson, and a family member."

Zak's mother's face lit up. "That's a wonderful idea."

Mr. Andrews glanced about, taking the temperature of the room. "But only for three weeks," he said, pointing an index finger at Mrs. Andrews.

"Yes, yes," Mrs. Andrews said.

Helena glared at Mr. Andrews' finger. Zak wondered what Helena was thinking. Perhaps, the many ways in which she might snap that finger in half.

– 25 –

ONCE ZAK AND his mother settled into Helena's condo, Helena rushed out to Whole Foods. If she was going to have two houseguests, she was determined to stock the refrigerator. Large containers of broccoli cheese, chicken noodle, and Thai Tom Yum soups were the first items in her cart. Would Zak enjoy mac and cheese? Or should she buy a whole pizza? Maybe she should just grab a few premade chicken teriyaki bowls. As she rounded the corner toward the bakery, her eyes zeroed in on the stacks of cookies in clear containers. Chocolate chip, oatmeal raisin, and snickerdoodles. She might handle everyday shopping at Safeway, but for special treats, it was Whole Foods all the way. Or, as she joked, Whole Dollar. Expensive, it certainly was. But to her, it was worth every penny to entertain Zak and his mom in the proper style.

Back at Ventana, refrigerator stocked, Helena made her way to the dining room on the eleventh floor. "Where have you been?" Cynthia asked, seemingly disgusted that Helena had once again arrived late for dinner. "We've already finished our salads."

"I'm sorry," Helena apologized as she locked eyes with Aggie and waved hello. "I had to pad the pantry. You can't have guests and no food in the house."

"Guests!" Babs practically shrieked. "Who, what, when? Tell us everything."

Helena unfolded a while napkin and draped it across her lap. "Remember the young man who was losing his hearing?"

"Of course," Donna said. "So sad for a young man to face such adversity."

"The operation was a success," Helena explained as she reached for the breadbasket. "And now, he will convalesce with me."

Babs passed Helena the butter. "But you said guests, plural."

Helena hesitated. How much should she share? Zak's family dynamics were so fraught with tension. "I invited his mother to come and stay too. I'm sure she'll do much of the hands-on care."

"You'll have a full house," Donna remarked as if people their age never had company.

"If his mother is there, what will *you* be doing?" Cynthia asked with a scowl.

Helena wondered if Cynthia had been told when she was a child to stop smiling. Perhaps that explained why she never smiled as an adult. "Whatever I need to do to make them comfortable."

Cynthia balked. "That doesn't seem right. Surely there are enough hotels in Tempe to house a boy and his mother. Why should you be expected to open your home? It seems like a major imposition."

"Oh no," Babs countered. "It's a good deed. Hotels are expensive. Meals out can really drain your finances."

"They'll certainly be more comfortable with Helena than at a hotel," Donna added.

"Still," Cynthia said with all the gravitas of a displeased matriarch, "that shouldn't be on you. It's a lot of work for an older woman. Shame on them."

Helena was taken aback. "You didn't think it was unfair when it was just Zak."

"That was different. He was all alone. But now his mother is in the picture. Ventana is for those who are fifty-five plus. That young man and his mother are certainly younger than fifty," Cynthia sniffed. "We're not running a halfway house for people who don't match our demographics."

Helena couldn't believe her ears. "We're not running a halfway house! Who is this 'we'?"

Cynthia straightened her back, drawing herself up to full height. "We all have families. We didn't move to this lovely setting to host relatives. What happens if we make an exception for you? What if my son decides he wants my grandchildren to move in with me? Or, God forbid, he loses his job and eyes my guestroom. Do I have to take his squadron of grubby little thumb-suckers into my small space? Not to mention that fishwife of a daughter-in-law. Oh no. The rules protect you and me from unwanted squatters," she said with the wave of an index finger. "Especially, family."

"Oh, Cynthia," Helena said, "I don't believe for a moment that you would deny your family the comfort of your home if the need arose."

"Now, that's where you're wrong."

"*Cynthia*," Babs and Donna said in unison, as if by invoking their friend's name, Cynthia might revoke her opinion.

"I'm not the bad guy," Cynthia insisted. "We all made the same decision when we moved here. No one under fifty-five. And if we have company, it's limited to seven days."

"Seven days is not enough time for Zak to heal," Helena explained.

"Well then, you run the risk of someone filing a complaint."

"Oh, you wouldn't," Helena said.

Cynthia didn't immediately respond. Instead, she tapped her spoon repeatedly on the table as if thinking about it. "No, I wouldn't," she finally agreed, chin high. "But not everyone is as sweet as I am."

Helena smiled. If not filing a formal complaint with Ventana management about Zak and his mother was considered sweet, Helena was willing to concede that Cynthia positively reeked of sugar. Though not everyone had such an intense mix of sweet and sour in their personality as Cynthia. Thank goodness!

Aggie made her way across the room, pitcher in hand, stopping at a nearby table to fill a waterglass. She and Helena exchanged glances. Helena winked. Aggie winked back.

"Are you ready to order?" Aggie asked as she assumed her regular position next to Helena's chair. "The special tonight is meatloaf. If you're concerned about your weight, get the gravy on the side. It's made with heavy cream."

"It's about time you showed up," Cynthia hissed under her breath.

Aggie ignored her.

Helena had always liked meatloaf. "That sounds lovely. Thank you for the recommendation."

"Would you like me to send something up to the condo for your guests?"

"My goodness," Cynthia burst forth, "does everyone know about your houseguests?"

"They're okay for now," Helena told Aggie. "I brought in dinner for them from Whole Foods."

"Good for you," Aggie said, touching Helena's arm. "Have you ever tried their chicken alfredo? It's wonderful."

"No," Helena answered. "Isn't it very rich?"

Cynthia rolled her eyes. "Helena, can you please order. We don't need to go through a roll call of the best dishes from Whole Foods. Really! We're trying to eat dinner here."

"Fine," Helena answered. "Meatloaf and a glass of the house red."

As Aggie hurried off, Helena turned to Cynthia. "Why do you dislike her so? What has she ever done to you?"

"I don't dislike her," Cynthia balked. "I just think she's here to do a job."

"You're abrupt with her," Donna agreed.

"And it's not like she's unpleasant," Babs pointed out. "I often enjoy talking to her."

Cynthia clicked her tongue. "Well then, you can all be best friends with the help. But as far as I'm concerned, you three are my friends. Not that waitress. I just wish she was better at her job."

Helena couldn't resist. "Perhaps she might be, if you weren't always barking at her."

Cynthia held a palm to her chest. "Me? Why, I've never barked at anyone in my life. And certainly not a waitress who can't figure out which way to enter and exit the kitchen."

Helena had noticed Aggie going in and out of the same side of the split swinging doors. A definite waitress no-no. "Well, you should still be nice to her," Helena warned Cynthia. "Especially because we all know what happens when you upset the kitchen staff."

"What?" Babs asked.

"Now that's just hearsay," Donna added. "I worked in a kitchen when I was in college and nothing of the sort ever happened."

Cynthia shifted in her seat. "What are you two talking about? Spit it out."

"Exactly," Helena said with a smile. "Right into your food."

Cynthia gasped. "That would never happen here. Aggie would never . . ."

Helena suppressed a laugh. "You're not so sure, are you?"

"Oh, that's ridiculous," Cynthia said as her gaze shifted down to her salad.

It was eight o'clock when Helena returned to the condo. All was quiet. The door to the guestroom was closed. Helena imagined Zak resting comfortably while his mother sat in the corner chair watching him. In anticipation of Zak's arrival, Helena had turned down the guest bed and made sure the proper toiletries were available in the guest bathroom. She cleared off the decorative pillows from her living room sofa so Mrs. Andrews would have a comfortable place to bed down. It was odd to have strangers as company. Over the years, she'd become accustomed to living alone. Doing as she wished. Now, it felt as if she was supposed to be doing something. Something to amuse her guests, but she wasn't sure exactly what. With Zak's mother in the picture, there was simply nothing to do. No one to look after. Nothing to worry about. Her role had been reduced from patient advocate to mere innkeeper. The hostess who sets up breakfast. Makes recommendations for lunch. Provides suggestions for dinner. All the while making sure there were plenty of clean towels on hand, or anything else her guests might need, including the blanket, pillow, and clean sheets that Helena had laid out on the sofa for Mrs. Andrews.

After setting up the coffee pot for the morning, Helena checked the refrigerator again. Yes, there was plenty of milk. She opened the fruit bin. It too was full. As she contemplated turning in, there was a knock at the door. *Who the heck can that be?* she fretted as she checked her watch. It was eight-fifteen in the evening. Hardly late, unless you were living in a fifty-five-plus building where everyone raced back to their units to catch the evening telecasts of *Jeopardy* and *Wheel of Fortune*.

"I trust your guests are settling in," Gilbert Goldfarb said, wispy white hairs flying about as if he were standing in a windstorm, though the only breeze produced was when Helena opened the door.

"Yes," she said as she stepped into the hallway, pulling the door halfway closed behind her. "What are you doing here?" As soon as she asked the question, her face burned. Her tone was a bit harsh. Unbecoming of a woman her age when talking to an acquaintance.

"I was just wondering," Gilbert said with a Cheshire smile, "perhaps you might want to have a nightcap. I saw you at dinner. You came in late. Otherwise, I would have asked you earlier."

"Why not just stop by the table and say hello?" Helena said. "You could have asked me then."

"Oh, I didn't want to disrupt your meal. Besides, I don't think those ladies like me."

Helena searched her memory. Had anyone ever said anything negative about Gilbert? They'd implied that he was the lothario of the building. But what harm was there in that? Surely, any man of advanced age would be flattered if the women even noticed him. "Oh, no, Gilbert. That's not true," she quietly protested, before remembering the negative comments about his mah-jongg skills. "Everyone likes you."

"You're just being nice, or you'd tell me."

"I'm not that nice," Helena warned. Her face was growing warm.

"So, will you join me for a nightcap?"

Helena gave it a moment's thought. Everything was certainly under control. She wouldn't be sitting in her living room if Mrs. Andrews was going to commandeer the sofa. She'd just sequester herself in the bedroom. And though she had a good book she'd just started, Amor Towles' *A Gentleman in Moscow*, perhaps it was still a bit too early to turn in. "Okay," she said as she cinched the door lock so she could slip back in later without a key. "I could use a little something."

Gilbert's eyes lit up like two firecrackers on the Fourth of July. "Marvelous. If you like, we can sit outside on the roof terrace and enjoy the night air."

"Why not?" she answered, amused to find herself in the company of a man who seemed interested in her. "But aren't I really too old for you?" she teased Gilbert as they walked toward the elevator.

"Too old?" He seemed to ponder the question with a mischievous grin. "I think we're close to the same age. Give or take a year."

Helena burst into laughter. "Absolutely not. I'm years younger than you. Still, I am one of the oldest women in Ventana."

"I like a woman with experience. None of those sixty-year-old babes."

"Babes?" Helena couldn't help but find the term offensive. "Now surely you don't call women babes. It's so disrespectful."

Gilbert took a breath. "No, I don't really use that term. But aside from a woman's beauty, nothing is more endearing than an intelligent mind."

"Really," Helena said as the elevator doors opened and she stepped inside.

"That and a kind heart," Gilbert quipped as the doors closed and the elevator ascended.

⌘

Helena wished she'd brought a light jacket when she and Gilbert stepped out onto the roof deck to enjoy the night air. She wrapped her arms about her small frame as Gilbert, ever the gentleman, slipped off his sports coat and placed it over her shoulders. She'd been so preoccupied with Zak, his story, and now his mother's arrival, that she hadn't had much time to consider her own life. Perhaps that was best. But sitting with Gilbert at a small wrought iron table, sipping a glass of merlot, she couldn't help but wonder what the future might hold. Or even if it was wise to think about the future beyond waking up every morning and trying to be productive. She'd already done more than she'd ever thought possible by just moving to Ventana. She'd started a column in the student newspaper, and though she'd written the first few chapters of what she hoped might be the next Great American Novel, finishing a novel required a significant commitment of time and energy. Was she up to such an undertaking? Was that how she really wanted to spend the next few years? Wrestling over a manuscript that might never be published?

When she'd been younger, she'd measured her life in ten-year increments. On each birthday, she'd review the past and think about the future. But now, ten-year increments seemed like a fool's game. If her health scares had taught her anything, it was to stay in the moment. Enjoy the now. Focus on what's in front of you. Still, she couldn't help but wonder if there was more. More to do. More to learn. More to share. The candle that had burned brightly inside her when she was twenty was still burning brightly, and though the wax might be running low, the heat remained intense and ever- glowing. She knew she wasn't done. Moving to Ventana had miraculously revitalized her. And then, she met Zak. The experience of helping him had awakened something inside. She felt useful. A feeling she hadn't felt in a very long time. Whatever might lie ahead, she hoped it could still be glorious. Miraculous. She refused to feel sad about whatever little time might be left. Though even at eighty-three, she wanted more life. More fulfillment. More time.

"A penny for your thoughts," Gilbert said as he inched his wrought iron chair closer to the table, creating a high-pitched squeak.

"A penny," she quipped. "No one uses a penny anymore. Even the Federal Reserve has done away with the penny."

Gilbert cocked his head. "I have a PayPal account. Will that do?"

Helena giggled. "PayPal. Aren't you modern! If you have Venmo or Zelle, we might be able to hatch a deal."

Gilbert pressed on, his expression one of disappointment. "Of course, you don't have to tell me what you're thinking. I certainly don't want to invade your privacy. I hope it isn't about me. Unless they're good thoughts. Then, that's okay."

Helena rolled her eyes. Why do men always think everything is about them? "It's not about you," she assured him. Though it was on the tip of her tongue, she didn't add, *you silly man.* It seemed unkind, and she'd no intention of being unkind to Gilbert. He appeared far too vulnerable to withstand teasing. Instead, she opted to open up and allow Gilbert in on her thoughts. "Here we are at this advanced stage of life. What we once knew about the world, well, it's all changed."

"Why so sad? That's a good thing."

"Is it?" she asked as she looked up at the sky. "The stars are the same."

"Some things never change."

"I don't remember worrying about time when I was younger," she admitted. "I seem to be thinking a lot more about it now."

"Of course you are. We all are."

"I'm not sure I'm making the best use of it. Does that make any sense?"

Gilbert sipped his wine as he processed Helena's question. His eyes twinkled as if he'd finally come upon a reasonable response. "There's no one best way to make use of time. Just being here should be enough. Who needs the added pressure of assuming something else must be done? Life isn't about scoring goals. There comes a time when it's okay to sit back and just watch the game."

"That's exactly what I'm struggling with. I'm not good at sitting back and watching life happen. I've just *got to get in there*," she said so loudly that a bird perched nearby on the terrace railing took flight.

"Well, good for you. That's fine. That's who you are. We're all different."

"How are you different?" Helena asked, turning her attention to Gilbert as if he were a guru about to reveal the secret to a happy life.

"I've made my peace."

Helena tilted her head. "What exactly does that mean?"

"Oh . . . I recognize that I've come to the end of a long struggle. Decades to be sure."

Helena sipped her drink as she examined Gilbert's face. Barely a line. Quite remarkable for a man in his late eighties.

Gilbert rubbed his thigh as he stretched a leg out. "I've tried to make something of my life, and I have. I've made enough money to be comfortable. But I've also lost a lot along the way. My first wife died when I was in my forties. Breast cancer. The love of my life. I wish I'd spent more time with her instead of working all those late nights. After that, life lost its sweetness. I remarried two more times, but it was never the same. I was lonely. I learned the hard way that it's not smart to be with someone you don't love. It's a mistake. The marriage doesn't last. At least, it didn't for me."

Helena found herself sympathizing. Such a sweet man. So much pain. "You've had your heart broken."

"A few more times than I care to admit. Now I float from flower to flower, never lingering too long, because I don't trust myself. You see, I've learned that I'm vulnerable, and being vulnerable has cost me a pretty penny." Gilbert looked off into the distance. He seemed unable to meet Helena's eyes. "I forgot. You don't like pennies. Anyway, I'm too old to entertain any more heartache. I don't want that in my life."

Helena understood. "You're scared. So, am I your latest flower?"

Gilbert seemed surprised by Helena's directness. "Well, in a manner of speaking."

Helena nodded. At least Gilbert was honest. Still, she doubted he was as innocent as he portrayed. "I bet you're not half as sweet as I imagine. You're probably breaking hearts wherever you go."

Gilbert straightened up, thrusting his shoulder back, head high. "Ahh . . . see? You imagine me sweet. That's part of my charm."

Helena couldn't help but feel sorry for a man who had such a low opinion of himself that he couldn't trust his own instincts. "You're really a sad figure."

"And lonely," Gilbert added, undeterred by Helena's criticism.

"Wait a sec," Helena burst into laughter. "That was a little too fast. Are you handing me a line? Are you working it?"

Gilbert's eyes glowed. "Of course not," he said with a frown, his voice low and serious. But then his voice modulated, hitting a higher tone. "But *is it working?*"

Helena nodded. "It's totally working. Perhaps it's the wine, but you've completely mesmerized me."

Gilbert raised a brow. "Can't it be both?"

Helena was on to Gilbert now. A lothario making his moves. "I think we'd better call it a night," she suggested as she got to her feet. "Thank you for inviting me to go stargazing. Maybe we can do this again soon. But first," she said, an index finger wagging, "I'll have to decide if I want to join your garden club."

"There's always room for one more flower," Gilbert quipped, glass held high in a toast. "Here's to brighter buds."

Helena glanced one last time at Gilbert as she crossed the roof deck and made her way toward the elevator. Gilbert caught her eye. His jubilant smile reminded her of youth itself. Yes, Gilbert Goldfarb was an attractive man. Perhaps she was being foolish, but even at the ripe old age of eighty-three, a woman might need a bit of male attention from time to time. As long as she didn't have to bring Gilbert home, prepare his meals, handle his laundry, watch over him when he was sick, and do all the things that husbands expect of their wives . . . she'd be fine. Age be damned. A little flirtation now and then certainly was nice.

━━⌇━━

When Helena returned to the condo, Zak's mother was sitting on the sofa in the living room reading a book. Helena hoped to keep the conversation short and sweet as she passed by, determined to make it quickly to her bedroom. "Good evening," she said, not wanting to appear rude. "Is Zak asleep?"

Mrs. Andrews closed the book. "He just drifted off."

Helena spotted the title: *Conversations with God.* She'd read it years ago; about a man's spiritual journey to discover the meaning of life through a dialogue with God. "I loved that book," Helena said. "I even purchased the CD set when it came out. Ed Asner and Ellen Burstyn alternatively narrated the part of God. I thought it was brilliant to have God switch genders."

Mrs. Andrews seemed pleased. "I love the message: everyone has the power to affect their life which is why God provides us with free will. I gather you're a religious woman."

Though Helena wasn't sure about the existence of God, the book had intuitively made sense to her. "Well, no," she admitted as she wondered what role religious faith might have played in Zak's family's reaction to his gay orientation. "I like to think of myself as spiritual."

Mrs. Andrews didn't seem to register the difference between religious and spiritual. "Aren't we lucky to have that kind of grounding?" she said, patting the sofa, inviting Helena to sit down.

How awkward, Helena thought. *A stranger in my home with whom I am now compelled to make small talk.* She ignored Mrs. Andrews gesture, and instead pointed toward her bedroom; her hint that she was heading to bed. "Can I get you anything before I turn in? A cup of tea, perhaps?" She hoped the question would be answered with a resounding *no.*

"Can we talk?" Mrs. Andrews asked, pulling the folded bedding Helena had left on the sofa closer to make room for Helena to sit down.

Helena had an uneasy feeling. What was she about to get herself into? Instead of sitting on the sofa, she took a seat in her favorite club chair across from Zak's mother. It was the chair where she preferred to read. The chair with extra padding which made it a pleasure to sit in. The curved back hugged her body, so even as she held her breath in anticipation of a difficult conversation, she felt supported.

Mrs. Andrews crossed her arms and leaned slightly forward. Her voice was a whisper. "How long have you known my son?"

"Not long," Helena admitted. She'd decided to keep all her answers short and to the point to avoid conflict. The less said, the better.

"I'm grateful he has someone to look after him."

"You can thank Dr. Peterson and Julie for that. They worked out the details."

"Julie?"

"The activities director here at Ventana. Very energetic. Very resourceful. Very determined," Helena said. "She arranged for me to volunteer as a patient advocate. Zak is my first client."

"And what have you come to learn about my son?"

Helena hoped she didn't look as stressed as she was beginning to feel. Warning bells were going off. She was reminded of the physician's Hippocratic Oath: do no harm. "Frankly," Helena admitted, "your son is a stranger to me. I know little about him beyond his next doctor's appointment and that he likes PB&J sandwiches. We discussed that in preparation for his stay."

Mrs. Andrews appeared genuinely surprised. "He never mentioned his parents?"

"Not that I recall," Helena lied, unwilling to enter a subject mined with booby traps.

"Then you don't know that our family has struggled with Zak being gay."

There it was. A direct hit. No beating about the bush. How should she answer? Stay above the fray? Pretend ignorance? Or jump in and seize the opportunity to help Zak? She thought for a moment, unsure which direction to take. Ruthie's voice resonated in her head: *Don't be such a freaking coward. It's too late to back out. You're already in.* "Dr. Peterson told me the family wasn't in the picture. Julie also mentioned it."

"Oh God," Mrs. Andrews sighed. "Everyone knows our business."

Oh no, Helena thought as Mrs. Andrews held her gaze. *Now what?* "Was it supposed to be a secret?" she asked, doubting a complicated family matter which required a patient advocate to step in could be kept a secret for long.

"It isn't just that," Mrs. Andrews admitted. "What we did to Zak was . . . well . . . it was terrible. Terrible."

Helena was thankful the stranger on her sofa was showing remorse over an act that Helena had found particularly odious. That was a relief.

Mrs. Andrews covered her mouth with a hand. Her voice soft; barely audible. "Do you have children?"

"Yes," Helena answered. The air in the room seemed to grow heavy. What did her life have to do with Mrs. Andrews bad behavior? *Tread carefully,* she thought, wary of becoming Mrs. Andrews' confidante.

"Sons?"

Helena nodded. "Two. Happily married with families of their own."

Mrs. Andrews locked eyes with Helena. "Do you see them often?"

Helena sighed. There it was. The million-dollar question. *Why,* she wondered, *do some people, when cornered, decide to corner others?* No, she was not going to talk about her disappointments with a stranger. And certainly not with a woman who'd abandoned her son when he revealed he was gay. Oh no. Not going down that rabbit hole. "I'd like to think so," she lied.

Mrs. Andrews's voice grew more confident. Her energy shifted. She was no longer the embittered mom. She was now the conniving prosecutor, and Helena sensed she was about to be cross-examined. "But you're not sure."

"Mrs. Andrews . . ." Helena began.

"Please, call me Betty."

"Betty, I really don't want to discuss my life with you. That isn't why you're here in Arizona."

"No, of course not," she agreed. "But from one mother to another, you must know the disappointment Zak brought into our home. He's our only child. We'd expected . . . no, hoped, for a certain life for him. Perhaps if he'd listened to us, he wouldn't have this hearing problem now. He's never been very good at listening. Maybe this is God's way of shaking him up."

In all of Helena's life, she'd never heard such a load of crap. And though she knew this was not her fight, she couldn't help but feel angry. "Mrs. Andrews . . . I mean Betty, this is none of my business."

Mrs. Andrews inched forward on the sofa as if to close the gap between her and Helena. "Forgive me. I didn't mean to drag you into this."

Helena doubted that was true. She braced herself. Despite her best judgement, she was going in. She just could not help herself. "Yes, well, you did, as you say, drag me into this. So let me say there's absolutely nothing wrong with your son. He's a wonderful young man. And very brave, if you ask me. He was willing to share some personal information in the hope of building a closer relationship with you. But you seem to think his goal was to sabotage the relationship. Nothing could be further from the truth."

Mrs. Andrews sat quietly, as if the weight of Helena's words had actually penetrated. Helena was almost certain they had. But then Mrs. Andrews appeared compelled to argue the point. "I'm not sure you're correct," she said, her voice quivering. "This gay thing isn't right. You know that. None of this is right."

"And why is that?" Helena asked, bound and determined to plant doubt in Zak's mother's mind that her viewpoint was wrong.

"We didn't raise him that way."

Helena tried not to frown. But it was impossible to keep a poker face. "What does that have to do with it? Could you have raised him to be taller or shorter? To have brown or blond hair?"

"You think this is all genetic."

"I don't know what causes sexual identity," Helena admitted. "Frankly, it doesn't matter. Because it just is."

"You make it sound like it's immutable. That you approve."

"My approval, or anyone else's, has nothing to do with whether he's gay. One day, we'll both be dead. Long gone. How he lives his life will be up to him. Not you. Not me. Only him."

"While I'm alive, I can't accept it."

"Then don't," Helena theorized. "You wouldn't be the first parent to disapprove of their child. So what? That doesn't mean you can't love and support your son. He still needs you."

"You don't understand. Gerry and I have an understanding . . ."

Helena had already heard too much. "Please. Don't say another word. I'd like to stop the conversation before it gets heated."

Betty looked askance. "I'm not sure you're a very good influence on my son."

"Well, Mrs. Andrews, frankly, I don't care about your opinion. So, before I say anything that I'll regret, I'm going to say goodnight. Should you need anything else, please feel free to raid the closet in the guest room. I have extra blankets and pillows there. Otherwise, until tomorrow, goodnight."

Helena stepped over the threshold of her bedroom and shut the door. Sweet privacy. No Betty or Gerry Andrews to deal with. Poor Zak. His mother had seemed so intractable. Set in her ways. Now she wondered what her sons might say about her.

The next morning, when Helena stepped out of her bedroom with every expectation of hosting breakfast, she was surprised to find the blanket and sheet she'd taken out for Mrs. Andrews neatly folded on the sofa with the pillow balanced on top. "Where's your mom?" Helena asked Zak when he emerged from the guestroom.

"She's gone," he answered.

Helena guessed Mrs. Andrews had gotten up early and headed to Starbucks. "To grab a cup of coffee?"

Zak grunted something or other as Helena poured a bowl of Honey Nut Cheerios. Had Mrs. Andrews told Zak about their discussion the night before? Helena wished she'd kept her mouth shut, but Mrs. Andrews had asked for it.

"Did something happen between you and your mother?" she probed as she passed the bowl of cereal to Zak. *I should have held my tongue. Said nothing. Me and my big mouth!*

"Yeah," Zak said, his mouth full of cereal. "You happened."

Helena stopped in the middle of pouring herself a cup of coffee. "I'm so sorry, Zak. I didn't mean to . . ."

"She came to talk with me after you went to bed. She told me about your conversation."

"Listen kiddo, I don't know what she told you, but honestly, I was on my very best behavior."

Helena heard Ruthie laughing.

Zak shrugged. "She just decided to leave. No big deal."

"Oh no." Helena moaned. "That's terrible."

Zak scratched his forehead. "I know," he whispered, his voice faltering. "But there was no other choice. I am who I am. I can't change."

Helena came around the counter and hauled herself up onto the adjacent stool. "Now, you listen to me. You shouldn't ever have to change. You're perfectly wonderful exactly how you are."

Zak nodded as tears gathered in his eyes. "That's nice of you to say, but I don't know what to do. I have nowhere to go. I don't have the tuition for next semester. I'm not even sure that I can finish this semester. I'm completely lost."

Helena placed a hand on his and gave it a squeeze. He was in an awful situation and there was little she could do or say to comfort him. What choices did he actually have? "How about if we take it one day at a time? I know you've got a lot on your plate, but I've often found that when things become overwhelming, it's best to narrow your focus. Figure out the next step for that day, and then just do it."

Zak nodded, though he didn't appear comforted.

She felt a terrible sense of failure. After all, Zak's problems were troubling. Real life coming up against the challenges of youth. Zak certainly wasn't the first nor would he be the last youngster to be abandoned by their family. Surely there had to be more she could say. It was infuriating to feel so helpless.

"I could couch surf until I get back on my feet," Zak said as he talked through the choices. "Maybe Marshall will let me crash with his family."

Helena watched in awe as Zak struggled to work through the potential options.

"I'm sure Melinda would take me back at the bar. Maybe I could even bartend. Those folks do okay financially. I could clear enough money to at least stay in Tempe until I can go back to school. If I have to, I could transfer to a community college. I hear they're cheaper."

"You could do that," Helena agreed. "But why did you want to go to ASU in the first place?"

"Honestly? To get as far away from my folks as possible," Zak admitted. "I thought if I studied pre-med at ASU, I'd have a better shot at getting into the new medical school they're opening. I always knew I'd need to support myself. Being a doctor seemed the logical route. I still have four years to decide before I apply, but I'm not sure how it will play with medical school admissions if I wind up at a community college."

Before Helena knew it, the words flew out of her mouth. "Oh no, you don't. You're going to finish at ASU, even if I have to pay for your next semester's tuition."

"I can't let you do that."

"Well then," she said with a firm tone, "you can sign a promissory note to pay me back."

She'd said the very same words to her boys, and still, they'd never paid back a dime. She knew once money was loaned to a family member, the chances of ever seeing it again were infinitesimally small.

Zak's expression fell flat, as if he might have taken the money as a gift if she'd insisted. Helena suppressed a laugh. Oh, to be young and idealistic. "Nothing given freely is ever truly appreciated," she admonished, while resisting the urge to pull out her checkbook and write him a check outright. "Things need to be earned."

Zak seemed perplexed. "Did you make your sons pay for everything when they were growing up?"

Helena gasped. Zak's blunt assessment made her sound awful. Like the worst of mothers. "No, of course not," she defended herself. "But you, young man, are not my son."

– 26 –

ZAK ANDREWS PUT on a brave face, and with the help of Helena, managed through the wake of his mother's departure. Though he'd left his family at the end of high school and moved in with Allison, that had been about self-survival, not punishing his parents for their backward views. This time around, he couldn't avoid the truth. His mother's hasty exit proved the ultimate rejection. A cutting of ties when he was most vulnerable, leaving Zak in a depression he couldn't quite shake off.

Helena did her best to ensure Zak's friends remained close. She opened up her condo to Marshall and Chuck for frequent visits and spontaneous meals. Melinda often stopped by for a cup of coffee and to see how her favorite *Andy boy* was doing. Even Allison, the girl who sucked the oxygen out of the room and should have been in New York City studying theatre arts, could be found late at night sitting on Helena's sofa whispering with Zak.

"I've made up my mind," Allison announced as if Zak should be honored to be included in her momentous decision. "I'm transferring to ASU."

Zak stifled a gasp. He'd been wondering why Allison was still in Arizona. She'd booked a nearby motel room using her father's credit card. The Visa provided in case of emergencies. Zak had no doubt the card was getting quite the workout, especially when Allison showed up in a beige Winslet cashmere cardigan coat. "Whoa," he'd said as he touched the soft cashmere material. "This thing is gorgeous. It must have cost . . ."

"I know," Allison impishly moaned.

In truth, Zak's patience was wearing thin with his high school buddy. Or was he just jealous? Allison knew he was strapped for cash and here she was blowing through money. Plus, it required a huge effort on Zak's part to bolster Allison's ego as she rambled on about the boys she'd met in New York City, the classes she excelled at, and how she was going to build a career on the Broadway stage. Zak wished she'd stop making every conversation about herself. After all, no one could possibly have as interesting a life as Allison pretended. "That coat's very New York City," he said about the cardigan. "But out here, everyone is dressed in jeans and T-shirts. Besides, you love New York City, and that's where all the theater jobs are," he reminded her, wondering if her mind was really made up about transferring. He hoped not.

"I'm tired of New York. It's loud and dirty. I need to get away. Do something entirely different." Allison's eye tic was back, vibrating feverishly.

Zak couldn't imagine Allison doing anything different. If she couldn't be the center of attention, how would she survive? "You can't build a career at ASU," Zak said as he tried to understand why she'd made such a rash decision. "New York City is where you belong. You are New York!"

"I don't need New York," she pouted. "Emma Stone's from Scottsdale."

Zak knew nothing about Emma Stone or Scottsdale. So, he punted. "Sure, she was raised here. But she lives in Los Angeles. Does an actor even need a college degree to succeed?"

Allison was not to be deterred. "Jodie Foster has a BA from Yale. Mayim Bialik, a BA and a PhD from UCLA. It certainly didn't hurt them. Once I'm done with my BA, I'll move to Los Angeles to scout jobs."

Zak wasn't exactly sure who Jodie Foster was, but he was aware of Mayim Bialek from her run on *The Big Bang Theory*. But what was the point in arguing? Clearly, Allison had made up her mind. "What will be your major?"

Allison pursed her lips as if Zak was the dumbest boy in the world. "English, of course."

"English," Zak repeated. "You don't even like to read!"

"Don't worry about me," she said. "I'll be fine. But what about you? What are you going to do?"

"Helena and I spoke to the dean by conference call yesterday. He agreed to the extension on my midterm exams. At first, he argued, but Helena was not about to take "no" for an answer. It was impressive. I then set up a Zoom call with each professor and asked if I could take my midterm next week. Marshall and Chuck helped with those calls. Each professor agreed. How lucky was that? When I catch up on the semester, I'll look for another job. But first things first. As Helena says, one step at a time."

Allison ran her fingers through her blond hair, giving it a shake. Zak wondered if that particular move had any effect on the men of New York City. It certainly didn't work on him. Why did she seem so bored by Zak's recap? More importantly, what was at the root cause of Allison leaving New York City? "Have you flunked out of school?" he asked, taking a wild guess.

Allison dodged the question. "Have you heard from your mother?"

Zak tried not to think about his parents. What was the point? It only sent his mood into a tailspin. Still, he couldn't help but feel tremendous guilt as if he'd done something wrong.

"There's no point in going there," he said, hoping to change the subject back to Allison. But Allison was not about to let it go.

"At least your parents are still married. My folks have already moved on with their very separate lives. My Dad took a job in California, leaving my mom to fend for herself. As far as he's concerned, I don't even exist."

Zak doubted that was true. "Your dad? No way. He loves you. Besides, he didn't leave you. He waited till you were out of the house. Away at college. And let's not forget that Visa card you've been waving around."

"He still left me," Allison insisted. "It's not like I can hop on a plane and visit him."

"Why not? You had no trouble visiting me in September. And now you're back in November. Why not go see your Dad?"

Allison's lower lip trembled. "I can't," she said, shaking her head.

Here we go, Zak thought as he pressed ahead. "Your parents' marriage ended. That isn't exactly a rejection of you."

"Oh, isn't it?" Allison said in a rush.

Zak's temper flared. Why was Allison making her parents' divorce about her? Yes, it was sad. But they still loved her. Clearly, they were financing her life in New York City. He could only imagine what that monthly Visa bill must look like. "When they tell you they don't love you, and don't want to see you again, then you can come crying about your parents' rejection. Until then, get ahold of yourself. You have your life, and they have theirs. I think you're lucky."

Allison wiped away a tear. Her bubbly demeanor, gone.

"You need to grow up," Zak counseled. "You're a young woman who can manage her own life."

Allison looked as if Zak had slapped her across the face. "That's a nice way to talk to a friend."

"Hey," Zak countered, "I'm just keeping it real."

"And what's so *real* about your life?" Allison wanted to know. "You're living with an old lady in a luxury condo. She takes care of you like you're her grandson. I'd say that's a pretty sweet deal." She looked about. "Why shouldn't I want the same for myself?" she asked as if coming up with a brilliant idea. "Do you think once you vacate, Helene might take me in?"

"Her name is *Helena.*"

Allison waved a hand. "Whatever."

"No. Not whatever. And stop referring to Helena as an 'old lady.' She's been amazing to me. Without her, I wouldn't have had the surgery. She's even offered to loan me the money to continue my education. She's been a true lifeline."

Allison seemed to listen, but Zak wasn't sure she grasped the magnitude of Helena's importance to him. "Is she your new best friend now?" Allison giggled, mocking him.

Zak's heart pounded. Was it time to tell Allison the truth? Would this be the ultimate breaking point in their friendship? "There's something seriously wrong with you," he said. It was a bad way to start. "How could we have ever been friends? What could have made me want to hang with you? It's always about you, isn't it? You can't be that insecure and needy."

"Me?" she shot back. "Have you looked in the mirror lately? You're all about your hearing, parents, and ASU. It's exhausting being your friend. You've worn me out. I've tried to be supportive. Honestly, we're all exhausted by you," she shrieked.

"We?" He quickly realized it was the wrong question to ask of the wrong person at the wrong time.

"Marshall and Chuck agree. We're all so over you."

Zak weighed her words. Was she telling the truth? Or was she just trying to get even? He wasn't sure.

"I think we're done here," she said as she lifted herself off the sofa. "Enjoy your life. But don't get too comfortable. You know how you are. No family. No friends. No money. I wouldn't be surprised if you wind up homeless."

Zak watched as she made a hasty exit, slamming the door behind her. He tried to soothe himself. *She's mean. She's not a good person. She's hardly in a position to judge me.* Still, he couldn't help but wonder if she was right. Had his friends grown tired of him? Would he soon be homeless? That certainly was a possibility. He'd seen people standing on corners with signs begging for money. Hands extended in a silent plea for help. Was that his future?

The next morning, Zak sat quietly at the kitchen counter poking at a bowl of cereal as Helena jabbered about her plans for the day. She'd go to the library to work on a new blog for the student paper and then head to a lecture on Egyptian art history by some renowned professor brought in by the ASU faculty. "So how late did you stay up last night talking with Allison?" she asked as she rinsed a coffee cup in the sink.

Zak wasn't in the mood to talk. He didn't sleep well. Allison's prediction about his future was still reverberating in his head. "Late."

Helena slipped the coffee cup into the dishwasher. "She's a very pretty girl."

"Looks aren't everything," Zak answered as he pushed the half-eaten bowl of cereal away.

Helena leaned against the counter, crossing her arms as she studied her houseguest. "Is everything alright?"

Zak shook his head. How could he share with this wonderful lady that he was afraid? It didn't seem right to burden her with more of his problems. Hadn't she already done enough for him? "I'm fine," he said, looking down. He could feel her eyes drilling into him.

Helena took a breath. "No, my darling. Fine, you are not. Tell me what's wrong."

"It's nothing," Zak insisted. Tears filled his eyes.

"You seem awfully upset over nothing," Helena said in a gentle, soothing voice. "We shouldn't have secrets. After all, we're housemates. Now, let me see. What could be upsetting you?" She came around to Zak's side of the counter. "Your hearing has improved. Dr. Peterson said your right ear is now eighty-five percent. That's miraculous. Something to be excited about. You're all set with your professors. I've seen you studying for your midterms. Marshall shared his notes. It's fortunate you two have the same classes. And we've discussed next semester's tuition. I've agreed to loan you whatever you need. So that's covered for the moment. Oh—I know. This is about your parents," she said putting a palm on Zak's back. "You're upset about your folks. Well, given time, they might surprise you and come around. Many parents eventually do."

Zak shook his head. "It's not about my folks."

She sat down on the barstool next to him. "Okay. Then tell me. I'm all ears."

Zak looked away. "I just feel lost. How am I going to manage in the world? I'm all alone."

"You're not alone," Helena insisted. "You have friends. You have me. We're all here."

"My friends . . ." Zak said as he leaned over, his forehead touching the counter, "don't really like me."

"Now where did you get that idea?" Helena asked, indignation in her voice as she encouraged him with a tap on the back to sit up.

"Allison told me."

"Oh, honestly. How would that girl know anything? She's too busy looking in the mirror. I've seen your friends. Marshall and Chuck like you. They wouldn't be hanging around here if they didn't. Melinda too. You're doing just fine with friends. Yes, indeed. Just fine. I'd be proud to have any one of those three as a friend." Helena draped an arm about his shoulder and pulled him in for a hug.

Zak lingered in her arms for a moment, grateful for her affection. When he pulled away, he stared into Helena's eyes to see if she was being sincere. "You're not just saying that to be kind."

Helena hopped off the stool and walked around to the other side of the counter to face him. "Now you're just being tiresome. You've got to stop listening to what others say. Take it from me. You have a long life ahead of you. If you need every Tom, Dick, and Harry to love you, well, you're sunk. It won't happen. You have to be your own man. You have to decide whether *you like you!* The real question is, why would you put your trust in Allison? That, I don't understand."

Zak certainly knew the answer. "She was there when I needed someone. She took me in when I came out. She supported my move to Tempe. Encouraged me to go to ASU. She was my rock in high school."

Helena raised a brow. "Maybe it's time to crawl out from under that rock."

Zak shook his head. "I don't know."

"Okay. She's been good to you."

"She has."

"I'm sure in many ways you've been good to her. But you're no longer in high school and people change. You can't be her cheering section for the rest of your life. And that doesn't give her license to tell you things that aren't true. Someone who does that isn't a friend."

Zak wondered if Helena was right. Had Allison said those things to get a rise out of him? To get even with him? Was she someone he really wanted to continue to be connected to?

"As you get older, you'll find that we have friends for a reason, and friends for a season. If we're very lucky, friends for a lifetime," Helena said. "I like to think people show up when we need them the most. Some friends slip away, and that's fine too. From every connection, we learn a little something about ourselves."

Zak nodded. He liked that way of looking at things.

The following week was off to a fast start as Zak sat for his midterms. He'd moved back into his dorm room, and with the help of Marshall's notes and late-night cramming, managed to wrap up his exams. Once again, he attended the large lecture halls, but this time, without a late-night job to keep him up to all hours, he arrived early to class and sat in the front row. Dr. Peterson had assured him the tumor was gone, but Zak couldn't quite shake the fear that any day he might lose his hearing. That fear propelled him forward, and with it, an intense desire to learn everything he could while he could.

When biology class ended, Zak looked for Marshall. Before Zak's hearing loss, they'd sat together, and while deep in conversation, walked to their next class. But now, Marshall was missing in action. Something had changed in the friendship. Zak remembered Allison's words. Maybe the friendship had been too one-sided. Marshall giving and Zak taking. When viewed in that light, Zak understood why Marshall would keep his distance. *I should have been a better friend*, Zak thought as he made his way across campus. Yet, he couldn't help but feel a growing sense of confidence in being alone. There was no need to make small talk or try to fit in. He didn't have to worry whether he missed any part of the conversation or needed a copy of Marshall's notes. He could relax and be his own person with his own thoughts, processing the world as he encountered it. Alone, Zak was the master of all he thought and said, and happily, he could hear everything perfectly.

— 27 —

Helena grabbed the towel bar and held tight as she waited for the current episode of dizziness to pass. Dizziness had become a fixture in her life, always taking her by surprise. Fortunately, her most recent episodes had happened when she was home. She'd just grab a seat and wait until the cloudy headache passed. Still, she feared a repeat of the time she fainted at Starbucks when she was due back at Dr. Peterson's office to meet Zak. The anticipation of such a public display filled her with dread. She may have relocated to Ventana with its various levels of care to ensure her safety, but she wasn't quite ready to take advantage of the help or admit her dizzy spells were getting more frequent. Instead, she kept her episodes a secret.

Seated on the edge of the tub, she caught her breath. Her doctor had yet to find an explanation for the dizziness, so she shopped for second opinions. One internist offered a particularly sympathetic look, which read: *you're old . . . what do you expect?* Another doctor dismissed her inquiries by explaining everyone in Arizona was lightheaded from the heat. He recommended that she drink more water. Was she dehydrated? She didn't think so. A third doctor, young enough to be her grandson, attributed the dizziness to failing vision. "As we age," he advised, "we lose focus." She'd never heard of such a thing. The boy genius wasn't even an ophthalmologist! Could it be that she'd entered the twilight zone of aging where every ailment was a mystery? Was Rod Serling hanging around the corner waiting for her to implode? Maybe it was just the human experience. Live long enough and you're bound to become a medical enigma.

She thought back on the stages of her life. In her forties, the doctors recommended hormone replacement. In her fifties, she'd undergone small surgeries. A tummy tuck. D&C. A bladder lift for good measure. In her sixties, they cited her mental health, recommending Prozac and Wellbutrin. She passed on that suggestion. In her seventies, the doctors became testy, annoyed that she asked so many questions about her repeated urinary tract infections and painful hip. Didn't she understand the human body was built to go only so many miles? In her eighties, her concerns fell on deaf ears. Who wanted to listen to an old woman struggling with mysterious symptoms? Was she making it up in a desperate bid for attention? She hadn't considered it a possibility until a doctor offered the diagnosis. Was he correct? Was she so desperately lonely that she needed to schedule endless medical appointments to try to get to the root of a problem she'd only imagined had bothered her for over a year? That made no sense. It didn't sound like her at all. But once the doctor said it, she couldn't help but wonder if perhaps there was some truth to it.

Ruthie's voice boomed in her head. *You're not crazy.* Helena didn't know what to think. *This is how doctors silence women. I'd like to see those men manage with our reproductive system.*

Imagine the complaining if they had to go through our monthly cycles, childbirth, or menopause. And you better believe that if men had ovaries, ovarian cancer would have been cured by now. They certainly put enough money into Viagra and all those male potency drugs. As if anyone ever died of erectile dysfunction.

Perhaps that was all true, but it didn't help with Helena's dizziness. Should she go back to her family doctor? Change doctors? See a cardiologist? Visit a neurologist? Did she need a female physician? She had no clue which way to turn. "Why do physicians assume old age is incurable?" she called out in frustration as she continued to balance on the edge of the tub. She immediately caught the irony in her statement. If the only cure for old age was death, that made old age the most curable of all conditions. *If stroke, heart attack, or cancer don't get you, old age is sure to bring up the rear,* she thought, as she decided to once and for all put the dizzy spells out of her mind. She'd already spent too much time focusing on a problem she'd no control over. Perhaps it was time to make peace with the new normal. Give up and assume from here on out, dizziness was going to be part of her life. If so, she'd have to adapt. No more taking the stairs. Far too risky. She'd sit down whenever she got dressed. She'd have to be more mindful of the location of her grab bars, grateful her condo had grips throughout. *Yes,* she thought. She'd befriend the dizziness, if such a thing were possible. Accept it and move on.

⚘

Helena checked the mirror. A little face powder, blush, and lipstick, went a long way. She'd never been one to use a lot of makeup, but now, she realized if she looked better, she'd feel better. And she was all about feeling better.

"You're late," Cynthia complained when Helena arrived for dinner.

"I know," Helena said, as if being ten minutes late for dinner in a place where nothing much was going on was such a terrible sin.

"Were you tending to your young man?"

"He's gone." Helena answered, happy that Zak was better, but missing his company. "He left a few days ago."

"Oh no. So that's why you've been so quiet. Why didn't you tell us?" Donna asked.

Helena shrugged. She hadn't wanted to talk about it.

"Then he's well now," Babs added. "Back on his feet. Back with his friends. That's good news. It's too bad we never got a chance to meet him. I was hoping you'd invite us for coffee."

Helena sighed. They'd been pestering her to meet Zak since the day he arrived. But it didn't seem like the right thing to do. She didn't want to expose him to a lot of questions, especially in light of his troubles with his parents. She couldn't be sure the ladies would be tactful. She didn't want anything said that might upset him. "He wasn't quite up to it," she explained, hoping to sidestep any further questions. But like a dog with a bone, her friends weren't quite done discussing Zak.

"Perhaps we can meet him when he next visits," Babs suggested.

"There are no plans for him to visit," Helena clarified, feeling awful about it. "He's a busy ASU student. I was merely his patient advocate. Now that the job is done, there's no need for any further connection."

"It sounds like you'll never see him again," Donna said.

Helena smarted. Gosh, how the truth hurt. "A young man doesn't want to hang around with an old lady. He's got a life to live. I have no expectations of seeing him again."

"It's always best to have no expectations," Cynthia remarked. "Otherwise, you risk getting hurt. People will always disappoint you."

Donna rotated her water glass. "After all Helena's done, it doesn't seem right for that young man to simply walk away."

"Ladies," Helena said, unable to hide the exasperation in her voice. "That young man has a life. He needs to get on with it. I'm the least of his concerns. Besides, whatever I did was out of the goodness of my heart. He owes me nothing."

Babs recoiled. "Maybe he enjoyed getting to know you. Isn't that enough to maintain a friendship?"

Helena shrugged. How very silly these women could sometimes be. "What does an eighteen-year-old boy and an eighty-three-year-old woman have in common? When you were eighteen, were you even aware of anyone over thirty? I certainly wasn't."

"Helena's right, ladies," Donna said. "We shouldn't expect young people to behave differently than we did when we were their age."

"Are we all so old that we've forgotten what it is like to be young?" Helena added.

The conversation died as Aggie approached. "Are you ladies ready to order?"

Helena took the bull by the horns and opted for the chef's special, eager to redirect the table conversation. That was how it tended to go at dinnertime. The mere mention of food could change the tempo of any discussion as the four friends, after a lifetime of preparing dinners in their own kitchens, reveled at being served a delicious meal in a lovely restaurant perched high above the city of Tempe.

By eight o'clock, Helena was back in her condominium sprawled out on her sofa, watching television, when the doorbell rang. "What the heck?" she complained as she knotted a robe about her waist and padded off to the door in her bare feet. She looked through the peephole. A wisp of white hair waved at her. "For goodness' sake," she moaned, contemplating not opening the door. After all, when someone showed up uninvited, it was well within a homeowner's right to ignore them.

"I can hear you," came the familiar voice on the other side of the door.

Helena covered her mouth. Too late. Gilbert Goldfarb was back. "It's late," she said, as if that might deter him.

"No, it isn't. I'm looking at my watch."

"But I'm already undressed and ready for bed."

"That's alright," Gilbert assured her. "It's not like you have anything I haven't seen before."

If he hadn't been on the other side of her door, she'd have pinched his arm. Hard. Leaving a bruise for him, over which to ponder his bad behavior. "I'm not seeing visitors now. Call me tomorrow and we'll schedule a time."

"I don't want to," he quickly said. "I'd like to talk now."

Honestly, Helena thought. It was a new level of rudeness. She'd heard about not taking a hint. But she wasn't hinting. She couldn't have been more direct had she opened the door and thrown a cold glass of water in his face. "I'm not opening the door, Gilbert. If it can't wait, tell me what you have to say." She fiddled with the bobby pins she used to set the curls in her hair, removing one at a time in case Mr. Goldfarb, with the mighty strength of a man in his late eighties, kicked down the door and made his way inside.

"There's a dance coming up, next week. I want you to go with me."

Helena hadn't heard anything about a dance. But then, she'd been so busy with Zak, she hadn't paid much attention to the Ventana social schedule. "I don't dance," she said.

"You have to go," he pressed.

"There are plenty of other women to ask."

"But I want to dance with you."

Helena blushed. What had she done to attract this roving lothario?

"Say you'll go, and I'll leave you alone."

"How about if I say no and you leave me alone?"

Goldfarb laughed. "That isn't how this works."

Helena was growing tired of the back and forth. Besides, it wouldn't be so terrible to spend an evening at a dance. Actually, it sounded quite nice. A departure from the norm. "Well, okay," she relented, "as long as you promise to leave me now in peace."

"Of course," he uttered as he backed away. "Consider the evening once again yours."

⌘

"I know it sounds foolish," Helena admitted as she and Aggie enjoyed an early morning coffee at the Starbucks around the corner from Ventana. "I'm just not interested in all of that lovey-dovey stuff anymore. I'm not sure I ever was. I think I've outgrown men. Correction—I've definitely outgrown men."

"I think it's kind of sweet," Aggie said as she popped the lid off her coffee cup and inspected the contents. "I hate when they put milk in it for you. It's either too dark or too light. Why can't they leave the milk out like they used to, instead of having the barista add it?"

Helena had an idea. "You don't think kids will fill up their thermoses with free milk if they leave it out?"

Aggie leaned forward and let out a gasp. "Oh my God. Of course. Seniors take the sugar packets from the dining room. Kids must swipe the milk."

They shared a laugh at the absurdity of it all. "We're really not that different," Helena admitted, "college kids and seniors. I keep finding these points of commonality. Just the other day, I was thinking about it for my next blog. There's a real sense of anxiety among these kids. Maybe it's about school and grades, or social connections. I'd forgotten how scary it is to be young and on your own. It's like being old and on your own."

Aggie tilted her head. "I'd never consider someone like Cynthia scared."

"Oh, trust me," Helena advised. "That one is all about fear. The louder they roar, the more frightened they are. And I can't blame her. No relatives nearby. No one to count on. But then, I have sons, and I'm alone."

"Oh, no," Aggie disagreed. "Not you. You're too lovely a person."

Helena sighed. "It's not anyone's fault. I did my best. Or at least I thought I did. It's a strange thing being a parent. One day they grow up and leave. That's how it's supposed to be. And even though you love them, they have their own lives. You really can't be the center of their world. You're lucky if you're a little star off in the distance. But that doesn't mean you don't miss them. Still, in the end, you're on your own. Just like these kids," Helena said as she looked about the Starbucks. "Navigating the world without a compass. Picking up friends here and there." Helena reached over and grabbed Aggie's hand. "Like me, lucky to have found a friend in you."

"And then Mr. Goldfarb comes along," Aggie teased. "You are a lucky girl!"

Helena gave Aggie's hand a shake. "Oh, what to do about Gilbert?"

"If I were you, I'd scare him off."

"He's too sweet. I'd hate to do anything to upset him."

"Sweet! That old rooster has been twice through the hen house. There's nothing sweet about him."

Helena thought of the wispy white hairs atop Gilbert's head. His ebullient smile whenever she crossed his path. His dark emerald-green eyes. His gentlemanly way. So outdated. Almost corny. Yet somehow endearing. "I couldn't hurt his feelings."

"Then he'll be forever around your neck."

Helena let out a nervous laugh. The very thought of Gilbert in her life was unnerving. "I'm just not going there. Besides, who needs a man at this point? Someone to take care of. Oh,

I don't think so. I want to be free. Do the things I want to do. I don't need a man," she said a bit too loudly.

An ASU student sitting nearby caught Helena's eye. "I don't blame you," she said as she leaned forward. "Men need to learn how to take care of themselves."

Helena offered her new friend an enthusiastic fist bump. "See Aggie, this generation of women has their act together," Helena said as a young man plopped down in the seat across from Ms. Fist Bump. The young man fumbled to secure the lid of his coffee cup and Helena's *sister in self-reliance,* who'd just advocated for men doing things for themselves, grabbed the cup and with a snap, secured the lid.

"And that," Helena whispered to Aggie, who'd also watched the exchange between the two young people, "is the problem right there."

Aggie nodded. "We wind up doing everything for them."

"Because they're so damn helpless."

"I guess, in some ways, they are."

"Well, I'm not here to bail Gilbert Goldfarb out of his old age."

Aggie laughed. "He just asked you to go to a dance. Not get married."

Helena caught herself. Aggie was right. Still, she had no intention of sacrificing her life for the needs of a man. This was her time to take care of herself. If she wanted to read a book or take a bath or sleep late, she didn't want to ask anyone for permission. And she certainly had no interest in anything physical a man might want to do, even if he were still able to do it. She suddenly laughed at the thought of a naked Gilbert Goldfarb. She imagined a wrinkled Char Pei. But then, she wasn't exactly a sprite Toy Poodle herself.

"I have to get going," Aggie said as she checked her watch. "If you're joining us today for lunch, the turkey pot pie is delicious."

Helena waved as Aggie rushed off. She was glad to be alone with no need to make further small talk. Strange how life is, she thought. No place important to be. Nothing scheduled for the day. Still, there were things she could do. Write her next blog or continue working on her novel. She might take a walk along Mill Road and peek into the little shops that lined the street. She could catch a ride to Whole Foods and do a bit of shopping. She could head over to Tempe Marketplace, eat lunch, and maybe see a movie. The day was hers and that was a good feeling. She could come and go at her leisure, happy to enjoy her own company.

She took the last sip of her coffee and stood up. She spotted the trash can by the wall. She took a step forward. And then another step. By the fourth step, her headache was back. The familiar thick fog settled in as she struggled to maintain her balance. All the seats around her were taken. She reached forward, hoping against hope to find anything to lean on. The last thing she heard was the scream of the young woman who had proclaimed no interest in taking care of a man.

– 28 –

Alone at his desk, Zak searched the Tempe online job board. With Christmas just a few weeks away, and the end of the semester in sight, he'd have to quickly figure out a way to pay for next year's room and board, not to mention ASU's tuition fee of $15,000 for the semester. Though Helena had offered to cover it, it just didn't seem right to take her money. He scanned the job listings. Wetzel's Pretzels at Tempe Marketplace offered part-time hours. Circle K needed extra hands at the car wash. Safeway advertised for clerks to load grocery shelves at night. Sure, he could do any of those jobs, but none allowed him to earn the kind of money he'd need to stay enrolled at ASU.

He thought about his parents. They might help him if he pretended to be straight. Had he changed so much that he couldn't step back into the closet? He wished things were different. He wouldn't be in this quandary had he kept his mouth shut and just came out after graduating college. But he'd felt like a fraud in high school, closely monitoring everything he said and how he acted. Keeping his parents at bay. Lying to them. Keeping his emotions locked away. No, he couldn't be the old Zak. Some things in life just couldn't be wished away. Not even for $15,000. The situation was hopeless. No job and no scholarship. Worse . . . no future. He'd arrived at a point in his life where he could only hope that something positive might turn up. But could hope ever really be a successful strategy?

His friends were so lucky. Marshall had a secure home life with his parents. Melinda had her Freddy. Allison, well, she had her father's credit card. And Chuck! Lucky Chuck. He imagined Chuck without a care in the world, coming and going as he pleased with an athletic scholarship. An admired jock on campus, Chuck could go to the library and study without being concerned about working. And it hadn't taken Chuck long to make a whole new circle of friends, which meant Zak saw less and less of him. The elusive Chuck was truly blessed.

Zak closed his laptop. He was tired. Something *had* to turn up. But wishing and worrying had never solved anyone's problems, and soon enough, he'd worn himself into exhaustion. Fully dressed, he slipped over to his bed, falling backward until his head rested comfortably on his pillow. It was eight-thirty when he'd closed his eyes. When he awoke, Chuck was back, poring over a textbook at his desk. Zak blinked hard, trying to clear his head. "Hey guy. How have you been?"

Chuck looked up. "Better than you. When did you start sleeping in your clothes?"

Zak smirked. "I'm practicing for when I'm homeless. I better get used to it. January is just around the corner."

Chuck grimaced. "Come on," he said in an exasperated tone. "That will never happen."

Zak was serious. He'd spotted homeless kids on campus. Young men and women who looked strung out on drugs. Could they have once attended ASU and found themselves in a comparable situation? No job. Unable to continue their education. Out of money. "If I don't figure something out soon, you'll have a new roommate next semester. I don't have the money to pay for my spot in the dorm, never mind tuition."

Chuck squished his face up as if he'd sucked on a lemon. Zak had seen Chuck make the same face when watching video replays of past wrestling matches. "Maybe you should create a GoFundMe page."

Zak shrugged. "Okay. But how would I get anyone to contribute?"

Chuck glared. "Hey, bud. I can't think up everything. You need to do the work here. Like get up off your butt and act instead of feeling sorry for yourself. I just suggested the tool. You figure out how to get it funded."

Zak sat up. "I'm sorry. I didn't mean to . . ."

"You give up so easily. You just took your midterms and you're back on track with classes. Marshall and I helped when you were struggling with your tumor. Okay. I get it. You couldn't hear. You needed help. We were glad to do it. But honestly, for all the work we did for you, you didn't seem appreciative. Now, you're bitching and moaning about the next problem. *Poor me. I'm going to be homeless.* Life is tough. But you've got to get your sorry self together. No one is going to do it for you. Figure it out."

Zak was shocked. He knew he'd been a self-centered pain in the ass. Of course, he had. And now, here he was imposing again. "You're right," he agreed. "I've been self-focused. I haven't thanked you or Marshall. I haven't been a good friend."

"No. You haven't," Chuck agreed.

"Are we still friends?" Zak wondered aloud.

Chuck offered an exasperated look. "Yes . . . but you better stop feeling sorry for yourself." He pointed a pen at Zak. "This whole *sorry for yourself* shit is not a good look."

Zak laid back down. Chuck was right. He needed to take charge and pull together a GoFundMe account. But could he raise the thousands of dollars needed to stay in school? Sure, it was a large sum. Maybe he could talk to Melinda about helping him sponsor a fundraiser. Perhaps he could even get Helena to bring her friends from Ventana. He started to get excited. *I'll start tomorrow with a to-do list. Yes, tomorrow will be soon enough. Who knows, by the end of December, with a little effort, I just might have enough money to stay at ASU. Nothing's impossible. It's certainly worth trying.*

⁓

Zak was surprised how easy it was to set up a GoFundMe account. He knew his financial target, added his high school graduation photo, and uploaded a quick video he did on his iPhone explaining his dilemma. Check, check, check.

Now he needed to share the GoFundMe page.

He had less than thirty TikTok followers; high school contacts who were mostly Allison's friends. He couldn't imagine anyone contributing. He was sure that if he did reach out, his GoFundMe account would become a GoUnfriendMe experience. Depressed, he walked the campus until he found himself wandering over to Ventana, wondering if Helena might have time to visit. She'd been a true friend when he needed her, and though he didn't want to impose on her good nature by accepting a loan, he was getting scared. Was the loan still available? Or had she thought better of offering money to a college kid without a job or any resources to pay her back? "You'll get a job," she had said. "Have a little faith in yourself." But that was just it. He didn't have any faith. Not in himself, his future, his friendships, or even the longevity of his hearing. At the tender age of eighteen, any faith he'd once had was long gone. As the Ventana high-rise came into view, Zak was gripped by a terrible mix of fear and sadness. Fear that he was out of ideas and resources. Sadness that he was very much on his own.

"Hello," he said to the receptionist at the Ventana front desk. "I'm here to see Helena Greenblatt. My name is Zak Andrews. I thought I'd surprise her. Can you let her know I'm here?"

The young woman, an ASU student working the desk as a part-timer, recognized Zak. "Are you her grandson?"

Zak was taken aback. "No. We're friends."

"But I've seen you before."

"Right," Zak admitted. "I've stayed here with her."

"That's it," the young woman said. "I asked my boss, Alan, about you." She blushed.

Zak smiled at her obvious interest.

"Have a seat," she said. "I'll be back in a minute."

Zak perused an AARP magazine as he waited in the lobby. The issue featured Sally Field on the cover. There were other stories on Diane Keaton, Clint Eastwood, Liza Minelli, and Dennis Quaid. None were familiar names to Zak. He wondered how they could truly be famous.

"Excuse me," a man's voice interrupted. "Are you waiting to see Helena?"

"Yes," Zak said as he got to his feet. "I'm Zak Andrews. Helena and I are friends."

"Please, sit," the man instructed as he sat down next to Zak. "I'm Alan Lane, executive director at Ventana. Were you the young man who had the ear surgery?"

"That's me," Zak answered, uncomfortable at being known for his hearing impairment.

A young woman with spiky blond hair made her way across the lobby. Alan introduced her. "This is Julie Gold, our activities director."

Zak remembered seeing Julie from a distance when he'd first come to Ventana. He'd been deaf then and Helena, sensing his discomfort, had spared him the struggle of an introduction. "It's nice to finally meet you," he said.

Julie smiled, then nodded to Alan.

"Can we speak to you privately?" Alan asked.

Zak's stomach lurched as he followed the two to a private meeting room. "What's going on?" he asked as he took a seat at the conference table.

Julie answered. "Helena took a bad fall two days ago."

"It's serious," Alan added. "She hit her head on the edge of a table. She's in the hospital."

Zak winced. "Is she okay?"

"We shouldn't be telling you this," Julie whispered, as if lowering her voice made it okay. "It's confidential. But I know how much she cares about you. I thought you might want to visit her."

Zak's heart skipped a beat. "Of course I want to visit her. Which hospital is she in?"

"There's more," Julie warned. "She may not know who you are."

Zak didn't have a clue what they were talking about. "I don't understand."

Alan took the lead. "She's been babbling. Talking to a woman named Ruthie."

Zak nodded. "Ruthie. That's her mother." Julie and Alan exchanged glances. Zak wondered if he'd said something wrong. Based on Alan and Julie's surprised reactions, he guessed he had.

"How do you know about Ruthie?" Julie asked.

Zak remembered Helena's reluctance to admit she had psychic abilities. In truth, he hadn't believed her. He'd heard about older people getting confused. Having delusions. He remembered his parents discussing an elderly aunt who purported to have had an affair with Fidel Castro. His parents had laughed about it. Still, Helena wasn't nutty like that. But then, he didn't know any older people. "She told me about her mother," he said, trying to keep his answer brief.

"Was she talking to her mother when you were staying with her?"

Zak said nothing as Alan and Julie once again exchanged glances.

"Oh boy," Alan said as he scratched his head. "This isn't good."

"Maybe it doesn't mean anything," Julie said.

But Alan was not about to let it go. "You and I both know exactly what it means."

"I don't know what you two are getting at," Zak said. Why had he said anything about Ruthie!

Julie answered. "Assisted living."

Zak looked askance at them. "You mean the third floor?"

"We also have memory care unit on that floor," Alan clarified. "It's a separate section; a lockdown unit for patients who might wander."

Zak refused to believe Helena needed that accommodation.

"I know it sounds extreme," Alan told Zak, "but it's our responsibility to make sure she's safe. And if she can't manage independent living, we're going to move her."

Julie nodded, but based on her expression, Zak could tell there was no pleasure in her agreement.

"We've gone through this before," Alan confessed. "A senior we've come to love and care about suddenly takes a downward slide. That's the odd thing about aging. Life can turn on a dime."

"Turn on a dime?" Zak had never heard that expression.

"In all fairness," Alan pointed out, "it could happen to anyone. You could cross the street and be hit by a car. You're standing in the wrong place at the wrong time, and a tree limb falls on you."

Zak understood. "Like losing your hearing before midterm exams."

Julie and Alan nodded. "But this setback might just be temporary," Julie suggested. "Short term."

Alan rubbed his temple. He appeared genuinely upset. "Or it might have triggered another issue."

Zak's mind raced. "Like what?"

"Confusion is the beginning," Alan explained. "There might be an underlying condition. The start of dementia with an inability to care for yourself."

"No," Zak said, fearing the worst.

"We can always hope it isn't so," Alan added.

Zak didn't like the word *hope* when it came to measuring someone's future. He didn't like having to rely on hope to get him through his financial challenge. He certainly didn't like hope as it applied to the woman who'd taken such great care of him when he needed it the most. "Tell me which hospital she's in and I'll Uber over now."

"No need," Julie said. "Give me a minute and I'll grab my car keys. You can ride with me."

– 29 –

When Helena awoke, the room was dark. She blinked but was unable to move. She was in a hospital bed. That much she knew. But why? There was a stabbing pain in her right arm. No. Not the arm. The right hand. She wiggled her fingers. An IV needle was embedded above the knuckle of the middle finger. *That'll make a nice purple bruise*, she thought. The side of her head was throbbing. Had she been in a car accident? Fallen down the stairs? She tried to remember. Within seconds, the flashback: Starbucks, coffee, Aggie, dizziness. The scream. Helena sighed. *Getting old is a bitch.*

Day turned to night and back again, as various nurses and doctors marched through her room. They scribbled their names on a whiteboard hanging across from the bed, and even though they used a black marker and wrote in large letters, she was unable to focus. They raised her bed, lowered it, and then raised it again. They poked and prodded. Reflexes were studied. Eyes examined. Questions asked. Simple questions to which she knew the answers but couldn't find the words or voice to answer.

What day is it?
That she didn't know.
What time is it?
How could she tell? She couldn't see the clock and the venetian blinds were closed. Wait. Had they just brought breakfast? Or was that lunch? She couldn't remember what was on the tray. She wanted to be helpful, answer their questions, but she found herself useless. Instead, she slept. Until the next person woke her up. She wondered, is this what it's like to be given up for dead?

⁓

Entering the hospital with Julie at his side, Zak was flooded with memories of the days before his ear surgery. How miserable he'd been, isolated in his dorm room with only Chuck and Marshall to lean on. In hindsight, he realized the stress he'd put them under. Expecting they'd provide his meals so that he didn't have to interact with the world. He'd been so difficult. Impatient. Demanding. Certain they couldn't understand his situation. Was it any wonder Chuck and Marshall had given up on him? Chuck, busy with new friends. Marshall, missing in action. Both had avoided him since midterms and who could blame them?

"I think she's sleeping," Julie said as she peeked inside Helena's dark hospital room.

Zak stood behind her. "Why are the blinds drawn and the lights off? It's nearly noon."

"Maybe we should come back later," Julie suggested.

"The last thing she needs is to be left alone." Zak pushed past Julie and called out Helena's name. There was no response. Zak adjusted the blinds, flooding the room with light. Helena was lying flat on her back, eyes wide open.

"Oh my God," Julie whimpered.

Zak jumped into action. "Let's sit her up." With the push of a button, the back of Helena's bed rose until she was in a seated position. "There," he said. "That's better."

Julie tugged on Helena's blanket until it covered her legs. "How did you know how to adjust the bed?"

Zak looked at Julie as if she'd just asked the dumbest question ever. "I was in a bed like this only a few weeks ago. Trust me. I know how everything in this room works."

Julie gripped Helena's bed rail. "She looks really out of it."

Zak lifted Helena's limp hand and held it in his. "Don't say that. She can hear you."

Julie covered her mouth. "I'm sorry," she murmured.

"I bet she's thirsty. Let's get her a glass of water."

Julie looked about. "I don't see a cup."

"They'll have one at the nurse's station."

As soon as Julie left, Zak whispered into Helena's ear, "Alone at last." He remembered Helena laughing when they'd watched an old movie together and the actor had whispered romantic nonsense into the heroine's ear. Sure enough, the corner of Helena's mouth curled slightly upward as she squeezed his hand.

By the time Julie returned with a cup of water and a straw, Zak was sitting on the side of Helena's bed and gently massaging her arm. Julie passed the water to him. Zak brought the cup to Helena's mouth, placing the tip of the straw between her lips. Helena immediately started to drink. "There you go," he said as Julie looked on. "You were thirsty."

"You're a natural," Julie said.

"I learned everything I know from her. She took terrific care of me when I was here. Barely left my side. I told her to go home, but she wouldn't. I can't tell you how many times she helped me. Once, they left my lunch on a tray near the bed, but I couldn't reach it. Another time, they left the lights on in the room when I was trying to sleep. She brought in dinner when I thought I couldn't eat another bite of hospital food.

Helped me to the toilet when I was dizzy. She did so much for me. And then, she let me stay with her at Ventana. I owe you a great deal. Don't I?" he said, turning to Helena, realizing he was talking about her as if she wasn't in the room. "Well, I'm here now. You're going to be fine. I'm going to see to it."

Helena assumed she was hallucinating. After all, the IV was pumping all sorts of drugs into her system. Or perhaps Zak was one of those ghostly visitors from her childhood. So many strangers had passed through her bedroom back then. Lying in her pajamas, half-awake in the darkness, the visitors lurked nearby. Scared, she would hide under the covers and wish the apparitions away. Was Zak one of those visions? But then she felt the straw in her mouth and took her first sip of cold water. She knew instantly Zak was real. *Thank goodness*, she thought as Zak settled in and shared the details of his day, the things he was learning in class, and his memories when he was in the hospital. He asked her no questions. Instead, he talked about his friends; brought her up to speed on Chuck, Marshall, and Melinda. It was a blessing to have him nearby. Even if she was unable to speak, she could listen. Yes, they were truly friends, and a friend knows what the other friend is thinking even if they're unable to speak, because much can be known just by looking into a friend's eyes. "I'm here, Helena," Zak said, as he massaged her arm. "You're going to be fine. Don't you worry. Just rest."

She relaxed, comforted by Zak's presence. She hadn't expected it, but now she knew Zak would be there for her. She decided as soon as she was able, she'd amend her will. She'd add Zak as a beneficiary. It'd be a secret she'd share only with her attorney. Zak didn't need to know the details. She felt an immense allegiance to this fine young man who despite his own problems had come to her aid.

You'll beat this, Ruthie's voice echoed in her ear. *This isn't the end.*

Helena nodded, grateful for the assurance.

———◆———

The first few days in the hospital were a blur of visitors. Much to Helena's surprise, Cynthia, Donna, and Babs showed up to sit with her, each taking a morning shift. The afternoons were alternatively covered by Julie and Alan when Zak couldn't be present. Aggie, too, made time in her busy schedule to drop by, once even dragging poor Gilbert Goldfarb, who despite his insistence that he hated hospitals, seemed perfectly comfortable asleep in the corner chair of Helena's hospital room. If she'd been able to speak, Helena would have expressed her genuine appreciation, honored to see the round of visitors. But it was when Zak walked through the door that she teared up, keenly aware that Zak was the glue that held together her visitor's schedule.

"Are you okay?" Zak asked, startled by Helena's jerky movement.

Helena nodded, though she wasn't fine. She was unable to speak, trapped in her small body—and after years of ignoring her family situation, forced to confront the nature of her relationship with her sons. It was one thing to have moved into Ventana to assure her independence. Quite another to realize that when it came to her sons, she was very much on her own.

"We'll get you through this," Zak said, assuming her tears were for her current condition. His warmth radiated through her hard shell of disillusionment. "You'll be talking again. You'll see. We'll get you out of this bed. Try not to worry. Before you know it, you'll be back to normal."

By the fourth day of Helena's hospitalization, Zak's prediction came true. Speech slowly returned as she struggled to grab the words floating about in her brain and direct them onto her tongue. The connections were still there, but the battery was running on low voltage. She was able to move without any lingering paralysis, though there was an awkwardness to her gait. The doctors assured her it was temporary. They recommended a walker to make certain she had adequate support once she returned to her Ventana condo.

As Helena practiced using the walker, Ruthie closely watched over her daughter, making certain Helena was aware of her presence. *See? Just as I told you. You're going to be fine.*

But Helena didn't feel fine. She hated the walker, which symbolized another aging milestone she wasn't quite prepared to accept. Despite what the doctors said, she worried that she might become dependent on the walker. She made up her mind: that was not going to happen.

"You're certainly doing well," the doctor said as he checked her reflexes. "You had us worried for a while."

"Did I, now?" she answered, her speech slightly slurred.

"May I talk in front of your guest?" the doctor asked, acknowledging Zak's presence.

"Oh yes," Helena answered. "We have no secrets."

"I initially thought you had a mini stroke, but I've changed my mind. It was a TBI."

"TBI?" Zak asked.

The doctor spoke directly to Helena. "A traumatic brain injury suffered from a fall."

Helena balked. "That doesn't sound good."

"We can discharge you, but I'm concerned about your being on your own. I know you live at Ventana. I'm going to recommend the staff admits you to their special care unit and makes certain you're monitored."

"That won't be happening," Helena responded.

The doctor took a breath as if by doing so Helena might change her mind. "I'm sorry. I can't release you in good conscience to your own care. You'll need someone with you in case you fall. We don't want you hitting your head again."

Zak approached the bed, taking Helena's hand. "Don't worry about a thing," he said to Helena. "We're going to get you back home and I'm going to stay with you."

Helena shook her head. "Oh no. You have classes."

"I can do both," Zak insisted. "When I can't be at the condo, we'll ask the others to help out."

Helena sighed. "Well, I suppose that might work."

"Of course it will," Zak said. "Everything will be fine. You'll see."

⌁

On the day Helena was discharged, Zak escorted her home. They shared an Uber back to Ventana where Julie and Alan greeted them as they entered the lobby. Though Helena was happy to be back, Alan's expression was unmistakable. Something was wrong and it wasn't just that Helena was using a walker. Helena had hoped to go straight to her condo and lie down. She'd fantasized about the moment, covers pulled up about her neck, head on a soft pillow, as she drifted peacefully off to sleep. But she realized upon seeing Alan's expression that there might be others plans for her return.

They gathered together in a small conference room. Alan led the discussion as Julie, Zak, and Helena listened. Beads of sweat gathered on Alan's brow. "Helena, we've agreed it would be best for the foreseeable future to have you on the third floor where we can look after you."

Helena's heart dropped. She'd already made up her mind. She was going home. "Absolutely not," she blurted defiantly. She had no intention of going anywhere but back to her condo.

And though she tried to keep her tone even, she was unable to hide her irritation. "Who are you to tell me what I need to do? I'm an adult. Completely capable of making my own decisions."

Alan clasped his hands together as if were bolstering himself for a difficult discussion. "When you had the TBI, you were unable to speak. We had to make the decision to move you to the third floor in your own best interests."

"But you have no right!" Helena said, struggling to keep her tone civil.

"It's the recommendation of your doctor and reflects the arrangement we have with you," Alan clarified. "If your medical condition deteriorates, we're required to provide the proper level of care."

Helena refused to be infantilized. "But I'm on the mend."

Alan blushed. "I totally agree. But we made these arrangements before we knew that."

"Well, unmake the arrangements," Helena insisted.

"We can't," Alan apologized. "At least, not today."

Helena reeled as if she'd been slapped in the face. She was certain this would never have happened if her sons were nearby. But they weren't. And how could she blame them? When they were young, she'd been so busy with her career. Come to think of it, when was the last time she'd spoken with either son? She'd been so consumed by rearranging her life: downsizing and moving to Ventana, working on making friends, and then helping Zak. She remembered earlier phone calls. Her boys had mostly talked about their families. They'd never expressed much interest in her life. She'd been hurt, but she covered the pain. What could possibly be gained by being upset? She'd tried to remain involved in their families, but it was impossible to remember the names of the great-grandchildren she'd never met. Was that the reason why they'd drifted apart? Because she'd expressed so little interest in their families? No matter how she thought about it, the distance between them had to be her fault. Something she'd done wrong. A lack of focus. An oversight that had created the gap in the relationship.

Oh, stop it, Ruthie implored. *It's not your fault. Not everything that goes wrong in the world is your fault. All that negativity will get you nowhere. Face the facts: your sons are stinkers. They always were. They always will be. You did the best you could. I say good riddance to bad rubbish.*

Helena fumed. She didn't agree with Ruthie. "I won't stop it!" she suddenly yelled, surprising everyone in the room.

"I'm sorry," Alan said, a troubled look on his face. "What won't you stop?"

Helena wrung her hands. "My mother thinks I'm making a big deal out of nothing. But it isn't nothing. My sons have abandoned me. If they were here, I'd be back in my condo right now, resting."

Alan looked nervously at Julie. Julie leaned forward as if she might reach out and touch Helena. Zak blinked twice, seemingly unable to get his bearings.

Helena dropped her facade of politeness. "My mother thinks you're all lying."

"Your mother," Alan repeated as he stared at Helena. "Are you okay?"

Julie's spiky blond hair seemed to sag in the face of Helena's confusion. "I think Helena needs to lie down. She must be awfully tired. After all, it's been a busy morning."

Helena refused to budge. "I'm not going anywhere until I'm assured that I'm returning to my condo."

"She's upset," Zak said. "Moving her to the third floor can't possibly be helpful."

Helena turned to Zak. "It's my mother who has upset me. She won't stop talking about my boys."

Alan and Julie excused themselves, leaving Helena and Zak alone. Afraid they might be overhead, Zak whispered, "If you mention your mother again, they're definitely going to put you on the third floor for observation. I know we've discussed your gift, but I don't think Julie and Alan are believers."

Helena tried to calm herself. "You're right. I shouldn't have mentioned her. I just couldn't help it. She's been talking to me so much lately. It's difficult to tune her out."

"You've simply got to," Zak stressed.

"Yes," Helena agreed. "No more mother comments."

Sure enough, when Alan and Julie returned, the news wasn't as Helena hoped. There was no way she could go back to her condo. She'd need to check into the third floor, and after a day or so, when the Ventana medical director made his rounds and cleared her to be on her own again, she could return to the condo.

"There you go," Zak said. "That's a reasonable compromise."

Helena was too tired to argue. "Okay," she said. "But I want to see the medical director as soon as possible."

———— ∾∾ ————

Helena tried not to panic. Her newly assigned third-floor room was painted a shade of institutional pink. Gosh, how she hated pink! The space contained a hospital bed, an oak nightstand, a three-drawer dresser, and a tan La-Z-Boy tucked in a corner. Instead of carpet, there was beige tile. Even the one picture on the wall, a photo of a seagull in flight, looked like standard-issue artwork sold at HomeGoods. The room was so institutional that Helena wondered how anyone could enjoy staying in such an environment. But then, it occurred to her that many of the folks on the third floor suffered from dementia. Was it easier to make the rooms look standard issue rather than putting money into a décor patients couldn't appreciate? Was pink the preferred choice to keep everyone calm? Or were the rooms decorated to the tastes of women who tended to outlive the men?

"It's not too bad," Zak said as he looked about.

"Easy for you to say," Helena grumbled, holding tightly onto her walker. "You're not sleeping here."

"I'm sure there are worse places. Like being homeless."

Helena hated false equivalents. "Well, that isn't a fair comparison."

"I'll tell you what," Zak offered. "If you think this is so bad, I'll stay with you."

"Don't be silly. You can't stay here," Helena scoffed.

"Why not?" Zak pressed. "We can push a cot up against the wall. They must have a roll-away bed somewhere."

"Absolutely not," Helena repeated, feeling guilty about making a fuss. "It's not so bad. And I should be out of here in a day or so."

"True," Zak agreed. "But I don't like you worrying."

Helena was losing her patience. She didn't want to stay in the room, but she also didn't want Zak to feel obligated to join her. "I will make the best of it," she concluded. "Now, don't you have classes?" she asked, hoping Zak would take the hint and get on with the rest of his day, leaving her in her misery.

Zak arched a brow. "Are you trying to get rid of me?"

Nothing could have been farther from the truth. If anything, Helena wanted to hold onto Zak a bit too tightly. There was no denying she'd become dependent on him. Scared when he was out of sight. How could she explain the feeling? She realized the special bond when he'd shown up at the hospital to visit her. She might not have been able to talk then, but she was certainly able to feel. How lucky she was to have him in her life. It was as if Ruthie had ordered him up directly from central casting. Clean cut, infinitely kind, and with a smile that could melt the coldest heart. To think this fine young man carved time out of his day to look after her! What had she ever done in her life to be so lucky? How could she express her gratitude to him? "I'll be fine," she assured him. Now, if only she could believe that!

Zak checked his watch. "I do have class on the other side of campus. I better go. But I'll check back with you later. Meanwhile, try not to worry."

Helena chewed on her lower lip. She had to be strong. She had to do what was best for Zak. "Thank you for helping me out, but I really can't take up any more of your time. Shouldn't you be in the library studying?"

Zak flashed a hurt look. "You don't want me to come back?"

Helena instantly realized her faux paus. "Did I say that?"

"It sounded like it."

"I just don't want you to feel obligated to take care of me. It isn't your job."

"Don't be nervous," Zak teased. "I'm not adopting you. But no matter what you say, I will be back. At least until you're up on your feet, one hundred percent."

Helena was grateful for Zak's resistance. As much as she wanted him to get on with his life, she wasn't ready to let him go.

"Now before I head out, let's get you settled," he said, pointing at the bed.

Helena kicked off her shoes and slowly made her way over to the edge of the bed with the help of the walker. She turned about and eased herself down onto the bed while continuing to hold onto the walker. Zak took the walker and parked it within arm's reach. As she swiveled about, he lifted her legs until they rested on top of the comforter. "I am tired," she muttered as she relaxed, her head finally coming to rest on a pillow.

"Sure, you are," Zak said as he made his way out of the room, closing the door gently behind him.

– 30 –

Zak grew tired of reaching for the impossible. There was no way he was going to get a job on campus. Even if he did, he wouldn't be able to come up with the funds needed to stay at ASU. He had only one choice: finish the semester on a high note by making sure his grades were top-notch. As for living arrangements, he'd cross that bridge when he got to it. In the meantime, he scanned his chemistry notes. Where to start? What would be on the final? He'd come to the library to try to review it all but found himself distracted by the other students prepping for finals. How were they getting ready? Did they have any tips to share? He looked about the large study hall to see if he could pick up any clues, but there was nothing to be gleaned from the top of the heads of students leaning over textbooks. Not a darn thing!

A familiar voice: "Long time, no see."

Zak turned. Marshall was squatting behind Zak's chair. "Hey," Zak said, feeling suddenly shy.

"What are you studying?"

"Chemistry. Electrons, protons. Atoms."

"Right," Marshall said. "Why not join me in the back of the stacks? There's a small table there. We can study together."

"Are you sure?" Zak asked.

"Of course," Marshall said.

Seated next to each other in a hidden corner, Zak with his notes and Marshall with an open textbook, Zak felt compelled to clear the air. "I want to apologize for being such a jerk."

Marshall nodded. "Yeah. You were a jerk."

"I'm sorry," Zak whispered.

"I'll admit it. I was mad. But I've thought about it. I get you were frightened."

Zak nodded. Marshall did understand.

"But now, you're fine."

"I am," Zak agreed as he turned to look at Marshall.

"Good. Then, let's start over," Marshall said, his blue eyes piercing Zak's soul.

"I'd like that," Zak said, unnerved by the intensity of Marshall's stare.

Perhaps there was more to their friendship, Zak thought, as Marshall shifted his attention to the open chemistry textbook and offered a suggestion. "I think the final will include a section on the periodic table. I say we go through the table and make sure we can identify all the elements based on their chemical properties."

Zak struggled to concentrate. The nearness of Marshall was unsettling. He couldn't help but notice the adorable way Marshall's blue hair, the color for December, fell across his brow. Or the sensation of Marshall's knee pressed against his. As they huddled together examining the periodic table over the shared textbook, Zak caught a whiff of Marshall's musk. He struggled against leaning in and kissing the stubble on Marshall's chin as he grew dizzy from reviewing the noble gases, wondering what chemical property Marshall was exuding that made him so darn attractive.

Marshall broke the silence. "By the way, what's happening with Allison?"

Zak shrugged. He'd no clue. He'd last spoken to her the night that she'd stormed out of Helena's condo, upset about her parents' divorce. He'd lost patience with her. Pushed back on her decision to transfer to ASU. Perhaps he'd been too direct. Too harsh. Should friends always support each other, even if they disagree? He wasn't sure. "I don't think I'll be hearing from her again. We had another fight. A doozy."

"Too bad," Marshall said. "She really cares about you."

Zak sighed. "Does she? Or was it all about her?"

Marshall leaned against Zak. Their shoulders touched. "She's in love with you."

Zak could barely contain his shock. "Me? Never."

But Marshall was not about to concede. "You're wrong. I've seen the way she looks at you . . ."

Zak stared at the open book in front of him. He couldn't imagine anyone being in love with him. It didn't seem possible. "I'm sure you're wrong," he said, directing his comments to the page.

Marshall whispered in Zak's ear. His breath sent a shiver through Zak's body. "You're very easy to love. I should know." And there, in a quiet corner of the library, Marshall placed his hands on either side of Zak's face and pulled him in for a kiss as the elements of the periodic table seemed to explode into a combustible mix of intense desire.

***

"Is Helena sleeping?" Zak asked the nurse's aide stationed by the third-floor elevator. He could see Helena's room in the distance; the door was closed.

"She prefers her privacy. We've been instructed to knock before entering. And who can blame her? She doesn't belong here. She's too alert for this floor. Do you know she writes a column for the student newspaper? She told me that she was a real live author, so I looked her up. Such a beautiful lady. Have you seen pictures of her when she was young?" She reached for her iPhone and Googled Helena.

"Whoa," Zak said as he held the aide's iPhone and scanned the Wikipedia page. "I had no idea."

"Right?" the aide said. "She's a celebrity."

Zak was in awe. How could he have known so little about Helena? Sure, he knew she had two sons she rarely saw and that she was a grandmother. But those were only the sketchiest of facts. Like someone knowing he was an ASU student.

Zak swiped through the iPhone. There were images of Helena marching in Washington for women's rights holding up a picket sign: *If Not Now, Then When!* Another photo showed her standing with a group of women: Betty Friedan, Shirley Chisholm, and Gloria Steinem. Zak didn't recognize the names, but assumed they were important. Then, a snapshot of Helena giving a speech on the Washington Mall. "Holy crap," he whispered, coming to terms with the historical importance of the woman he'd befriended. "I guess I was too focused on myself to know . . ."

The aide beamed. "I just ordered her first book. I can't wait to read it. All about a single woman who raises two children on her own and struggles to become a successful writer. I bet it's really her autobiography disguised as fiction."

Zak scanned Helena's author page on Amazon. "She's written eight novels!"

"It just goes to show you," the aide said, sticking her chin out. "You never know who anyone really is in this place. We forget that the elderly were once young and vibrant. You'd be surprised how many people come through here who've lived fascinating lives. I've Googled every last one."

"They all can't be famous."

The aide seemed annoyed. "You don't have to be famous to have lived an important life. Some were adored brothers and sisters. Others, beloved parents who were the backbone of their families. And the tumultuous times they've lived through! It's a history lesson when you get to know them. Some honorably served their country in wartime. Others raised children who went on to make a difference in the world. Each of them has touched the lives of others in a profound way. We think of their lives as being so terribly sad because they wind up here. But nothing could be farther from the truth."

"But they're ill," Zak said, stating the obvious.

"Sure, they are," the aide agreed. "So what? Does illness erase your humanity? Because you're not well, does that mean you shouldn't be championed for all you've done in your life? Do you know how many elderly people have been hidden away? It makes me angry when I hear people say *this one is too old* or *that one is too slow*. My goodness. This older generation has a tremendous amount of knowledge and though it's true some people here are unable to manage by themselves, there are those who can manage quite well. Their brains are still healthy. Like your Helena."

Zak looked about. "How many folks are on this floor?"

"There are fifty beds."

"Beds?" Zak asked. "They've become furniture instead of individuals?"

The aide laughed. "Oh, you got me on that. That's *institutional speak*. Bed count is how we define healthcare facilities."

Zak looked down the hall toward Helena's room. "I'd like to stay overnight with her in her room. Can I do that?"

"I don't see why not. We can pull in a rollaway for you."

Zak imagined himself using a walker to get around. "Helena says that the healthy folks in Ventana are afraid to wind up here."

"That's because they think it's the last stop on the *aging* train. Being here means you need more hands-on care with bathing, dressing, and personal matters than can be managed in independent living. And sometimes, they move along to Memory Care for advanced dementia. That's tough to watch. It's rare for anyone to come here and then return to independent living."

Zak didn't like the sound of that. "Do you think Helena belongs in assisted living? She doesn't want to be here."

"That's for the medical director to decide. But the truth is, none of us lives forever. If we're lucky, we grow old, and along with that comes nature's challenges. But so many people view the third floor as a storage closet for the broken and lost. I like to think of the third floor as a place of peace for those who've had busy and exciting lives and now need to rest. I'm honored to look after them. It's a privilege."

Zak couldn't have agreed more. He certainly felt privileged to spend time with Helena. To be allowed in her orbit. "I think she's expecting me; I'll just go on over and knock on the door."

"You do that," the aide concurred. "She'll be happy to see you. She's such a lovely lady!"

⌇

Helena answered Zak's knock with a loud, "Come in!"

"They can hear you in New York City," Zak teased, happy to see Helena alert and propped up in bed, wearing a purple tracksuit. Zak touched the sleeve. "Velvety. I bet that's comfy."

"I bought it at Saks last year for lounging. I asked a staff member to grab it out of my closet upstairs. I hadn't even taken the price tag off yet." She pulled out the tag from where she'd stuffed it inside the sleeve. "Today is its fashion debut. I wonder: Is it ridiculous to see an old lady in a tracksuit? I'm not exactly Wilma Rudolph!"

Zak thought the tracksuit was pretty. "I like it. But who is Wilma Rudolph?"

Helena balked. "Don't they teach anything in those public schools about the amazing women of the twentieth century? Wilma was a sprinter who overcame polio as a child to become an Olympic champion in track and field. I met her once. Such a lovely lady. Anyway, this is the closest thing I have to pajamas. Look around and you'll see most people here aren't really dressed. At least, not in a presentable way. Before I shut my door, I saw the staff chasing after a man who refused to wear pants. He slipped into my room to hide."

Zak was shocked. He couldn't imagine such goings on. "Were you frightened?"

Helena made a face. "Only when he showed me his weenie."

Zak covered his mouth with his palm. Laughing seemed wrong. "What did you do?"

Helena rolled her eyes. "What do you think I did? I Invited him in for tea!"

"You didn't?" Zak said, bent over in convulsions of laughter.

"Of course, not," Helena said. "I shrieked, 'Get out!'"

"Did you scare him?" Zak asked playfully.

"Oh, you," she answered with a shake of the head. "Don't make fun. One day, if you live long enough, you might wind up in a place like this too. And then, you'll understand why I want out."

"Do you think the guy will run by again?" Zak asked as he glanced out the open door into the hallway. "I'd like to catch the show."

Helena rolled her eyes, but her voice was serious. "I don't belong here. At least not yet."

"Funny," Zak answered, "the nurse's aide said the same thing."

"See?" Helena edged forward on the bed. "But what will it take to get me out?"

"You could start by never mentioning your mother to Julie or Alan again. Pretend you were hatched from an egg."

Helena held a palm to her chest as she stifled a chuckle. "Don't try to cheer me up when I'm miserable."

Zak sat down at the foot of Helena's bed. "It doesn't seem so bad. You have a lovely room. The staff, or at least the aide up front, likes you. If we hung up a poster or two, this room would be nicer than my dorm."

Helena sneered. "Your dorm is a pit."

"Maybe we should switch places."

Helena chortled. "Can you imagine the look on Chuck's face if I became his roommate?"

Zak couldn't imagine. Though he'd bet Chuck would probably prefer the company of Helena to Allison. "Thank goodness you're only here for another night or two. Strictly for observation."

"I've become a scientific experiment in my old age. Watch the old lady. See if she falls. Ten points!"

"You've fallen before," he reminded her. "It's not like it can't happen again."

"So have you," Helena snapped as if her health was akin to that of an eighteen-year-old's and nothing to be concerned about. "People walk. People trip. People fall."

Zak stuck out his chin. "I don't."

"You mean to tell me, you've never fallen?"

Zak thought about it for a moment. "Sure. When I lived in New York City and slipped on the ice. But we don't have ice in Tempe, unless it's floating in your drink."

Helena clicked her tongue. "Well, live long enough and you're bound to fall. You still have plenty of time to eventually find yourself flat on your ass."

"I hope not," Zak replied, keenly aware Helena was growing testy. Maybe he should stop teasing her. "I do have a surprise for you. We're going to have a sleepover."

Helena cocked her head. "What the devil are you talking about?"

"I'm staying the night."

She shook her head vigorously. "Oh no, you're not."

"Yes. I am. They're going to bring in a cot for me."

"You won't be comfortable."

"Of course I will. I can sleep anywhere. Besides, it'll be good practice for when I'm kicked out of student housing and have to live in a homeless shelter." His tone dripped with sarcasm.

"Oh, Zak," Helena moaned. "That won't happen. I won't let it."

"Okay, okay," he said, conceding the point. "But for now, I'm taking care of you, just as you've taken care of me."

Helena warmed to the idea. "Alright," she acquiesced. "Maybe, one night."

"Good. It's settled. I'll head back to the dorm and grab a few things. You sit tight and *I'll be right back.*"

⸺⸻⸺

When Zak returned to the dorm, he felt like a stranger in a strange land. Despite his kiss with Marshall in the library, he couldn't shake the feeling that Marshall and Chuck might have hooked up at some point. He might have once been unable to hear, but his vision had always been fine. More than fine. The way they looked at one another. How they physically connected with a hug when meeting up. It may have been a friendship born out of a shared concern about Zak, but given time, they seemed to be genuinely into each other. And though Chuck and Marshall had been kind to him when he needed them, he couldn't move forward with Marshall unless he knew the truth. He hadn't asked Marshall questions about Chuck when they were studying in the library. The timing just didn't seem right. Certainly not after Marshall kissed him. It would have been too awkward. And he didn't want to appear desperate and needy, though of course, he was in fact very desperate, and awfully needy.

"Hey guy," Chuck said as Zak walked through the door.

Chuck's demeanor had changed since the last time they'd talked. He seemed casual. Nonchalant. Books open on the desk, an empty Red Bull next to his laptop, the college jock was preparing for finals week. Did someone with an athletic scholarship really need to study?

"I was hoping we could grab a bite together," Chuck said without looking up. He underlined something in the textbook with a yellow magic marker.

Zak lingered in the doorway. "I thought you were over me."

"I was," Chuck admitted, as the two exchanged glances, "but then Marshall filled me in on how you stepped up to help Helena. That's so great."

The mere mention of Marshall's name and Zak lost it. "Are you two together?" Zak asked, his tone accusatory. As soon as he asked the question, he felt like a damn fool. So much for trying not to appear jealous.

Chuck leaned back in the chair and crossed his arms. "Marshall and I are just friends. That's it. Besides, Marshall's into someone else."

Zak shrugged. "I should have known."

Chuck broke into a smile. "It's you, idiot."

Zak's heart skipped a beat. "How do you know?"

"He told me."

"And what about you and me?" Zak asked.

Chuck held his hands up in the air. "Hey man, I'm not into you at all."

Zak smiled. "That isn't what I meant. Are we still friends?"

"Yes, of course we're friends. And talking about friends, Melinda was here yesterday looking for you."

Zak dropped into his desk chair. It suddenly felt right to be back. His hearing restored. Chuck across the way. It was like starting over again. "What did she say?"

Chuck glared. "Do I look like your freaking secretary? I didn't take a detailed message."

Zak stuttered. "I . . . didn't . . . mean—"

Chuck laughed. "I'm just busting your chops. She said she was thinking about you and to stop by the bar when you can."

Zak exhaled. "God, I hope she found a spot for me. I could take next semester off and save up some money."

"What about your ear? The noise?"

"I spoke to Dr. Peterson. As long as I keep an earplug in, I should be fine."

"But if you take the semester off," Chuck reminded Zak, "you can't stay here. The dorm is only for registered students."

Even if Zak could get his old job back, there was no way he could ever make the kind of money he needed for tuition, plus room and board. The option remained to borrow from Helena. But she was now in assisted living. He couldn't impose on her. "I hate being me," he whispered, elbows on the desk, hands covering his face. "Why is everything so complicated?"

"That's life," Chuck answered without a bit of sympathy. "We're supposed to struggle, so when we triumph, we've learned something. That's why we're young. We have the energy to do this. Like cramming for finals."

"I want life to get easier," Zak moaned.

"It will. It just takes time."

Zak hoped so, though Helena was old and she still had plenty of problems. "I wonder if it's true that things get better. I can't take much more of this *being young*."

"Don't be so dramatic," Chuck said, hopping out of his chair. "It's not the end of the world. We'll figure something out. But for now, let's head over to the cafeteria. Your problems have made me hungry."

As Zak stood up, he had an idea. "Okay. But let's stop by Windy Canyon first and find out what Melinda wanted. It just might be good news."

———— ✧ ————

Zak had never been inside The Windy Canyon Bar in the early afternoon. It was so quiet. There were just a few customers, and

The Dirty Toenails weren't playing. Thank goodness. Still, old habits die hard, and Zak couldn't help but notice a table here and there that needed a thorough wipe-down. He stopped short of peeking into the bathrooms. There was no point in going there. Some awful places, he guessed, never changed.

"This place reeks," Chuck said as the sour odor, a lethal combination of stale beer, cigarettes, pot, and a hint of vomit, hit Zak's nose.

Zak wondered if things were just different in the daylight. "It doesn't smell this bad at night. They usually have the AC and fans going, which helps move the stench around. And all the ladies with their different perfumes help cover it all up."

Chuck looked about. "Where's your friend?"

Zak made his way back toward the kitchen, waving at Chuck to follow him through the swinging doors. They walked past a series of prep counters, then a massive double-doored refrigerator and stove, before heading down a hallway cramped with boxes. Zak knocked on the first door to the right marked *Private*. There was no answer.

"Sorry man," Zak said to Chuck, "I thought Melinda would've been here."

In the next moment, the door opened. Melinda stood before them, her eyes lit up like the fourth of July. "Well, look at you," she practically shouted. "My handsome, *Andy boy*."

Chuck made a face. "Who's Andy?"

Zak rolled his eyes. "It's a long story."

Melinda laughed. "It's *my special name for Zak*." She jabbed a finger into Chuck's chest as a warning to never use that name for Zak. "I'd invite you to come in," she said as they gathered in the cluttered hallway, "but there's no room." Her private office was barely large enough to hold a small desk and chair. She flashed Zak a smile. "I heard about Helena."

Zak was surprised. "How?"

"We've been texting. How do you think I knew about your surgery? Do you think I just showed up at the hospital to check on you because I dreamt about your pretty face? And now, you're helping Helena," Melinda said, her voice warm, almost maternal. "I was thinking, what if we held an event here? A welcome home for her; glad you're better. Invite the folks from Ventana."

Chuck laughed. "Old folks in The Windy Canyon Bar."

"Sure," Melinda said. "Why not? They drink. And they like music."

Zak couldn't believe her suggestion. "You think they'd enjoy an evening of The Dirty Toenails?"

Melinda chuckled. "Hardly. I don't even enjoy an evening with that band. But maybe we can do it earlier in the day when the place is quiet."

"Good idea," Zak said.

"And I could pipe in sixties rock n' roll on Spotify."

Chuck bobbed his head. "That might work."

"But there's one problem," Zak pointed out. "She's in assisted living. I'm not sure they're going to let her out to attend."

"I thought she had her own place."

"She does," Zak explained, "but after the fall, she started to talk about her mother, and now they've decided it's better for her to be where she can be watched. They think she's becoming confused."

Melinda seemed surprised. "She never mentioned anything about assisted living. How is she managing? Have you spoken to her?"

"I'm with her every day. As much as I can."

Chuck put a hand on Zak's shoulder and gave it a squeeze. "That's a great thing to do."

Zak bristled. "Hey, let's be clear. This is not about me being a terrific guy. Helena was amazing to me through my surgery. She was totally there for me every step of the way. If anything, I owe her."

Melinda crossed her arms. "You don't owe her, honey bun. She didn't do it to get paid back. She did it because she's a loving person and you needed help. That's how kind people behave in the world. When they see someone in need, they act."

Chuck nudged Zak. "Gosh, you're a dope. Do you think Marshall and I helped you hoping you'd do something for us?"

Zak did believe that relationships were transactional. Wasn't that true of his parents? Be a good straight boy . . . and we'll support you financially. But then, Helena was a stranger, and she'd welcomed him into her life. What possible motive could she have had?

Melinda tugged on Zak's arm. "What do they mean by confused? Does she have dementia?"

"From what I can tell, not at all. But I'm worried," Zak admitted. "Helena's afraid she'll never leave assisted living. That she won't ever see her condo again."

Melinda balked. "Then we should talk to whoever's in charge at Ventana and discuss the matter."

Zak wondered if Alan and Julie might be willing to meet. "Let me see if I can set something up."

"Terrific. Schedule the meeting," Melinda said. "We'll see what we can do to move her back where she belongs. And what about next semester? Have you figured out what you'll do?"

"I don't know," Zak answered, though he knew only too well that he had no job, no tuition, and no room and board. "Is there any chance you might have a job here for me?"

Melinda shook her head. "Your job is already filled."

"Then what did you want to tell me when you stopped by the dorm?"

Melinda released a loud *humph*. "I stopped by to check on you. I missed you and was worried about how you were doing. I care about you!"

"You really are a dope," Chuck said as he gave Zak another elbow to the rib.

"So how are you doing?" Melinda asked, a concerned look on her face. "You seem to be fine. You can hear."

"Oh, I can hear," Zak said. "But I've run out of money and I'm not sure what I'll do next semester. I can't pay the tuition. If I don't stay in school, I have no place to live."

Melinda furrowed her brow. "Well, we can't let that happen."

"I know," agreed Chuck.

"I just don't have anything around here for you," Melinda admitted. "Have you tried getting another job?"

"That's what I've been trying to figure out between classes and hanging out with Helena," Zak said. "I just go from one challenge to the next. It's getting pretty tiring."

"Well, hang in there, kiddo," she said as she pulled Zak in for a tight hug. "You're a wonderful guy and I just know something is bound to turn up."

Zak squirmed. *Welcome to another moment of magical thinking!*

– 31 –

WHEN HELENA FINALLY opened her eyes, it was mid-morning. She rolled onto her side. Zak's empty cot sat by the window. The blanket, askew. He'd stayed the night but had already left for morning classes. Chemistry lab, he'd said. She tried the night before to talk him out of staying but he had insisted. He said something foolish: that he was determined to be by her side until she was back in independent living. She thought it sweet. They stayed up late talking and he asked about her family and why they weren't around. She'd struggled to answer, flattered by his attention but uncomfortable discussing her sons. It wasn't as if she and her sons had exchanged angry words or actually had a falling out. How could she explain it? Whatever the relationship was, it had long ago petered out. Perhaps it was her fault. When her boys lived under her roof, she was rarely home. She was busy building a career, attending meetings, writing another novel, or off to an important speaking engagement. When her sons left for college, it was a relief to be an empty nester. The burden of motherhood lifted as her chicks flew free. She'd taken their independence as a sign that she'd done something right. She'd been an excellent mother. But now, their disinterest signaled a different reality. She'd been reluctant to look too closely at the gulf in the relationship. She'd pretended all was well, afraid to ask them too many personal questions about their disinterest in her life. The lack of intimacy created an ever-expanding chasm, which she now imagined was too wide and too deep to surmount. The night with Zak, discussing the past, had left her emotionally depleted. By ten in the morning, she was still in her nightclothes as she napped on and off, furrowing under the covers.

"Good morning, Mrs. Greenblatt," the aide called out as she came through the door. A new day. A new aide. Helena had requested the staff knock before entering, but with the shift change, the request was overlooked. "I'm going to open the blinds and let the sun in," the aide said without waiting for Helena's response. "It's a lovely day and we don't want to miss it. We have all sorts of activities planned. But first, we have to get you bathed and dressed." The aide examined the breakfast tray. "Good. You ate your yogurt and cereal. Wonderful."

Helena smiled, knowing full well Zak had scarfed down her breakfast before leaving for class. She was in no mood to be pandered to and thought herself perfectly capable of attending to her own ablutions without the assistance of an aide. "Thank you," she said, "but I think I'll sleep a bit longer."

The aide's smile was gone. The happy air of frivolity dropped. "Now, Mrs. Greenblatt, we have a schedule to keep. There are other patients to attend to. I've already let you sleep way too long. I can't be fooling around with you all day. It's well past the time for you to be up." She pulled the covers back, exposing Helena to the cool morning air.

Helena's temper flared as she pulled the covers back. "Ex-Cuse-Me," she said, irritation leaching through her enunciation. "I'm not a child and you're not my mother." As soon as the words left her mouth, she felt a distinctive chill in the room. Sure enough, Ruthie was sitting in the corner chair.

You tell her. Who does she think she is?

"Okay," the aide conceded. "I'm not going to fight with you. But I will make a note in your chart. This behavior is uncalled for."

Ruthie blew a phantom kiss at the intruder. *Get lost, sweetheart. We'll call you when we need you.*

As soon as the aide left, Helena started to fret, worried about the documentation in her chart. What would the aide write? How would it reflect on her ability to get back to her condo? She decided nothing good could come from such an interaction. How many more nights would she need to stay on the third floor before returning home? Perhaps one more night until the medical director floated through the unit to sign her out. But how often did the medical director visit the unit? Helena wished she'd asked the question.

What are you so worried about? Ruthie wanted to know.

Helena gasped at what seemed obvious to her. "Have you seen this floor?"

I see it. The interior designer must have been blind to select that color for the tile.

"Not that," Helena said, exasperated to spell everything out for her mother. "This is a special floor . . . unit," she whispered as if telling someone she had cancer. Why did people always whisper that diagnosis? "For people who can't take care of themselves."

Well then, it's simply lovely. Do you remember the horrible place we put Grandma in? The Death Valley Inn or something like that. The smell alone could have killed you. But why are you here? What did you do? Have you been a bad girl?

Helena gritted her teeth. Leave it to her deceased mother to describe her eighty-three-year-old daughter as *a girl*. "I've been having dizzy spells. If you'd paid attention to what's going on, you'd know. Remember my bathroom floor? The EMTs?"

No sooner had she spoken those words than the aide was back, this time with her hands on her hips, a suspicious look on her face. "My goodness, honey. Who are you talking to?"

Helena wished she had a quick answer, but the aide had caught her by surprise. "Just little old me," she lied. "It's something I do to keep myself mentally engaged."

"You talk to yourself in complete sentences?"

"Certainly. That way, I can follow the conversation."

The aide frowned. "That doesn't make any sense."

Helena smirked. "It makes as much sense as me being on this floor."

The aide eyed Helena in her bedclothes. "I don't know about that. You're still not dressed."

Screw off, Ruthie blurted out.

Without a moment's hesitation, Helena turned to the empty chair. "Mother, please!"

The aide nodded. "Hmmm."

Helena blushed. "It isn't what you think."

The aide shook her head and offered a world-weary expression as if she'd seen it all before and there was nothing Helena could do to surprise her.

Helena winced. Now she'd done it. She'd given the woman ammunition. Confirmed that she must have a screw loose and actually belonged on the third floor. That wouldn't do at all. She'd have to figure a way to cover for talking to Ruthie. Nothing immediately came to mind. So instead, she excused herself to take a shower. Maybe the hot water might birth an idea.

If only.

⁓

"I've been foolish," Helena admitted when Zak showed up after lunch. She paced back and forth, no longer in need of her walker. "I think I've made things worse for myself."

Zak dropped his bookbag on the cot. "What do you mean?"

"That woman outside caught me talking to myself."

Zak flopped down on Helena's bed. "Is that all? I talk to myself. So what?"

"But you're not eighty-three returning from the hospital after a head injury. And even though you slept here last night, there's no expectation you'll spend the rest of your life on this damn floor."

"Now you're exaggerating," Zak said with all the certainty that someone who is young and naïve can muster in the face of threats outside their realm of imagination. "You're as sharp as ever. What if you talk to yourself from time to time? It's not illegal."

"But . . ." Helena held her breath for a moment as she anticipated what Zak's reaction might be to the next piece of information. "I'm not really talking to myself."

Zak shrugged. "Well, just tell them you're talking to Siri."

"Siri?"

"You know. The assistant on your iPhone."

Helena had no idea what Zak was talking about.

"The clearinghouse for information on your iPhone. You ask a question, and Siri answers."

Helena had heard her phone speaking, but hadn't realized the voice had a name. She shook her head. "It's not Siri."

Zak leaned backward and rested on his elbows. "Then tell them it's the television. Everyone talks back to the television."

God, how Helena wished she'd thought of that when the aide had come in. She could have lied and said she'd just turned the television off. The same argument could have been used with the radio. She was always talking back to NPR, exasperated that the world was so screwed up. "But I was talking to Ruthie."

She'd spoken extensively to Zak about her childhood with Ruthie, the take-no-prisoners kind of mother who could as easily cut you with her sharp tongue as love you with her warmth.

Zak sat up. "We agreed. You weren't going to mention your dead mother. Remember?"

Of course she remembered. But what did that have to do with anything?

There was silence between them as Zak appeared to think through the challenge. He ran his fingers through his dark hair as if he might shake out a possible solution to Helena's awkward dilemma. "How often do you talk to her?"

It was an honest, direct question without any tone or judgment. As factual as one might ask how often you go for a daily walk. Nothing alarming about the topic at all. Helena felt the tension in her shoulders ease as she realized the extent of her trust in Zak. "Whenever she shows up. Or if I need her."

Zak rubbed the back of his neck. "For real? That's kind of nice. I know we've talked about it. I just didn't know it was truly possible."

"It is for some people," Helena answered, as if they were talking about being double-jointed. She, herself, could wiggle her ears. Not many people could do that. Did that make her strange and different? Well, maybe different. "People don't always approve."

"Of you being psychic?"

"They don't understand."

"Really? With all the famous psychics out there. Have you ever watched Tyler Henry? Or that blond gal from Long Island?"

Helena was shocked someone so young could know two psychics.

Zak seemed surprised that Helena was surprised. "My mother loves those shows. My gosh. The minute they start reading someone, she starts to cry."

Helena had watched a few of those people over the years. It had made her increasingly uncomfortable. She didn't want to be known as kooky. Or edgy. Or odd. All that attention from admiring fans only brought about the naysayers. The ones who complained that money was being made off of the fears and pain of those grieving. "I'm not a television personality with a psychic gift," she reminded Zak. "I'm a real person, just like you. If anything, I'm a serious woman who has had a career as an author. I've been a lecturer. A speaker. I've marched for civil rights and the ERA. I'm not a kook. I might be a serious-minded leftie, but I'm not insane," she said with a laugh. "I'm very proud to be *awake*."

Zak scrunched up his face. "Awake? I think you mean *woke*. Not awake."

"Whatever," Helena said with a wave of the hand.

Zak offered a smile. "Whoever said you were a kook?"

"People don't have to say it. I know what they're thinking."

"You can read minds too?"

Helena blushed. "Well, of course not."

"Then you're probably making too much out of this. So what if you're psychic and talk to yourself now and then? Welcome to the human race. Everyone's probably a little psychic. Why should you be any different?"

Maybe Zak was right and she was making much ado about nothing. It certainly wouldn't be the first time. And probably she'd taken the nurse's aide's comments out of context. It wasn't like they'd ordered a psych evaluation. Or put her into a strait jacket. Perhaps she needed, in Zak's words, to just chill. Not be so uptight. Soon enough, she'd be back in her own place and could rest. "You're a marvel," she said to Zak. "I already feel calmer. Thank you."

Zak beamed. "Glad to help. Now, how about we order from the café downstairs? Something sweet. I vote for a chocolate malted."

Helena lifted the phone to place the order. "I think we ought to have them toss in a scoop of ice cream for good measure."

"That's the best idea yet."

On the second day of Helena's stay in assisted living, she awoke early and quickly dressed. When the social worker arrived by midmorning, Helena was in the activities room watching as the third-floor residents engaged in a stretching class. "Hands over your head," called out a young woman in a pink yoga outfit. She instructed the group with the enthusiasm of a kindergarten teacher. "Now, wave to the stranger across the way," she said as palms flapped and voices were raised in a chorus of giggles. The seniors were arranged in a circle. Some, seated in folding chairs. A few had walkers parked in front of them. Others were in wheelchairs, brakes securely locked.

Helena closed her eyes. She didn't belong here. She no longer needed to use a walker. Instead, she'd placed it in the bathroom to hang dry her delicate washables.

Miss Pink Yoga Lady clapped to get the group's attention. "Alright, everyone. Next, we're going to do a sing-along. I'm going to pass out sheet music. Doesn't that sound like fun?" The instructor provided each member of the circle with a handout and then stepped out of the circle to give a sheet to Helena who was sitting nearby. "Be sure to join in," she cooed.

Helena grimaced as she scanned the words to The Beatles' song, "She Loves You." She could remember the British Invasion of the 1960s when they'd first performed on *The Ed Sullivan Show* and then at Shea Stadium in Queens.

"She loves me, yeah, yeah, yeah," the young woman sang, waving her hand like a baton as she tried to keep the group in harmony. But it was no use. High notes, low notes, altos and bass, blended into a cacophony of sound. Disgusted, Helena headed for the exit. "Wait," the instructor called as Helena opened the door to leave. "We have three more songs. We're not done yet."

"You are as far as I'm concerned," Helena said as she stormed off.

"Helena," a voice rang out as she made her way down the hall. "I'd like to speak with you."

Helena turned. A woman with Bettie Page bangs was following her. As she came closer, Helena spotted a tattoo of a snake wrapped around the woman's neck, the mouth open, fangs bared as if reaching up to devour an earlobe. "Do I know you?" Helena asked as she eyed the horrible tattoo.

"We haven't met. I'm Marlene. The social worker at Ventana. I was hoping we might have a chat," she said with a smile. "If you'll follow me, we can step into my office. It's just around the corner."

Office, Helena thought. *This sounds official.*

The office was a small beige space that held a metal desk, a filing cabinet, and a small side chair. The nameplate on the desk said *Marlene Lesser, M.S.W.* in gold letters.

Helena took a seat as Marlene opened a folder. Was this her psych evaluation? Was it Marlene's job to determine who stayed on the third floor and who could leave?

Marlene cleared her throat as she glanced down at the file, avoiding Helena's gaze. "I understand you've had some problems with dizziness."

Helena nodded, determined to say as little as possible.

"And that you've recently been hospitalized."

Again, Helena nodded. As long as the questions were yes or no, she was confident the interview would set things straight and she'd be back in her condo in no time.

Marlene focused on Helena. "Do you remember how many days you were in the hospital?"

Helena had no clue. She thought it might have been three, but then, she wondered if it had been four. There was a period when she'd been unable to communicate. Had that been for a day? Or maybe, that was two days. In truth, she couldn't exactly recall the timeframe. But wasn't that to be expected? After all, she was in the hospital. But did she have a TIA or was it a TBI? It wasn't a TSA. That had to do with the airlines. No, it was definitely a TBI. Anyway, she'd fallen and hit her head. But what had the doctor said? "I really can't say for sure," she admitted to Marlene. "More than two days, but less than a week." she said as she leaned forward. "But don't you know? It must be in your paperwork."

Marlene jotted a note down in the file.

"Is this an evaluation of sorts?" Helena asked, concerned Marlene was gathering documentation.

"It's just a friendly chat," Marlene said as she continued to scribble.

"Now that's absurd," Helena answered. "If it were a friendly chat, we'd be sitting in the lobby and you'd be telling me about the weather or why you selected that dreadful snake tattoo." Helena's busy mind poured over the possible reasons for the tattoo. Perhaps Marlene fancied herself Eve, lost in the Garden of Eden. Or maybe, she loved snakes and had one at home in an aquarium. Or it might be that the dreadful tattoo was her way of keeping the world away. Like wearing a sign that read *Stand Back or I'll Bite You.*

Marlene's hand went to her neck, unsuccessfully covering the reptile. She didn't offer any explanation. "Helena, we're here to discuss you."

"Well Marlene, if you'd like to know about me, let's begin by using my proper name. I'm Ms. Greenblatt." Helena's heart raced as Marlene scribbled away. She didn't enjoy confrontations, but clearly there was no way to avoid this one. "Why, for goodness sakes, are you taking such copious notes?"

Marlene seemed caught off guard, as if when friends visited, she normally took notes, and no one had ever complained. "I just need to be sure I'm catching your words correctly."

"But why?" Helena insisted on knowing.

Marlene looked at Helena askance. "Is this making you uncomfortable?"

"Oh, don't turn it around on me," Helena said. "You invited me here for a *friendly* chat, and then you started taking notes. I want to know exactly what's going on. What is your intent?"

Marlene blushed. "I just want to ask you a few questions."

"And why is that?" Helena said, wishing her tone had been softer.

"You seem upset," Marlene remarked. "Do you lose your temper easily?"

Helena balked. "If you think I'm angry now, you've lived a sheltered life. Where I come from, anger is expressed by shouting. I've yet to raise my voice. But what I'd like to know is . . . do you always avoid answering questions? If so, that would make you a very annoying person."

Marlene took another note.

"Oh my God," Helena blasted as she got to her feet. "What is wrong with you?"

"We're not done here," Marlene said as if such a statement commanded Helena to sit back down.

"Yes, we are. And by the way, if you want people to talk to you, I'd get rid of the snake," Helena said, pointing at the woman's neck. "It's not only distracting, it's absolutely repulsive. I'm shocked your mother, if she's still alive, hasn't bothered to tell you."

<p style="text-align:center">~~~</p>

I'm in trouble, Helena thought as she shut the door to her room and looked about. My life has come down to a bed, chair, and dresser. How could I have gotten myself into such a situation? And more importantly, how the hell do I get out of here? Maybe I should call the boys. And yet, she resisted getting her sons involved. Would they even come to her rescue? She'd been afraid before, but not like this. She'd lost control of her life. Why had she handed herself over to strangers, placing them in control of her destiny? Beads of sweat broke on her brow as panic settled in. How could she have been so foolish?

Ruthie was back, seated in the corner chair. *How you get yourself worked up! Breathe!*

"Where have you been?" Helena pressed, ignoring Ruthie's pulmonary suggestion. "Things just couldn't be worse. I don't understand what's happening. How could I have wound up here?"

It's not so very hard to imagine. There are three levels of care: independent, assisted, and skilled. You've already done independent, so it's natural the next step would be assisted. By the way, catch me up. Have the doctors figured out what's going on with those dizzy spells?

Helena shook her head.

Of course not. You're at that age when the old machine gets rusty. Nothing works as it once did.

"Oh, I don't believe age has anything to do with this."

You don't. Now who's being naïve?

"It's just complicated."

When you get to a certain age, they think, 'Well, this one is checking out soon. We don't need to work too hard to find what's wrong.' Besides, Medicare pays a lump sum. Extra hospital days or additional tests come out of that one-time payment. It makes financial sense for them to limit services.

Helena was surprised to hear her mother speak about the intricacies of Medicare. "Oh, Mother. Why do you always focus on the negative?"

You don't believe me about Medicare. You'd be surprised what I've come to learn. For instance, the JFK assassination . . . I know who did it.

Helena *hmphed* as she crossed her arms. "Okay. Tell me."

Not on your life. You don't even believe me about Medicare.

Helena rolled her eyes. "So how do I get out of this mess?"

The way you got into it. Use your brain. Think it through. And for God's sake, don't hide in here. Get out of this room and play along with whatever they want you to do. Try to be yourself. The charming, intelligent girl I raised. And let that young man help you.

"How can he help me? He's only eighteen."

Ruthie closed her eyes. *Oh yes. But he's a good soul. He's going to surprise you. Now, go back to that group of aging ragamuffins and participate. Smile. Be helpful to others. Now, go on,* Ruthie shooed her. *Out the door with you.*

– 32 –

WHEN ZAK SHOWED up at Ventana, it was mid-morning, and though he wanted to see Helena, he decided to hold off until after his eleven o'clock meeting with Alan and Julie. He hoped by then to have good news to share with Helena.

He checked his watch. Melinda had promised to meet him at the Ventana cafe so they could talk through strategy, though he wasn't quite sure what Melinda had in mind. After all, Helena was perfectly capable of moving back into her condo. He'd stayed with her for a few nights, sitting up late, talking about life, trying to understand how anyone as lovely as Helena could wind up alone. It just didn't make any sense that her family wouldn't be there to support her. And when the nurse's aide had done her evening rounds, Helena was already in her PJs and bathrobe, the perfect guest on the third floor. In Zak's opinion, there was no point of assisted living if Helena didn't actually require assistance.

Sitting alone at a corner table, Zak worked his way through two bran muffins and two cups of coffee before Melinda arrived. "Didn't you eat breakfast this morning?" she asked as she spotted the empty muffin wrappers.

"I did. But the muffins looked so good. And I wasn't doing anything. Besides, you're late."

Melinda checked her watch. "Not that late. You must have wolfed those muffins down in record time. I thought we were going for lunch after this meeting."

"We are," Zak confirmed. He doubted two bran muffins would slow him down when it came to lunch. "Marshall took me out last night to a great Mexican place. Maybe we can grab lunch there. The tacos and salsa were unbelievable. Really hot and spicy."

Melinda squinted as if too much of a good thing was just too much. "Are you sure you want to eat Mexican again?"

Zak shrugged. He loved Mexican and wasn't that what Arizona was all about? The best darn Mexican food. "Why not?"

Melinda shook her head. "Men. You eat anything and everything in sight and never gain a pound. It's so unfair. But wait a second—what's this about Marshall? I thought that friendship was over."

"It's back on," Zak proudly announced, wishing he didn't blush so easily.

"Really?" Melinda said as she broke into a busybody kind of smile. "Is there more . . ."

"Can we please focus on why we're here today," he said, regretting the mention of Marshall's name. "There's really nothing more to tell," he said, hoping to change the subject.

But Melinda was not put off by Zak's shyness. "Oh, yes, there's more. You two did the nasty. I can see it in your eyes."

Zak scoffed. Yes, they'd hooked up. It happened after class. Chuck had been at wrestling practice, which allowed Zak and Marshall enough time to have the room to themselves. "Does there always have to be more?" Zak said, hoping there'd always be more. Lots more.

"What about Helena?" Melinda asked. "Is she loaning you the tuition money?"

Zak sighed. He wasn't sure how to answer. Helena had said she'd loan him the money, but it didn't feel right asking her when she was initially released from the hospital. And now, she was holed up in assisted living. "How comfortable is your living room sofa?" he half-joked. "I have a terrible feeling I'll be couch surfing come January. Either that or living on the streets."

Little lines popped up on Melinda's forehead as she scrunched up her face. Her lighthearted manner was gone. "Stop it, now. You're not going to be homeless. That's just crazy. We'll figure something out."

Zak ran a finger along the edge of the table. "Something interesting came up this morning. Remember my friend, Allison? She's transferring to ASU next semester. I was certain our friendship was over. We had this terrible fight. But I got a text from her. She's taking a place off-campus and invited me to stay with her."

Melinda grimaced. "Oh no. Not her, again. That girl is obsessed with you."

"Me?"

"Of all the places in the United States, tell me why she's coming here, if not for you?"

"ASU has a great film school. She's switched majors from performance to screenwriting. She initially wanted to be an English major, but that was nuts."

Melinda shook her head. "Be careful."

Zak had no idea what there was to be careful about. Wasn't he the liability? The problem at hand? He considered himself lucky that anyone, no less someone he knew as well as Allison, would allow him to stay should he need a place to land. But today was not about him. He rubbed his palms together. "What should we say in the meeting?"

Melinda didn't miss a beat. "You're going to tell them how well she's doing."

"Right! But why would they listen to me? I'm no one."

"That's why I'm here. I want to be sure they hear you out."

Zak felt a sudden, uncomfortable rumbling in his gut. Had the bran muffins disagreed with him? Was he getting a bellyache? Perhaps it was nerves. "I appreciate your help. I know Helena will too."

Melinda sighed. "Do you remember when we first met?"

Zak nodded. Melinda had been ornery. Downright unpleasant. Nothing like the friend who now sat across from him.

"I'd just come back from my grandmother's funeral in Chicago. She'd had surgery for a broken hip and was transferred to a rehab facility. My grandmother was allergic to nuts. The staff failed to properly monitor her meals, and she had an allergic reaction and died. Now, I'm not saying Helena is in the same situation, but I've come to understand how important it is for a family member to be present. Helena rallied around you when you needed help, and we know older people are prime targets for scam artists. Now, I'm not sure what's going on at Ventana. Maybe everything is on the up and up. I wasn't there for my grandmother, but I can sure as hell be there for Helena. I love how you've stepped up to help her. You're a special guy. Not everyone would have done what you're doing."

"Kindness doesn't always win the day," Zak said as the ache in his gut exponentially intensified. He winced at the next cramp. "Better to be a little cutthroat, I think," he gasped.

Melinda sat back in her seat as she pondered Zak's words. "You'd think so. But the truth is, good people always find good people. That's how life works. Let's hope Alan and Julie are good people." Melinda got to her feet. "I think it's time for the meeting."

Zak squeezed his eyes shut. It didn't seem that the pain in his gut could get any worse. And then, it did. "Oh, my God," he squeaked as he leaned forward, pain ripping through his intestines.

"Are you okay?" Melinda asked, a concerned look on her face as Zak raced to the men's restroom, certain he was about to give birth to an alien.

Alan and Julie couldn't have been friendlier as Melinda and Zak joined them in a small conference room. Alan, much to Zak's surprise, told Melinda how terrific Zak had been through Helena's illness, visiting Helena every day at the hospital and making sure when he couldn't be there, that others were. Julie bragged that she'd been the one to set Helena up as Zak's patient advocate, taking credit for connecting the two. And though both Alan and Julie were upbeat, the conversation struck Zak as odd, as if both were appealing directly to Melinda since she, and not Zak, was the adult in the room—though it had been Zak who'd scheduled the meeting.

"I was hoping you might clear something up for us," Zak finally said as he turned to Melinda, including her in the *us*. "Why is Helena still in assisted living? She's able to take care of herself and she wants to go back to her condo."

Alan and Julie exchanged troubled glances. "Well," Alan began, "it's not that easy."

Zak's chest tightened. There was a visceral pressure to the frustration. A lack of breath that was either the beginning of an asthma attack, which he'd once had as a child, or a keen awareness that he'd have to push for Helena's freedom. Was Alan going to explain why something simple had become so complicated? Did Alan think that by saying it wasn't easy, Zak would give up? "Of course it's easy," Zak countered, struggling to stay calm. "She gets on the elevator and presses the button to the tenth floor. What could be simpler?"

"We have protocols that need to be followed," Alan explained. "Once there are signs of cognitive disability, we move a resident to assisted living. We don't typically move someone with cognitive disabilities back to independent living."

Melinda knitted her brow. "But we thought assisted living was a short-term solution until she was back on her feet. Once she no longer needed the walker."

"Back on her feet," Alan repeated. He looked at Julie as if the two were co-conspirators collecting metaphors to describe their dastardly deeds. "What makes you think she's okay to be on her own?"

"Because she is," Zak said, his tone emphatic. "I've stayed with her. She might get dizzy from time to time, but that doesn't mean she belongs in assisted living."

"Ahh," Alan sighed. "That's where you're wrong. All you need to do is read the Ventana guidelines that every owner signs and agrees to when they buy into the complex. We're obligated to move her to the proper level of care based on her health status."

The tone of the meeting changed as Melinda became more forceful. "I'd like to see those guidelines."

"Are you a relative?" Alan asked, knowing full well Melinda wasn't.

"You know we're not related," Zak said, alarmed that Alan may not be as nice as he pretended.

"Then I'm sorry," Alan continued. "I know how much your friendship means to Helena . . ."

"That makes no sense," Zak said, cutting Alan off. "She wants to go back to her condo. That's what she wants."

Alan took a deep breath, as if by doing so it might give everyone a moment to cool down. "I'm not the bad guy here," he said, defending himself. "When Helena moved into Ventana, she signed a power of attorney. She doesn't get to make the decision."

"You're talking as if she's not competent," Melinda pointed out.

"What about her sons?" Zak asked. "What if they interceded on her behalf? They're relatives."

Julie shifted about in her chair. "Sons. What are you talking about?"

Had Zak stepped into a minefield? Both Julie and Alan seemed confused. Melinda picked up the thread. "Surely her sons should be able to override any decision."

Alan slipped backward in his chair as Julie leaned forward. "She doesn't have any sons," Alan clarified.

Zak's heart skipped a beat. "Of course she does. Nick and Ben."

Julie looked over at Alan, who seemed to take her cue. He directed his next question to Zak. "Did she also tell you that she speaks with her mother?"

Zak wasn't sure how to answer. Was this a trap? A way of getting him to admit Helena was incompetent, unable to care for herself? His silence required no confirmation.

Melinda put a hand on Zak's shoulder. "Maybe there's more here than we know."

"No, no, no," Zak kept repeating. "She's fine. I don't know about her sons, but you can't blame her for living in the past. Pretending her mother is still alive. Maybe it comforts her. Like . . ." Zak struggled to think of a parallel. "Like humming. Some people hum to reduce stress. It's possible that speaking to her mother is a way of comforting herself when she feels stressed."

"Sure. That's possible," Julie admitted. "But she hides it. Like she's keeping a secret, knowing it's kind of crazy. If she was comforting herself, she'd own up to it. Laugh about it."

"Says who?" Zak argued. "You have no idea how someone might behave when they're comforting themselves."

Alan cleared his throat. "We know that with the onset of dementia, some adults start to act strangely. They speak to people who are no longer here. They forget the time and place. It's not uncommon for them to ask for their mother. They might even call out to their mother for help. Or see and hear visions. And believe those visions are real. Pretend they have children who never visit. Spouses that have died years earlier."

"You're making too much of this," Zak said, desperate to convince them that they were wrong. "You're attributing behaviors to her that she doesn't have."

Alan offered a sympathetic look. "I know you care deeply for her. But you have to consider what's best for Helena."

Melinda sighed. "Hold on. You're in no position to make an official diagnosis. Who are you two? An administrator and an activities director."

"We had her evaluated," Alan said.

"By whom?" Melinda demanded.

"A member of our staff who provides psychological support."

"This is ridiculous," Melinda pressed. "Shouldn't you have an independent third party make that assessment?"

"Why?" Alan asked.

Melinda didn't miss a beat. "Well, it seems to me that you have a financial incentive to move her from her condo into assisted living."

Zak cringed. He'd no idea what Melinda was about to say, but based on Alan's expression, he doubted it was going to play well. "Never mind," Zak said, hoping to derail Melinda. But Melinda was mad. Zak was afraid she was ready to burn the place down.

"So let me understand this," Melinda said. "Helena buys this gorgeous condo in your building. Sinks a lot of money into it. Then, the moment she falters, you move her so that you can resell the unit. The condo is *the big-ticket item.* That's where you make your money. No offense Alan, but that's probably how you earn your bonus."

Zak was grateful his hearing had been restored as silence fell over the conference room. Otherwise, he might have assumed he'd once again gone deaf.

"That's outrageous," Alan finally said. "We'd never do that. We have a responsibility to the welfare and care of our owners. We're about helping people."

Melinda turned to Julie, whose mouth hung open. "You don't look so very certain. Maybe I'm a little right."

Zak wondered if Melinda had stumbled onto something Helena had never considered when she bought into the senior living model. That once she moved to another level of care, she wouldn't be able to return to her condo.

There was a sweet sadness in Alan's voice. "We're not the villains here, no matter what you think. We agreed to meet with you because of all you've done for Helena. We admire that. But since neither of you have any legal standing regarding Helena, this meeting is officially over." And with that final statement, Alan stood and left the room, leaving Julie behind with Zak and Melinda.

"That can't be true," Julie mumbled mostly to herself. "I don't believe there is a profit motive involved here."

"Maybe there is and maybe there isn't," Melinda said. "But I've been texting with Helena. She's not demented. She's as sharp as a tack. Zak knows for sure. He's stayed with her."

"What about the sons? And her talking to her mother?" Julie asked.

Zak had no idea how to explain about Helena's sons. But he did know about her mother. "She's psychic," he said. "She doesn't like to share that, but I've known it since we met. She believes she can speak to the other side."

Now it was Melinda's turn to be skeptical. "Really . . . she told you that?"

"She's always had the gift," Zak confirmed. "From the time she was a child."

Julie offered a sympathetic smile. "No matter what you think is going on here, we all care about Helena. Including Alan. He's a good man. I wouldn't work here if he wasn't. Still, this kind of setup is relatively new. There might be a bug or two to work out. But just because you think we're railroading her doesn't mean we're actually doing it."

Melinda blinked hard. "That makes no sense. You either are, or you aren't."

Julie sighed. "If only the world was that simple. So very black and white."

"It is," Zak answered as he thought about his own situation. No job, no money. No money, no tuition. No tuition, no place to live. No place to live . . . well . . . he didn't want to consider what that might mean.

"How about if you two give me some time to talk with Alan? See what we can figure out."

"I don't get it?" Zak said, unwilling to accept any further delay. "What more do we need to do?"

"You don't understand. The transfer to assisted living has triggered a relocation clause in her Ventana contract. There's a set amount of time before we have to vacate the unit."

Zak gasped. "Vacate the unit. You mean, sell her belongings."

"Sell the condo," Julie clarified. "We have no interest in her personal belongings."

Melinda shook her head. "Because you've already taken possession of her most valuable asset. The condo!"

"I know it sounds terrible, but that's what happens when people buy in. You see, we're more than just real estate. We're a health insurance model. You're investing in the possibility that should you get ill, we'll take care of you."

"But you're not doing that strictly out of goodwill."

"I'm afraid not. The money you spend for the condo is invested in a fund that generates income for your future healthcare needs as you live out the remainder of your life."

Melinda held a hand to her chest. "My God. It's too gruesome. You're hoping Helena will die."

Julie seemed shocked by the mere suggestion of such a notion. "Not at all. But everyone does eventually die. It's just a reality. So instead of winding up in a nursing home with no money and living on Medicaid, you have the option of being cared for here in a lovely environment, and when you die, sixty percent of the value of your initial investment, the condo purchase, goes back to your heirs. That's a very fair bargain."

Zak felt his heart drop. "Does that mean it's too late?"

"I don't know," Julie admitted. "I just started working here a few months ago. I've never been through one of these triggering events."

Zak didn't like her answer. "We definitely need to get to the bottom of this."

"Yes," Melinda agreed. "The sooner, the better."

Zak's gut rumbled. The intense pain was back again. "Excuse me," he said, a desperate look on his face. They hadn't solved the issue with Helena, but at the moment, he had bigger fish to fry. He wasn't sure he could make it all the way back to the bathroom by the café. "Can you direct me to the nearest restroom?" he asked Julie, praying that the facilities were closer. Much closer.

"Just across the lobby, you can't miss it—"

And like a jackrabbit, Zak was gone.

⌇⌇⌇

The Perfect Pear Bistro in Tempe was crowded with its usual eclectic lunchtime crowd of business folks, college students, and mommies who lunched with baby strollers parked tableside. The noise level was a bit much for Zak, so he and Melinda opted to sit in the courtyard which was still decorated with carved jack-o-lanterns and ghoulish masks, even though Halloween had long since come and gone. "I think you'll like this place," Melinda said. "It isn't Mexican, but you've had enough Mexican for the moment."

Zak couldn't agree more. He felt as if he were a survivor of Mount Vesuvius. "That bran is poison."

"Poor baby," Melinda chuckled as she eyed the menu. "Are you hungry?"

Zak wasn't sure, though he imagined his system was like a gas tank, currently running on empty. If he wasn't hungry now, he'd be later. "I can always eat."

Melinda looked up with a smirk. "*Men!* Which reminds me—do you have plans for Christmas?"

Zak fumbled with the oversized menu. "Marshall asked me to his house, but I don't want to leave Helena alone."

Melinda swatted at a fly circling the table. "That's noble, but maybe this is Marshall's way of introducing you to his family."

Zak hadn't considered that. "After the way my family behaved, I'm scared to meet his folks. He says they're *accepting*, like being *accepting* is a good thing. Why do people feel they need to *accept* other people, and that once they do, they should get credit for it? I think it's off-putting. Like me saying to you, I'm *very accepting* of redheads."

Melinda nodded. "That does sound condescending."

When the waitress approached, Zak, mindful of his limited funds, ordered only a cola. Melinda, in contrast, ordered a grilled cheese sandwich with a bowl of tomato soup and a side of sweet potato fries.

"What should we do about this whole Helena thing?" Melinda asked, once the waitress withdrew. "Between her invisible sons and that dead mother, it sounds like an impossible situation."

"I have no idea," Zak admitted. "She doesn't want to be there, and I don't think she should be. But she does get dizzy. I don't want her to fall and get hurt. Julie said someone had evaluated her and decided that she needed to remain in assisted living. I'm torn. Is that the safest place for her?"

Melinda rubbed her chin. Her freckles seemed to almost light up, giving her skin a healthy glow. "Just because she's in assisted living, doesn't mean she won't fall again. She can't be wrapped in plastic and kept safe for the rest of her life. Falls happen. People get sick. Old folks die. Should everyone at risk be locked up?"

"Maybe we need to get another opinion," Zak wondered. "Right. But from whom?"

"What about my ear surgeon? Zak suggested. "Helena volunteered with him as a patient advocate. I bet he could help us."

Melinda's eyes lit up. "A doctor's opinion would carry weight."

"Sure," Zak agreed as the waitress appeared with Melinda's lunch order and Zak's cola.

"Oh, my word," Melinda said with a laugh. "Did I order all this food? What was I thinking? Do me a favor, Zak. Split the sandwich with me and take the soup. We can share the fries."

As Zak bit into his half of the sandwich, he wondered if Melinda had intentionally ordered it to share. "Thank you," he said as his eyes welled with tears. He didn't want to cry over Melinda's kindness, but he couldn't help himself.

"Now, stop that," Melinda said as Zak struggled to get ahold of himself. "I don't want you to worry about Helena, or your tuition, or what you're going to eat. I'm going to take you home with me for the holidays and we'll figure it out together."

Zak didn't know what to say. He wiped his eyes. Wasn't he lucky? Melinda was now the second invitation for a home visit. But tempting as it was, he couldn't leave Helena alone. In an odd way, he'd adopted her. Or had she adopted him? He couldn't decide. But did it really matter? As long as they were together, he was certain the holidays would be a joyous time. If Helena had to stay on the third floor at Ventana, he'd join her. "I think I should go see Helena after we finish eating. Let her know what we've been discussing."

A concerned look crossed Melinda's face. "What are you going to tell her?"

"The truth," Zak answered, as if any other option was inconceivable.

"Maybe I should go with you," Melinda suggested.

Zak shook his head. "No need. I've got this."

—❧—

When Zak stepped off the elevator onto the third floor, he headed straight for Helena's room, only to find it empty. He wandered down the hall, following the sounds of laughter, until he came upon the activity room. There, he spotted Helena at the front, reading aloud from the newspaper, acting out parts of a story by modulating her voice. It took Zak a moment to realize she was reading from the newspaper's "Peanuts" comic strip to the other residents. When Helena spotted Zak, she waved and finished up in her best Charlie Brown voice before heading to the back of the room where Zak had taken a seat. "Hey there, kiddo," she said as she sat down next to him.

"That was nice," he said.

Helena nodded. "I thought I'd help out. After all, not everyone here is still reading. There's a lot of dementia," she said in a hushed tone, "and others are extremely infirmed. But do you want to hear something strange? I'm glad I had a chance to see what the third floor is all about."

Helena's comment surprised Zak. Had she had a change of heart? Was she planning to stay in assisted living? "Then you're okay with all of this?" he asked as he looked around.

"Sure. For those who need it. It's a wonderful place. But not for me. At least not yet. I might need help now and then, but that can be provided in the privacy of my condo. I'd pay extra for that. But I don't need the extensive attention to dressing, bathing, and eating, like the folks here."

Zak thought about the conversation with Alan and Julie. Alan was convinced Helena was in the right place with the right level of care. Zak hoped that with Dr. Peterson's help, he might change Alan's mind. But would Peterson help? Zak had tried to get an appointment to see him, but his office had said the next available appointment was two months away. By then, Helena's condo would surely be sold.

"Okay, out with it," Helena demanded.

Zak shrugged. "What?"

"I can tell something's up."

"It's going to take a bit more time to get you back into your condo. At least according to Alan."

"I don't understand."

"Neither do I," Zak admitted. "But it stems from your talking to yourself. More specifically, to your mother."

"Damn," Helena said, as she appeared to put two and two together. "Well, what am I going to do? I can't stay here."

"At least for the next few days, you have no choice."

"Hmm . . ." Helena tapped a finger to her temple.

Zak tilted his head. "What's going on? What are you thinking?"

"As the kids used to say, that's for me to know and you to find out."

"Oh no," Zak moaned. "You can't do anything to undermine your place here. Please, don't do anything rash. I was talking with Melinda, and we think if we can get Dr. Peterson to weigh in and clear this whole matter up."

"I don't think so," she said in a singsong voice. "His father never approved of him taking over that practice. There's a definite negative vibe happening over there."

Zak did a double take. They'd only talked about her gift abstractly. But now, Helena was talking to him as if he were a confidante. As if he believed her. And he wasn't sure if he did. It was one thing to talk objectively about her psychic gifts. Quite another to have it expressed so plainly, and in such direct terms about Peterson, someone he actually knew. It sounded crazy. "I don't get it. What's his dad got to do with it?"

"When I was there, his dad was circling the office. There's a lot of spiritual energy in that place."

Zak gasped. "Oh my God. Are you serious?"

"Would I say something that wasn't true?"

Zak wondered if there was a fine line between *thinking* something was true and *knowing* for a fact that it was. Could a deeply held belief be enough to make an impression a fact? "You wouldn't lie to me?" he said as he questioned his own judgment. Had he totally misread the situation? Was Helena indeed losing it?

"Peterson's dad," she whispered, looking about as if someone might be listening, "in life, hated him."

Zak couldn't imagine that a well-respected surgeon might have a father, much like Zak's, who didn't like his son. "You're kidding. That's terrible."

"Right," Helena agreed. "At first it caught me off guard until I realized the father was in spirit. Then, the whole conversation with him made sense. You see, Peterson's dad is trying to guide Peterson from the other side. Help him. Undo the damage he did during his lifetime."

Zak was unsure how to tactfully approach the real issue at hand. "If you're going to talk like that, we're never going to get you out of assisted living."

Helena straightened her back. "I have another idea. What if we launch a protest? That ought to get me out of here."

Zak was frightened. Why did Helena seem so unhinged? He remembered her talking about the peaceful marches she participated in with the women's movement. But to organize a protest for a senior stuck on the third floor of a luxury adult community? The idea was absurd. Even delusional. Perhaps Helena was further gone than he'd imagined. "Maybe we can work this out without any trouble."

"Zak," Helena said, a finger pointing upward. "There are times when civil disobedience is the only way."

Zak shook his head. The conversation was getting nuttier and nuttier. "But who are we going to get to march? Certainly not the people on the third floor. Everyone's infirmed."

"I'll need you to get a message to my friends in the dining room. That'll start the ball rolling!"

"How can I do that?" Zak asked, certain he'd lost control of the conversation.

"Simple. You'll eat dinner with them at the penthouse restaurant."

"Helena," Zak objected. "I can't afford to eat there."

"You're going to take my place at the table with Cynthia, Donna, and Babs. Talk to them. Tell them what's going on. Tell Aggie to charge the meal to my account."

Zak doubted he could have much pull with the ladies. "Are they really going to listen to me?"

"It depends on how you bait the hook," Helena said with a glint in her eyes. "I have a few ideas to get them moving in the right direction."

"I can't leave her there," Zak moaned as he and Marshall walked out of the chemistry lecture hall. "Now she wants me to meet up with her friends for dinner."

Marshall slipped an arm about Zak's shoulder and pulled him close. "I know you want to help, but this is not the best time. You have finals coming up. You've got to think of yourself first."

Zak pulled away. His body, rigid. His jaw set as the two stopped walking. "You don't understand," he said as he faced Marshall. "The clock is ticking. They're going to sell her condo right out from under her unless we do something."

"I know she's important to you, but we have to study. And you still don't have a job. What will you do next semester? You have more important things to worry about than Helena."

Zak shook his head. Marshall was not getting it. "I can't think of anything else right now. She depends on me. She's the first adult who's ever spoken to me as if I were her equal. Isn't that crazy? She's more than sixty years older than me, and I feel so close to her. I can't explain the attachment, but it's there. It's strong and I'm worried about her. I can't abandon her. I can't."

"She's a lovely lady. I like her too. But you can't sacrifice your future to solve her problems."

Zak didn't think it was a *this or that* kind of choice. "I know. But it's hard to concentrate on getting anything done knowing she's in trouble."

"Well then, what about your idea to go to Dr. Peterson?" Marshall pushed open the double doors as they exited the building and stepped into the cool December air.

"You have to make an appointment, and he's booked solid for the next two months."

"But you're his patient."

"So what?"

"Did you tell them that?"

"They didn't ask."

"Well, that's ridiculous. Get your phone out."

Together, they huddled on a bench. Zak got out his phone and pulled up Dr. Peterson's contact information. Marshall extended a palm and Zak passed the phone over. Zak watched as Marshall initiated the call. "This is Zak Andrews," Marshall began once Peterson's office answered. "I'm a patient of Dr. Peterson's. I had surgery three weeks ago and I'm having a problem."

Zak tried to grab the phone.

Marshall swiveled, turning his back to Zak. "Can you squeeze me in today to see the doctor?"

"Oh, no. Don't," Zak whimpered, hands covering his face. "I'm okay. The ear is fine!"

Marshall waved at Zak. "Yes, I had a tumor removed in the right ear. The ear is hurting."

Zak jumped up from the bench and leapt in the air, arms flailing, trying to get Marshall to stop.

"Three o'clock?" Marshall beamed as he watched Zak's manic spinning. "That's perfect. See you later."

As Zak completed his final twirl, hands up, breathless, Marshall held the phone out to Zak. "There you go! Your appointment is set. You can thank me later."

– 33 –

ELENA FINISHED HER chocolate ice cream cone in time
to help Della, a third-floor nurse's aide, clean up after
the weekly ice cream social. "Thank you," Della called
out to Helena who was busy on the other side of the room
wiping faces and hands with a wet washcloth.

Time passed slowly as Helena committed to engaging with
the activities on the third floor. She hadn't written a word in
weeks. Her laptop remained locked in her condo. If she had
access to a laptop, she imagined that she could write a terrific
piece on assisted living, just as Nelly Bly, the Nineteenth
Century investigative journalist had done when she went
undercover in a New York City insane asylum to document
the horrendous abuses. Though the thought of writing an
exposé thrilled her, in truth, the staff on the third floor were
perfectly lovely and the residents were well cared for. Della
was certainly a doll. Despite the journalistic possibilities an
exposé might inspire, after devouring a chocolate ice cream
cone with sprinkles, Helena found herself no longer interested

in challenging the status quo. Any institution that nurtured her sweet tooth deserved her undying admiration. "It's hard to complain," she said to Della, "when everyone makes such a concerted effort to take such good care of me."

Della smiled an elfin grin as she crossed the room to join Helena. "I can't understand why they haven't sent you back to your condo. You shouldn't be here. You're much too *with it.*"

Della's diagnosis was such a welcome relief that Helena insisted on hearing it again. "Am I?"

"I'll miss you, when you go," Della answered as she knelt beside a resident asleep in her wheelchair. Della carefully removed the empty ice cream cup from the woman's hand.

"I can always come back and volunteer," Helena suggested. "Now that I've seen the work you do, I'd be proud to spend more time here."

Della got to her feet. "I've been trying to get Julie to find us volunteers, but management says folks don't want to experience the third floor."

"You mean they don't want to see firsthand, the ravages of time," Helena snapped sarcastically.

Della shrugged. "But you don't mind."

Helena imagined it was because she saw a need, and where there was a need, she felt compelled. She'd always been that way. Looking out for the underdog was what had driven her to the civil rights, and then the women's movement. When race or gender prohibited talented people from succeeding, she couldn't sit back and do nothing. And now, in her golden years, she felt proud as she reflected on her life. She certainly hadn't done anything singlehandedly, but she'd stepped up. Isn't that what life is about? Making a difference.

"When I was young," Helena remembered, "people were proud to volunteer. JFK gave the most marvelous inaugural address. 'Ask not what your country can do for you. Ask what you can do for your country.'" Just repeating the words sent a shiver up Helena's spine. "There are so many worthwhile organizations to give your time to. Wouldn't it be beautiful if everyone in America who was retired, committed to helping people at least one day a week? Think how we could change the world for the better."

Della smiled. "That's a lovely thought. You know, I Googled you when you first arrived on the floor. I do that with all the owners. I watched a few videos of you being interviewed. You can see them on YouTube. You might've been younger, but that fire is still there."

Helena embraced Della in a hug. It was sweet to be appreciated. Even sweeter to know that she'd found an ally and a friend. "When they move me back," she promised, "I'll just be an elevator ride away. You only have to press the *up* button . . ." The timing of Helena's statement couldn't have been more prescient as the ding of the elevator down the hall announced the arrival of a new visitor to the third floor.

Could that be Zak back so soon?

⌁

Aggie emerged from the elevator as if she were a time traveler entering another dimension known as *The Third Floor*. "What are you doing here?" Helena said as she rushed to her friend's side. "Aren't you working today?"

"There you are!" Aggie said with relief, a hand on her chest. "Well, you look just fine."

"Of course I'm fine," Helena answered, forgetting for the moment the events that had brought her to the third floor. "It was just a bump on the head," she said as if her fall had been nothing to be concerned about, dismissing her stay on the third floor as an overabundance of caution and a nuisance to boot.

Aggie took Helena by the arm. "I just can't tell you how worried I've been. I assumed you were convalescing in your condo and not ready for visitors, but then this morning Julie shared with me that you were actually here." She looked about with a sour expression. "What are you doing in assisted living?"

Helena wanted to laugh. Aggie was so dramatic. So very over the top. Why did the third floor make everyone so nervous? The food was great. The staff, impeccable. Yes, it was a step away from skilled nursing care and the Memory Care Unit, but it wasn't like she was in prison. Or on the moon.

"This is a terrible turn of events . . ." Aggie caught herself when she saw Della within earshot.

"It's okay." Helena said, dismissing Aggie's concerns and nodding in Della's direction. "This is Della. She's a good egg."

Aggie continued. "Everyone has been asking about you. It's like you simply disappeared. Like you were abducted by aliens. We were told you were having your meals sent in. Those ladies, that awful group of women you've befriended, haven't mentioned a word to me about you since you disappeared. Do they know where you are?"

Helena assumed they did.

Della interrupted. "I doubt they would."

Aggie turned and gave the young woman her full attention.

"When an owner moves to assisted living, it's regarded as confidential."

"But why?" Aggie asked with indignation, as if news of the owners should be privy to everyone.

"It's got something to do with HIPAA."

"Oh," Aggie snorted. "Like that makes any sense."

In the course of their short friendship, Helena had yet to see Aggie so riled up. "But now you've found me." Helena pulled Aggie farther down the hall. "That's all that matters."

Aggie remained in a huff. "Why is everything such a goddamn secret around here?"

Helena hadn't quite thought of it that way. But now that Aggie mentioned it, it did seem as if the third floor was a mystery unto itself. A place where people were shut away because they'd suffered some physical setback. That hardly seemed right. Could someone's poor health be the sole reason to be sequestered? Out of sight, out of mind. Where were the visitors? It seemed so wrong for adults to be isolated and left to wither away in a single room with barely enough space to hold their worldly possessions. Even though Ventana had the good judgment to hire excellent people like Della, Aggie, and Julie, it still seemed as if something wasn't quite right. "This is just temporary," Helena told Aggie as she showed off her quarters, certain her time on the third floor was soon coming to an end.

Aggie didn't hold back. "Helena, this is not much bigger than a hospital room."

"In a very upscale hospital."

"And that's a hospital bed," Aggie pointed out, touching the side bars that were currently down.

"I don't need those bars, thank goodness," Helena explained. "Come see the bathroom."

Aggie stepped into the bathroom. "There's no tub."

"But there's a great shower," Helena assured her.

"I see. And a nice bench to sit on."

"What more could a girl ask for?" Helena joked, trying to keep it light. There was no point in acting like she was staying forever. The possibility was absurd. The furthest thing from Helena's mind, though Zak had warned her about the interview with the social worker that had landed her on the third floor and the challenge she'd face in overturning that ruling. She still wasn't scared. Why would she be? Even Della knew she didn't belong on the third floor. She was certain it was a matter of time before she was back sleeping in her own bed. Enjoying the privacy of her kitchen. Brewing her own coffee. Sitting on her terrace watching the planes land and take off at Sky Harbor Airport. Surely Ventana wouldn't keep her on the third floor. It didn't make sense.

Aggie rocked side to side. "I don't know, Helena. If I were in your shoes, I wouldn't be so easygoing about all this."

"And what would you have me do?"

"I'd march right over to that elevator and get on it. Then, I'd go directly to Alan's office and try to find out what the heck is going on and how to get back into your condo."

"Or I could just get on the elevator and go home," Helena said, realizing for the first time that there was nothing stopping her from leaving. Why did she feel she needed to ask anyone's permission? What was she afraid of? Upsetting someone's feelings? Making a bad impression with Julie and Alan? Or was she scared to be perceived as disobedient? The bad little girl that no one liked because she was loud, creating a scene and insisting on what she wanted. Surely life had taught her about the importance of owning her voice. Facing up to authority. Speaking her mind. Not being intimidated by men who were all too happy to dominate meetings, voice opinions, and interrupt women. Yet here she was. Eighty-three years old, experiencing the same lesson all over again. Allowing Alan to call the shots about where she should live. Standing down as Ventana dictated her present and future.

Helena felt a surge of adrenaline. It was time to put a stop to all this foolishness and get back to her life. She stepped out into the hallway. Della was no longer at the front desk. Probably called away to attend to a resident. Helena grabbed her purse. She beckoned Aggie to follow. They made their way down the hall to the elevators as if on a secret mission for the State Department, Russian spies monitoring every move.

⸎

As the elevator doors closed on the third floor, Helena wondered why she hadn't done this sooner. No one was standing guard over her. She hadn't been tethered to her bed. There was no monitoring bracelet about her wrist or ankle. If anything, she'd been complicit in her own detainment. At any time, she could have taken the elevator back to her condo. Waiting for someone, anyone, to give her permission, now seemed like the height of foolishness. Why had it taken Aggie's outrage for her to see her circumstances clearly?

The elevator passed the fourth, fifth, and sixth floors. Helena could hardly wait to be back in her condo. It was as if the last few weeks had happened to someone else. She couldn't help but wonder how she'd arrived at this moment in time. Who was that woman who'd given up her power so easily? Who, after a lifetime of standing up for herself, acquiesced so willingly to the decisions of others?

When the elevator doors opened on the tenth floor, Helena steadied herself. She was nearly home. She calmly walked down the hallway, Aggie tagging behind. Key in hand, Helena reached for the doorknob and attempted to open the door. But something was wrong. Try as she might, the key wouldn't slide into the lock.

Aggie gave it a try. "Oh, no," Aggie said as she too failed to open the door. "They've changed the locks!"

Helena broke into a cold sweat, beads of perspiration gathering on her forehead. "That's not possible."

Aggie arched a brow. There was no need to speak. Wasn't it obvious? Someone had entered the premises without Helena's permission. Stood inside her entry way, knelt down, and with a screwdriver, switched one lock out for another.

"What am I going to do?" Helena said, without any expectation of an answer.

Aggie was quick to respond. "You're going to get mad."

"And then what?"

"You're going to march yourself down to Alan Lane's office and have it out."

Helena took a deep breath. She was too old for all this drama. She hadn't moved to Ventana to fight with management.

She'd come to be cared for; tended to in her dotage. Had she been a fool to think strangers would be truly concerned with her well-being? She hadn't considered anyone would make a decision that wasn't in her best interests. How could she be so trusting? So naïve? And now that the damage had been done, could she correct the situation?

"Are you okay?" Aggie asked. "I feel awful. I had no idea they would have done such a thing."

Helena nodded, much too focused on her plight to worry about Aggie's feelings. At the end of the day, no matter what happened, Aggie could go home. She could spend the evening in the comfort of her own living room in proximity to her possessions. But where were Helena's things? Her laptop. Her checkbook. They were secured behind a front door with a new lock. And she didn't have the key. Or had her things been boxed up and moved to storage? Was that possible? She shuddered at the thought of someone going through her closets and drawers, as if her life had become an estate sale, girdles and panties marked down for quick disposal. No, she assured herself. They can't sell my things. They might move them into storage, but they can't sell them. Absolutely not. Still, the idea of a stranger's grubby hands touching her possessions filled her with disgust. "They're my things," she said, much as a child might complain about their toys being put away without their consent. "Mine alone."

"Do you want to talk with Alan?" Aggie asked, her tone modulated. The indignation, gone. Her voice had taken on a gentle, soothing quality, as if she recognized something in Helena had changed. There was now a frailty of spirit as if the intractable key had thrown Helena off her game. Broken her spirit. "Maybe we should go back to the third floor so you can lie down," Aggie suggested.

Time seemed to stand still as Helena weighed her options. She could go to Alan and complain, revealing she'd broken the rules, left the third floor, discovered the locks had been changed, and demand access to her condo even as she threatened to call a lawyer. Maybe she could use the gentlemen who'd handled the sale of her home. No wait. That was a realtor. Then who was her lawyer? She had one. She was sure of it. The fellow who'd updated her will and estate papers. What was his name? She couldn't remember, but she was certain the info was in her kitchen drawer where she kept a roster of contacts for electricians, plumbers, and other handymen. But now, she'd have to manage without the list. Wait. She just needed to look at her Ventana paperwork from the closing. Her lawyer's name was on that document. *Oh no*, she realized as she leaned against the locked door. *I gave the paperwork for safe handling to Ventana at the closing.*

"Dear God," she whimpered. "I'm screwed."

– 34 –

"STOP BEING SO dramatic," Marshall said to Zak as they stood in the lobby of Dr. Peterson's medical office building. "You can do this."

Zak shook his head as if trying to clear the cobwebs. "I'm not sure what to say."

Marshall wasn't taking any guff. "Just tell him she's in trouble. She needs his help. It's that simple. Now go ahead. Get on with it." Marshall checked his watch. "It's nearly three and they're expecting you."

Zak was surprised to find Dr. Peterson's waiting room empty. But then he remembered they'd squeezed him in on a surgical day when the doctor wasn't seeing patients in the office. "I'm Zak Andrews," he announced to the receptionist.

"Sign in and have a seat," she said. "We'll call you shortly."

Zak watched an old episode of *Love It or List It* on the widescreen television, trying to follow along with both the sound and the closed-captioning. Odd, he thought, how many mistakes he caught in the closed-captioning. He turned away. His head hurt from trying to keep pace with the program.

"The doctor's running late. He'll be with you shortly," the nurse said when she showed him to an exam room. As soon as she left him alone, pulling the door closed behind her, Zak regretted his decision to come. Being back in the office stirred up bad memories. Specifically, the way he treated Chuck and Marshall when he was deaf. Yelling. Losing his temper. Making up stories in his head about what was going on with his friends. He'd assumed they were hooking up. That they didn't want to be around him anymore. His confusion was fed by fear. Fear that he'd never hear again. Fear that his life was out of control. Even his jealousy was based on fear. He wished he'd handled it better. Perhaps this was his chance to even the score. To prove, he wasn't afraid. After all, wasn't Dr. Peterson just a man? Sure, he'd done amazing work with a scalpel, but at the end of the day, he was like everyone else. And maybe the doctor was also afraid at times.

A brief knock on the door and Dr. Peterson stood before Zak who was seated on the exam table. "What's going on, Zak?" he asked as he took Zak's chin between his thumb and index finger, swiveling Zak's head to the left to get access to Zak's right ear.

"My ear's perfectly fine," Zak admitted.

Peterson pulled his hand back. He offered a quizzical look. "Then what's the problem?"

There was no way to sugarcoat it. Zak blurted out the truth. "My friend, Helena, is in trouble."

Peterson stepped back a bit. "What kind of trouble?"

"They've placed her in assisted living, and she doesn't belong there."

"Who did?"

"The management at Ventana."

Peterson winced. "I'm not following any of this. Start from the beginning."

Zak took a breath. He needed to calm himself. "She sometimes has these fainting spells, and after she fell, she was hospitalized for a few days. She hit her head, and they were concerned she might have had a stroke. But she was fine. Confused a little, but she is eighty-three years old. When she was released from the hospital, they put her into assisted living, and now, they won't move her back into her condo. She's a prisoner."

Peterson rolled his eyes. "A prisoner. I doubt she's a prisoner."

"Okay," Zak conceded. "But they won't let her go back to her condo."

"Has someone evaluated her?"

"They say so," Zak admitted. "There's this social worker."

Peterson raised his hand. "Look, I'm not exactly sure why you're telling me all this."

"Because you know her," Zak pressed. "She helped me through my surgery. She was at the hospital every day when I needed someone to look after me. She stepped up. She's, my friend. She's been there for me. I have to help her."

"It doesn't sound like she needs your help. Ventana can certainly look after her needs. If they think she should be in assisted living, that's good enough for me."

"But they're wrong!"

Peterson softened. "I know how you must feel. You're grateful for her help. But older people have physical limitations. Bodies break down. Minds wander. That's why we have senior facilities. Places that specialize in the care of our older citizens. I know your heart is in the right place, but she's probably exactly where she needs to be."

Zak swallowed hard. Helena had warned him he might have a problem convincing Peterson. *Medical professionals tend to stick together*, she'd said. *Don't be disappointed if he doesn't come through.*

"I wish I could help," Peterson said. "But I really can't take any more time . . ."

Zak hated to bring it up. He was afraid to say anything that might alienate the doctor. Make him angry. But it was worth a shot. No matter how crazy it sounded when Helena had whispered it, he knew it was his last chance with Peterson. "Your dad wants you to do it. He likes Helena and he's upset about the way you're managing the practice. Spending so much money on frivolous things. Like the new espresso machine in the breakroom. And you're too familiar with the staff."

Peterson froze. His face registered alarm. "What did you say?"

Zak blushed. "Please," he begged. "Don't make me say it again. Just visit Helena at Ventana. That's all I ask."

⸙

Marshall's eyes lit up when he spotted Zak coming into Starbucks. "How did it go?" he asked, an iced green tea in hand as Zak slid into the chair next to him.

"I don't know. Peterson seemed totally blindsided."

"Do you think he'll visit Helena?"

Zak shrugged. "I hope so."

"What now?"

"Dinner."

"It's only four o'clock," Marshall said, checking his watch.

"I know. But four-thirty is when Helena's gang gathers to eat on the eleventh floor. I told her I'd have dinner with them."

Marshall nodded. "You're a good guy."

"Eating dinner doesn't qualify anyone for an award."

Marshall conceded the point. "I don't know if I'd be doing what you're doing."

"You mean, getting involved?"

"Right. Especially with all you have on your plate."

Zak hadn't forgotten about his own problems. "Worse comes to worst, I can move in with Allison next semester. I certainly can't go back to New York City. Allison appears to be my only solution."

Marshall rolled his eyes. "Oh no. Not, her."

"I know. It's like going backward."

"Well, you'll figure something out."

"Or I won't," Zak said sarcastically. "Anyway, I better get over to Ventana. I told Helena I'd stop by before dinner."

"Just make sure you're taking care of yourself too," Marshall advised.

"I'm not sure what that even means," Zak answered.

"You're putting in a lot of effort into Helena. And though it's noble, let's be honest. She's an old woman. Maybe she belongs in assisted living. Perhaps that's the best place to keep her safe."

Zak had heard the argument before. Alan and Julie had made it. So had Peterson. Is that what's expected when someone gets to a certain age? That everyone wants to keep them safe? And what exactly is safe? Should older people be locked up in their homes? Tethered to a room? Closely guarded twenty-four seven? Did that make any sense for someone who was still sharp as a tack and physically capable? It seemed a sad reality after having lived an independent and successful life.

"I don't know," Zak pushed back. "Shouldn't she make the decision for herself?"

"Maybe that's the problem. She can't."

Zak bit his lip. It was all so damn confusing. Was he overstepping his bounds, interfering where he didn't belong? Maybe everyone was right. After all, what the hell did he know? He couldn't even scrape together enough money for the next semester's tuition. Still, he knew they were wrong about Helena. "Nope," he said as he stood to leave. "She doesn't belong there."

"Okay, tiger," Marshall conceded. "If you're determined to help her, you better get a move on. Dinner is in fifteen minutes."

Zak touched his stomach. "Oh my God. I barely have an appetite. Who eats dinner at four-thirty?"

The dining room at Ventana was abuzz with activity when Zak arrived. Seniors gathered at tables of four and six, meeting up for a meal after spending the day doing whatever retired people do. Before searching for Helena's table, Zak checked out the activity calendar posted on the board by the elevator. Some had spent the afternoon attending a lecture by a local professor on educational opportunities in ASU's Lifelong Learning Series. Others had gone on a three-hour shopping trip to Tempe Marketplace where the Ventana bus deposited them at the entrance to Target. Still others had taken advantage of the new Restorative Yoga class in the gym, followed by a massage and a visit to the steam room.

Zak looked for Helena's table. She'd described her friends, but to Zak, all older women looked alike. He racked his brain for the hints she'd provided. He remembered her saying they never changed tables. That they were sitting at one of the tables abutting the windows. Or was it the table *across* from the windows? And then he spotted a woman with dark hair taking dinner orders. Ahh, he thought. That's Aggie! "Excuse me," Zak said as he sidled up to Aggie who was in the middle of jotting down an order for veal scallopini. "Can you point me to Helena Greenblatt's table of friends?"

"You must be Zak!" Aggie said so loud that Zak blushed. "Helena was right. You do look like Keanu Reeves. I'm so glad you're here. Are you looking for Helena? Because she's not—"

"I know," Zak said, interrupting her. "She asked me to have dinner with her friends."

"Oh, no. Not that dreadful threesome."

Zak was immediately on guard. Helena hadn't mentioned her friends were unpleasant. Surely, they'd welcome him. Didn't grandmotherly types love young men who were respectful? He hadn't anticipated any other reaction. But then, his own family had behaved terribly when he came out. Perhaps he should stick to the script Helena had provided. Not say anything about himself. Or was it too late? Had Helena already shared his story?

Aggie pointed. "They're right over there. The third table by the window. Beware the one with the horse face. She's mean."

Zak spotted the table. The three women were engaged in lively conversation and failed to look his way as he approached. He slipped into the empty chair which he assumed was Helena's.

"Excuse me, young man, but what do you think you're doing?" asked the woman with the long narrow face, her tone sharp.

"Helena sent me," he answered as if he were *Austin Powers: International Man of Mystery*, a movie he'd watched often with his father.

"How is she?" the blond with the curly hair asked.

"Not too good," he quickly admitted, hoping to curtail small talk.

"You're Zak?" the third woman guessed. "You texted us about visiting Helena when she was in the hospital. We were there when you were in class. Julie told us all about you."

Zak blushed. What had they heard? That he'd gone deaf and needed surgery? That he was gay and his parents had kicked him out? That he'd lost his job and was broke and unable to pay tuition for the following semester? That he'd have no place to live come January? No matter what he imagined they knew, it was all too shameful. Information he'd never share with strangers. Facts that he believed reflected poorly on who he was. But then, he wasn't quite sure who he was. For the moment, he was all those depressing things.

"Are you having dinner with us?" the long-faced woman asked.

Zak nearly laughed. Of all the questions he'd anticipated, he hadn't expected to be asked anything so obvious. Before he could answer, Aggie was by his side, a fairy godmother assigned to protect the innocent prince. "Have these old buzzards introduced themselves yet?"

Zak's face burned with embarrassment. He hoped Aggie wasn't planning on making him squirm as she poked fun at the ladies.

"You're awful," the horse-faced woman said to Aggie. "We should report you to management. It's about time they got rid of you."

Aggie offered an indignant *humph*. "Cynthia is the old one here. Babs is the friendly one. Donna, well, she's over there," Aggie said, pointing at poor Donna, who hadn't even merited a description. "This young man is our Zak," Aggie said in such a loving tone that Zak wondered if she'd let him crash with her come January. "Well, go on," she said to Zak as she stepped away to attend a patron at the next table.

Zak had thought he might have a moment to acclimate himself, but he could see it wasn't in the cards. He cleared his throat. "Helena's in trouble," he squeaked, surprised by the high-pitched tone of his voice. "They've moved her to assisted living and won't let her go."

Babs spoke. "But we understood she needed to be there. Something about a stroke."

"That isn't true. She did fall and hit her head, but there was no stroke. Or heart attack. Nothing that required follow-up care."

Cynthia frowned. "We heard she was mentally out of it. That she was talking to herself."

"Have you never talked to yourself?" Zak asked. "I do."

Donna shifted. "It's not a psychotic break?"

Zak had no idea what that was, but it sounded bad. "Uh, no," he answered.

"Then why is she still in assisted living?" Cynthia wanted to know.

Zak shrugged. "I have no idea. But that's why she needs your help."

"But what can we do?" Babs asked as she looked at Cynthia and then Donna.

"You can visit her on the third floor," Zak shot back.

"Oh, I don't know," Cynthia said.

"Not me," Babs echoed.

Donna just folded her hands and placed them in her lap.

Zak was flabbergasted. Why would three seemingly intelligent women refuse to visit their friend? It didn't make any sense.

"Have you been to the third floor?" Cynthia asked. "It's not a place for healthy adults."

"But Helena's fine," Zak implored. "I've stayed the last few nights with her. She's perfectly healthy."

"Then why is she there?" Babs asked.

"That's a really good question," Zak answered. "One I've been trying to figure out myself."

"If she's on the third floor, there's a good reason," Donna finally said, as if she'd been searching for some way to contribute to the conversation.

"Of course," Cynthia insisted. "Assisted living is for those who need hands-on care."

Zak couldn't believe what he was hearing. The three friends had already written Helena off. It was the strangest interaction he'd ever had. It was as if they were afraid. But afraid of what? There was nothing scary at Ventana. The setting was lovely. The style, first class. Still, the ladies resisted getting involved with the third floor. Or was it that they didn't like Helena? He couldn't figure out the reason for their reaction.

Aggie returned to take the table's dinner order. She directed her attention to Zak. "Have you made any headway here?"

"Not really," Zak answered, struggling to figure out how to get the ladies at the table engaged to visit Helena.

"Maybe that's because they're afraid of winding up on the third floor if they don't behave themselves."

"Now wait just a minute," Cynthia snapped. "You don't know anything about us."

Aggie threw back her head and laughed. "Are you kidding? I know all about you. You might ignore me when I'm working, but I can see and hear you three perfectly. Helena was too good for this table, and if you know what's good for you, you're going to do as this young man asks."

"Insufferable," Donna huffed.

"Who are you to tell us what to do?" Cynthia practically growled.

"I'm in charge of the food that comes out of the kitchen. Need I say more?"

"What are you implying?" Babs wanted to know.

"Fool with me, and you'll find out."

⚯

The next morning, Zak caught Julie outside of Ventana as she arrived for work. He stopped her before she entered the lobby. He'd last seen her in the meeting with Melinda and Alan and sensed she was sympathetic to Helena's plight. Perhaps he could pick her brain. Understand a bit more about Ventana and how they made their placement decisions. Surely, there was a way to figure out some solution without creating a lot of conflict and drama. At least, that was his hope. "I don't know if you remember me," he said, certain she must.

"Of course, I do. But shouldn't you be in class?"

"I have a bit of time yet." He checked his watch. He'd have to make a mad dash across campus so as not to miss his last biology lecture before finals. But if Julie could help, it'd be worth it. "Can we talk for a few minutes?"

Julie looked about, as if she didn't want to be seen with Zak. "Let's walk over to Starbucks," she suggested. "We can talk there."

Seated in matching lounge chairs, Julie untied the scarf wrapped around her neck. "There," she said as she stretched. "It's cold this morning."

Zak felt the tension ease. *She wants to help.* "I need to figure out a way to get Helena back into her condo. She doesn't belong in assisted living. You know that, and I know that. It's just not right. And I don't think your boss has any intention of fixing the mistake. I hope I'm wrong, but before this gets out of hand,

I want to make sure we've done everything possible to manage the situation without making a huge mess. I don't want Helena to get hurt in any way. She lives in Ventana, and once they move her back to independent living, there can't be any hard feelings."

Julie rubbed her temple as if she might have a headache coming on. "I've been looking into her case since we last met. Can she manage on her own? I'm not sure. It's not as if we have a crystal ball. We're doing the best we can. And there are moments she seems out of it. Confused."

"I've stayed overnight with her. There's no confusion. If there was, I'd know it."

Julie leaned forward as if sharing the code to America's nuclear arsenal. "But she's talking to herself."

Zak wasn't sure why she seemed so concerned. "So what? Is it hurting anyone? I'm sure a lot of lonely people talk to themselves."

"But not to their mother!"

"How do you know? Do you know every lonely person in America?"

"It's just not right," Julie clarified. "We're worried that it's the beginning of . . ."

Zak finished the sentence. "Dementia."

"It could be."

"Isn't it enough that she can manage on her own and doesn't need the services in assisted living? Why would anyone expect her to stay there? If it is the beginnings of dementia, there'd be time enough to move her. When she truly needs it."

He could tell he'd scored a point.

Julie relaxed back into the chair; eyes glued on him. She seemed to be thinking about his argument. Or was she thinking about something else? "But doesn't it bother you about her sons?" she finally said.

Zak hadn't forgotten about Helena's sons. But what was the point of bringing up her sons? If they'd cared about her, they would be around. But they weren't. "Why does that matter?"

Julie persisted. "Because there are no sons!"

Zak rubbed the stubble on his chin. There had to be a reasonable explanation.

Julie cocked her head. "You didn't know that. Or did you?"

Zak struggled for a moment, wondering what to say next. "Okay. But does it really matter?"

Julie pursed her lips. "It should."

Zak countered. "Why? She didn't have sons when she purchased the condo and was living independently. So really, nothing's changed."

Was he making headway? Did Julie's concerns truly make a difference? Yes, Helena could be strange at times. He'd concede that. But was her odd behavior enough to make her a prisoner on the third floor?

"Okay," Julie agreed. "You're right. So what? How many people stretch the truth about their families? Or talk to themselves."

Zak leapt out of the chair. He could hardly believe it. He'd won Julie over to team Helena. "I'm running late for class, but I'll be in touch," he said with the energy of a newly-minted superhero as he dashed out of Starbucks, feet barely touching the ground.

– 35 –

WHEN DR. PETERSON showed up at Ventana in the late afternoon, Helena was sitting alone in the third-floor lounge looking at an old issue of *People*. She was surprised to learn that Matthew Perry had died. *Such a shame*, she thought. But she wasn't surprised to see the young doctor. She knew he'd be intrigued by what Zak had shared. Though Peterson was a man of science, he'd remember their first meeting when Helena had mentioned his father, a man with whom Peterson had a troubled past. The conversation had unnerved the good doctor and so Helena had used Peterson's father as bait. The rest, she hadn't quite worked out, but in the end, she was certain he'd help her. Isn't that what being a physician is all about? Helping your fellow man . . . or woman?

"You wanted to see me?" Peterson said as he hovered nearby, clearly unwilling to sit down.

Helena detected a hint of irritation in his voice. She chose to ignore it. She was thrilled to see him. "Thank you for coming."

Peterson rolled his eyes. "Are you going to tell me what this is about?"

"Didn't Zak explain my situation?"

"I think so," he said. "You want me to intervene with management to transfer you back to your condo."

"Correct," she said, offering her warmest smile.

Peterson remained standing, unwilling to yield to the visit. "What makes you think I have any pull?"

"Well, you're a respected surgeon. Certainly, your word must count for something."

Peterson's voice grew louder. "It does. As a neuro-otologist. Not a psychiatrist. I don't have training in that field."

"Psychiatrist!" Helena couldn't help but be insulted. "I don't need a psychiatrist."

"But you are delusional," Peterson whispered as if the preliminary diagnosis was confidential. "I can't help you."

Helena shifted her gaze and stared across the room. It was time to use the information that Peterson's father had earlier shared. "He means well," she said as if she were communicating with someone, though no one was there.

Peterson spun about. "Who are you talking to?" he demanded to know.

"Your father," she lied. "He wants to know why you've been taking that new receptionist to lunch at the hotel. Is the food really that good?" Helena struggled not to laugh.

"That's ridiculous," Peterson said. "I'm a happily married man."

"I'm just passing along what he tells me. By the way, you've been taking a bit of money off the top. He doesn't approve of falsifying expenses. What would the IRS say if they found out?"

"Oh," Peterson said as he eyed Helena. "So that's how you're planning to play this little game. Am I really to believe you have a direct line to the cemetery?"

Helena corrected him. "You mean, the other side. There's no one at the cemetery."

"What does it matter?" Peterson said as he glared at her. "Get on with it. What do you need me to do?"

"A letter requesting the Ventana board reverse their decision."

"And in exchange?"

"Nothing," Helena said. "Just my undying gratitude."

Peterson's eyes glimmered. "I bet," he muttered.

***

By the time Zak showed up on the third floor, Helena was getting ready for bed. The moment she answered the knock at the door, she sensed something was off. "What's wrong?" she asked as he settled into the corner chair.

"Julie told me the truth," he said, his voice so low she struggled to hear him.

Helena sat down on the edge of the bed, unsure what Zak was getting at. "Is there a truth? Something I've missed?"

Zak tilted his head as if seeing her in a new light. "I thought we were friends."

What could this be about? she wondered. "Of course we're friends."

Zak looked away. "You know, when you're gay, you grow up keeping secrets. You pick up signals that it's not safe to be who you are. So, you hide. You don't want to be judged. You learn to shut down an important part of yourself. At first, it seems fine. It's not like others feel compelled to reveal the intimate details of their life. Deep down, you know the truth. You're different. You're forced to keep your family at arm's length so they can't hurt you, and in the end, you pay the price for hiding. There's always a price."

Helena was confused. Why was he telling her this? What was this all about?

Zak turned to look at her. His stare, intense. "I came out and I lost my family, security, and possibly my future. Was it worth it? Right now, I don't think so. After this semester, I'm kind of screwed. Was there another choice? Perhaps. But I couldn't go on lying about myself. And now, I'm facing the consequences."

Helena had never seen Zak this serious. She already knew about his parents and their rejection. She'd come face to face with their intolerance after his surgery. It broke her heart to think parents could treat their child the way Zak was treated. She hoped her presence in his life had cushioned some of the pain, but she knew better. No one could make up for the loss of a parent. Even if that parent was a bad parent.

"I'm disappointed you never told me *your truth*," Zak added. "I would've understood."

Helena was unclear what Zak was getting at. Julie must have told him something that had upset him. But what could that be? And how could that have any bearing on their relationship?

Zak blurted it out. "I know you made up that whole story about your sons. They don't really exist."

Helena nodded. There it was. The truth she'd kept buried. What had possessed Julie to reveal that to Zak? He looked so hurt. Why would Julie paint the picture as if Helena had deliberately lied to Zak. But then, she did lie to him. But no more than she'd lied to herself.

Helena struggled to find her voice. "It isn't what you think," was all she could manage to say.

"Then tell me," Zak pressed. "Do you have sons or not?"

Helena exhaled. How could she explain to this young man about her life without coming across as a horrible human being? After so many years of lying to herself, she wasn't certain anymore about the truth. What first had started as a little white lie to protect herself had morphed through the years into a big black hole in her heart. A painful gap that she'd tried to fill with half-truths and pretending. After all, she was an author. She knew how to create other worlds in her novels. Surely, she could manifest an alternative world for herself. A better world. A world where she felt safe and loved. A world where she was blameless. And so, she'd done it. She'd worked hard to build a cocoon, never imagining she'd have to confront the truth at this late stage of life. "I do have sons. Two fine young men," she rambled, struggling to think about the best way to tell the story. If only she had a typewriter in which to write it all down. She could stare at a blank sheet of paper and tell the story instead of looking at Zak's hurt expression. In that way, she could spin the backstory so that it came out with the proper detail, editing along the way to offer it in the most favorable light.

Zak perked up. "So, you have sons. That clears that up."

Helena nodded tentatively. How could she explain? Why did she have to explain? It didn't seem fair after all these years to make excuses. No. She wouldn't take that route. No more excuses. Not now. Still, she'd no idea what to say. The truth was so . . . permeable.

"If you have sons, why did Julie tell me you have no family?"

Helena felt the tension on her chest as if she were lying under a boulder, struggling to breathe. Was it possible for two truths to exist side by side? Does a half-truth still make you a liar? And what exactly is a half-truth? An error of omission?

Zak cocked his head. "Did you deliberately lie to Julie?"

Helena remembered the intake process when she'd sat with Alan and filled out the original paperwork to buy into Ventana. There had been a section asking about next of kin. Helena had opted to leave it blank. Instead, she'd provided the name and phone number of her attorney. "I didn't lie," she answered, feeling so very tired that she feared the movement of her pinky might consume all her energy. Why did she have to go through this all again? And yet, in Zak's eyes, she could see the hurt her fabrication had caused. He thought she'd lied. Lied to him. And for someone like Zak, who lied to survive his teen years, lying was the worst of all sins. And so, she decided to tell the truth. A truth she'd kept buried for years. A truth she wasn't proud of. She took a deep breath. Hopefully, Zak wouldn't judge her too harshly. Hopefully, he wouldn't judge her at all. She gathered her courage and finally said it. "My sons want nothing to do with me."

Zak shook his head as if he'd misheard. "I don't understand."

"How can you?" she said, wringing her hands, knuckles all red. "But it's true," she confirmed.

"Sons love their mothers," Zak whispered.

Helena closed her eyes. There was a time when her sons had loved her. Or at least she thought they did. But how could she explain the pain she'd inflicted on her children? She'd been careless. It was the carelessness her sons had found so very unforgiveable. Though she'd been angry at first by their dismissal of her, the years had offered another perspective. She'd come to understand their point of view. That lesson didn't come easily or cheaply. Years of therapy were required to dig into the nature of her failure as a mother.

Zak waited, his eyes signaling a willingness to understand whatever she might say.

"It wasn't one thing or another. It happened over the course of many years. I had a career. I had a life. I made mistakes. I . . ." She searched for the right words that could explain what she couldn't quite explain, even to herself. "I wasn't there when they needed me."

"So, they stopped talking to you?"

"No," Helena said, afraid he might impugn her boys for the choices they'd made. "Not at all. It was more of a drifting away. It happened slowly. At first, I didn't notice. I had a busy schedule back then, and as I became a well-known speaker, I traveled a lot. The boys spent quite a bit of time on their own. They were capable, responsible, young men, so I thought, this is good for them. They're growing up to be independent. And so, they were.

And as their lives became more complicated with their own families, we drifted, unable to get back the time we should have spent together. I was already out of their lives by then."

Zak's eyes searched her face as if there had to be more.

"I don't know if I can explain it any better. My sons were no longer interested in me. They had busy lives, so I didn't press them. What right did I have? I wasn't there when they were growing up. How could I expect them to be there for me? When I decided to move to Ventana, I was embarrassed. I thought it best not to mention the boys on the intake form. I didn't want to explain their absence. How I'd failed them. How they'd failed me. What was the point? It was already old news."

"Something more must have happened. An argument. A confrontation."

She wondered how she could expect him to understand what she herself was still grappling with. She hadn't wanted to think about it. But now it was too late. There was no turning back. "Years ago, I authored an article about college-educated women who opt out of the workforce to stay home and raise children. At the time, I thought it a perfectly good waste of an education to trade a career for housekeeping and changing diapers. It concerned me that so many women could have made a real contribution to society instead of being sidelined by what I referred to as the *baby glass ceiling*."

Zak shrugged his shoulders. "Okay, so you wrote an article."

"I then followed it up with a book. Television interviews. Even a controversial appearance on *Phil Donohue*."

Zak didn't understand the reference. "Who?"

"Never mind. I was interviewed in the Sunday *New York Times* and a host of other publications. Interviewed is a nice way to put it. I was vilified. The press had a field day. But so did many women of the day who had opted to raise families. Behind the backdrop of all this noise, my boys were caught in the middle. You see, I was advocating that if professional women must raise children, they should only have one. That didn't go over well with my sons who already felt neglected."

Zak perked up. "Did you neglect them?"

Helena covered her mouth as she considered Zak's question. "It depends on who you ask. My sons had their opinions. It was certainly different from mine. But what does it matter?" Helena said with a quick wave of a hand as if by doing so she could end the conversation. "What's done is done. I can't fix it. God knows, I've tried. But some things in life can't be fixed. It's a hard lesson to learn. And unlike that fly that repeatedly butts up against a closed window trying to escape to the outside, there comes a time to give up. When it no longer makes sense to try. Otherwise, you'll have no energy left for anything else."

Zak nodded. "I understand. It feels that way with my parents. I'm not sure there is anything I could do to save the relationship."

"Well, now," she gently corrected him. "That might change. If you give your parents time to educate themselves, they might come around. You're still young. There's hope."

"But there's no hope for you?"

Helena winced. "I think not. I'm already at the end of my story. You're just at the opening chapter of yours."

"Perhaps," he said, "there's still time for my parents to make amends. I guess it's possible."

Helena smiled. She was grateful he understood. It wasn't an easy concept to convey and certainly not what you'd expect to hear from someone her age. Though she missed her sons, she didn't think it fair to try to get them to reengage with her. Whatever the past, the present was up to her. She couldn't expect to mend relationships at this late date.

Zak wrinkled his brow. "There are just some losses in life that are forced upon us. My parents. Your sons."

"That doesn't make us bad people," Helena added. "We all do the best we can. You're a remarkable young man who happens to have a same-sex orientation. I'm a gifted writer who refused to bow to the patriarchy. Somehow, both of us managed to get into trouble based on who we are. Aren't we lucky to have found each other?"

———◆———

When the news story broke, Helena was in the activity room with Della helping her set up for bingo. "Check this out," Della said as she pointed at the television. Helena covered her mouth, collapsing into the nearest chair as she watched six adults marching in a circle at the entrance to Ventana carrying picket signs that read *Free Helena*. Della turned up the volume as a reporter stepped in front of the picketers. "Can you tell us what's going on here?" the reporter asked, a mic held up to Zak's face. "We're here to protest management's decision to keep a capable senior, Helena Greenblatt, hostage in assisted living, instead of letting her return to her condo." The reporter faced the camera. "Ms. Greenblatt is a resident of Ventana, a Tempe retirement community. How do you know Ms. Greenblatt?" she asked Zak as she turned back to him. "We met through a Ventana volunteer program. She helped me through a bad period of my life when I needed surgery. Helena stepped in and became my family, and now it's my turn to help her." The reporter again turned to the camera. "This is quite a special young man, Zak Andrews, with an interesting story of intergenerational support."

"How did they manage to get this on the news?" Della asked as the station transitioned to the weather report.

"You can thank me for that," Julie said as she walked into the activity room, surprising both Helena and Della. "I pitched the story to a local news team when I found out Zak had organized a protest. I knew it was too good for them to pass it up. Human interest and all."

"You're a rebel at heart," Helena said as she wagged a finger in Julie's direction. "Oh, what we could have done with you back in the seventies."

Julie beamed with pride. "But what I can't figure out is how did Zak ever get those women to march with him? And who are the other two young men?"

Helena laughed. "Aggie is probably responsible for convincing the ladies. She must have used her dietary responsibilities as an influence."

Della looked puzzled. "I'm not following."

"Cynthia, Babs, and Donna love to eat. And since Aggie is in control of what comes in and out of the kitchen, she had them . . . let's say . . . eating out of her hand."

Julie seemed astonished. "Aggie would never put anything in their food."

"Of course, not," Helena agreed. "But the mere threat was enough to engage them."

"And those young men?" Della pressed. "Who are they?"

"Two of Zak's friends. Marshall and Chuck. And the other young lady, Melinda, runs The Windy Canyon Bar." Helena thought Zak had done a masterful job recruiting his friends.

A call came in on Julie's iPhone. From the sound of Julie's voice, Helena could tell it was good news. She hoped the picketing had proved successful and the call was from management announcing Helena's move back to her condo. Julie's eyes were as big as saucers. "Who is this?" she asked the caller again as if she'd misheard the name. "Robin Roberts!" she said with excitement. "Are you serious?"

Della and Helena both gasped.

"Yes. Certainly," Julie said as she disconnected from the call and let out a shriek. "Oh, my God. ABC wants to interview you and Zak together for a human-interest piece."

Helena held a palm to her chest. "I don't know. That seems so . . ."

Julie shouted out the word. "BIG!"

By the time the ABC interview aired, Helena was back in her condo, happy to be finally home. Even though Alan had insisted plans were already underway to move her back ahead of the broadcast, she doubted that would have happened without the intervention of Zak, Aggie, her dining room friends Cynthia, Babs, and Donna, and of course, Zak's friends, Marshall, Chuck, and Melinda. Plus, she couldn't forget the wonderful Dr. Peterson and his protest letter to the Ventana management board. But most of all, she was grateful to Zak and Julie for believing in her and acknowledging that even though she was a bit different, it didn't mean she was experiencing the onset of dementia. To prove it, Helena dedicated herself to continuing to work with Della and the Ventana staff to demystify the third floor, which included arranging for other seniors, including her dinner companions, to regularly rotate through the floor as volunteers. This was especially poignant when Ventana's resident Romeo, Gilbert Goldfarb, took a bad tumble, broke his leg, and had to be installed on the third floor for three weeks as he learned to get around on crutches. The ladies took turns spending time with Gilbert, and although he flirted shamelessly with all four, Helena captured his true interest. Much to her surprise, Gilbert proposed, though it wasn't quite up to Helena's standards, and not because he was unable to get down on one knee. She just thought it too ridiculous for a man of Gilbert's age to expect a woman of Helena's age to consider marriage. After all, Helena had no intention of sacrificing any of the time she had left to catering to the needs of the male species. No . . . she'd never again appear undressed in front of a man, unless of course, he was an EMT who was there to pick her up off the bathroom floor. For those heroes, she was willing to throw caution to the wind and make an exception.

As for the ABC interview, the ripple effect turned out to be astounding. The interview was done via satellite so neither

Zak nor Helena needed to travel to New York City. Together, from the comfort of Helena's condo, they told the story of how they'd met and how circumstances had shaped their unlikely friendship. The show booker had been briefed by Julie about Zak's troubling backstory, a gay kid who'd been rejected by his family and was facing an uncertain future. Much to Zak's and Helena's surprise, Zak's GoFundMe page went viral, and before Zak could say thank you, his ASU tuition and room and board were covered for the next four years.

In celebration, Marshall invited Zak out to dinner to the local Culver's, and just after they'd finished eating their ice cream sundaes, asked Zak to be his steady guy. Zak didn't hesitate to answer yes, hoping that given time, they'd soon be living together. Meanwhile, Chuck surprised Zak by coming out to his wrestling coach and teammates. "It was about time," Chuck said, inspired by Zak's visibility and the warm response he'd received.

As for Zak's parents, he wasn't sure if they'd seen the ABC interview. Allison claimed to have told them about the high-profile story, though why she was still in contact with his parents was a mystery to him. It wasn't long after that conversation that Zak decided it was time to move on from his friendship with Allison. Things change. Friends change. He'd changed.

"Thank goodness I was wearing my Life Alert the day I fell in the bathroom," Helena told Robin Roberts. "I thought my life was over. I'd no idea that my decision to move to Ventana would be so life changing."

Robin paused, adding weight to Helena's statement before turning to Zak. "And what is your major takeaway from all this?"

Zak turned to face the camera. "That no matter the age difference, we can all be friends. When I think about what Helena went through when she moved into Ventana, and then the challenges going on in my life at the same time, well, we were both in the midst of a crisis. I was lucky to have her. She helped me see that no matter what life puts in front of you, you can turn it around. I hadn't thought someone of Helena's age would be able to appreciate my struggles."

"Or remember them," Helena interjected with a giggle. "But it's true. We're all going through challenges. It's wonderful to connect with another generation and see the world through their eyes."

Roberts had the last word. "Two generations. Two sets of problems. And yet, the ability to solve their issues together through love and mutual respect. How wonderful!"

How wonderful indeed, Helena thought.

ACKNOWLEDGEMENTS

To Jules Hucke of Red Pen Refinery who was my editor on this novel. I'm grateful for her attention to detail and guidance with storytelling. Every insight made the novel better. To Megan McCullough who created the design and layout for the paperback and ebook. A very humble thank you. To Lily O'Brien for her copyediting skills. If you find a typo in the novel... call Lily. To Jennifer Stimson who designed the cover. Wow! And to Yucel, the photographer who snapped the photo of me on the back cover. Ah, the wonders of Photoshop.

If you enjoyed reading *Friends for a Season:*

1. Please rate the novel on Amazon and Goodreads.
2. Join Brad Graber's email list at www.bradgraber.com and sign-up for his humor blog: ***There, I Said It!***
3. Recommend the book to your local book club.
4. Invite Brad to be a speaker at your next community event.
5. Send Brad a note at brad@bradgraber.com – he loves to hear from fans.

If a stranger knocked

on your door, would

you welcome them in?

When Dave and Charlie relocate to Phoenix, Daisy shows up at their door after a long illness unaware relatives have sold her home. Charlie assumes the older woman is Dave's aunt from Chicago and happily ushers her into a guest room. **Tales of the City** meets **As Good As It Gets** in this heartwarming page-turner about love, friendship, and the family we choose.

What happened to
Rikki's mother?

Rikki can't remember her mother. When she asks her grandmother a question, the older woman refuses to discuss the past. Desperate to learn the truth, Rikki embarks on a journey to meet Harry, a writer who is struggling with his own issues of identity, in this psychological tale of love, loss, and forgiveness.

Humorous Observations on Modern Life!

Ever wonder why a fly is circling the deli? What you can learn from your dog about aging? If Mahjong is the true game of champions? Wonder no more. If you're a fan of the Chicken Soup series, love Erma Bombeck, David Sedaris, and Larry David, you'll enjoy these seventy essays on life, love, and the pursuit of dairy products that don't spoil.

How does a widower

start over?

George Elden's world is turned upside down when his golf buddy suddenly dies. Why did the family stay away from the funeral? Why did the check to the mortuary bounce? And why did George, who is on the verge of bankruptcy, kick in the pay for the funeral? More important, what can George learn from his former friend's life to escape making the same mistakes?